# THE
# MIRROR
# MAN

# THE
# MIRROR
# MAN

## JANE
## GILMARTIN

mira

ISBN-13: 978-0-7783-0964-2

The Mirror Man

This edition published by arrangement with Harlequin Books S.A.

For questions and comments about the quality of this book, please contact us at CustomerService@Harlequin.com.

Mira
22 Adelaide St. West, 40th Floor
Toronto, Ontario M5H 4E3, Canada
BookClubbish.com

**Printed in U.S.A.**

In memory of my mother
and
David Bowie

# THE
# MIRROR
# MAN

# CHAPTER

# 1

## DAY 1

The first time he saw his own replica, laid out on a bed, its eyes closed as though it might be dreaming, Jeremiah choked on his own breath. He'd never seen himself from this angle before. There was a slackness to the skin around the jawline; it draped down slightly on either side of the face in a way that was distinctly unattractive. He was riveted—enthralled and repulsed all at once.

"It's uncanny, isn't it? The resemblance?" Dr. Charles Scott spoke with his typical detachment, which, in the moment, Jeremiah wished he could share. But that was his own image he was looking at, exact in even the smallest detail. For him, detachment was impossible.

His eyes zeroed in on a dry, pinkish patch on the clone's left cheek and Jeremiah absently lifted a hand to the same spot on his own face, where he'd scraped himself with a worn razor just a few days ago. Uncanny resemblance didn't begin to describe what was on that bed.

It was uniquely unsettling, like standing on the face of a mirror. His mind couldn't work out where his own body began and ended.

"Is it… Is he alive?" Without thinking, without actually wanting to, he reached a tentative hand out to touch his double.

Scott deftly blocked Jeremiah's hand with his own. "Oh, yes, very much alive. At least in a biological sense."

His eyes wandered from the face for a moment and only then did Jeremiah notice the steady, slow rise and fall of the clone's chest.

The thing was breathing.

"What other kind of alive is there?" he asked.

"At the moment, the clone is nothing but a shell. He has no mind, no inner workings. He's empty." Scott looked quickly from the clone back to Jeremiah, with an expression that suggested smug satisfaction. "Once we input your neural platform—your memories and synaptic patterns—then he'll be alive in a more definitive manner."

"Unbelievable," Jeremiah said. "It's really unbelievable."

"And the whole process shouldn't take more than a couple of hours," Scott told him. "Once we administer the Meld you will be neurologically connected until the procedure is complete."

Almost as if on cue, Dr. Philip Pike entered the room, setting down a tray with two syringes. He barely acknowledged Jeremiah's presence with a nod, but immediately checked the clone's pulse and then dispensed something from a dropper into each of its eyes. He made a careful scan of the medical monitors around the clone's bed and jotted hurried notes on a clipboard. Once he seemed satisfied with whatever the readings told him, he began to affix a tangle of colored wires to various points on the clone's head. He did all of this in silence and at a pace that might have suggested he had somewhere more important to be, although Jeremiah knew that was certainly not the case. At the moment, he thought, this small hospital room, tucked away in a hidden basement of ViMed Pharmaceutical, was the epicenter of the entire scientific universe—and only a handful of people were privy to that fact. Somehow, inconceivably, Jeremiah was at the heart of the whole thing.

"So, during this transfer," he asked of no one in particular, "am I supposed to think about anything specific? Is there something I need to focus on?"

"Not really, Mr. Adams." It was Dr. Pike who spoke, and Jeremiah noted again the tinge of a British accent, something softened and obscured by years of living in the United States. "But you may want to think about a pleasant memory—something you can easily recall—to help with the initial disorientation you may experience under the Meld."

The prospect of taking the drug again made Jeremiah's stomach churn. He'd taken it once already with the project's psychiatrist without any lasting effects, but it had been a strange experience, and he couldn't shake the idea that it was risky. His fears were ironic, to say the least. As one of ViMed's marketing managers, he was literally paid to dispel those very notions, persuading the public and the bureaucratic watchdogs that Meld had been thoroughly tested and was perfectly safe. But when illegal street use had erupted in a rash of baffling suicides, his job had grown progressively more difficult. And the most recent suicide wasn't "just" another junkie. It was a forty-two-year-old housewife from New Jersey who had stabbed herself in the throat with a corkscrew while in the throes of an intimate moment with her husband. The media had gone crazy, and Jeremiah had become acquainted with migraines under the burden of finding a positive spin. She was a regular person, some poor slob who thought a little jolt of Meld might put some magic back in the bedroom. If it could happen to her, he thought, it could just as easily happen to anyone. It could happen to him.

It was one thing to sway public opinion. It was proving harder to suppress his own doubt, though—especially since he now knew the whole truth about Meld—that it had been specifically created for this project, especially made for him, in a way. And he'd have to take it multiple times over the next twelve months. Beside the doctors who were using it in practice, no one had ever done that before, as far as he knew. The implications of being the guinea pig sat on his shoulders like lead.

"Is it okay to take it again so soon?" he asked. "I mean, it hasn't even been a month since the last time. Are you sure this is safe?"

"Perfectly safe," Dr. Pike told him. "Under proper medical supervision the chance of any serious side effects is virtually nonexistent."

The words offered little comfort. Jeremiah had written that company tagline himself. He'd believed it at the time. He had been just as impressed as everyone else at the prospect of a drug that could literally allow a direct link to the human mind. But now, as he waited to be injected again, he couldn't help but see the whole thing from a different perspective. What if there really was something to it? What if Meld really *was* doing something to make people want to kill themselves? He didn't harbor any such desires—not that he knew of at least—but that did little to calm his nerves as he stared at the syringe.

His thoughts must have been evident on his face.

"Mr. Adams." Charles Scott's tone was laced with a hint of irritation. "Our scientists have just created an exact replica of you. You are staring into the face of a scientific miracle. A perfect human clone. The Meld should be the least of your concerns. If the FDA can see fit to keep Meld on the market, there is obviously nothing for you to worry about. Of all people, I'd think you'd be the last one to doubt the Meld."

Jeremiah took his place in a chair next to the bed and tried to swallow his worry. He nearly gagged on it.

Dr. Pike began to connect Jeremiah's brain to that of his empty double, and he felt a bit as though he were about to be syphoned like a gas tank. But he knew it didn't work that way. In actual fact, he supposed, it was more like being copied. He began to wonder what his clone would do with all the conflicted thoughts swimming through his mind, all the personal turmoil and philosophical struggle he'd faced in the weeks leading up to this moment. He'd agreed to have himself illegally cloned. He was walking out on his family and leaving a replica in his place. It hadn't been an easy few weeks. What a thing to wake up to, he thought.

"What's with all the wires? There weren't any wires when I took it before."

"This is a different kind of connection," Pike told him. "Normally, Meld acts as a neural stimulant on the brains of both subjects. The clone has no active neurons yet. This is a one-way thing. Think of it as a download. The physical connection is necessary."

"Besides," Scott said, "hardwiring prevents the accidental input from anyone else in the room. It wouldn't do to have the clone picking up random thoughts from me or Dr. Pike."

Jeremiah nodded and turned his attention to something he hoped would be easier to grasp.

"Does it have to be so cold in here?"

"For the moment, yes," Pike said without explanation.

"Mr. Adams," Scott said tersely, "please relax and allow Dr. Pike to do his job."

He couldn't relax.

"If the clone is going to know everything in my mind, doesn't that mean he'll immediately realize he's a copy?" Jeremiah asked. "Won't he remember everything that's happened up to this moment? The agreement? Our conversations? All of it?"

"I will make sure that doesn't happen, Mr. Adams," Pike said. "I'll be connected to each of you so I can monitor everything that's going into the clone's mind. Everything will go from your mind, through me and into the clone. I'll have full, precise control over the entire thing."

"When we implant the memories," Scott added, "we can be as selective as we need to be. All the information about the cloning—every thought you've ever had about it—will be withheld from what we insert into his mind. We can filter it. Everything else will be preserved. He will wake up thinking he is—and always has been—Jeremiah Adams. He will remember leaving for work this morning, exactly as you do, and he will remember a car accident. It will all make perfect sense to him."

"A car accident?"

"We needed some sort of reasonable explanation for the lapse in time," Scott told him. "We will transfer him to a secluded room in a nearby hospital, which is where he will wake up. There needs to be a reason for that. We have someone taking care of the corresponding damage to your car as we speak."

"Damage? I'm still making payments on that car!"

"It is unavoidable," Scott said. "Stop worrying about the trivial."

"So, he's going to remember something that never even happened?"

"It's a false memory," Dr. Pike explained. "Something lifted from someone else."

Jeremiah was shocked. "You can do that? You can pick and choose what he's going to remember?" A whole new set of worries seeped into his mind.

"It is an amazing achievement, that little drug," Scott said as though that were what Jeremiah had implied. "If we were so inclined, Mr. Adams, we could be just as selective with you. We could wipe out every memory you have of this whole arrangement and even you wouldn't realize you'd been cloned. But, of course, that wouldn't serve our needs for the project at all, would it? We need your mind intact." He shot a tense smile at Jeremiah, which did little to lighten the weight of the insinuation. If Meld could be used to implant precise, tailored memories, the possibilities were endless. And sinister. It made his skin crawl.

If the public had even an inkling of what Meld could actually do, the suicides would almost be beside the point.

Meld had been fast-tracked from the start, and the medical community had gone giddy at the drug's potential. The ability to actually see into a patient's mind—even the somewhat foggy glimpse that Meld offered—had implications for all manner of physical and psychiatric mysteries. Jeremiah hadn't been surprised at how quickly the drug had been accepted. It was a marvel. But had they seen the other edge of that sword, he wondered, or known what Meld was really for, would it have passed the initial trials? More to the point, he thought, would he have been so keen to help push it on the public?

Charles Scott glared down at him with a glint in his green eyes that felt like a warning, and Jeremiah replayed in his head the man's ambiguous threat during their first meeting several weeks before.

*"You now know as much about this project as anyone else involved,"* he'd said. *"It wouldn't do to have too many people walking around with this kind of information. Our investors have a tendency to get nervous."*

Although Scott had quickly followed that remark with the matter of Jeremiah's substantial compensation, there was no mistaking the implication: the moment he'd been told about the cloning project Jeremiah was already in. That first meeting hadn't been an invitation so much as an orientation, and the contract he'd later signed had been a formality, at best. And the entire thing had done nothing but gain momentum from that moment on.

Dr. Pike continued to affix the wires to Jeremiah's head. Jeremiah focused on the man's gleaming black hair and the deep brown of his sure, professional hands, and he struggled to remember the allure of the $10 million payout he'd get at the end of the whole thing. That kind of money could fix a lot of problems. It would change things. The prospect of that fortune had been enough to make him turn away from principles he thought were unshakable. Every man has his price, he supposed.

Somewhere in the back of his mind he also acknowledged the real temptation of a twelve-month sabbatical from his own life. It had seduced him every bit as much as the money had. Maybe more. Between a job that had already begun to make him question his own morals, and a marriage that felt increasingly more like a lie, stress was eating him alive. And into his lap fell a chance to just walk away from all of it—without consequence and without blame. A free pass. He could simply walk away without anyone even knowing he was gone. There isn't a man alive, he told himself, who would have refused. Despite the ethical question, despite that human cloning was illegal the world over, it would have tempted anyone.

Dr. Pike injected the clone with Meld and then turned wordlessly to Jeremiah with the second syringe poised above his left shoulder.

Jeremiah closed his eyes and rolled up his sleeve.

After the initial stab of the needle, he felt nothing. Which is not to say he didn't feel anything; he literally *felt* nothing. Seconds after the injection, he became aware of a total emptiness, like a towering black wave that threatened to sink him into an immeasurable void. The experience was unlike anything he'd ever known. He imagined an astronaut suddenly untethered from his ship, floating helplessly into unending darkness. Without thinking, he immediately felt his body recoil. His mind screamed against it.

*I'm dying!*

From impossibly far away, he heard Dr. Pike say something about a heart rate and felt the slight pressure of a hand on his

shoulder. He couldn't see anything of the hospital room anymore. He was drowning in the blackness. His chest felt suddenly
constricted. He fought just to find his breath.

"This is all perfectly normal, Mr. Adams. You have nothing
to worry about. Concentrate on the sound of my voice. Nod if
you can hear me."

With considerable effort, Jeremiah managed what he hoped
was a nod of his head. He was suddenly gripped by the alarming certainty that if he couldn't communicate somehow, he'd
be lost—swept away forever.

"Good. Good. Listen to my voice. It will keep you grounded."
Pike still sounded far away, but Jeremiah nodded again and strug-
gled to focus. "What you are experiencing is to be expected.
Do you remember when you took the Meld with Dr. Young?
Do you remember the way you could feel her thoughts for the
first few minutes?"

He nodded. It had been an unnerving thing to perceive her
consciousness mixing with his like that. Flashes from her mind—
odd, alien things like the feel of a blister on the back of her right
heel, the familiar gleam in the eye of an old man he'd never
seen—had swirled into the very structure of his own mind and
fought for a place to settle. He had railed against that, too, and
she had grounded him by flashing a penlight in his face, making him focus on that while the Meld took effect. Afterward,
once he had sunk in, it had been easier.

"This is no different than what you experienced then," Pike
said. "This time, though, you are connected to an empty mind.
There's nothing there. But the more you resist, the longer this
will take. You need to relax, Mr. Adams. Give in to it."

Jeremiah nodded again and then shook his head with as much
grit as he could muster. How does one give in to this? He didn't
think he could do it.

"Once your thoughts begin transferring into the mind of

the clone it will be easier for you," Pike urged. "Focus on a memory, as I suggested. Something vivid. It will help to fill that void you're experiencing now. It will give you something to hang on to."

Without the benefit of his full faculties, Jeremiah had little choice but to grab the last thing he'd been thinking about—his initial conversation with Charles Scott, the day all of this began.

He'd been surprised when he'd received an invitation to lunch from ViMed's head of Engineering. The man was an icon in the science world, and although he'd quoted him a hundred times for the company, Jeremiah had never actually met him. He'd been intrigued enough to accept the invitation, especially when Scott had told him it involved a "proposition that could make him a very wealthy man."

Flashes of that encounter and snatches of conversation now flitted through his mind like so many fireflies. He fought to catch them.

*"We've been watching you, Mr. Adams."*

*"All we ask is one year of your life. Isn't that worth $10 million?"*

*"We can do this. The science exists. And with Meld, the clone will even share your thought patterns... Your own mother won't know the difference."*

*"This is sanctioned by powerful people—we have millions in secret federal backing. There are billions more in eventual funding... There's no need to be so suspicious, Mr. Adams."*

From somewhere far away, Jeremiah heard Dr. Pike repeating his name. He had been so engulfed in his efforts to hold on to the memory that he'd almost forgotten where he was. As soon as he realized it, the void loomed again in his mind.

"Mr. Adams," Pike said, "you've got to listen to me. The clone cannot pick up on any memory of the experiment. What you're thinking about is not going to help. You need to think about something else, some memory that won't be filtered. His mind is still empty."

Jeremiah panicked. He couldn't think. And now that he wasn't focused on anything, the blackness began to take over again, creeping closer and threatening to swallow him. He fought for breath.

"Relax, Mr. Adams," Pike said. "Think about your job here at ViMed. Remember something the clone can actually use. Something he'll need to know."

He felt a dull jab at his shoulder.

"This should help. I've given you a mild sedative. Take a few deep breaths. Concentrate on your breathing."

With everything in him, Jeremiah tried to turn his mind away from the void that seemed to be all around him. He inhaled deeply and tried to focus on the rise of his own chest. Exhaled, and he felt his chest fall.

"Very good, Mr. Adams. Very good. Pulse is returning to normal. Deep breaths. Now, think about a typical day at work. Something ordinary and mundane."

Inhale. Exhale. After a moment, Jeremiah began to relax and, as the sedative took hold, he found he could let his mind wander without the frantic thought that he'd never get it back. An oddly comforting fog seemed to expand in front of him, pushing the blackness away slightly, and Jeremiah retreated into it.

He began to think about the morning of the Meld fiasco— the day the New Jersey housewife had killed herself. The press had been circling. He'd arrived at his office with a terse mandate from his superiors to "get these fuckers off our back" and no idea how to accomplish that. It hadn't been lost on him that not a single soul seemed bothered enough to stop and feel sorry about it, and he'd taken a quick moment behind his office door to offer silent condolences. It wasn't thirty seconds before someone had come knocking, pushing him to get something done.

Weeks before, he'd heard talk of Meld being used to detect brain activity in a sixteen-year-old football player who had been comatose for nearly six months. Time to cash in. He tracked down the doctor somewhere in Delaware and the man started gushing about Meld, calling it "magical," "a godsend" and "the most important medical advance of a generation."

"After so many weeks," he said, "the parents were hopeless."

Meld was a last resort before pulling the plug, and it gave them the first clear signs of neural activity in the boy.

"Not only was he aware and awake in there, but he was cognizant of everything that was going on around him—including the fact that his parents were losing hope. He even heard them talking about funeral arrangements at one point. The kid was scared, terrified. He was begging for his life in there. That's what I saw when I took the Meld with him. Meld absolutely saved his life. There is no doubt in my mind."

Jeremiah had almost smiled. It was pure gold. A few hours later, the story was in the hands of every major news outlet, and that doctor was spending his fifteen minutes of fame touting Meld as "a medical miracle."

Jeremiah focused on that now. Maybe Meld did have some silver lining, after all, he thought. Maybe it *was* miraculous.

# CHAPTER
# 2

Jeremiah had no idea how long he'd been under the Meld when Dr. Pike's voice began to penetrate his mind again.

"Mr. Adams. We've finished the transfer. We're done here. Wake up."

Jeremiah shook his head in an attempt to disperse the fog in his mind and felt Pike's hand on his shoulder easing him to a more upright position in the chair. He must have fallen completely asleep under the sedative, he realized, and that possibility touched on a vague sense of worry in the back of his mind.

"It's time to go, Mr. Adams," Scott said. "The clone will be waking up soon and we can't have him wake up to your face. I will take you to your new home now."

"I just need a minute." Jeremiah closed his eyes again and fought a sudden wave of nausea.

Charles Scott took a slight step back, afraid, no doubt, that his four-hundred-dollar shoes were at risk.

After a moment, Jeremiah stood up slowly and followed Scott down an intricate puzzle of intersecting hallways and through doors that were opened by a wave of a key card in Scott's hand. When they finally arrived at the living quarters, Jeremiah couldn't have retraced their steps if he tried for the entire year. At the moment, he didn't care. His head ached and all he wanted was a place to lie down.

They entered through a nondescript door into a generous room, furnished with two light-colored leather couches, low tables and a desk in the corner outfitted with a sleek, all-glass computer terminal. Discreet overhead lighting cast everything in a pleasing glow. But despite the size and opulence, the room felt closed in. Two walls were lined with shelves of books and a third was almost entirely filled with a six-by-eight-foot screen, which, at the moment, was turned off and blank.

"That's quite the TV," Jeremiah said with some surprise.

"That monitor is where you will watch your clone each day, Mr. Adams. Four hours, every day, for the next 365 days. It is controlled remotely, but when not in use for its intended purpose, you can certainly watch television as you desire."

"Bugs Bunny will look terrifying on that thing."

"This monitor will also serve as a window to the outside, Mr. Adams," Scott said, ignoring Jeremiah's attempt at levity. "It can provide you with a real-time view of just about any place on Earth equipped with a camera feed." By way of demonstration, Scott picked up the remote and revolved through vistas of an African wildlife sanctuary, an outdoor market in Amsterdam and a convenience store that could have been somewhere in Detroit.

"You're going to be secluded within these walls for a rather long time," he said. "We thought this technology would at least give you the illusion of more expansive surroundings." Scott nodded toward a treadmill in the corner with a helmet-like device hanging from its handlebar. "That's the latest in virtual reality tech," he said. "Put that on and you'll swear you're walking the streets of Paris, jogging in Central Park or whatever else you're inclined to do."

"An exercise wheel. You equip all your lab rats like this?"

"You are not a lab rat, Mr. Adams. But surely you can appreciate the importance of maintaining your current physical condition. We can't have you returning home suddenly twenty pounds heavier than your clone. That might raise some eyebrows. It is imperative that you and your double remain exactly that—doubles."

"How did you get it to grow so fast? I mean, this thing is my age. You only took the cells a week ago."

"With a bit of tweaking," Scott said, "it appears the neuroendocrine hypothesis was essentially sound."

Jeremiah shook his head.

"We extracted secretions from your own pituitary gland," Scott explained. "That compound contains human growth hormone, which we then genetically hyperstimulate, at a systemic level, during cell division. The process allows us to increase the maturation rate and create a fully grown replica in about forty-eight hours."

"You went from a couple of cells to a forty-seven-year-old human in forty-eight hours?"

"Science, Mr. Adams, is a wonderful thing. But to ensure our efforts remain intact, you will be put on a strict regimen of exercise. Dr. Pike will monitor everything with periodic visits."

"It looks like you've thought of everything."

"We want you to be comfortable here. This is your home, not a cage."

Jeremiah noted the total lack of windows and the fact that the front door didn't even have a doorknob.

"I'd say that depends on your vantage point," he said.

"Seclusion is paramount to this project, Mr. Adams. We simply cannot risk any contact with the outside world."

"Well, at least there's the internet, I suppose. I assume the Wi-Fi is state-of-the-art down here."

"Yes, yes, of course," Scott said. "You'll have full access to the web. But I'm afraid there is no outgoing signal. No email or text. And no camera. You understand. You will not be able to communicate with anyone other than our immediate team."

"Then what's with that thing?" Jeremiah nodded toward an old-fashioned landline telephone on the desk in the corner.

"That line will connect you with an administrative assistant on the project," Scott told him. "You can use it to make any requests for specific foods, personal necessities and so forth. Or in the case of an emergency, of course. But we don't foresee anything like that. You will be well looked after during your time here."

To Jeremiah's ears, Scott's words sounded more like warning than solace.

"Looked after? Do you mean you'll be watching me, Dr. Scott? Will I be monitored in here?"

"Monitored, yes, but we won't be spying on you," Scott said. His expression reflected bewildered affront. "Besides, we have no need for anything like that. Brent Higgins will be here with you for a good part of every day, and he reports to me. You'll also have regular psychological sessions with Dr. Young throughout the process. We'll be keeping track of your exercise, food intake, sleep patterns, that sort of thing—but we have no need to do anything quite so covert. We're scientists, not secret agents. You don't need to be suspicious."

It wasn't suspicion so much as it was amazement that he had been selected at all. He still had no idea why they'd chosen him for this role. There must have been better candidates than him. Someone younger, stronger, better connected. Scott's only explanation was that he'd been "vetted" by those involved and had proven he could be trusted and was loyal to ViMed interests.

*"We tested you repeatedly to see how you'd react,"* he'd said, *"and every single time you protected the company. Even when people started dying. You toed the line, Mr. Adams. You soldiered on."*

The explanation, like much of what Scott had to say, had sounded to Jeremiah like a veiled threat. And it didn't answer his questions. Of course he'd protected the company. That was his job. That's why ViMed paid him. From the very beginning, he'd had the feeling that all of this had been decided without him, a long time ago. But he was content with the fact that they'd selected him, no matter their reasons. It was an opportunity beyond anything he'd ever expected.

He walked farther into the room and took a closer look. The decor leaned toward the masculine, with bronze and glass accent pieces dotting the shelves and walls the color of sand. On the side wall, closest to the kitchen, there hung an oversize framed painting—an abstract array of varied circles done in grays and blues. The effect was dizzying and, silently, Jeremiah decided he didn't like it. He was startled to see, on one of the coffee tables, the exact book he'd been straining to finish for the past two months at home. He picked it up and thumbed through it, relieved to find no page corner had been turned back exactly where he'd left off.

"We've supplied you with a range of reading materials," Scott said. "You'll have a lot of free time on your hands, I'm afraid. Any specific requests can be handled, of course. Our sources suggested you prefer the physical books over the reader tablet, but we could get that, too, if you like."

"No, it's fine," Jeremiah said, wondering who these "sources" were and how they knew anything at all about his reading habits. He let it go for the moment and walked into the kitchen. Scott followed. The room was a small but opulent galley, gleaming with glossy appliances and stainless-steel countertops.

"Now this," Scott said, encompassing the room with outstretched arms, "is very impressive. The latest smart home tech—much of it generated specifically for the project. There isn't a kitchen like it anywhere in the world. You'll barely need to lift a finger."

Scott described appliances that were smarter than the average teenager. A refrigerator that would keep track of—and actually place orders for—groceries, and an oven that could set precise temperature and cooking time based solely on the weight and type of food you put into it. Someone must have known, he thought, that he wasn't much of a chef.

"And these devices actually get smarter the more you use them, Mr. Adams. They will learn your particular tastes and adjust accordingly—right down to the precise temperature you prefer your coffee."

"Well, it looks like I won't starve to death, anyway."

"You may explore the rest of your accommodations at your leisure." Scott glanced at his watch. "I believe the clone will be waking up soon and I've arranged for us to witness that. It's quite a significant moment. Historic, I dare say."

Jeremiah followed him back into the living room, where the video screen had just switched on of its own accord, and sat with him on one of the leather couches.

On the wall, Jeremiah watched as his double opened its eyes and attempted to ease itself up in its hospital bed. Dr. Pike was still there and was immediately at the clone's side with a hand on its shoulder.

"Mr. Adams, I am Dr. Evans," Pike said. "You're in the hospital. There was a car accident, but you are not seriously injured."

"A car accident?" Jeremiah had the impression of listening to a recording of his own voice—recognizable, but slightly unfamiliar in tone. It spoke almost in a whisper, as though waking from a long sleep, but it was undeniably Jeremiah's own voice.

"Can you tell me what you remember?" Pike prodded.

"A car accident? Was anyone else hurt?" the clone asked, sudden alarm evident in his tone.

"No, there were no other injuries. What can you tell me? What do you recall?" It was obvious to Jeremiah that Pike was trying to ascertain the success of the Meld procedure.

"I don't know," the clone started. Pike helped it into a sitting position, propping a pillow behind its back.

"Try to remember, Mr. Adams. It will help us to determine if there is any head injury."

"Head injury?" The clone put a tentative hand to its forehead. "All I remember is that I was at a stop sign. The one at the end of the exit ramp. I was hit on the passenger side. I think the air bag deployed. Did I hit the air bag?"

"I believe that's what rendered you unconscious, yes. But we've already run scans. There is no interior bleeding and no outward signs of neurological damage. We'll run a few more tests and keep you here for observation for a few hours just to be sure. But to test your short-term memory, could you state your full name and address for me?"

"Jeremiah Adams. Twenty-two Dorsey Road in Riverdale." The answer was correct and fully automatic. "I should call my office," the clone said, "and my wife."

Scott switched the monitor off but continued to stare at the blank screen with something approaching amazement. The expression seemed unnatural on his face. When he turned back to Jeremiah, he was fully composed again, his features aligned in their usual studied neutrality.

"Seems to have worked," he said. "The clone has remembered the accident exactly as it was recorded, and there is no sign of amnesia."

"Remarkable." Jeremiah shook his head. "It's absolutely incredible."

"And a promising start to our adventure. I'll leave you to rest, Mr. Adams. I imagine you must be tired from the morning's activities. The bedroom is just through there." Scott nodded toward a closed door on the far side of the room. "And remember, if there is anything you need, use the phone."

Scott left, swiping the key card against a panel to open the door. It closed behind him with a quiet but significant click.

# CHAPTER
# 3

Jeremiah stood in the middle of his new living room. There was almost complete silence, except for a steady hum coming from somewhere above his head. It must have been some sort of air circulation, he decided. He began to explore his surroundings.

He was happy to note a few of his favorite authors on the bookshelves and delighted to see a complete set of Shakespeare, small books bound in ancient-looking cracked red leather. In the kitchen, he opened the refrigerator and found it stocked with all the necessities, but in a wide enough array to cover any taste: three kinds of milk, five different juices and an assortment of fruits and vegetables, many of which he didn't even like. There were two six-packs of beer from a microbrewery he'd never heard of. At least, he thought with some relief, Scott had stopped short of hiring someone to snoop through his home refrigerator and duplicate its contents here.

In the bedroom, he sat tentatively on the edge of the king-size bed and noted the total lack of any feminine touches in the decor. There was no vanity table or makeup mirror, no tall lingerie chest like the one Diana had at home. The attached bathroom was bigger by far than the one they shared and had both a shower and a claw-foot tub, as well as a doored-off toilet. High shelves in a walk-in closet held a full wardrobe in his exact size. He absently fingered the assortment of khaki pants and jeans, T-shirts in every color and a hanging rod that held about twenty-five casual buttoned shirts. There wasn't a suit or tie to be seen. He wouldn't need business attire for a solid year, he realized.

Back in the living room, he picked up the landline phone. It had no dial on it, no way to call out. Before he even put it to his ear, he heard a woman's voice on the other end.

"Hello, Mr. Adams. Is there something I can help you with?"

"Oh, n-no," he stammered. "I was just testing the phone."

"I see. Have you had a chance to go through your provisions? Is everything satisfactory?"

"Yes, yes, fine. They seem to have thought of everything."

"Well, if you should ever require anything from the outside—specific food, books, even furniture—all you have to do is pick up the phone and we can usually arrange it for you," she said. "We can handle most requests."

"Well, I might let you know I probably won't eat the asparagus. You can cross that off the shopping list."

"I'll make a note of it, Mr. Adams. Anything you don't eat you can deposit in the composter. There's a small door just behind the kitchen sink."

"I'll make a note of *that*," he said. "Oh, and that beer you got me, I prefer something simpler. Budweiser would be fine from now on."

"Noted," she told him. "But that request was from Mr. Higgins."

"Mr. Higgins?"

"Yes, Brent Higgins. He's the data analyst that will be working with you each day. He's scheduled to come and see you this afternoon."

"I know who he is. I just wasn't aware he was going to be making beer requests."

"Since he's going to be spending so much time in there with you, I suppose he has a few extra benefits," she said. "I can get that beer to you by this afternoon. Is there anything else I can do for you?"

"Something for a headache, maybe?"

"The medicine cabinet in the bathroom is fully stocked. You should find what you need."

"I'll look, then. Thanks. Sorry to bother you."

"It's not a bother, Mr. Adams. It's my job."

"I didn't catch your name."

"I'm Andrea," she said. "I'm the day shift. At night, you'll speak to someone else."

"Thanks, Andrea."

There were at least three different things in the medicine cabinet that he could have taken for a headache. He was also covered for a sprained ankle, allergies, upset stomach and, apparently, a sudden attack of killer zombie bees. It was as well supplied as any pharmacy. He swallowed two tablets with a glass of water. Then he loosened his tie, took off his work shoes and stretched out on the mammoth bed. It was unexpectedly comfortable.

Despite the headache and the after-effects of the sedative, Jeremiah's mind raced. He was amazed at the exactness of the clone. Everything about the appearance was precise, right down to the smattering of gray in the hair. And when he'd heard the thing speak for the first time on the monitor, he was struck not only by the voice but the intonation and the slight hesitation before it spoke. It was a habit Jeremiah had noticed in himself. It was positively eerie how accurate it was. And he knew for a fact that the similarities didn't end there. Aside from the Meld duplicating thought patterns, behavior and the rest, the clone was a perfect copy of Jeremiah inside as well—right down to the molecular level, right down to the slightest cellular makeup. Dr. Pike had seen to that.

The first time he'd met the good doctor, for what Jeremiah had assumed would be a simple routine exam, he'd been put into a room-size scanner, strapped into a severe-looking chair that jerked around by way of hydraulics and had his entire medical history recorded. The machine, created by a team of ViMed scientists and specifically for use in this project, had completed a medical probe unlike anything in history. It detected everything, and left Pike with an exhaustive list of every childhood illness Jeremiah had ever suffered, every metabolic imbalance, every virus, vaccination and injury. It had even picked up on the fact that Jeremiah had broken the same arm twice, once at the age of seven, and again at twenty-two. The injuries had left him with the disturbing ability to rotate his left arm several degrees farther than his right. His clone, Pike had told him, would be able to do the same thing.

"Where did ViMed get the funding to develop tech like this?" Jeremiah had asked, astonished.

"Meld is quite a profitable drug, Mr. Adams," Pike told him. "Its release provided substantial cash flow for other avenues of research."

"And just in time, it seems."

"There are also some well-endowed investors behind this project. Interested parties with deep pockets," Pike said.

After the scan, Jeremiah had been injected with experimental nanotechnology that had served as a vaccine against any further viral infections and most bacterial illnesses from that point up until the cloning. The measure ensured that he and his clone would start out medically identical in every way. The idea of microscopic robots swimming around inside him had unnerved him, but Scott had only scoffed when Jeremiah asked about it later.

"It's perfectly harmless, Mr. Adams. If it makes you feel better, I've tested it on myself without adverse effect."

It hadn't made him feel better at all. In fact, he found it disturbing that Scott would subject himself to untested technology when he must have had a lab full of rabbits at the ready. There was so much about him that Jeremiah found disturbing, though.

It was reasonable, he supposed, in the quiet of the room, that his thoughts drifted to his family. He'd left them that morning and wouldn't return for an entire year. He hadn't even been able to say a proper goodbye. During his walk with Louie that morning, he'd lingered a bit longer than he usually did, allowing the dog to sniff every tree they passed and giving him an extra lap around the block. Scott had cautioned him to act normally, not to give anything away by altering his usual routine. But Jeremiah had found that almost impossible. He knew that an imposter—an inhuman copy—would be coming home in his place for dinner that night. He was leaving them in the hands of an untested science experiment. How does anyone act normally knowing that?

So, as Parker brushed by him out the door to make the school bus, Jeremiah had given his son a quick, impulsive kiss on the top of the head, a gesture so out of character that both Parker and Diana had paused and stared at him like he'd just lost his grip on reality. Jeremiah had made a show of shrugging it off. But what, he wondered now, would his clone do with that memory? They had erased the memory of why he'd done it, certainly, but Parker and Diana had seen it. Presumably, the clone would need to remember that moment in case it ever came up in conversation. The effort of wrapping his brain around that enigma wasn't going to help his headache, he decided, and he almost welcomed the disruption of someone knocking at his front door.

Before he could get himself out of bed and into the living room, Dr. Natalie Young had already let herself in. She'd have to, he figured, since he was incapable of even opening his door from the inside.

"I wasn't expecting you, Dr. Young." He looked down at his shoeless feet with some apprehension.

"You have just seen the clone for the first time. I thought it might be a good idea to have a talk, Mr. Adams," she said, and motioned for him to take a seat on one of the couches. She sat on the other, directly across from him. She crossed her legs at the ankles, adjusted her computer pad on her lap and smiled at him in a way that was at once demure and expectant.

Just like the first time he'd seen her, Jeremiah was struck by the idea that she looked more like a model playing a scientist in some rock video than she did an actual scientist. She was a beautiful woman for her age, which Jeremiah guessed was near either side of forty. The fact that she sported black-rimmed men's eyeglasses and wore her silvery-colored hair pulled back in a tense knot behind her head was an obvious attempt to work around her looks. It almost had the opposite effect.

But Natalie Young was all business and a woman of few words, as he supposed most psychiatric doctors needed to be. She seemed to be waiting for Jeremiah to say something.

"Have you seen it?" he asked.

"I have, briefly."

"What did you think?"

"I'm more interested in your thoughts," she said.

"Well, they got the nose just right."

"And everything else, I'd say."

"Yeah, everything else. It's strange to think that thing will be going home tonight, having dinner with my family, walking my dog."

"How does that make you feel, Jeremiah?"

"I don't know, nervous, I guess. But this is what I signed up for, right?" He tried to smile but he had the sense it didn't come across right.

"Why don't you tell me how you spent the last night with your family. What was that like?" she asked.

"It was just normal, I guess. A normal night. You know, dinner, some TV."

"I can't imagine it felt very normal for you," she said. "You are literally being replaced, Jeremiah. You must have been feeling something on your last night with your wife and son. Did you do anything special? What was going through your mind?"

In fact, there had been a great deal going through his mind the night before. On his drive home, he had thought of soldiers. How many times had he seen on the evening news the syrupy stories of young men or women returning home from war to welcoming crowds and weepy families? How many times had he cringed as the cameras invaded the intensely private moment when a father or mother sought to surprise a young child with a visit to a kindergarten class? He was always struck by how silent a child's joy could be. Most of them just ran into the arms of a parent and burrowed in with hardly a word, lost in some transcendent relief. And despite the fact that he always felt like he was intruding, watching something that no one else should be witness to, he typically choked up at the sight and couldn't look away. It was brilliant media manipulation, something he could admire.

But what the cameras never captured—what they never seemed to care about—was what came beforehand. How did these people say goodbye? He doubted that was as silent a thing. More likely there were moments of tension and fiery exchanges. Fear and uncertainty coming out as unintended anger, the way it had for him in the weeks leading up to the cloning. He imagined frustrating, terrible things that no one would want to watch. But at least, he thought now, those were shared fears. Jeremiah hadn't even had that comfort. He couldn't even tell his family he was leaving. He couldn't say goodbye to them.

He would have liked his last night at home to be special somehow, even if he was the only one who knew why. He had come home with a decent bottle of wine and stopped short of buying flowers for Diana. If anything were going to make her suspicious, he realized, it would have been flowers. He hadn't done anything like that for a very long time. Neither had she.

"I suppose I would have liked to explain a few things to them," he told Natalie Young. "I sort of feel like I was cheated out of that."

"What would you have explained?"

"Well, it hasn't been easy these past few weeks, you know. I've been a little on edge with all of this. I haven't been easy to live with."

"Go on."

He recounted for her an evening about a week before when he had gone upstairs to Parker's bedroom door fully intending to maneuver his way into playing a computer game with him.

Parker hadn't even looked up from the screen when Jeremiah spoke to him from the doorway. It was like he wasn't even there, or like he was a figment that couldn't penetrate the laser fire and bomb blasts of the game. So, without even meaning to, Jeremiah had let everything inside him come out in a burst of anger that—to Parker—must have looked like it came out of nowhere. And once it began, Jeremiah hadn't known how to reel it back in.

"You're on that thing twenty-four hours a day! You're wasting your life with this crap!"

Parker had said nothing, but Jeremiah saw his face redden with a tormented mix of anger and the frustration that comes from not being able to do anything with it. Jeremiah could see that his son was fighting to keep himself quiet.

"From now on there are going to be rules. You hear me?

You're not going to be on that computer whenever you want. You can play for one hour after school and then one hour after your homework is done. Do you understand?"

"My homework *is* done," Parker said without looking up. "I already finished it."

"Good. So, turn that goddamn thing off and clean your room or something. Read a book. I don't care what you do, but just turn it off."

He turned on his heels and almost ran into Diana, who was standing in the hallway with an empty laundry basket, her eyes wide in quiet surprise. Jeremiah just shook his head and skirted past her down the stairs where he sat heavily on the couch and turned on the TV. She followed him.

"What on earth prompted that?" she asked icily. "What's gotten into you lately?"

"Nothing's gotten into me," he snapped. "The kid needs to grow up. Someone around here has to be the bad guy. It might as well be me."

"Oh, come on. That's ridiculous. He's not doing anything wrong. He's a kid. He's playing his games. What's so bad about that? You think he's the only kid his age who does this?"

"Yeah, well, I don't care about other kids. We need to have some limits."

"Jesus, Jeremiah. There *are* limits," she said. "He knows that, and you would, too, if you bothered to pay attention. I've already told him that he can play until he goes to bed once he's done his homework. He needs his downtime, you know."

"Yeah, well, now there are more limits. What's so wrong with that?"

Diana had called him unreasonable. Looking back on it, he could understand why.

"I would have liked to apologize," he told Dr. Young now. "I should have said something. But what could I say?"

Dr. Young was quiet for a moment and looked at Jeremiah as though she might have something comforting to offer. But in typical fashion, she didn't, and only gave him another question.

"How long have you and Diana been married?"

"Almost sixteen years." As he said it, he was struck by the fact that it would be his clone celebrating his wedding anniversary in a few months.

"And Parker, he's sixteen?"

"Yes, last month actually." Jeremiah noted a look of mock surprise on her face. "I think I can see where this is going," he said. "Yes, we got married in a hurry. But you do what you need to do, right? I don't think any of this is relevant to the experiment."

"Everything is relevant to this experiment, Jeremiah. I'm simply trying to establish some background. We need that."

"Seems to me you got all the background you needed when we took the Meld together. Wasn't that the idea of taking it before the cloning? To get a baseline? Some background?"

"Well, yes," she said, "but the Meld doesn't always give a complete picture. And what we do glean from it is somewhat dependent on what you're thinking about at the time it's administered. It isn't a precise science."

"From what they told me this morning, that drug is a hell of a lot more precise than I ever thought it was," he said. "Did you know it can be used to implant false memories? That's what they did to the clone."

"It works differently in that scenario," she explained. "With a physical connection everything can be recorded and manipulated as needed. The way you and I use it, it isn't anywhere near as exact. I can control it, but not to that extent."

"What good is it, then?"

"It's extremely useful," she said flatly. "It offers a sharing of feeling, thought processes, impulse reactions, things like that.

More importantly, for our purposes, it illuminates self-perception and self-awareness. It affords me a glimpse of how you see yourself in the world."

Inwardly, Jeremiah began to understand how Meld could be so dangerous. It seemed like something no one ought to see.

"How?" he asked. "I mean, how the hell does it actually *do* that?"

"The science is hard to explain in laymen's terms," she began. "But essentially, Meld does different things to the brains of the people who take it—the Meld I take chemically stimulates mirror neurons in my brain. That's what makes empathy possible— like when you see someone yawn and then you can't help but yawn yourself. That's because of mirror neurons. It gives me a picture of what's going on in your mind and, in a way, lets me experience it."

"And what about the drug you give to me?" he asked. "What does that do?"

"Among other things, it inhibits your own self-perspective. It filters out all those little lies we tell ourselves about who we are, how other people see us. It allows me to see the truth. And to some extent, it allows you to see it, too."

"It sounds a little invasive when you put it like that."

She smiled slightly. "I suppose it is," she said. "But Meld doesn't divulge everything. And because of the interplay between our minds, it's never as exact as I'd like. There's always the need for me to interpret some of what I see. If you want the more specific background, the details, sometimes simple conversation is still the best route."

Jeremiah had the impression that no conversation was ever simple where Natalie Young was concerned.

"Well, there's your specific background, then. Diana got pregnant and we got married. We were already talking about it, anyway. This sort of thing happens all the time. It's not a big deal. Plans change."

"What sort of plans changed, Jeremiah?"

"You know, just normal plans. We were going to go to London. I had an offer from a newspaper there. But it was risky with a baby on the way, you know, up and moving to another country. She got nervous. So, instead we got an apartment. I got a job on a paper here. We had to put things on hold."

"For a long time, it seems," she said.

"We have a son to raise. You make sacrifices. I don't think that's so hard to understand, Dr. Young. I certainly don't think it's a bad thing."

"No, of course not. On the contrary. Do you consider yourself a good father, then?"

"Yes," he said pointedly. "Actually, I do. I've been there for Parker."

"And is that the most important thing?" she asked. "Being there?"

"Well, I'd say it's a pretty damn good start. That's what you do if you're a father."

"Your own father left when you were…how old?" she asked, looking down at her notes. "Four years old?"

The expectant look on her face gave Jeremiah the impression she was waiting for him to make some breakthrough connection about overcompensating in his role as a father. But he wasn't going to give in to her cheap psychoanalytic tricks.

"I guess he didn't want to make those kinds of sacrifices," he said. "He left my mother to do it on her own. So, I suppose, yeah, I'm one up on him."

"You've told me she was a good mother to you."

"She was," he said. "She did a good job with a bad situation. But yeah, she was always a good mother. She *is* a good mother."

"And what about Diana?" she asked at last. "Has she been a good mother to Parker? Has she had to make sacrifices, too?"

"Of course she has," he said. "She was going to go to law school. She wanted to travel. We've both had to make sacrifices. That's what you do."

"What else have you sacrificed?"

"Well, for one thing, I gave up a career in journalism to work for ViMed. For God's sake, I just had myself cloned! I'd call that a sacrifice."

"So, you did this for your family, then?"

"In a way, I suppose so. The money they're paying me for this will solve a lot of problems."

"I wasn't aware you had financial troubles."

"We don't. That's not what I mean." He tried not to raise his voice, but it was getting more difficult. It seemed like she took everything he said and turned it around to imply something else. He hated talking to her.

"What sort of problems will the money solve?"

"A lot of things. We can travel now. If Diana wants to go to Europe we can just go. We can take Parker with us as soon as he graduates. If that can make her happy, we can do it now."

"So, she's unhappy?"

He could feel his face getting hot. How much had Natalie Young learned from him when they took the Meld? She seemed to be dancing around the edges of Diana's affair, trying to move him toward the topic. That was off-limits. He didn't have the strength to discuss it with his own wife. He certainly wouldn't drag it into this experiment. It had nothing to do with anything, as far as he was concerned. So, whether she knew about it or not, he wouldn't discuss it with Natalie Young.

"I never said my wife is unhappy," he told her with what he hoped was some level of finality.

"Are you happy, Jeremiah?"

"Yes," he said flatly. "Perfectly happy."

"Okay, then," she said after a pensive moment. "Why don't we leave off for now. I'll see you in a couple of days in my office."

"I'm counting the minutes," he told her.

# CHAPTER

# 4

Just before one o'clock that afternoon, Brent Higgins let himself into Jeremiah's living room with an almost simultaneous knock. Jeremiah began to wonder why they'd equipped him with a door at all. Everyone seemed to waltz in exactly as they pleased.

Brent was nothing like what Jeremiah had expected. He looked to be about twenty-five years old, half the age of anyone else on the team, and was dressed casually, in jeans and sneakers. His red hair was in need of cutting and he sported a close-cropped beard, a shade darker, that was an oddly complicated thing: a sizable bare spot smack on the ball of his chin gave the impression of a pair of sideburns that had migrated down his face in an attempt to sneak away. Brent flashed an easy smile at Jeremiah and held his hand out by way of introduction.

"It's great to finally meet you in person, Jeremiah," he said. "I'm Brent Higgins. You and I are going to be spending a lot of time together over the next twelve months. I'm looking forward to it."

"Likewise, Mr. Higgins," he said.

"Might as well call me Brent."

"Might as well. And you've already decided, apparently, to call me Jeremiah. So, Brent, do we begin today, you and I? Now?"

"We're scheduled for our first viewing shortly," he said. "They've discharged the clone from the hospital, and we'll pick him up when he gets home. The monitor will go on when it's time. I thought I'd come a little early so we could get acquainted, go over the basics and all."

"Great. Can I get you anything? Coffee? They got the beer you asked for. It's in the fridge."

"Oh, yeah. Sorry about that. I hope you don't mind. It's not for when I'm on duty, you know. But as I understand it, we'll have a bit of downtime. I'm here for six hours every day. Dr. Scott is fine with it, but if you have a problem, that's okay."

"It's no problem. So, the basics? Don't we just watch the clone together? Is there more to it?"

Brent went to a closet near the kitchen and took out a white lab coat, which he donned over his T-shirt.

"A little," Brent said. "As you know, we will be watching the monitor for a different four-hour period each day. I'm basically here to observe your reactions to the viewing and note any relevant changes in your reactions. Pretty straightforward, really."

"That's nice work if you can get it."

"Actually, it's a fairly critical aspect of this whole experiment," he said, a hint of injury in his expression. "After all, Jeremiah, the point of the whole thing is to watch *you* as you're watching your clone. You know, to gauge whether it's an exact duplicate in thought and action. You're the expert on that. It's key. I mean, it's one thing if it can convince the people on the outside. It's another thing if it can convince you."

"Of course. Sorry. I didn't mean any offense."

"None taken," he said. "Anyway, the point is, part of my job is getting to know you on a more personal level. I need to do that if I'm going to be able to accurately assess your responses to the clone."

"Sounds reasonable."

"So, essentially, we'll be watching together, and I'll follow up each viewing with a series of questions for you. Once those answers are put into the system, we'll get the schedule for the next day's viewing. The exact times are selected randomly." Brent took a seat on one of the couches and opened up his laptop. The monitor on the wall went on almost at the same instant, so that anyone watching might have been forgiven for thinking Brent Higgins had turned it on with his own computer.

"Time to get to work," he said to Jeremiah, and motioned for him to have a seat.

On the wall, Jeremiah watched as the image of an unfamiliar car pulling into his garage snapped into focus. It must have been a rental, he thought, and he wondered about the condition of his own car. He was watching from an angle near the back wall of his garage as the car pulled in and the taillights flicked off. A moment later, the clone stepped out, dressed in exactly the same suit Jeremiah had on that very moment, the only difference being that Jeremiah didn't have his shoes on. Seeing his replica in his own home like that was jarring, and he felt a sudden stab of finality. *This is really happening,* he thought. *He's there. He's up and walking and he's going into my house.*

As the clone opened the door into the kitchen, the scene changed suddenly so they were viewing the clone head-on, from a camera located somewhere just above the refrigerator, Jeremiah guessed. When, he wondered with some concern, had they put all of this monitoring equipment up in his house? And how could they have done it without his knowledge?

It was just before two o'clock in the afternoon. Jeremiah wasn't usually home at that time of day. Parker would be at school for another two hours, and Diana was evidently still at work, though he half expected her to be home after she'd heard about his car accident. Maybe the clone had downplayed it, he thought. He would have.

He heard the familiar jangle of Louie's tags as the dog came rambling down the stairs and into the kitchen, eager to greet him and, no doubt, excited by the unusual timing. Typically, when Jeremiah came home at the end of the day, Louie was already waiting by the door, anticipating his arrival by way of some canine radar. Diana found it uncanny the way he sat there even before Jeremiah's car pulled into the garage. "It's like he's got you on GPS or something," she'd said. Jeremiah watched and felt his own muscles tighten as he waited for his dog's usual greeting, which involved jumping up and putting both paws hard on Jeremiah's chest and licking his cheek. But today Louie stopped as soon as he turned the corner into the kitchen, his claws scraping against the floor as he slid to a halt and eyed the clone with a slight twist of the head, as though he had a question. This was more than just the odd timing throwing the dog off, Jeremiah thought. It was a look he'd seen in Louie before. The dog was hovering, torn between aggression and friendly greeting, the way he acted when Jeremiah would allow the pizza guy—an unwelcome stranger in Louie's mind—right into the kitchen. To Jeremiah's astonishment, at the first sight of the clone, Louie stood still, lowered his head and growled, just a little, while his eyes and his other canine senses fought for some sense of resolution. His tail wagged tentatively while his ears twitched in alert. The clone took a step forward, leaning down, hand out in invitation, but the dog wouldn't even come in for a quick sniff. Finally, after a moment, Louie retreated backward and went back up the stairs. He was definitely frightened.

Louie knew. That dog knew in a single instant that it wasn't his master who had just walked through the garage door. The very first real test, and it had failed utterly.

Jeremiah said nothing. He was gripped by a sudden alarm. If that dog cost him this $10 million, he could kiss those expensive organic dog treats goodbye.

He turned to Brent with what he hoped was an expression of casual exasperation and tried to explain it away.

"I'm sure he was expecting Parker at the door," he said. "That dog's whole world revolves around Parker. He barely tolerates anyone else."

Brent said nothing but offered a half grin, which Jeremiah took as a good sign. He turned back to the image with some relief.

The clone closed the door behind him, put his keys down on the counter and called to Louie without success. He then went to the refrigerator and took a bottle of water. Jeremiah noted that a different camera seemed to pick up his movements almost seamlessly as he walked through the house. There was never a time when he was out of view. Only the angles changed, blending together almost like a professionally edited film. He couldn't understand how they did it. He watched from behind as the clone climbed the stairs and, when he reached the top, had a front view as the clone walked across the hallway into his bedroom.

"Is there someone operating these cameras?" he asked Brent.

"No, it's all automatic—sensors pick up the clone's movements and the next camera is cued from that. It's pretty neat, huh? This is the first time I've seen it in action. It's flawless."

He was slightly shocked when he realized that he had a clear view as the clone took off his jacket and tie in the bedroom.

"How many cameras, exactly, are in my house?"

"A lot," Brent told him. "We can see him anywhere in the house and all around the property. There's even a camera in your car and, of course, there's a whole separate system so we can watch him at ViMed."

"And in the bedroom, I see."

"Oh, don't worry about that. There's a fail-safe installed so we won't be able to see anything private. It will fade out if anything, you know, physical happens. And there are no cameras in the bathrooms."

Jeremiah was glad to know they wouldn't be watching the bedroom, but more because of what they wouldn't see rather than anything else. What Brent didn't know was that Jeremiah had insisted, right at the start of this whole thing, that the clone be prohibited somehow from any physical relations with Diana. Scott had assured him it was possible with a little tweaking of the clone's physiology, and reinforced by suggestion during the initial Meld. Sexual desire for her had simply been wiped out of the thing. As for Diana, Jeremiah doubted it would even be an issue. Those cameras would never have the need to fade out.

"What about my family, though? I don't really like the idea of them being watched like this. I had no idea it would be so… intrusive."

"The cameras are only activated by the clone, Jeremiah. It's all done by facial recognition. State-of-the-art. No one's going to be watching your family, except for when they're interacting with the clone. That's all we care about here."

Jeremiah turned his attention back to the wall where the clone was just picking up the remote control and switching on the TV. For the next few hours, they just watched as he sat there, propped up against the pillows on the bed, and channel surfed the unfamiliar landscape of afternoon television. The image on the wall was close up and six feet tall and, in the lull of any activity, Jeremiah found himself scrutinizing his own familiar face in all its uncomfortable detail. It was both fascinating and a bit unnerving. He could see every pore in his own cheeks, every unruly gray hair at the temples, every crease around his eyes, every pockmark. He noted with some dismay that his shoulders looked small and slightly hunched over. *Do I look like that?* He put a hand under his own chin and made a mental note to look up a suitable exercise for a saggy neck. He never realized he'd gotten so soft. At one point the clone fell asleep and Jeremiah was shocked to see his own slack-mouthed expression and hear the sound of his own snoring, which nearly drowned out the TV. How the hell did Diana ever get any sleep? Jesus!

After a while the kitchen door opened, and the clone got up when he heard Louie's tags jangling again in a jubilant ruckus down the stairs.

"Parker?" he called. "Is that you?"

"Dad? What are you doing home?"

The clone walked down the stairs to meet the boy in the kitchen, cameras following so that Brent and Jeremiah could track his progress without interruption. Jeremiah braced himself. Would his son react the same way that Louie had? Would he know the clone wasn't really him? This entire thing, he thought, could be all over before it even began. He might be home for dinner, after all.

"I had a little car accident this morning. I'm fine," the clone told Parker. "But the doctors at the hospital told me to take the day off, so I did. I'll be back to work tomorrow, though."

"Whoa! You were in the hospital?"

"Just as a precaution, it's nothing serious. They checked me out. I'm okay."

"Did you total the car, Dad?"

"Not sure yet, but I think so. Probably. Shouldn't your mother be home by now?"

"Nah," Parker said, opening the refrigerator and turning his attention to the pressing matter of what he would eat. "She's working late."

That was news to Jeremiah.

"I thought you had something at school tonight," the clone said, echoing Jeremiah's own thoughts right down to the word.

"It got canceled. I texted her and she said she might as well stay late tonight."

"Did she say when she'd be home?"

Parker shrugged and poured himself a glass of milk to wash down the eight or nine cookies he had snagged from a cabinet. "I don't know," he said. "Hey, if we get a new car can we get a convertible?"

There wasn't a hint of suspicion in Parker's face. In fact, Jeremiah was stunned at how readily Parker had taken the clone for him. His every reaction and expression, every gesture, was exactly what Jeremiah would have expected. His son interacted with it in exactly the same way he would have done with Jeremiah. As impressive as it was, it hurt. Dr. Young's words echoed in his mind: *"You are literally being replaced, Jeremiah."* That thought hit home watching the clone talking to Parker.

"We'll see," the clone said. "Where have you been? Did you miss the bus or something?"

"Nah. I stayed after school with some friends."

"What friends?"

"You don't know them. Kids from school."

"What were you doing?"

"Nothing much, just hanging out."

Parker turned to head upstairs, eager, no doubt, to begin his usual hour of gaming before dinner. But the clone stopped him.

"Hey, do me a favor and take Louie out for a walk. He's acting strange. I hope he's not sick or something."

At that moment, the cameras stopped and the monitor on the wall blinked off just as abruptly as it had switched on four hours before.

Brent stood up from his place on the couch with a slow stretch. Jeremiah was still staring at the blank wall in front of him.

"That was," he began, shaking his head to find the right word, "absolutely bizarre."

"I bet," Brent said. "It certainly looks like an exact copy. So, down to my questions and then we can kick back for a while, have some dinner." He didn't seem genuinely fazed by what they'd just seen.

"Yeah, sure. Go ahead."

Brent sat back down and pulled his laptop closer. When he spoke, his voice had assumed a more solemn, businesslike manner.

"During the viewing did you note any actions of the clone to be unexpected, atypical or otherwise out of the ordinary?"

"The whole thing was a bit out of the ordinary from where I'm standing," he said. "But no. I suppose he acted just the way I would have under the same circumstances."

Brent typed and then looked up at Jeremiah.

"At any point during the viewing did you note an instance where you would have acted in a manner different from the clone?"

Jeremiah honestly tried to settle on something he might have done differently. But the clone had done everything exactly as he would have done—from the things he'd said to Parker to the way he'd fluffed the pillows behind himself, stacking them at an angle to support his shoulders and upper back. It was almost spooky.

"No," he said at last.

"Finally, did the people interacting with the clone display any indication that they recognized the clone as an imposter?"

"No," he said. The question had referred to *people*, after all, so technically, Jeremiah reasoned, he wasn't lying when he failed to mention Louie's reaction. He felt justified in his answer. And in terms of Parker's interaction with the clone, it was definitely the truth.

He'd been struck, in fact, by the way Parker hardly seemed to look at the clone when he talked to him. Parker acknowledged his father only as much as he needed to and nothing more. It hadn't always been like that.

Jeremiah's mind turned to a camping trip they'd taken together when Parker was about ten years old. Jeremiah had never been camping in his life and never had any desire to try, but at the first mention of the idea from his son, he'd rushed out and spent a small fortune on anything he thought they might need: a top-of-the-line tent, subzero sleeping bags, a book of campfire stories, several cans of bug spray and a portable stove. They ended up at a campground in central Maine, slightly off-season, with a persistent light rain that stayed with them the entire weekend. He wasn't surprised they'd had the place almost exclusively to themselves.

The trip wasn't the idyllic adventure Jeremiah had imagined it would be. It took him three tries to get the tent up and even then it ended up lopsided when one of the poles wouldn't stay put. They couldn't get a fire started until the owner of the place felt sorry for them and finally helped to put up tarps in the trees above their campsite. But Jeremiah had never felt closer to Parker than he did during those damp, chilly two days in the middle of the woods.

"It's a good thing it's just me and you, Dad," Parker had said while they listened to the rhythm of the rain on the tent. "I don't think Mom would be able to handle this like we can."

"Yeah. She's not much for roughing it," he agreed. "She'd need her pillows and a place to plug in her coffeepot."

"And her makeup," Parker added, "and her TV."

"And her shower," Jeremiah said.

"And her clothes dryer!"

"And about six pairs of shoes!"

"And basically the whole house!"

They'd fallen asleep that night laughing, and as Jeremiah pulled the sleeping bag up under his chin against the cold, he couldn't remember ever feeling more completely content and comfortable.

The tent and all that expensive gear never made its way out of the attic a second time.

After watching the strained exchange between his clone and his son, Jeremiah felt the full force of regret like a weight around his neck.

"No," he said again to Brent. "Parker treated the clone just the way he should have."

# CHAPTER

# 5

The next morning, Brent came to the lab early, only a few minutes before the day's viewing was scheduled to begin. Groggy and still half-asleep, Jeremiah dragged himself to the living room couch and looked at the wall just as the clone was pouring himself a cup of coffee in the kitchen. The typical commotion and rush of his family's weekday morning routine played out in front of Jeremiah and had an almost immediate effect. He could feel his own adrenaline kick in as he watched them hurrying to beat traffic and make the school bus. Diana, a blue sweater slung over one arm, was digging in her purse for Parker's lunch money and Louie was leaning up against her knees in a futile attempt to get her attention.

"Have you checked on the car?" Diana asked the clone without looking at him. She handed Parker three crumpled dollar bills.

"I'll call today," he said. "It's at the shop near my office."

"I have to stay after school for a makeup quiz in English," Parker said, slinging his backpack over one shoulder. "Can I get a ride?"

"I won't be home until after four today," Diana said. "Can you get a ride from someone else?"

"Yeah, probably. I guess so."

Parker heaved his shoulders to settle his mammoth backpack behind him and stuck the buds of his headphones in his ears before bolting out the door and down the street to catch the bus. Diana downed the last of her coffee and struggled her sweater on.

"You've been taking on a lot of extra hours lately," the clone said to her. "You worked late yesterday, too."

"Well, there's a big case and they need me," she told him. "It's mainly just a lot of research. It won't be for too much longer. How's your head?"

"Fine," the clone said. "Doesn't hurt anymore."

"That's good." She rinsed her coffee mug and left it in the sink. "I've got to go. I'm late."

The clone poured the last of his coffee into the sink and followed her to the door leading to the garage. Louie took a tentative step after him, but then seemed to think better of it and walked back to his dog bed in the corner of the kitchen and lay down.

"I think Louie might be sick," the clone said. In the lab, Jeremiah cringed, hoping Brent wouldn't pick up on all the talk about the dog.

Diana stopped and turned toward Louie with a hint of confusion on her face.

"Really?" she asked. "He seems fine to me. He ate his breakfast. Was he okay on his walk this morning?"

"He wouldn't come on the walk with me," the clone told her. "That's what I mean. He just didn't want to go. Dug his heels in. I just let him out in the yard on his own. He was acting strange last night, too."

Diana's brow wrinkled. "I'll make an appointment for him later this week," she said, and walked into the garage.

The clone followed and closed the door behind him. Another camera, situated somewhere above the garage bay doors, immediately picked him up from another angle in an almost seamless cut.

Diana got into her red Subaru and waved at the clone as she closed the door. Jeremiah saw with some unease that she hardly looked at him as she did so. He'd never noticed while he was actually there with her, but she hardly looked at him at all anymore. There's guilt in her, he thought. The clone waved back, and Jeremiah noticed that his gaze lingered for just a moment longer than it should have. The realization that he knew exactly what was going through its mind in that moment was slightly disturbing to him. It was definitely someone at her office she was having an affair with. He had never met anyone from the law firm, knew them only from her sporadic mentions of them: four lawyers, three of them men, two other legal secretaries, one of them a much younger man, and two receptionists, both female. He should have done something. He should have confronted her. He didn't know why he never had. It wasn't as though he needed any more proof. He had been sure of it for a while, several months at least. And, he realized now, the clone shared that certainty. He found himself wondering if his double would somehow muster the resolve to do something other than wait and pretend. He wondered if he even could.

"I'm going to make coffee," Brent said, startling Jeremiah out of his contemplations.

On the monitor, Jeremiah watched as the clone got into the rental car, started the engine and backed into the driveway. He drove to work listening to news radio and sighing occasionally at the traffic on the highway. How the hell had they gotten a camera into the rental car?

Brenda, the bubbly, flame-haired receptionist for ViMed's

Communications department, greeted him at the office in typical exuberance. She wore an equally brash outfit, featuring a
pair of oversize kelly-green hoop earrings that were specifically
distracting.

"Good morning, Mr. Adams," she said, handing him a single
slip of pink paper. "Walt Thompson from the *New York Times*."

"Thanks," he said, looking her directly in the ears. "Anything else?"

"You have that editorial meeting at 11:15 and the printer will
be here at noon to go over the proofs of the newsletter. Other
than that, pretty quiet so far."

The clone nodded and headed into his office. He closed the
door and the camera angle shifted. This one, if Jeremiah had to
guess, was located in one of the paintings on the wall directly in
front of him and afforded a clear view of the desk and a head-
on view of the clone.

Walt Thompson was a science editor for the *Times* and Jeremiah's former classmate and one-time colleague on a Boston
paper. There was a chance the call could have been a social one,
but Jeremiah suspected it more likely had to do with Meld. Even
without a current storm over the drug, Walt had been keenly
preoccupied with it, writing no fewer than four stories on the
drug in the past two months. He was probably still chasing it.
The clone sighed and picked up the phone to dial.

Jeremiah could hear only the clone's side of the conversation, but it was relatively easy to figure out that his suspicions
had been correct.

"Give it a rest, would you, Walt?" he said. "If you want another angle, why don't you talk to that doctor in Delaware again?
I hear he's using Meld more and more. There's your story…

"What am I hedging about? I don't have anything new.
There've been no more suicides, no incidents at all since New

Jersey. Maybe the kinks have been worked out. Maybe the cops are doing their jobs…"

Maybe, Jeremiah thought in the lab, it was just a stroke of dumb luck.

"You're being ridiculous. You're starting to sound like one of those conspiracy theorists. I think you need a vacation…

"Look, I can put you in touch with someone else from the science end, but I think you're barking up a dead tree here, Walt. There's nothing new to report…

"I'm not defending anyone. This is my job…

"Yeah, yeah, the award thing. No, I haven't forgotten," the clone said, his tone shifting from the defensive for the moment. Walt had been after him to attend an award dinner in New York City at the end of the month. Jeremiah had no inclination of going.

"Diana is checking her schedule. I'll get back to you on it." He hadn't even mentioned it to Diana.

The last thing Jeremiah wanted was to drive four hours and schmooze with a roomful of journalists, most of whom he could have reported circles around in his day. He had no desire to banter about who got which promotion and listen to all the righteous First Amendment-Fourth Estate pontificating. And he certainly wasn't itching to see Walt get a second Hearst Award for Excellence in as many years. Jeremiah had been nominated himself three times but missed out on each one. If he had to hear one more person say to him what an honor it was "just to be nominated" he'd likely start throwing punches. Besides, with the Meld scandal, he'd be a goldfish in a piranha pool, and that wasn't something he was about to walk into casually.

"Yeah, I will," the clone said into the phone. "I'll call you later this week."

For the remainder of the viewing, Jeremiah and Brent watched the clone work silently in his office, lead an uneventful editorial meeting and decline an offer for lunch with two of his younger coworkers, saying he had a lot of busywork to catch up on. When the monitor switched off, he was eating a soggy tuna sandwich alone at his desk and staring, unknowingly, directly into the camera.

# CHAPTER
# 6

## DAY 30

It was a novelty to live in the lap of high-tech luxury without the responsibilities of work and family. Jeremiah wasn't used to so much free time, and in those first weeks he wallowed in it. He stayed up late, well after midnight, watching old movies and reruns of TV shows he hadn't seen since he was a kid. He ate unconventional meals at odd hours and burned them off on the treadmill in virtual locales as exotic as he could think of. He read newspapers—the *Washington Post*, the *Wall Street Journal*, the *Boston Globe*, even his hometown weekly—from cover to cover. They delivered the actual hard copies, like he'd asked. He started reading the books they'd supplied him with and toyed again with the idea of writing his own novel. A year of this could go far, he figured, toward finally setting that idea in motion. But what would he write about? Titles took shape in his mind: *Clone Alone; Cloney Island; The Year of the Clone.* He doubted Charles Scott would approve. Still, he thought, it could make for a good read.

After a while, though, too much free time begins to feel more like empty, wasted hours, and Jeremiah got antsy, the way one does when a vacation has gone on too long. He craved his old

routine. More than anything, he wanted a walk. Not the aug-
mented reality kind he could get on the treadmill, an actual
walk in the woods where he could feel the breeze on his face
and the crunch of the leaves underneath his feet. It didn't help
matters that he was made to watch his clone doing all the ordinary activities he was beginning to miss. He started to fixate
on things that shouldn't have bothered him. He hated that the
clone was left to choose a new car to replace the one that was
wrecked. A dark blue Lincoln town car? Really? It looked like
something a G-man would drive. Although he knew he would
have ended up with the same car—sedate, appropriate, not too
flashy—he had to wonder why he'd suddenly started eyeing a
lemon-yellow European sports car while he watched the clone
haggle at the car dealership. He found himself wishing the clone
might at least have taken it for a test drive.

The days went by, in what felt like four-hour stretches to
him, and Jeremiah was repeatedly astonished by how exact
this replica was. In those first days, they watched it in a variety
of activities: leading editorial meetings at ViMed, walking the
trash to the curb on a Monday morning, stammering and fidgeting through casual office conversations in the hallways of his
office. Each time, Jeremiah had the feeling he was watching a
television show he somehow had forgotten he'd written. It got
to the point where he could mouth the words of every other
thing the clone said, both at home and at work. *No, I don't want
any pie… Let's put some polish on this write-up… Have you finished
your homework yet?… Yes, dear… No, sir… I suppose you might be
right, dear…* No wonder Diana and Parker had been so totally
and utterly fooled by the thing. He was almost fooled himself.
It was a marvel, to be sure, but increasingly unsettling to him.

"This is stupendous, Mr. Adams," Charles Scott exclaimed
during a random check-in.

*This is pathetic*, Jeremiah thought.

"And what's truly remarkable," Scott added, "is that the clone seems to be perfectly convinced himself. He actually believes he is you." Scott shook his head in a show of unexpected amazement. "He doesn't know the difference at all. Everything is working exactly as we hoped. He has no idea he's a copy."

"Yes, well, except he *is* a copy. He's not really me."

Scott waved a hand in annoyed dismissal and sat down on the edge of the couch. "Yes, yes, of course. But don't you find it fascinating that he has no awareness of that? Isn't it intriguing that he could, essentially, continue living your life for, well, for the rest of your life? And no one would know. Not even the clone."

"I don't know if *intriguing* is the right word," Jeremiah said. "Disturbing, maybe. Scary as hell. 'Breach of contract' springs to mind."

"I'm not suggesting anything quite so nefarious," Scott scoffed. "I'm not talking about you. But consider the possibilities, Mr. Adams. Think about what this could mean."

"Why don't you illuminate me? What could it mean exactly?"

"It means an end to needless suffering," Scott told him. "It means we are no longer chained to the random failings of our imperfect bodies. This can change everything, don't you see that, Mr. Adams? This is a second chance." Something in the man's tone, the way his eyes seemed to focus on something far away as he spoke, made Jeremiah pause.

"What do you mean, a second chance?" he asked carefully.

"Exactly what it sounds like. Imagine the implications if every man, woman and child could have a perfect, healthy spare. For God's sake, man. Use your imagination! Blood transfusions, organ transplants, even stem cell therapy—all of it would be as simple as going to the dentist."

"So, what?" Jeremiah asked uneasily, "This is spare parts? That's the way you see this? And to hell with the moral implications?"

Scott's face reclaimed its usual austerity and he looked Jeremiah hard in the eyes.

"Morality isn't always the best judge of what is right, Mr. Adams," he said stiffly. "And the medical implications, that's just one benefit. There are other interested parties who see even more potential in what we're doing, and they are providing the bulk of our funding for this entire endeavor. Those deep pockets might suddenly dry up if this experiment were to fail somehow. But so far, it's been an astounding success. It's working seamlessly."

"If it's working so perfectly already," Jeremiah said, "why do we need an entire year for this? Why not three months? Why not just end it now?"

"Science takes time," Scott said. "Besides, there are other factors at play here. It's more than just the behavioral aspects we're monitoring. We need to ensure that the clone is physically viable, as well. There have been some issues with vital organs in earlier attempts. Nothing for you to be concerned about. Dr. Pike seems confident that these issues have been addressed. But we need to be certain. We need the full year, as your contract clearly stipulates."

Scott turned quickly and retreated out the door without another word, leaving Jeremiah with an unnamable feeling in the pit of his stomach and a sudden resolve to prove the man wrong. This clone couldn't be an exact duplicate of him.

He began to scrutinize the clone during every viewing, trying to decipher some flaw, some minuscule difference. Something wrong and unexpected. *I don't walk like that... That tie? Really?... I would have used a different word there... I'd take the back roads if I were him—doesn't he know the traffic will be murder this time of the day?...* But every single time, without fail, the clone did everything exactly as Jeremiah would have done himself. He could *say* he would have made a different choice, done a different thing, but there wasn't a single time that this was actually true. On one morning, in fact, Jeremiah got up early and made himself waffles for breakfast, something he never ate during the workweek, preferring instead just a quick coffee. Implausibly, on the monitor an hour later, the clone popped a frozen waffle into the toaster. Diana had looked mildly surprised but didn't question it. Jeremiah was absolutely shocked.

"Is it startling to you to see all of these similarities?" Natalie Young always began their sessions with a question. They had begun meeting twice weekly in her small office located on the same basement floor as his apartment. Despite the fact that it was only down the hall, she always came to escort him. He wasn't allowed to go even that short distance on his own.

"No. Not surprising," he said. "Just, I don't know, getting annoying, I suppose. I know everything he's going to say, exactly what he'll do. I yell at the monitor for him to call a specific person at work, for a quote or something, and before I finish talking, he's dialing the number."

"And that bothers you, Jeremiah?"

"Wouldn't it bother you?"

"Not if that were the very central idea of what we're doing here. I'd consider it a success. Don't you think these similarities point to success?"

"Well, yeah. It does. But sometimes I almost wish it wasn't so successful, you know?"

"Can you elaborate?" she pushed.

"I keep wishing he'd slip up or something. I wish I'd see him do one thing—just one thing—that's not exactly the same thing I think he's going to do. I wish someone would realize that it's not me out there."

"You told me before that you were glad your family wouldn't miss you. You said that's what made this easier for you. Has that changed?"

"No," he said, "that's not what I meant. I'm glad they don't know. I guess I just keep waiting for someone to notice something. I mean, you'd think at least Diana would notice something! We've been married a long time. You'd think she'd realize it isn't her husband sleeping next to her in the bed. But she doesn't even notice it."

"Is there something that you think your wife ought to notice? Be honest, Jeremiah. Be objective. This is very important to the experiment. This is crucial. *Are* there any noticeable differences between you and your clone? Is there something you think Diana should pick up on?" Something in her face alarmed him instantly. There was a certain intensity in her eyes that felt almost like a warning to him. What would Charles Scott actually *do* if someone started to catch on, if he thought his funding was at stake?

"No," he said finally. "I don't think there are any differences between me and the clone. I think the whole thing is a raging triumph. Someone ought to break out the champagne."

She looked at him for a long moment and pursed her lips in that way she did whenever he attempted sarcasm.

"I might think you'd be relieved that your clone is doing such a good job of things for you. He's carrying out everything in your life just as you, yourself, would do."

"Yeah. It's all good." Inside, Jeremiah was silently celebrating the fact that at least Louie wasn't fooled. It made him feel marginally better to know that someone out there knew he'd been replaced. But he said nothing of this to Dr. Young.

Sensing he was done talking for the day, she reluctantly closed her laptop. She escorted him back to his apartment, where Brent was already sitting on the couch engrossed in some war zone computer game. He maneuvered the controller wildly with both hands and wore a headset that partially covered his eyes and ears. On the wall monitor was an eight-foot-tall, high-definition image of an animated soldier, deftly sidestepping grenades and gunfire and blasting enemy squadrons. Jeremiah could hear a muted racket coming through Brent's headset and he felt the vibrations through his shoes.

"Working hard, I see." Jeremiah grabbed a bag of potato chips from the kitchen and then took a seat next to him on the couch. "What's this, then?"

*"Infinite Frontiers,"* Brent told him with a quick glance. "It's awesome."

His momentary lapse in total concentration was evidently enough for a misstep and his avatar exploded in a serious blast of blazing debris on the wall.

"Shit!" Brent slammed back into the couch as though he'd suffered the same blow as his soldier and removed his headgear.

"You want a game?"

"Nah," Jeremiah laughed. "I'm not much for these things. I doubt I'd be a worthy opponent."

"C'mon," Brent persisted. "We'll team up."

"I'd probably make an even worse ally," he said. "I've been wondering why they supplied me with all this gaming gear. Now I know."

"It's all top of the line, too," Brent told him. "Some of this stuff isn't even on the market yet. But there's no outgoing signal on this setup, so I have to play against this moronic AI soldier. I need a real adversary. Maybe I can figure out a way to tap into the beta platform when it launches, find someone to play." He switched off the game and the wall went blank again.

"The only thing I know about these games is the ridiculous amount of money I've spent outfitting my son," Jeremiah told him. "Besides, don't we have to get to work?"

"Still an hour almost until the next viewing. I thought I'd come in early just to hang out."

"Hang out? I have never met anyone who would voluntarily

come early to work to hang out. Don't you have a life outside of ViMed?"

"Yes," Brent said. "In fact, I do."

In the span of forty-five minutes, Jeremiah learned more about Brent Higgins than he knew about people he'd worked next to for almost ten years. Brent was raised in a suburb of Chicago, an only, adopted child to parents who were deeply religious, and he was engaged to a girl named Melanie, whom he affectionately referred to as "Mel." Mel, as it happened, was firmly agnostic and, further, had once been employed as an "exotic dancer." Jeremiah resisted the urge to point out the obvious passive aggressive tendencies at play against his parents here, deciding it wouldn't be wise to so quickly alienate the only person he could count on for any kind of company and diversion. *But really*, he thought, *an agnostic stripper? Had the kid no sense of subtlety?*

"How did you get involved with this project?" Jeremiah asked.

"Sheer luck," Brent said. "I was one in a pool of twelve applicants for this position. We were recruited in-house, from all over the company. I think I had five interviews in total. It was brutal."

"For a data analyst? The competition was that tough?"

"This is kind of a big deal," Brent said, a shadow of injured pride pulling at his features. "They weren't going to hire just anybody."

"I didn't mean it that way, Brent," Jeremiah said. "I just can't believe they had that many people after the job. I suppose I just figured they'd handpicked everyone involved, the way they did me."

"Well, we were all asked to interview," he said. "So, I suppose, in a way, I *was* handpicked."

"Did you know what you were applying for, though? The details, I mean. If everything is so hush-hush, how could they afford to have that many applicants involved?"

"We had no idea what we were applying for. I had zero clue about the project until after I was actually hired. A few weeks afterward actually. All I knew was it was a special one-year assignment and that it was being run by the top brass. There weren't any details at all."

"And that was enough for you?"

"Hell, yeah, it was. I can write my own ticket after this. It's a pretty good feather in my cap, you know, being pulled out of a grunt job in the IT department into something like this. I have a graduate degree, you know."

"If any of this gets out you might be writing your own ticket to federal prison," Jeremiah said. "We're breaking a lot of pretty big laws here. Human cloning is illegal. Weren't you worried when you found out what it was you signed on to?"

"Maybe a little, at first," Brent said. "But there are a lot of very important people behind the scenes here. Powerful people. There are serious safeguards, believe me. And this is cutting edge, you know? This is the future, and what we're doing is helping to shape it. It's exciting. It's important work."

"You sound like you swallowed Charles Scott."

"Well, he isn't wrong, Jeremiah," Brent said. "Human cloning is coming, whether we like it or not. And you, of all people, must believe that. I mean, you're in this deeper than any of us."

"It was an offer I couldn't refuse."

"Tell me about it. You're making a tidy little sum off this, as I hear."

"Yeah," Jeremiah said. "That, too. But doesn't it worry you, Brent? I mean, human cloning. Don't you wonder what all of this is for? What it means?"

"It means a better world. This technology can solve a lot of problems."

"I suppose, sure. But don't you think it's dangerous? Especially if it ends up in the wrong hands. I mean, what if someone decided to clone the president? Or create a whole army of mindless, disposable people? You know what I mean."

"I don't think Scott is focused on anything like that," Brent said. "When he shook my hand, he told me I was helping to make a difference, helping put an end to human suffering. He seemed passionate about it. He sees this as a good thing. I believe him. I trust him. You should, too."

Jeremiah wanted to say something about the way Charles Scott had seemed almost too passionate about it, as though it was more than just the science driving him. But before he could say anything, the monitor switched on. Brent's posture straightened almost imperceptibly, morphing seamlessly from casual urban hipster to scientist. On the wall, they watched Jeremiah's double slog through another uneventful afternoon at ViMed and then sit silently in traffic, listening to news radio on the drive home. Before he even pulled into the garage, the monitor switched off again. Though he did nothing even remotely interesting—hardly uttered a word out loud, in fact—Jeremiah watched with his usual intensity, trying to find something—anything—that made him feel like he wasn't watching himself up there. Some tiny mistake. Some flaw. He didn't find it. He never found it. He might as well have been looking in a mirror.

# CHAPTER

# 7

By the time Jeremiah had entered high school, he had lived in six houses in four different towns. His mother liked to wander. Sometimes they'd move because she'd found a better job some-where, other times it might have been because she was just bored of the neighborhood. He'd never been in one place long enough to make a best friend, and honestly never understood the feeling of being settled. Until he spent four consecutive years at Boston University, in fact, he'd never fully understood the notion of feeling "at home." It was no wonder that he'd decided to stay in the area after graduating. He felt comfortable there, connected, and it seemed an obvious choice when he and Diana suddenly had to put down some roots. But even then, complacency never came easy to him. He could never escape the nagging feeling that things could change in an instant. Uprooting never seemed entirely out of the question to him. So, several weeks into the experiment, when he began to feel at ease and familiar with his routine and even a little bit comfortable with Brent, he should have been ready for the monkey wrench. But it caught him off guard, the way monkey wrenches will.

It was a Thursday, early evening, and he and Brent were

scheduled to watch the clone at home. Jeremiah had already secured the last of a half-gallon container of coffee chip ice cream
and had settled in on the couch.

"This is Family Dinner Night," he said with a roll of his eyes.
"Probably going to seem pretty lame to you."

"Why?"

"I don't know, it's just a silly weekly routine. Diana makes a
dinner, and we all have to clear our evening to make sure we're
there. It's our scheduled family time, you know, to catch up and
*talk* about things. You might find it sort of mundane, is all."

"I think it's kind of cool. My family never did that. What do
you talk about?"

"Normal stuff, I don't know. We're just supposed to talk, re-
connect and all that. Diana is a real stickler about it." He didn't
mention, of course, that it was really all a charade—that he and
Diana talked about pointless, useless things, avoiding discussion
of any real issues. Secretly, though, Jeremiah had been looking
forward to watching a Thursday dinner, eager, perhaps, for even
the false sense of family they'd become so practiced at.

And that's why he was so surprised when Diana wasn't even
there. The screen turned on to the clone and Parker sitting alone
at the kitchen table, eating slices right out of a pizza box.

"That's not like her," Jeremiah told Brent, "to miss Thursday
night. Where could she be?"

*He knew exactly where she was.*

"Maybe she had to work late?"

"That isn't usually an option," he said. "She'd never let me
get away with it. Where the hell is she?"

*Some romantic rendezvous with her secret lover.*

"This is kind of a treat," the clone said to Parker, "just the
guys, having a manly dinner."

Parker grunted and rolled his eyes. "It's pizza, Dad," he said.
"We didn't kill a wild boar."

"So how is school going?"

"It's going."

"Any plans for the weekend?"

"Nope."

"Maybe we should save a slice or two for your mother."

"I doubt she'd want cold pizza. I have homework. Can I take this upstairs?"

"Isn't that against the rules? Aren't we supposed to talk or something?"

"I don't know, Dad. I'd say this Family Dinner Night is pretty much a bust."

"Hey, just because Mom's not here doesn't mean you and I can't have a chat."

"A chat? About what?"

"I don't know," the clone said. "What's the latest in the gaming world?"

"There's a new one coming out, but not for, like, a year. It's called *Infinite Frontiers*. I was going to ask if I could get the beta next month. But I need to subscribe to this group."

In the lab, Brent shot a grin at Jeremiah. "The kid is plugged in," he said.

"And how much will that cost me?" the clone asked.

"Not much," Parker said. "I think it's, like, fifteen dollars a month."

"That's more than half your allowance. If you want to blow it on some game, it's up to you. But I thought you were saving up for a new monitor."

"I was kind of hoping the subscription could be, like, a birthday present or something. My birthday is next week."

"He's a good negotiator." Brent smiled.

"That sounds reasonable," the clone said. "I'll spring for a one-year subscription. Get me the details."

"Awesome! Can I go upstairs now, though? I want to finish my homework, so I get some game time in."

"Has Louie had his medicine? If we want that stuff to calm him down, the vet said he has to take it at the same time every day."

"I gave it to him," Parker said. "But if you ask me, it's just making him sleep too much."

Jeremiah rolled his eyes and hoped Brent didn't notice. His dog was on downers?

"Okay," the clone said. "Go ahead, then."

As the clone set about clearing the table in silence, Jeremiah felt oddly as though he were invading on someone else's awkward, private moment. He watched him sigh and wipe the crumbs off the table. The clone stood still for a moment as though he weren't sure what he should do next, and finally went into the family room, sat down on the couch and switched on the TV. Jeremiah wondered vaguely what was going through his mind. Somewhere along the line he'd come to accept his clone as a person, at least in some sense of the word. There were moments, like this one, when he almost felt sorry for him.

He wanted to turn the monitor off. But he knew the viewing would keep going for the complete four hours, so he and Brent played crazy eights and gin rummy while the clone rotated through TV channels and finally fell asleep on the couch, snoring again, much to Jeremiah's dismay. He was still there when Diana came home and shook him awake three hours later. At that point, the monitor switched off abruptly, the designated viewing time completed.

Brent and Jeremiah exchanged glances as the monitor went dark.

"That's it?" Jeremiah asked. "Can't we turn it back on? I want to see what happens."

"No," Brent told him. "There's no way to do that. We're just going to have to wait, I guess. What do you think was going to happen?"

"Well, I'd like to think she was about to explain where she was all this time. After all that and we don't even get to see where she was?"

"Yeah, kind of a bummer," Brent said through a yawn. "I'm exhausted. Let's get these questions answered so we can have something to eat."

"I'm not hungry," Jeremiah told him.

"Oh, come on," Brent said. "Watching them eat that pizza was torture. I'm starving. I'll make that macaroni and cheese you said you liked."

"I am too old to keep eating like this," Jeremiah said. "But, yeah. I could go for that."


"Displaced control issues" is the way Natalie Young described it during the next day's session. Jeremiah disagreed.

"What control issues?" he asked. "I don't have any control issues."

"Not when you were actually in control, no, but right now, Jeremiah, you're not really *in* control, are you?"

"Well, obviously," he snapped.

"Are you feeling angry?"

"Yeah, you know what? I *am* feeling angry. I'm pissed off, but I think that's pretty normal under the circumstances. I don't think that amounts to 'control issues' or anything quite so dramatic as that. I get that this is in your job description and all, but everything doesn't have to fit so neatly into your little psychobabble boxes."

"Who are you angry with, Jeremiah? Are you angry at your wife for missing the dinner? Are you angry at the clone for not doing something about it?"

"Well, I'd just like to know what was so goddamn important she would miss the one thing she never allows *anyone* to skip! And she doesn't get home until almost eleven? Where the hell *was* she all that time? She's an aide in a lawyer's office, for God's sake. It's a part-time job. She doesn't do anything that crucial. And she never worked nights before. I feel like I'm out of the loop here!"

"And this frustrates you."

"Yes, Natalie, it frustrates me!"

"Perhaps your clone discussed it with her after the monitoring was finished?"

"Well, if he did, I think I have the right to know what she said."

"Do you feel your rights are being compromised, Jeremiah?"

"I feel like I don't know where my wife was for half the night," he said. "I mean, first she starts working more and never even bothers to tell me, and then she misses Thursday night and I don't even get the satisfaction of knowing why? I want to know what's going on."

"Jeremiah," she said as calmly as always, "I am not saying you're wrong to feel this way. I am simply trying to help you to understand your feelings. That way I can help you to deal with them."

"I am dealing just fine on my own."

Even as he said the words, he knew it wasn't true. He hadn't slept at all the night before, and lately, there were more nights like that. Twice, in fact, Brent had had to come right into his bedroom and pull him out of bed for scheduled monitor time— and on one of those occasions, it was early afternoon. It seemed he was bothered by something else after every viewing. When he wasn't obsessing about whether the clone would remember to renew his car registration on time, he was questioning his apparent lack of preparation for an important meeting at work. He went to bed at night with his mind reeling over stupid, trivial things that never would have kept him awake before. Had the clone remembered to double-check the photo credits for the newsletter? Did he give Louie his flea medicine? Did he lock the garage door? Was it his turn or Diana's to get Parker to his guitar lesson on Monday night? Was he keeping up with the maintenance schedule on the new car? If he missed a single oil change, the warranty might lapse. And Jesus, he thought, was he taking it to the dealer? They'd rob him blind. He didn't trust his double to take care of things. This, coupled with the fact that Diana now seemed even more obvious about her transgressions—even at the expense of the family—had him stressed. It was starting to make a dark appearance on his face. He could see it every time he looked in the mirror.

"I don't know," he told Natalie Young. "Maybe I'm not coping as well as I should be. But it isn't easy. I feel trapped. Maybe you're right, I feel like I don't have any control. It's possible they chose the wrong person for this."

"I don't think Dr. Scott makes mistakes like that," she said. "He must have seen something in you that made you the right person for this."

"I don't know," he said honestly.

It was a question he still grappled with. Why the hell was he here? The entire affair had been so rushed after the first contact, everything happening so quickly, that he'd never had a chance to stop and question why he'd been chosen. Scott had said only that they knew Jeremiah would be loyal to the company, and therefore, presumably, to the experiment. But, in fact, Jeremiah held no great love for ViMed. If he had his way, he'd go back to newspapers in a heartbeat—get back to writing something that actually mattered, something that could make a difference. There was no denying, his heart was still back there. And as he considered this, he remembered what Scott had said to him at their very first meeting: *You did what was expected of you. You toed the line, Mr. Adams."* In that moment, Jeremiah felt suddenly very small.

"Maybe they just like me or something," he told Natalie Young.

"You are a likable person," she said with a tight, unconvincing smile.

Jeremiah said nothing and shifted his weight in the chair and looked away from her. This was getting him nowhere. He was through talking. In typical fashion, though, she decided differently and pushed on.

"Jeremiah," she said quietly, "I'd like to try an exercise with you. I'd like you to tell me one thing—one decision, one choice you made, anything—that you've done here that you might not have done before. It can be anything. It doesn't matter how small."

"What do you mean?"

"Well, for example, did you set an alarm clock this morning to get up?"

"No, I didn't need to be up early today. The viewing didn't start until after eleven."

"Really?" she asked in mock surprise. "No alarm clock on a weekday morning? Do you think your clone set his alarm this morning?"

"Okay, yeah, I see what you mean," he said. "But those things don't matter. Of course I'm doing things differently here. This is a different place, a totally separate situation. I'm not going to get up early every day and dress in a suit and tie just to hang out with Brent and basically watch TV."

"Hang out with Brent?" she asked, again with a look of exaggerated awe. "But he's your coworker, isn't he? And half your age. He doesn't seem like someone you'd even want to *hang out* with."

"Well, I don't have much choice there, do I? Look, I see what you're trying to do, but none of this really matters, Natalie. These are things I have no control over. It's not really up to me."

"I think you have more control than you realize, Jeremiah," she said. "You make your own decisions on a daily basis. And I'd wager a lot of those are very different from the decisions you'd make at home. Different from the decisions your clone is making."

"What, like I can take a shower whenever I want to?"

"Or not, if you decide. What else is up to you?"

"I suppose the coffee's better here. I don't have to drink that light roast stuff Diana likes."

"And do you suppose the clone is drinking light roast coffee?"

"Oh, I'm absolutely certain of it. Diana is very picky about her coffee."

"So, you see, you do have some control over your own life. You make your own choices, your own decisions here," she told him. "I'd like you to make a list, keep track of these sort of things for the next few days. I think it might help."

Jeremiah nodded and Natalie stood up, her usual indication that it was time to escort him back down the hall to his apartment.

Once he was alone, he brewed a half pot of French roast and took a long shower. Afterward he stood in front of the bathroom mirror, razor in hand, but he didn't shave. He stared at his own reflection for a moment and then he dropped the razor into the trash with a satisfying thud.

"Screw it," he said to his own face. "I'm growing a beard."

# CHAPTER

# 8

## DAY 56

When Charles Scott came to the lab apartment periodically to "chat," it never felt like anything quite so casual and spontaneous to Jeremiah. More often, in fact, he was left thinking he'd somehow managed to do something wrong. Scott had a way of making everyone around him feel like they weren't quite living up to his lofty expectations.

On a Tuesday morning, however, when Scott came in through the front door without knocking, Jeremiah was glad for the chance to talk to him. He had a growing list of questions of his own.

He poured them each a coffee, and they settled in on the leather couches where Jeremiah answered Scott's standard interrogation without discussion: *Yes, he was still convinced that the clone was a perfect replica of himself; No, he hadn't been surprised by any of the clone's actions in recent viewings; He was, indeed, getting enough exercise; Sure, he and Brent were getting along fine, no problems there.*

Before Scott could make a hasty exit, as he typically did once he was satisfied with these meetings, Jeremiah turned the conversation to his own concerns.

"You know, Dr. Scott, it's occurred to me that we never re-

ally discussed what happens at the end of this, once our contract expires."

"At the conclusion of the experiment you will be returned to
your own life, Mr. Adams, just as we've agreed. There's nothing to discuss."

"I mean the details," Jeremiah said. "We never talked about
how that is going to happen. When this year is over, what do
you do with the clone?"

"Do with him?"

"What happens to him? Do you just get rid of him?"

"If you're asking, Mr. Adams, do we kill him, the answer is
no. I assume you'd agree that wouldn't be the right thing to do."

Jeremiah was glad to hear it. Despite everything, the notion
had bothered him. The clone, after all, was blameless in all of
this, and in the clone's own mind, he was fully human. True
or not, that belief had to mean something. He *was* Jeremiah,
for all intents and purposes. It seemed unnecessarily callous to
just discard him.

"But there can't be two of us. How is it done, then?"

Scott took a measured sip of his coffee before he answered.
"They say everyone has a doppelganger somewhere in the world,
Mr. Adams. This will be yours. We will input a new memory
file into the clone, an entirely new identity, and send him on
his way. It's easily arranged."

The idea of his clone walking around freely somewhere in
the world was troubling.

"You just give him a new life?"

"Essentially, yes."

"Don't you think that's risky? What if he comes back? What
if we run into each other at the gas pump or something?"

"We have ways around that with the Meld. Stop worrying."

"I just want to be certain you've thought this through," Jeremiah told him. "He has my DNA, you know. He'll be walking around with my DNA. That's a problem."

"Why?"

"What if he decides to rob a bank? What if he kills someone?"

"He won't. We can see to that with Meld, as well. He won't have the inclination to do anything like that, or the capacity. We'll take care of it."

"What if he starts a family?" Jeremiah asked. "What if he has kids?" The idea, which had only just entered his mind, was positively frightening to him. Those would be *his* children, he realized. His own flesh and blood, essentially. Children who shouldn't be born.

Charles Scott dismissed the issue with a shake of his head.

"Sterilization," he said, "is a straightforward procedure."

"And what about me?" Jeremiah asked after a moment. "I'm just supposed to slip back into my old life with $10 million in my pocket? How do I explain that to my family?"

"You do like to dwell on the mundane, don't you? The winning lottery ticket has already been printed. Calm down, Mr. Adams."

Before Jeremiah could protest that he'd never purchased a lottery ticket in his life, Brent came in through the front door and Scott stood up to face him.

"Oh, I'm sorry, Dr. Scott," Brent said. "I wasn't aware you'd be here. I can come back."

"No need, Mr. Higgins," Scott told him. "We're done here. You have work to do."

As he moved toward the door to leave, though, Charles Scott's half-filled coffee cup dropped from his hand as though the man had simply let it go without a second thought. Coffee saturated the carpet, a dark spot expanding rapidly, and all three of them went momentarily still in sudden surprise.

It was Brent who moved first, rushing over and picking up

the toppled cup, while Jeremiah went to the kitchen to grab a roll of paper towels. Charles Scott, after a noticeable hesitation, bent down and began mopping at the spill with his own handkerchief.

"I'm terribly sorry, Mr. Adams," he said. The sincerity of the words sounded foreign coming from him. Scott wasn't prone to apologies. Jeremiah thought he seemed unnecessarily rattled over the accident.

"Don't worry," Jeremiah told him, pressing a thick wad of towels into the rug. "It's not my carpet."

Scott stood up and folded his soiled handkerchief into his fist. "I'm sure I don't know how that happened," he said. "I'll send someone to clean it right away."

His composure somewhat restored, Scott turned on his heels and left the room in a hurry, the front door closing behind him.

Brent looked down at Jeremiah and smiled. "That was strange," he said. "You think I make him nervous?"

"You aren't nearly as threatening as you think you are," Jeremiah said.

A half hour later, they were settled in front of the monitor watching the clone's uneventful morning at ViMed. Later, when Jeremiah returned from a late-afternoon session with Natalie Young, all evidence of the mishap had been erased from the carpet.

# CHAPTER
# 9

Whether it was because of Natalie's advice, the simmering worry inside him or just out of sheer boredom, Jeremiah didn't know, but late on a Friday afternoon a few weeks later, he found himself gleefully blasting virtual enemy soldiers into fiery bits in a game of *Infinite Frontiers* with Brent. He had to admit, there was a certain appeal to it. Teeth gritted behind his headset, he became slowly more comfortable with the intricate gestures and eye movements Brent had shown him to get his aim right. If Parker could see him now, he thought, he'd never believe it. And he was having *fun*.

They fought on the same side against a squadron of AI snipers and took turns ducking behind tanks and blown-out bunkers, shooting into the field so Jeremiah could get the hang of the most important aspects of the controls. Every now and then, Brent would send his avatar creeping out into the arena so Jeremiah could practice covering him against enemy fire. He wasn't very good at it and, more than once, Brent's player died an unceremonious death while Jeremiah failed to realize his weapon needed reloading. Every blast of machine gun spray and each explosion rocked through his headset and set his teeth on edge.

But his adrenaline was pumping like he hadn't felt it in months, and he sat on the edge of his seat as he practiced his aim. They could type to converse during game play, and Brent made him practice that, too. The letter selection was operated by the hand controller, which took some getting used to, so Jeremiah made his fair share of typos in his attempts at communicating, insisting several times that he needed more powerful *gums*.

After both soldiers were obliterated for the fifteenth time, Brent exited the game and switched the monitor to standby.

"Almost time for the viewing," he said. "Duty calls."

"I'd rather keep playing than sit and watch that clone for four hours. I can totally see how someone could get hooked on this stuff," Jeremiah said. He took off his headset and combed his fingers through his hair. He'd been letting it grow, along with his beard, for the past few weeks and it was long enough now to snag a bit in the back.

"I know, right? Maybe now you'll go easier on Parker when you get home."

At the mention of his son, a wave of regret washed over Jeremiah. Parker had been on his mind during the entire game. Part of him had picked up that controller in a futile effort to feel closer to him, but somehow, he felt more removed from him than ever. Why, just once, couldn't he have thought to join Parker in one of his games? Why had he let it become a wedge between them?

"Hell, I'll probably start pestering him to let me play," Jeremiah said sullenly. "You want to make some dinner before this thing turns on? I've been wanting to try lasagna."

"This is something I need to see," Brent said. "All this time I thought your specialty was toast."

"I'm branching out," Jeremiah told him. "You're rubbing off on me. Besides, I have so little to do around here that eating has taken on a whole new meaning. I like my food these days."

Brent followed him into the kitchen and went into the fridge to get them some beers while they worked on dinner. Jeremiah didn't know when, exactly, but they'd quietly begun opening their first even before the viewing started.

"Hey, what's with all the light beer?" Brent asked. "Where's the good stuff? You drinking my beers on me?"

"No, they're in there. Just look. While you're at it, get me the cheese, too."

"I am looking. It's not here. The only beer in here is this crap." Brent handed a package to Jeremiah and, with a grim expression, opened a can of light beer.

"This is fat-free mozzarella," Jeremiah said, tossing the package aside. "Is there anything else in there? What the hell is fat-free cheese even made from, anyway? I thought cheese *was* fat."

"That's it for the cheese. What gives, porky? You on a diet or something?"

"Not that I know of," Jeremiah said, and stuck his head in the fridge. "What the hell? What happened to all my food?"

There was no half-and-half, a piece of chocolate cake saved from yesterday was gone and the milk had been replaced with a carton of something that looked like it had been used to clean a paintbrush. There were more fruits and vegetables than an average horse could eat in a week. He checked the freezer. Ice cream had been replaced with frozen fruit bars and an entire stack of frozen pizzas had simply disappeared.

"Okay," he said, shaking his head. "Something's gone crazy around here. I have this thing programmed to order my food in a very particular way. None of this fat-free, diet garbage is on my list. That's for sure."

"That's weird," Brent said. "Maybe a malfunction or something?"

"That's quite a malfunction, I'd say." Jeremiah went to the

old-fashioned telephone and picked it up for the first time in more than a month.

A cheery female voice greeted him as soon as the receiver was at his ear.

"Good evening, Mr. Adams," she said. "Is there something I can help you with?"

"Yes, h-hello," he stammered, still feeling somewhat like he was calling room service in an overpriced hotel. "I wonder if you could tell me what's happened to all the food in my refrigerator. It seems to have been stolen and replaced with an assortment of inedible things. Fat-free milk, for example. And fruit."

"That was an order from Dr. Pike, Mr. Adams. He sent it down this afternoon. Is there a problem?"

"Yes," he told her. "The problem is I won't eat any of this stuff. The problem is I am going to starve to death in here. I'm no scientist, but I think that might be bad for this experiment."

"I'm afraid you'll need to speak to Dr. Pike about that, Mr. Adams. His order was very specific and I'm afraid I can't override it without express permission. If the food isn't to your liking, a new shopping list has been preprogrammed into the refrigerator. There are over one hundred and fifty items within the allowable parameters. Or I have a list of permissible items I can have sent to you right away, if you prefer."

"That list wouldn't happen to include any normal cheese, by any chance. Maybe a variety that is actually made from cheese? I'm trying to make lasagna."

"There are several fat-free varieties of cheese."

"Is there any decent beer on your list?"

"There are several selections of low-calorie beer, too. Should I read the menu?"

"No," he said. "Never mind. Thanks." He hung up the receiver and turned to Brent. "It would appear I've been put on a diet," he said.

"And me, too, it seems. This stuff is like dishwater." Brent poured the contents of the beer can down the sink. "There's some ham in there. I'll make us a sandwich. But I'm afraid the bulky rolls are gone. And there's no mayonnaise, either."

"Whatever," Jeremiah said. "I'll get Pike over here. I'll straighten this out."

They returned to the living room, set the food on the table in front of them and sat down just as the monitor switched on. Jeremiah was alarmed to see the clone entering his mother's room at the assisted living home. He hadn't expected that. He visited her every Tuesday after work, but never on a Friday.

"Hi, Mom," the clone said. Jeremiah felt a little sting on hearing that word come out of the clone's mouth.

His mother was sitting on the little stool in front of her mirror, brushing her hair in careful, smooth strokes. Her face was powdered and she was wearing a green dress with a silver brooch at the collar, in the shape of a star. She turned when she heard the clone come in and looked at him strangely for a long moment. So strangely, in fact, that for just an instant Jeremiah entertained the thought that she knew she was looking at an imposter. There was such a sense of confusion in her eyes and she scrutinized him silently.

"You're late," she said at last, and turned back to her own reflection. Jeremiah breathed a sigh of relief. He didn't want his mother dragged into any of this. "I can't seem to fasten this damn thing. If you'll just help me, I'll be ready to go in two shakes."

The clone walked over to her and took an ornately carved wooden barrette from her shaky hand. He said nothing as he gathered her auburn hair into a long ponytail, smoothing the sides of her head to catch the loose strands, and fastened it behind her neck.

"Thank you," she said, looking up at him without expression. "Now if I could just find my bag. I can never seem to find that thing." She shifted her gaze toward the doorway and then back at the clone. "You know," she said in a whisper, "I think they hide it on me. I really do. I think they're playing tricks on me."

"Who's hiding it? No one is hiding anything on you," the clone said.

She stood up and walked to her closet, shifting the rows of blouses and dresses in a flurry until she got thoroughly flustered.

"And someone has stolen my rabbit fur coat," she said.

"Rabbit fur?" the clone asked, confused. "Mom, you got rid of that coat thirty years ago. Don't you remember?"

Jeremiah remembered. She had been given the coat some years before, a gift from one of many admirers in her younger days. She loved it at first, and wore it everywhere, always commenting on how warm it was and how it was no wonder rabbits could stay outdoors all winter. She used to invite total strangers to run their hands over it. He didn't know when, exactly, she had a change of heart about it, but knowing her, it likely involved a wild rabbit spied outside the kitchen window. When he was sixteen, she made a very big deal about needing some sort of atonement for the transgression of owning a coat made from another creature's skin. She included Jeremiah in that endeavor, too, likely seeing an opportunity to instill something noble in her son.

She spent a great deal of time deciding how best to get rid of the now-offensive garment. In typical fashion, she wanted something symbolic and meaningful. At first, she looked into donating it to a homeless shelter, but quickly decided it wouldn't do to simply pass the sin on to some other poor, unsuspecting soul. She spoke briefly to animal rights' organizations, but they were too quick to chastise her for having the thing in the first place. Finally, she found a hippie priest woman or something, who presided over a complicated ritual that involved burning and burying the coat in an effort to return it to some animal spirit realm. He could still remember the smell and the oily black smoke rising up from the backyard. There was also chanting involved, he seemed to recall. Afterward, she wrote a sizable check to a local animal shelter and began leaving carrot sticks out in the garden in neat little piles—something she still did to this very day, even at the assisted living home.

On the monitor, his mother stopped and turned to look at the clone. Something in her expression looked lost for a minute, as though she might be remembering the exact same story, and then her lips straightened with a firm resolution.

"I know that," she said, and then repeated it as though to convince herself. "I know that."

"Why do you need a coat, anyway?" the clone asked, an un-easy smile curling the corners of his mouth.

"Well, I can't very well go to the party without a coat," she said. "It's the middle of winter."

"First of all, it's April, Mom," the clone said. "And what party? There isn't a party."

"Of course there's a party. There's always a party on Christmas Eve. Don't be silly."

"It's April," the clone told her again, quietly this time. "It's not Christmas Eve, Mom."

In the lab, Jeremiah put a hand to his forehead and said nothing. Brent shot him a concerned glance and then turned his attention back to the monitor.

"It's April?" his mother asked. "It's not. Are you sure it's April?"

"I'm sure," the clone told her. "Why don't you come and sit down for a while, Mom. Or maybe we could go to the dining room and get something to eat. Have you had dinner?"

"I'm not hungry." Her voice was hushed, and she avoided looking at the clone as she crossed the room and sat down carefully on the edge of the bed. "I think I'll just get some sleep. I'd like to be alone. I want to get out of this dress."

Jeremiah watched the clone and tried to compel him to do something other than stand there with a useless, blank look on his face. *Go over there*, he thought. *Put a hand on her. Hug her or something!*

But the clone remained where he was, his face cycling through several expressions in quick succession, settling at last on something that looked like defeat. Finally, he looked down at the floor and backed out of the room without a word. Just before he closed the door, Jeremiah could hear his mother say something else about Christmas Eve. Reluctantly, he realized that he would have reacted exactly as his clone had if he had been there himself. It was easy to judge from outside, but he knew that he would have stood there just like his double had done, looking at his shoes, clueless and utterly shaken. As if to demonstrate the point, Jeremiah closed his eyes and turned his head away from the monitor, without even realizing he'd done it.

When he looked again, the clone was in the hallway and the camera angle had shifted. He looked as though he weren't certain where to go and Jeremiah could feel his distress in the pit of his own stomach. He'd known for some time that dementia was likely, but he'd never seen his mother like this before. When had it gotten this bad?

After a moment, the clone was approached by Nichelle, the busty, plain-speaking head nurse with skin the color of bittersweet chocolate. He was never sure how she'd greet him when he came to visit: sometimes with a wide grin and a story about something funny that his mother had said, and sometimes with an exasperated sigh and a stern shake of the head. Today it was the latter, but it was mixed with a shadow of concern.

"Mr. Adams," she said. "Patricia's episodes are getting worse. Do you know she asked me to alter her wedding dress today?"

She didn't even own a wedding dress, Jeremiah thought. "And she practically accosted poor Dave the orderly this morning because she insisted he was her brother and he was very dangerous. And she keeps asking the doctors to drive her to the airport. I'm afraid Administration needs to see you before you leave."

Watching, Jeremiah said out loud that someone ought to check her medication. This had happened before, he told Brent, and all they had to do was increase one of her pills to three times a day. After a few days, she was back to her old self.

"Have they checked her medications?" the clone asked. "Maybe she just needs her meds tweaked or something. That helped before." Jeremiah nodded his head and looked at Brent as if to say, *See? I told you.*

"The doctors have checked her over," Nichelle told the clone, her face softening around the edges. "You can see for yourself what this is. It isn't a problem with her meds, Mr. Adams. This is her mind. We need to talk about a more suitable place for her. Come with me to the office. They're expecting you."

"Where would she go?" the clone asked as he followed her down another hallway behind the reception area. "She's happy here. She has friends."

"There are options. Good places with the right people. You'll see." Nichelle stopped momentarily and turned to look at him. "This is for her own good, Mr. Adams," she said. "We all want what's best for her."

The clone looked down at the floor again. In the lab, Jeremiah buried his face in his hands.

"I know," the clone said at last. The exact same words echoed in his own head. He knew.

Nichelle put a hand on the clone's shoulder and gave it a light pat, exactly the gesture that Jeremiah wished the clone had done for his mother, and led him down the hall where a thin, blond man was waiting in front of a closed office door.

"Hello, Mr. Adams," he said, extending a hand. "Dr. Tim Waterson—we've met before. You'll have to excuse the interruption, but for some reason they're installing a new phone system in my office at this exact moment. They should be almost done. I don't know why they couldn't do this later."

Almost as soon as he said it, the office door opened and two men in nondistinct gray overalls came hurrying out. In the lab, Jeremiah was vaguely perplexed, but if the clone shared those feelings, he said nothing.

"All set, Doctor," one of the men mumbled as they shuffled past. The doctor said nothing and ushered the clone inside.

The camera angle wavered slightly and then settled into a seamless view of the office. Jeremiah understood at once it wasn't a phone system they were installing.

"Does he have people waiting in the wings to put in his cameras?" Jeremiah asked Brent with some alarm. "How did they get it done that fast? How the hell did he even know?"

Brent shook his head and continued watching. "Charles Scott likes to cover all his bases," he said.

"Have you had a chance to visit with your mother yet, Mr. Adams?" Waterson asked the clone.

The clone nodded as he took a seat in front of the desk.

"And how did she seem to you this evening?"

"I'll agree she did seem a bit confused," the clone said, "but don't you think it's going overboard to talk about having her moved?"

"Mr. Adams, this isn't something we do lightly. You need to understand this is for her own safety and the safety of our other residents and staff. We are simply not equipped to handle cases of dementia here. We're a small, general assistance home. But there are a number of other facilities that specialize in these things. Some of them close by. She'd be much better off in one of those. Much happier in the long run."

"But she likes it here," the clone said. "Moving will be hard on her. Traumatic, even."

"There will be an adjustment, certainly," Waterson said. "But she'll be fine in due time. I don't see any other way. I'm concerned about her well-being here. She needs a certain level of care and monitoring that we simply cannot provide. If she were to become confused or disoriented, especially overnight when we're at minimal staff, well, I hate to think what might happen, Mr. Adams."

The clone frowned and leaned forward a bit in his chair. "So how do we go about this exactly?" he asked. "Do I just choose another facility? I'm not sure where to begin."

"I'm here to assist you in any way I can," Waterson said. "I have a few suggestions here that you can begin to look at." He pushed a handful of pamphlets forward on his desk. The clone took them and laid them in his lap without glancing at them.

"What are we talking about for a timeline?" he asked. "I mean, does this have to be tomorrow?"

"Regulation dictates that we allow sixty days for the transfer. I would suggest, Mr. Adams, that we move somewhat faster than that. We'll need to assign a dedicated nurse for your mother, around the clock, until she's moved. I'm afraid that will be your financial responsibility. It can be quite expensive, you understand."

The clone pursed his lips and nodded. "I'll start looking through the information right away," he said. "Do what you need to do. I understand."

The clone made a move to stand and Waterson put up a hand to stop him.

"One more thing, Mr. Adams," he said. "Before you select a facility, there is one procedure I'd like to try, something I think could be valuable in assessing her needs more exactly. It could help in placing her."

"What's that?"

"I presume you've heard of Meld?"

Jeremiah almost jumped off the couch. "He can't be serious," he said.

"You could say so," the clone told Waterson. "Actually, I work for ViMed Pharmaceutical, the company that produces Meld."

"Oh, I wasn't aware you were in the scientific field, Mr. Adams."

"No, I'm in the communications and marketing department. I've worked closely on Meld from that end, though. I know all about it."

"So, you're aware of the advantages here," Waterson said. "Meld would allow us a closer look at precise aspects of brain degeneration. We could pinpoint memory erosion, synaptic collapse, that sort of thing. It could go a long way toward tailoring her treatment."

"He's out of his mind!" Jeremiah shouted. "That damned clone better not let this happen!" Brent glanced at him and typed something into his laptop.

"Do you think it would be safe to use on her, under the circumstances?" the clone asked Waterson.

"Oh, yes," Waterson told him. "Under proper medical supervision, Meld is perfectly safe." Jeremiah saw an almost imperceptible smile cross the clone's face at the words, no doubt finding satisfaction at hearing his own jargon echoed back at him. Jeremiah felt like punching in the wall.

"Would you do that here?" the clone asked. "Are you equipped for that? As I understand it, there is a bit of training involved."

"Not to worry. I've already taken ViMed's course. I know how to use it. I think it would be useful to have it done before the transfer," he said. "Besides, to be perfectly honest, I've been looking for an opportunity to use Meld. It's a fascinating medicine, really. I think it's set to be a real breakthrough in dementia diagnosis and treatment. The first real break we've seen in the field."

"It's a miracle, all right," the clone said. "I don't see a problem if you think it could help."

Jeremiah watched slack-mouthed while his double signed a consent form that would let them submit his own mother to Meld. He wanted to scream. He could feel Brent's eyes on him, waiting to see if there was anything he ought to put in his report. Every muscle in Jeremiah's neck strained with the effort to contain himself.

"Jeremiah," Brent said, "am I correct in assuming you wouldn't have signed that consent? Would you have refused the Meld? Would you have acted differently from the clone?"

Jeremiah didn't answer right away. Eyes still glued to the monitor, watching the clone walk out of the office and stop with Nichelle in the hallway, he considered the fact that his double didn't have all the facts about Meld. Of course the clone wouldn't see the harm in it. In his mind, it was still the miracle drug Jeremiah had once honestly believed it to be. The clone didn't know the real reason behind the drug's creation. He didn't know what it could actually do. And he didn't know what it was like to take the drug. To him, it probably seemed like a good idea.

Jeremiah wished, for the hundredth time, that he could jump inside the image on the wall and shake his double by the shoulders.

"No," he said finally, and with a sorry conviction. "No. I suppose I would have done exactly the same thing in his place."

# CHAPTER
# 10

Jeremiah and Brent were quiet as they watched the clone drive home from the nursing home in complete silence, the pamphlets sitting next to him on the passenger seat and the radio turned all the way down. Jeremiah wondered what he was thinking about. When he got home, the clone opened the front door to a dark house, threw the pamphlets and his keys on the hall table and bent down on one knee in a useless attempt to entice Louie over for a pat. The dog just stared at him and lay down under the coffee table, eyeing him like the intruder he was.

"Hello?" he called as he switched on the lights in the living room. No reply.

"I don't know where everyone could be on a Friday night," Jeremiah said to Brent. "Why is he coming home all the time to an empty house now?"

Brent looked at him and shook his head. "Maybe things just get busy, Jeremiah. It happens."

"Never used to," he said. "Especially not on a Friday."

On the monitor, he watched the clone wander into the empty kitchen, Louie cautiously following from a safe distance.

"Have you eaten yet, pal?" The clone loosened his tie, picked up the dog bowl and filled it with two scoops of food from the bin on the kitchen counter. He put the bowl on the floor and took a few steps back so the dog would feel comfortable coming in to eat. Jeremiah sighed as he remembered the way Louie used to react to being fed, wagging his tail wildly and balancing on his hind legs in an exuberant dog tango. Now he took to it sluggishly and ate it in nibbles. It was probably the damn pills they had him on, Jeremiah thought. But he had to admit, his distrust toward the clone seemed less obvious now and that was one less thing to worry about.

The cameras followed as the clone went up the stairs into his bedroom. He changed out of his work clothes, carefully hanging his jacket and tie in the closet, and put on sweatpants and a T-shirt. He sat down on the edge of the bed and remained there for several minutes, resting one elbow on his knee with his fist curled underneath his chin. Jeremiah realized that he was sitting in the exact same position on the couch in the lab. He quickly raised his head and leaned back against the cushions and put his arms down at his sides.

For the next half hour or so, they watched the clone wander around the house and then finally settle in the living room and flip through the pamphlets they had given him. Eventually, Diana and Parker came noisily through the front door, greeted by the jangle of Louie's collar and tags. Both the clone and Jeremiah perked up at the sudden commotion.

"Where have you two been?" the clone asked.

"We waited for you," Diana said with a look that hinted at irritation, "but we were starved. We went out to eat. I brought you home my leftovers."

"Thanks," the clone said. "I was visiting my mother."

"You might have bothered to call and let us know. Why were you there on a Friday?"

"Yeah, sorry. They called me at the office just as I was leaving. She's having some problems."

Diana took off her sweater and walked into the kitchen with the little Styrofoam container of food. Parker put Louie on the leash and took him out to the front yard.

"What sort of problems?" Diana called from the kitchen. The clone got up and followed her, the cameras catching his movements seamlessly from room to room.

"I've got to move her," he said. "Her dementia is bad. She thought it was Christmas Eve."

"You're kidding." Diana shot a startled glance at the clone and then continued scraping the food onto a dish. "Move her where?"

"Well, they gave me some options." He tossed the pamphlets down on the kitchen table and took a seat. "There are places. I've been looking at them. I don't like them. They're expensive."

"I'll bet," she said. "But if that's what she needs, then that's what she needs. You just have to pick one and make it happen. She still has money in her savings, doesn't she? And this is a medical thing. There's help for that, you know."

"I was thinking," the clone said tentatively, "that maybe it would be better to have her live here with us. Just for a while."

Diana stopped what she was doing and turned around to look the clone straight in the eyes.

"Here? Jeremiah, she can't stay here."

"Why not?" he said. "We have the room and I just think it might be easier for her if she could make the transition slowly. I don't want her to think we're tearing her away from her friends, from her home. She's happy there."

"We can't take care of her, Jeremiah." Diana put his dinner into the microwave, turned it on and leaned back against the kitchen counter to face him again. "She needs someone with her and you and I both work during the day. And having her here would disrupt Parker's whole routine. No, she can't stay here."

Jeremiah knew Diana was right. It was entirely unfair to just spring this on her without any warning. It wasn't even something they'd ever seriously discussed. From the look on his face, he could see the clone knew it, too, so he was surprised to see him keep talking about it.

"You're home for part of the day," he said. "We could bring someone in to fill in the gaps. We could make it work. We could at least talk about it. She's my mother, for God's sake."

Jeremiah cringed at the look on Diana's face.

"And I'm your wife," she said coolly. "And we are talking about it. What do you expect me to say? I had no idea where you even were tonight because you can't be bothered to call me, then you waltz in here and drop this kind of a bomb on me out of nowhere? You know perfectly well this can't work, Jeremiah. It just isn't feasible."

"Well," the clone said, without meeting her gaze, "I suppose with all your extra hours at work these days, you're right. It just isn't feasible. You're not home a lot anymore, are you? If you can't be here for me and Parker, I don't suppose it's fair to think you could be home for my mother."

Jeremiah leaned in closer to the monitor. Of all the times for his double to man-up and finally nibble at the edges of Diana's infidelity, this probably wasn't ideal. She was already pissed off. This could backfire.

"Don't you dare make this about me," she said, her words coming out in severe, rapid succession. "Don't you dare turn this around. That is not fair, Jeremiah."

Jeremiah winced. The clone should shut his mouth about now, he thought, but he inched closer to the edge of his seat, eager to see just how far he would go with this. Was he going to come out and say it? Was he going to confront her with the actual problem? *Go ahead*, Jeremiah urged silently, *ask her who it is. Ask her.*

"I'm not turning anything around," the clone told her, mock innocence raising the pitch of his voice. "I'm just agreeing with you. How could I even think about adding this kind of stress to your life? There doesn't seem to be enough of you to go around as it is. So, you're right. It isn't fair of me. I'm sorry I brought it up."

Diana stared at the clone through narrowed eyes. Jeremiah shook his head and felt the full brunt of her anger right through the monitor.

# CHAPTER
# 11

DAY 81

The next day Jeremiah admitted to Natalie Young that he often worried about losing his mind.

"I think I'd rather my body went to hell than my mind," he said. "It's always one or the other in the end, but, to me, the mind has got to be worse."

"Why are you afraid of that, Jeremiah?"

"Oh, come on, Natalie. You don't have to be coy. I know it must be somewhere in that mammoth file of yours—my crazy uncle Charlie."

"I am aware of your uncle. And I would prefer you don't use the word *crazy*."

"He was crazy."

"He was a paranoid schizophrenic," she said. "That is an illness. Nothing more."

"And then, seeing it in my mother like that..." He shook his head and let out a long, slow breath. "It's not an easy thing to see."

"Dementia and schizophrenia are two completely different things," she told him.

"And it would appear that both run in the family," he said. "That doubles my odds. Beautiful."

"You may be genetically predisposed," she said. "But that doesn't mean anything. It's no more probable that you'll suffer from one of these afflictions than it is that you'll develop any other genetic trait. Arthritis and ulcers also run in your family."

"I'd rather have the ulcers, given the choice." He paused then and grew serious. "Do you think there's any risk, though? I mean, if these things are in my family, and I'm taking Meld so much, don't you think that poses a bigger risk?"

"Meld is perfectly safe when taken under the—"

"Yes, yes, I know," he interrupted, "when taken under the supervision of a medical professional. I know that. I wrote it, remember? But I am asking *you*, Natalie. Do you think it's wise, my taking Meld so often with this sort of thing in my genetic makeup?"

"I don't think the Meld increases your risk at all," she said.

"Have you seen anything—you know, warning signs, anything troubling—while I'm under the Meld with you?"

"Troubling, how?"

"Any signs of mental illness," he said. "Instability, wild thoughts, thinking I can fly, that sort of thing."

"No. Have *you* noticed anything like that in yourself?"

"Well, if I'm crazy," he told her, "I wouldn't be the best judge, would I?"

"Well, consider the more obvious things, then. Have you had any lapses in memory, headaches, anything like that?"

"No," he said. "I don't think so. Would that be a symptom?"

"Perhaps," she said. "Perhaps not."

"That's not much help."

"Well," she added coyly, "do you think you can fly?"

"I'm serious, Natalie."

"It is an imprecise science," she said. "And you are in a very unique situation here, Jeremiah. In your case, anything that might manifest could simply be a normal reaction under these circumstances. We really don't know because we have no basis."

"It sounds like you don't have any idea whether I'm crazy or not."

"I do not think you exhibit any symptoms of mental illness."

"But you don't know for sure."

"Jeremiah," she said, a hint of frustration in her voice, "this is precisely why using the Meld at regular intervals is so crucial to this project. Among other things, it allows me to see the first signs of any change in your psychological makeup. I really don't think you have anything to worry about. If something were wrong, I'd very likely see it under the Meld before you even begin to show outward signs. I'd know it before you do."

"And you'd tell me, right?"

"And I'd tell you," she said.

"I suppose I have no choice but to take you at your word, then."

"Tell me a little about your uncle, Jeremiah. We've never talked about him."

"I never knew him, really. He died more than twenty years ago. I only met him twice, and that was ages ago. He spent most of his life in and out of asylums."

"We prefer the word *hospital*," she said. "He was your mother's brother. Were they close?"

"Oh, she loved Charlie," he said. "She used to talk about him all the time, told me all these stories about his 'wild antics,' as she called them. I think he made her sad."

"I'm sure it had an effect on her. Watching someone you love spiral into the grips of mental illness is very difficult. You had a hard time seeing your mother just for a short while. Imagine watching that happen over the course of a lifetime."

"She used to say he could talk to the fairies," he said. "That's why no one else could understand him. Like he was on some higher plane or something, had some secret that all the rest of us could only dream about."

"That's a good coping mechanism."

"Thing is," he said, "I think she believed it. I think she was even a little jealous of it, if you want to know the truth. The stories she used to tell me, the way she talked about him. She made him seem sort of magical. She made him sound like he was lucky."

"What do you remember about him?"

"The first time I met him I was just a kid. My mother took me to visit him in some halfway house or something."

"And?"

"And he was sitting in the dark in this room and he didn't turn to look at us. He just stared at the wall and talked to us with his back turned. It seemed to me at the time that he must have had eyes in the back of his head."

"That must have been a little frightening to a young boy," she said.

"Not really, because my mother just talked to him like it was all perfectly normal, carrying on a whole conversation while he was turned the other way. And I asked him what he was staring at, if he was looking at the fairies, and my mother yanked my arm so hard I thought I'd fall over. But I really wanted to know. I remember that. After everything she'd told me, it seemed like a logical question."

"And what did Uncle Charlie say?"

"He laughed," Jeremiah told her. "He laughed so hard he started coughing and hacking. My mother went over to him and tried to calm him down. I just stood there, where she'd left me, wondering what to do. So finally, I went over to him, too, and he turned and looked at me and said, *'Yeah. The fairies. I'm looking at the fucking fairies. Don't you see them, kid?'* And then he leaned in close to me and grabbed my face in both his hands and started laughing again."

"Did that scare you?"

"Not really," Jeremiah said, remembering it so vividly in that moment that he could almost smell Uncle Charlie's vinegary breath and the sweat coming off his clothes. "What scared me more was my mother's reaction. She pulled at his hands and slapped them away and told him never to touch me again. She loved him, you know? But it must have scared her when he grabbed me like that. He told us to leave and we did."

"And what did your mother say about it?"

"Nothing," he said. "We never talked about it. I didn't see him again until I was much older—eighteen, maybe—my first summer home from college. He was at our house for a barbecue and I had a beer with him and listened to him talk about flies."

"Flies?"

"Yeah, for a good hour. How they see things in overlapping, fractured images because of the way their eyes are, so they can look at a person and see him from different angles at the same time. He said they know more because of the way they see things. He said he'd like to have eyes like a fly." He shook his head and smiled at the memory. "He was a real whack job. But at that age, I found him kind of intriguing. I never saw him again after that."

"Why not?"

"Because," he said, "a few weeks later he jumped in front of a moving train."

# CHAPTER
## 12

Later that same afternoon, Natalie came into his room and asked if he was all set to go.

"Go where?"

"You have an appointment with Dr. Pike today. I'll walk with you."

Jeremiah snickered. She made it sound like they were going for a coffee. She was, he knew, more guard than companion.

"Sure," he said. "That would be lovely."

They were a good five minutes early for the appointment and arrived to find the door to his examination room closed. As there was no waiting room, they stood in the hallway.

"Who's in there?" Jeremiah asked. As far as he knew, he was Pike's sole patient. Natalie shrugged her shoulders and looked at her shoes.

When the door opened a minute later, Jeremiah was surprised to see Charles Scott come out of the room, his suit jacket draped over his arm and his shirtsleeves rolled up above his wrists. Pike was at his elbow and both men looked momentarily flustered to find them there.

"Mr. Adams," Scott said, straightening his shoulders and assuming his usual air of supremacy in seamless transition. "Why on Earth are you loitering in the halls?"

"Sorry," Natalie said. Jeremiah noted that she seemed slightly rattled, as well. "Mr. Adams has an appointment. I think we're a few minutes early."

Scott offered her a cool expression. "You would do well," he said, "to adhere to your exact schedule."

She nodded and retreated back down the hall. Pike invited Jeremiah into the exam room with a flick of his hand, and Scott took a moment to button the cuffs of his shirt. As Jeremiah stepped around him to get into the room, he noticed a fresh cotton bandage adhered to the back of Scott's neck, at the base of his skull. About two inches in length, it was difficult to miss.

"I didn't know you were Dr. Scott's doctor," Jeremiah said when Pike closed the door hastily behind him.

"I'm not. He just comes in periodically for vitamin injections. He's something of a health nut."

Last Jeremiah knew, vitamins weren't typically injected into someone's skull.

He hoisted himself onto the table and watched with interest as Pike covered and then cleared away a metal tray holding implements that he'd presumably just used on Scott. Judging from the serious size of the needle and the amount of blood-soaked gauze, he was fairly confident Pike was lying to him.

Two hours later, alone at the computer in his rooms, Jeremiah thought he'd discovered the truth. A rudimentary search revealed the startling possibility that Dr. Pike had injected Scott's brain with stem cells. There was little else it could have been. There was a chance, he supposed, that it might have been a treatment for migraines. But Jeremiah knew about that kind of pain. Migraines were difficult to mask. It had to be stem cells. After that, Jeremiah kept landing on scientific journals that touted stem cell therapy as a promising treatment for various neuro-logical disorders.

He remembered now the odd change that came over Scott every time he spoke about the medical possibilities of human cloning, the way his eyes always seemed to gloss over with some-thing approaching desperation whenever he talked about it.

And he remembered the coffee cup.

Scott had all the early signs of a serious neurological dis-ease. Either Parkinson's or, far more likely, amyotrophic lateral sclerosis—ALS. In either case, it was going to get worse. In ei-ther case, he was dying.

It made sense. It answered a lot of questions. But as Jeremiah stared at the computer screen, it presented even more ominous ones: if Charles Scott was sick, what did that say about this ex-periment? What did that mean for him?

The realization hit him before he even saw it coming. Scott's own words echoed in Jeremiah's mind: *"Our work means every-thing, Mr. Adams. It means mankind can finally be free of all the ran-dom, senseless frailties of the human body. It means a second chance."*

The meaning of those words became suddenly crystal clear. Charles Scott didn't care about second chances for the whole of humanity. He wanted a second chance for himself.

Despite what he'd told Brent and everyone else, his motives weren't purely scientific. He was in it to save his own life. And that clock was ticking.

Charles Scott was a desperate man. Worse, Jeremiah real-ized, he was a desperate man with a lot of money at his disposal and in a position of considerable power. Jeremiah felt the hair on the back of his neck stand up: right now, Charles Scott con-trolled every aspect of Jeremiah's entire life and that fact prob-ably meant very little to him.

# CHAPTER

# 13

## DAY 82

On Sunday morning, Jeremiah picked up the landline phone and asked to see Dr. Pike as soon as possible. He knew better than to confront Pike with his suspicions about Scott, but he wanted to speak to him, to see if he could discern anything from the man's demeanor. An hour later, Pike had his head inside Jeremiah's refrigerator. He emerged with an expression of utter confusion.

"There are plenty of healthy choices here, Mr. Adams. I really don't think you're in danger of starving."

"I am if I don't eat it."

"I'm afraid your recent physicals have been unsatisfactory. You need to lose some weight. You are nearly seven pounds heavier than your clone. I've been telling you for weeks now to watch your diet and use the treadmill more. If you'd listened to my advice, you wouldn't be in this situation now."

"Can't you just fatten up the clone?" Jeremiah asked, only half joking. "Sneak in and switch a few things around in his fridge. He'll catch up in no time. And, that way, no one gets hurt."

"This isn't funny," Pike said.

"I'm not trying to be funny. Look. I have months left here.

Why is it so important that I catch up to the clone right this minute?"

"It's very important," Pike said. "If something were to happen, something which made it necessary for you to switch places with your double at a moment's notice, you'd have a hard time explaining to people how you managed to gain seven pounds in a matter of hours."

"Yeah," Jeremiah said. "I suppose. I just don't see why I have to be the one to suffer. I mean, I lead a very limited life here, Dr. Pike. Food is kind of the best part of my day. And you've stocked this place with things that taste like plastic and cardboard. Can we compromise? Just a little?"

Dr. Pike closed the refrigerator and turned to Jeremiah with a severe expression.

"I'm afraid not," he said at last. "This is too important. I'll make a deal, however. If you can shed five pounds by your next physical, in about one month, I will agree to some modest adjustments to your food selections. I'll let you select three things to put back in your diet. In moderation."

Jeremiah sighed. "I'm calling Dr. Scott," he said. "We'll see what he has to say about this. He's always telling me how he wants me to be comfortable."

"Don't bother Dr. Scott with something so trivial."

Jeremiah stared at Pike. He definitely noted something more behind his words. He was sincerely worried about the man.

"I'm calling him," he said.

"I believe you'll find he is in total agreement with me on this," Pike told him. "I'll see you at our next appointment."

"We'll see about that!" Jeremiah shouted before the door closed behind the doctor.

He picked up the landline phone again and put it to his ear.

"Good morning, Mr. Adams. This is Andrea. How can I help you?"

"I need to speak with Dr. Scott."

"I'm sorry, I can't connect you directly, but I could take a message for him."

"Why can't I just speak to him?" he asked. "It's important."

"He isn't in the facility at the moment."

"Then put me through to his ViMed office."

"It's Sunday, Mr. Adams. He isn't there. And even if he were there, you know I can't do that."

"No, I suppose not. When is he due back?"

"He won't be in today. I expect him to call later."

Jeremiah turned when he heard the familiar click of a key card opening the front door. Brent came in dressed in a wrinkled T-shirt, his red hair in its usual state of chaos.

"Okay, fine," Jeremiah told Andrea. "Just have him call me." He put the receiver back on its cradle and turned to Brent. "Charles Scott isn't even here today," he said. "Who's watching the monkeys?"

"He wasn't here yesterday, either," Brent told him. "I suppose he has other things to do. He is busy, you know."

"Other things? I can't imagine anything important enough to take him away from his precious experiment for two days in a row. You don't find that strange?"

Brent shrugged and walked into the kitchen. Jeremiah followed him and watched as he poured himself the last of the coffee from the carafe.

"You didn't want this, did you?"

"Does Scott go missing on a regular basis, then?" Jeremiah asked. "What if something happened here? What if there was an emergency or something?"

"There's such a thing as cell phones, you know. I'm sure he hasn't gone to the moon." Brent put two sugars into his cup. "What's the big deal?"

"Nothing," Jeremiah told him. "I just think it's odd that he isn't here for two days. He's in charge of all this. This is his show. Is he on vacation or something?"

Brent shook his head and took a sip of his coffee. "I doubt it," he said with some consideration. "I doubt he's taken a vacation day in ten years. He's probably just busy."

Jeremiah leaned back against the counter and stared at Brent. "Do you think he's sick or something?"

"I don't know, maybe." If Brent knew anything at all he showed no indication of it.

"He's been acting strange lately," Jeremiah said.

"What do you mean?"

"I don't know, like he's nervous or something, like he's got something on his mind."

"He's got a lot on his mind," Brent said. "He's in charge of this whole thing, remember."

"What if there's a problem we don't know about?"

"You're imagining things."

"I don't think so," he said. "I think something's wrong. And I'm starting to wonder if there's anything I should know. Do *you* know anything?"

"Nothing, Jeremiah. Calm down. You're reading too much into things that don't matter. It seems like you're the one with the problem."

"Easy for you to say. Sorry, Brent, but you don't have as much at stake as I do. And you're not trapped in this room all day. If something's going on, if something happened, I just think someone should let me know."

"What do you think happened?"

"I don't know. Maybe someone from the outside found out what we're doing and we're all going to jail? Maybe he's lost funding and has to put the brakes on the whole thing? How do I know? No one tells me anything around here. I'm asking you."

"And I'm telling you there's nothing to worry about. If it

were something like that, I would be told. Now, come on. The viewing's about to start."

"Would you tell me? If something happened?"

"Yes," Brent said with an exaggerated sigh. "I'd tell you. Now can we get settled before the monitor comes on?" He walked into the living room, and Jeremiah followed him, satisfied that Brent didn't know anything about Scott's illness. At least, he thought, that meant Brent wasn't in on it.

"I almost forgot," Brent said before taking his usual spot on the couch. "I brought us something." He unzipped his backpack and produced a white paper bag holding two absolutely mammoth chocolate-covered doughnuts. "Smuggled in something decent to eat."

"Pike's going to hand you your head if he finds out about this." Jeremiah took almost half the thing in the first bite. "He's all over me about my weight."

"I think it's definitely a risk worth taking. Maybe it's the diet that's making you all weird. Sit down, we have a show to watch."

"Bring me one with sprinkles tomorrow."

When the monitor came on, Jeremiah and Brent saw the clone and Diana at the kitchen table. He was doing a crossword puzzle. She was drinking iced coffee and flipping through the pages of a home decorating magazine, her eyes scanning the glossy photos with quick, critical precision.

"We should do the kitchen over," she said without looking up.

"Again?"

"That was ten years ago," she told him, as though this would serve as both explanation and final argument.

"Diana," the clone said, "I've got to figure out my mother's situation. It's going to cost me a lot more and they want me to move on it. Let's get through that first."

"There's always something more important," she said. She

got up from the table and began loading the dishwasher, still, Jeremiah noted, without even glancing at the clone.

"Last I heard," the clone said, turning now to fully face her back, "you were looking for a new house. We don't need a new kitchen *and* a new house, do we?"

"Well, there doesn't seem to be much interest in that, either," she told him. "I can't get you to even talk about it seriously. Forget it."

"You're never home to talk about anything seriously," the clone told her, and Jeremiah leaned slightly forward, paying careful attention to how this would play out. He was glad to see his double taking some initiative, even where he had been unable or unwilling to do so. But the clone was not confrontational, he was tiptoeing around the real question, just like he would have done himself.

She changed the subject.

"Louie has another appointment at the vet this afternoon. They might need to adjust his medication. Do you want to take him, or should I?"

"I think you better do it," the clone told her. "I can't get him to go in the car with me. Not even with a treat. I think that stuff is messing with him. He's not acting right."

Jeremiah shot a sideways glance at Brent. Every time someone started talking about Louie he got worried that there might be questions. But Brent wasn't typing anything into his notes. He just continued to stare at the screen. The comment had gone right over his head.

"It's probably just the new car," Diana said. "It smells different. Dogs can sense when something has changed. They don't like it. I'm going to take him for a walk." She closed the dishwasher and wiped her hands on a towel. "I'll be back in an hour."

The clone watched her leave and then went right back to his crossword. In the silence, Jeremiah looked at him and tried to recollect the exact moment he'd realized something in his marriage had changed. Diana's added hours at work had been noticeable, of course, but the first inklings of her infidelity had been subtle, quiet things. Something in her tone of voice, or her eyes, maybe. The way she started filling up long silences with pointless banter and conversations that led nowhere. He'd been staring at her one night as she sat in front of her mirror, combing her hair with a private, unexpected smile on her face. When she noticed him there, she put down her comb and left the room without a word. He had the distinct impression that he had intruded on something. That was the moment, he realized now, that *she knew he knew.* After that, they'd settled into a quiet, defeated sort of acknowledgment of the thing, without anger and without any words at all. It had become something they skirted around and averted, as though avoiding it might spare them some awful truth ten times worse. It was then, Jeremiah supposed, that he had stopped all attempts at intimacy with her, even small ones—reaching for her hand or brushing stray hair from her face. Eventually, that lack of physical contact began to feel normal. And that was the real charade, he thought, almost worse than the cheating itself. The knowing and not facing it. They were both guilty of that. And so, too, now was the clone. And in some way that he couldn't fathom, that aspect bothered Jeremiah more than anything else. Had he been harboring some latent hope that his clone would be stronger than he was? Did he think his double would have the guts to face things? To fix things? To do what Jeremiah himself couldn't do himself? He'd come closer than Jeremiah had, but he still hadn't said anything.

Jeremiah didn't pay much attention to the rest of the clone's Sunday morning. His double flipped through the pages of the newspaper at the kitchen table and then left in his car to do a few errands, the cameras losing sight of him each time he parked and got out, and picking him up again when he got back in.

Jeremiah felt like a silent passenger waiting in the car. He was relieved when the monitor switched off just before the clone turned into his driveway to pull into the garage.

"It's decently after noontime," Jeremiah said almost the instant the monitor switched off. "I could use a beer."

"We'll do the questions first," Brent said. "Then yes, I want a beer."

"I'll save you the trouble," Jeremiah said. "No, no and no. The clone didn't do anything surprising, I wouldn't have done anything differently and Diana certainly didn't show any signs she wasn't talking to me. Done. Get us a beer."

# CHAPTER
# 14

"How long have you been married, Jeremiah?" Brent asked a few days later over bland braised chicken.

"Sixteen years," he said. "In two weeks actually."

"Whoa, will clone boy remember?"

"I always do, so I assume he will."

"Sometimes I forget you're the same person."

"I wish I could forget," Jeremiah said.

"What does that mean?"

"I can't stand to watch him. He's weak. He's got no backbone. No guts."

"I think he has *your* backbone and *your* guts actually. Right down to the molecule, as I understand it."

"You know what I mean."

"I guess he does seem a little wimpy."

"Could you imagine sitting back like this with him, having dinner, just talking?"

"I don't know him the way I know you. Or rather, I suppose, he doesn't know me."

"You'd never be friends with him, not like we are."

"Well, we were sort of thrown together, you know? It's dif-

ferent," Brent said. "But he is you, Jeremiah. He's an exact replica. And you answer those questions every single day to prove
that. He's just the same as you."

"Yeah, well, I'm going to make some changes when I get
out of here. I can tell you that. I'm not going to be the same as
him anymore. I'm not going to be such a goddamn doormat,
always afraid of stirring up the pot. I'm going to say what's on
my mind."

"I think you're being too hard on yourself. You're lucky, in
a way," Brent said.

"Lucky, how?"

"Most people don't ever get to see themselves the way you
have. You get to see yourself from the outside. It's actually
pretty cool."

As soon as Brent said it, Jeremiah was startled by the idea that
this whole thing was very much like taking Meld. In an instant,
he could begin to understand how taking that drug the wrong
way might entice someone to suicide. Maybe it's better to never
know how the world sees you. Maybe no one should see themselves like that. It surprises you. You don't recognize yourself,
or maybe you do, and that's worse. The thought disturbed Jeremiah in a profound way. What was watching his clone for hours
every day actually doing to him? All he knew was that, as the
days went on, he liked what he saw less and less and tried to distance himself from the clone at every opportunity.

"I don't think it's cool at all," Jeremiah said. "I don't feel very
lucky."

"Maybe you're overthinking this," Brent told him. "Yeah, I'll
agree, the clone does seem like an asshole at times—way more
of an asshole than you actually—and he's sort of boring, one-
dimensional, but that is still you up there. That is the Jeremiah
Adams I first met. Maybe you've loosened up a bit in here, but
that could just be because of me, you know? Maybe I'm the el-

ement of change in this equation. You're still the same person. You're just better now. Maybe I made you cooler."

"Sometimes I look at him, and even though I know everything he's going to do, every single word he's going to say, if I could just switch places with him, sometimes I think I *would* do things differently."

"If that's true, then you need to tell me that when I ask those questions." Brent looked suddenly deadly serious. "That's important."

"I don't mean that he's doing anything unexpected," Jeremiah said. "I don't mean I actually *would* have done anything differently. I guess I just mean that I wish I *could*. I wish I had the chance. He is doing everything exactly as I would have done it. But maybe I've changed. I think the clone is incapable of that. I think he can only work with what he got from me at that point, at that *exact* point in time. That's all he'll ever have. He can't change. Maybe he's stagnant. But I'm not. And I'm different now."

Brent eyed him with measured attention, which made Jeremiah instantly uncomfortable. He wasn't certain, after all, how much he could actually trust Brent. Charles Scott still signed his paychecks.

"I don't know," he told Brent. "I'm not thinking clearly. I think I'm just tired."

He'd been living with these feelings for a while, wondering how it was possible to watch his own replica and not like him. Every day, as the viewing was set to begin, Jeremiah would feel his stomach tighten and his face harden into an expression of contempt, which he found more and more difficult to conceal. He watched with gritted teeth as his double wormed his way around his day, never fully engaging in anything, seemingly oblivious to the fact that his awkward insecurity came across as unwarranted conceit. In every conversation, he was only marginally there, only as much as he needed to be, never vested, and answering questions with abrupt predictability. He never pursued anything from anyone around him. Never initiated a discussion himself. He never asked a question or wondered out loud. At home, too, he seemed stuck on the edges, just halfway in. He wouldn't attempt any honest connection with either Diana or Parker and he all but pushed them away if they ever tried it with him.

"Can we go to a movie tonight, Dad?" Parker asked once. "We haven't been to a movie in ages."

"Anything you could possibly want to see ends up on TV for free in two months, anyway," the clone told him. "Nobody goes to the movies anymore." Jeremiah had been livid at that. It was a missed opportunity and he wanted to jump inside the wall and throttle that clone. He was an idiot.

Was he expecting too much of his double? Despite fleeting moments of a kind of empathy for the clone, he knew the thing on the wall wasn't really human. How, he reasoned, could something so unnatural even be expected to live and engage? He might walk and talk and breathe, but there had to be something missing from the clone, some elemental spark, some God particle, some essence. A soul?

Thoughts like that didn't typically clutter Jeremiah's mind and the fact that he thought about them now shocked him slightly. He had no unshakable faith in anything higher than the sky, but watching that clone haunt his own world, day in and day out, made him question things he'd never considered. It had begun to interfere with his sleep.

One morning, just after four, he gave up, threw back the covers and got out of bed. Better to just find something to do, he decided, rather than lie in bed wide awake. He didn't have a book he was reading at the moment and didn't feel like watching TV. He was antsy. He tried the treadmill for a few minutes and then gave up on that, too.

Finally, and without any conscious decision on his part, he found himself sitting on the living room couch, headset on and controller in hand, playing his first solo round of *Infinite Frontiers* or, as Brent had started referring to it, *IF*. Trying to recall the correct sequence of buttons it took to fire his machine gun and rummaging the 3-D war-torn landscape for med kits and discarded rations made for a good distraction. One needed to concentrate, after all, to avoid stepping on a land mine or getting shot in the head by some mindless AI sniper. It took effort, too, Jeremiah discovered, not to shoot his foot off with his own gun, a maneuver he seemed to have mastered without even trying.

After dying several unceremonious deaths and respawning in roughly the same spot he'd started at, he decided to work on his avatar instead. How many times had Brent chided him, after all, for continuing to play as the default image of a nondescript American soldier named Player 2?

The choices were many and intricate, starting with species and ending somewhere around eyebrow shape and shoelace color. If he wanted to, Jeremiah could literally have played the game as a bipedal alligator in an evening gown. But he went with something slightly more menacing.

Slowly, attribute by attribute, his avatar, whom he called Clyde, came into being. He was a stocky, stern-faced ex-marine (or so Jeremiah imagined) dressed in camouflage pants and a tattered Ramones T-shirt, which was bursting from the force of his muscular chest. He wore a military surplus helmet over messy, dirty blond hair, and goggles that looked like they were salvaged from an industrial waste site. He had a cache of weapons on his person that included an assault rifle, two handguns, a machete and a blade he concealed in one of his hobnail boots. Once he leveled up a few times, Jeremiah had his eye on a sweet

Uzi and a grenade launcher, but he didn't have the points for either yet. Standard-issue grenades were clipped in a ready row on his belt, and his pack contained ammo, med kits and rations enough to last a virtual month or more.

He sat and tweaked Clyde's appearance for over an hour, playing with the skin tone and trying out different placements for battle scars and tattoos. In the end, though, he opted to hold off on the ink altogether, deciding that tattoos would be used to mark his eventual kills. And Jeremiah planned on many victories, even if he hadn't come close to one yet.

When he finally positioned the nose just right and had firmly decided against a bandanna, the living room door opened without warning and Brent came whistling into the apartment. Jeremiah looked at the clock and was shocked to realize he'd been at it for four hours. It was nearly nine o'clock in the morning.

Brent smiled—almost laughed—when he turned and saw Jeremiah, still in his underwear, with the headgear on and controller at the ready.

"Practicing?" he asked.

"Yeah, well, I'm sick and tired of you whipping my ass every single time we play this stupid thing." He switched the system off, discarded his gear and went to the kitchen to make coffee. He'd wait until they were actually in battle before introducing Brent to Clyde. He wanted more practice, too. It wouldn't matter how fierce his avatar looked if he kept shooting himself in the foot.

"Yeah, well, I've been practicing, too," Brent said. "Still gonna whip your ass. Every single time."

# CHAPTER
# 15

## DAY 89

"Why do you get so bent out of shape when your wife works late?" Brent was attempting egg-white omelets for a late lunch. "I mean, Mel's out three or four nights a week, either working or out somewhere with her girlfriends. Doesn't faze me. She was out last night until all hours."

"It's different when you're married," Jeremiah told him. "Especially when you have a kid. And it doesn't help that I can't even ask her about it."

Jeremiah got up from the table and grabbed the orange juice from the fridge. They had a viewing scheduled for four o'clock and they still had almost an hour to kill. He was glad for the chance to get out of his own head for a while, so he didn't mind that Brent had decided to tread on what he considered personal territory.

"I don't know," Brent told him. "I just can't imagine me and Mel ever being that way, not even when we're married. I guess I just think two people don't necessarily need to be together every minute to be *together*."

"Like I said, it's all different when you're married. You'll see. We have an arrangement—I work, and she takes care of the family side. When she starts missing that, it's like she's not holding up her end of the deal."

"But she's working, too, right?"

"It was supposed to be a part-time job," he said. "You know, just something to keep her head in the game. And I make enough money. She doesn't have to work."

"Still," Brent said, shaking his head, "seems you're mad over nothing. I'm not going to be like that with Mel. I don't care what you say."

"You have any pictures of Mel?" Brent talked about her so often, working her into every other conversation, that Jeremiah felt he needed some point of reference.

Brent took out his phone, fingered the screen deftly and handed it to Jeremiah with a grin.

She was every bit as beautiful as Brent had built her up to be. Long waves of caramel-colored hair fell around light brown eyes and bright pink lipstick. She had four earrings in her left ear and the photo caught her in midlaugh so that even her personality seemed perfectly captured in still life—vibrant and confident and totally sure of her place in the world. She looked like the sort of person everyone else gravitated to in a crowded room. He could practically hear her laugh.

"How the hell did you land her?" he asked, handing the phone back. "You got some secret trust fund or something?"

"Nope," he said, waving his hands down the length of his body, "just all this awesomeness."

"Yeah, right. How did you meet? And don't say the strip club she worked at, because that would just be sad."

"No, we met through a mutual friend," he said. "And she wasn't a stripper, she was an exotic dancer, and she only did it to put herself through school. That isn't sleazy, it's a good work ethic."

"And where did she go to school?"

"She studied art history at Suffolk," he said. "She's an artist in her own right, though, and damn good." He nodded toward the abstract painting on the wall. "She painted that, you know."

"You're kidding." Jeremiah was glad he'd never thought to mention to Brent that he didn't like the painting.

"No, Charles Scott commissioned it himself when the place was being decorated. She's incredibly talented."

Jeremiah had trouble imagining that Charles Scott would concern himself with something as trivial as the lab's decor.

"Is all of her stuff abstract like that? You think you might be able to get her to paint something else for me? Like maybe a portrait of my dog or something?"

"Well, I can't do it now," Brent told him. "I'm not allowed to talk about you. It's in my contract. But afterward, I guess, when this is all over, I could ask her. Why the dog, though? I thought you didn't like that dog."

"N-no," Jeremiah stammered. "No, of course I like him. Why would you say that?"

"He doesn't seem to like you much."

Jeremiah swallowed hard. He hadn't meant to say so much.

"Well, he's really Parker's dog," he said. "I thought a painting might make a great gift for Parker when I get back."

"Sure, I'll see what I can do."

"So, does Mel just sit and paint all day? She makes enough money with that?"

"At the moment, she's working as an assistant in the press department of the MFA," he said. "But she does okay with her painting. She's had a few shows."

"In my day, nerds like you didn't get girls like her."

"I think we just sort of complement each other," Brent said. "Left brain, right brain sort of thing, science and art."

"Seems like the two things are mutually exclusive," Jeremiah said, more to himself than to Brent.

"Nah, it's like a balance. You need a little of everything in you, you know? And if you don't have it, you gravitate to someone else who does. Opposites attract, right?"

On some level, Jeremiah could understand that. When he'd met Diana all those years ago at college, it was her eccentricity and her absolute dread of the mundane that had drawn him in. In those first few succulent weeks, they'd lie awake in his twin bed talking by candlelight, and he'd listen with eager ears while she ranted about the hypocrisy of the American Dream.

"I don't ever want to be the kind of person who thinks it's important to keep up or get ahead," she told him. "We have to always be true to our *real* selves, to our own true destiny and desires. We can't ever give in to mediocrity. It's all so meaningless. It takes away so much."

She was so beautiful when she spoke that way, her eyes sparkling with some private fire and her whole body rigid with the strength of her conviction. He'd been mesmerized by her in those first weeks.

And he'd nod and agree and happily spit it all right back at her, all the while knowing that his own truest desires were laced with the trappings of everything she despised: family, stability, security, roots—all the things he never had growing up with his mother's whimsy. His mother didn't know the meaning of settling down. The very concept of laying down roots somewhere seemed as abhorrent to her as it did to Diana. She bounced from job to job only for the sake of "something new." She filled his head with stories and strung their yard with Christmas lights all year long "to lure the fairies." Quite unintentionally, it seemed, his mother had made him a serious man. It was no wonder he settled on studying journalism: he was pulled in by the allure of facts, the simple, plain language and the truth in it.

But there must have been something of his mother still inside him, and Diana, once, had fed that need in him. It was a sort of balance, like Brent said. But somewhere along the line, that balance had become skewed. Neither one of them had seemed to notice. Neither of them seemed to care.

"I suppose that's true," he told him now.

Inwardly, he marveled at how it had all changed. When Diana became pregnant with Parker, Jeremiah had insisted they settle down. He convinced her it wasn't giving in, that they'd still be their own *real selves*. He found them a decent apartment in a good neighborhood, and he helped her decorate it with Bohemian tapestries, curtains fashioned of Indian silk scraps and a secondhand red velvet couch. He landed his first real job on a newspaper. They got married with a small, civil ceremony. Then, before Parker was three, the rent was replaced with a mortgage and the velvet couch went to Goodwill. Eventually, it was Diana who convinced him that he'd make more money in marketing than he ever could in journalism and, reluctantly, he'd given in. After he started with ViMed, they moved to a better neighborhood and bought a bigger house with an extra bedroom. And though Jeremiah brought it up on a regular basis for a while, they never had another child. It was something he was sorry about from time to time.

When the monitor switched on, the clone was at his desk with his office door closed, his head bent over a short stack of pages. The muffled voices of his coworkers could be heard in the hallway, just outside. Brenda's voice rose above the din for a moment as she counted down the group to an uncomfortable delivery of "Happy Birthday" to someone called Tom. No one's birthday escaped Brenda's calendar. Nor their employment anniversary, promotion, new baby or impending retirement. She oversaw a collection schedule for the coffer and was on a first-name basis with a local bakery. Jeremiah had suffered through the ritual seven times himself. He'd smile and nod through the serenade and eat cake with a plastic spoon until, one by one, everyone figured out how to make a graceful escape back to their desks. When he could manage it, he tried to skip out on the gatherings for everyone else. It wasn't always an easy feat. On more than one occasion, he'd actually hidden in the bathroom.

Jeremiah watched the clone with a certain empathy and cringed when he heard Brenda's cheery rapping on his closed door. He almost laughed when he saw his double snatch the telephone receiver and hold it up to his ear. When Brenda poked her head in, he covered the mouthpiece with one hand and offered her a shrug of his shoulders and an apologetic expression. "Sorry," he mouthed. She nodded and ducked back out, closing the door behind her, and the clone slipped the phone back onto its cradle with a quick sigh of relief.

"You don't like cake or something?" Brent asked Jeremiah.

"It's the middle of the workday. Those things are a nuisance. One week there were three cakes in two days. He's got work to do. Can't blame him."

"Yeah, right, fake phone calls are so important. God, what a hard-ass." Brent chuckled. "It's cake. Loosen up a little, man."

A half hour later, when the coast was clear, they watched the clone slink out into the hallway and over to Brenda's desk. She smiled at him and handed over a paper plate with a lopsided slice of chocolate cake on it.

"I saved you some," she said.

"Thanks. I couldn't get away. Sorry about that. I'll be sure to stop by his desk when I get a chance. Tom, right?"

"Tom. Not the editing Tom, the one in Accounting."

"Got it."

"Oh, Mr. Adams," she said as the clone turned away, "while I have you here, I need to leave a little early on Friday, if that's all right."

"Sure," the clone told her, and attempted to walk away. She

came out from behind her desk and moved in next to him, brandishing her cell phone in one hand.

"My niece is coming in for the weekend," she told him, scrolling through her phone and then showing him a photo of a skinny, smiling teenage blonde. "She's visiting colleges. Can you *believe* it? They grow up quick, don't they?"

Jeremiah watched the clone smile lamely and inch away from her.

"Isn't Parker getting ready for the big college search?" she asked. Brenda made a point of knowing the names and approximate ages of everybody's children. "He's a junior this year, isn't he?"

"A sophomore," the clone told her. "Pretty soon, though, yeah." The clone smiled again and turned on his heels, sensing a reasonable escape. "Take whatever time you need on Friday," he called over his shoulder.

As the clone walked the short distance down the hallway back to his office, the ViMed camera hovered for another instant on Brenda, and Jeremiah saw something almost imperceptible change in her face. It stung him.

"That was kind of rude," Brent said.

"He's got work to do," Jeremiah protested. "People can't just sit around chatting all day, you know."

"Still."

Silently, Jeremiah agreed and made a mental note to look up Brenda's birthday before he got out of here. He realized at that moment that he couldn't remember a single one of those gatherings being organized for her.

After Brent left that evening, Jeremiah made a ham sandwich and nibbled at it absently as he took a closer look at Mel's painting on the living room wall. All this time, he'd looked at it with a casual distaste when he bothered to notice it at all. Now that he knew who the artist was, he felt obliged to at least give it a second chance. He'd never understood the appeal of abstract art. If someone put that much effort into a painting, he thought, it ought to at least resemble something familiar. To his eyes, this still looked like a jumble of circles, something a child might draw. They ranged in size from a dime to a dinner plate, painted in grays and deep blues. Some overlapped, some seemed to recede into the distance. Some were bordered in sharp lines, others had edges that bled into the background.

He positioned himself a few feet from the wall and stood there for a few minutes, tilting his head and squinting at it, but he couldn't recognize any form in the thing. If it was supposed to elicit something from him, he didn't know what it was, other than a slight sense of vertigo. Moving closer, he noticed there were places where the brush had pulled the paint up from the canvas in tiny ridges. Maybe it was meant to be tactile, he decided, and began to run his fingertips over it.

It was then that he noticed, camouflaged perfectly in the center of a tiny gray circle, the smooth glass lens of a camera. It had been almost imperceptible before. But when he saw the glint of it, he knew instantly what it was. He immediately pulled back his hands and took an unsteady step backward, turning his gaze away, suddenly overwhelmed by the feeling that he had been caught doing something he shouldn't have. In the grips of that absurd sense of guilt, Jeremiah sidestepped over to the bookshelf, out of the camera's view, and pretended to busy himself with the books. Every time he looked back at the painting now, his eye went directly to the camera lens, pulled there despite his best efforts. Now that he'd found it, it was the only thing he could see.

He wondered vaguely if there were other cameras hidden anywhere. Not likely in this room, he decided. The position of the painting would have offered a clear, sidelong view of Jeremiah as he sat in front of the monitor each day to watch his clone. He figured that was probably the thing Charles Scott wanted to see.

Still, he found himself examining the room, casually lifting books, fingering baseboards and checking the bulbs in every light fixture. He found nothing. A quick scan of the kitchen, with all its smooth, steel surfaces, offered no evidence of any additional devices. Even a tiny lens would have been readily visible in there, especially now that he was looking for it.

Finally, he retreated to his bedroom, quickening his pace slightly as he passed by the painting, and examined every corner of that room. After an hour, when he'd found nothing, he switched off the lights and climbed into bed, where he spent a fitful night tossing and turning, unable to shake the feeling he was being watched.

# CHAPTER
# 16

Brent wasn't due until after eleven the next morning, and Jeremiah spent three hours slinking by the painting between the bedroom and the kitchen. Ordinarily he might have passed the time reading or watching the news on the monitor, but he couldn't get himself to sit in the living room now that he knew Scott could be watching. So, instead, he ate three bowls of bran cereal standing at the kitchen counter and then took a shower until the water went cold. He was getting dressed when he heard Brent come in and went into the living room to meet him.

"Come into the kitchen for a minute." Brent was sitting on the couch, directly in line with the surveillance camera, and Jeremiah paused with his back purposely toward the painting. "I have a new smoothie recipe."

"Smoothie recipe? Okay, Jamie Oliver. But if it's made with that fat-free yogurt, I'll pass, thanks."

"I'm serious, it's good. Just come in."

Reluctantly, Brent got off the couch and followed him to the kitchen. Jeremiah poured half a carton of low-fat milk into the blender, tossed in a few ice cubes and switched it on.

"That's your recipe?" Brent asked above the din.

"I know this place is bugged," Jeremiah blurted. "I found the camera. In Mel's painting. I want to know if you knew about this."

"Bugged? What? There's no way." Brent looked at him with an expression of authentic doubt, enough to make him believe he knew nothing about it. It was possible, Jeremiah thought, that Brent was in the dark about a lot of things.

"Go see for yourself," he told him. "It's almost exactly in the center, inside one of those little circles. You can see it if you get up close enough."

Brent left the room and came back a few minutes later, shaking his head in a way that suggested he'd found it. Jeremiah put two more ice cubes into the blender and turned the setting up to Puree.

"I swear, Jeremiah, I had no idea." Brent held his hands up at his shoulders in a show of innocence. "I had no clue. Are there any others?"

"Not that I could find, and believe me, I looked. Why am I being watched?"

"I don't know. Maybe Scott wants to see what happens when you're watching the clone? The way the camera is facing, toward the center of the room, that's the only thing he could see, I think—us on the couch when we're watching the monitor." He paused and shook his head slowly again. "I'm being watched, too, I guess. Maybe he's doing it to make sure my reports are accurate. I don't know. But I swear I had nothing to do with this. I had no idea."

"So, what do we do? Cover it up? Take it out?"

"I don't think so," Brent told him. "I mean, that won't do anything but show Scott we're onto it. Maybe the best thing to do is just leave it there. For now at least."

"Doesn't it bother you?" Jeremiah asked.

"Of course it bothers me. But what else can we do? We just

have to be careful, is all. We just have to watch what we say in there. Maybe slow down on the beers, I guess. Besides," he added, "we're not even certain it's working. Maybe it isn't even hooked up. For all we know it could be a decoy, maybe he wanted us to find it just to keep us on our toes. We could test it, I think."

"How?" Jeremiah added more ice to the blender and let it go. If Scott could hear through that device, he certainly wouldn't hear them talking.

"Easy. I can take it out and hook it up to the monitor. It'll tell us if it's active or not."

"Won't he notice that?"

"He's not in the building right now. I just came from his office. He was leaving for a meeting. He won't be back until this afternoon."

Jeremiah switched off the blender. "Could have told me before I used up half my ice," he said. "But what if he has someone else monitoring the thing? How do we know he doesn't record it and watch everything later?"

"Look," Brent said, "we either do this right now or we don't. I say we do it. We have to find out."

He went into the living room and Jeremiah followed.

"Help me get this off the wall." Brent already had his hands positioned on one side of the mammoth painting. Jeremiah took the other end and, together, they lifted it up and off its hook. "Hold it there," Brent told him, peering behind the canvas. "Okay, it's definitely wired. Put it back, I'm going to take it out from the front."

Jeremiah watched as Brent gingerly twisted the tiny camera until it wriggled loose. He pulled it slowly outward, dangling by its wire, and then stopped to check something.

"Do you know what you're doing?"

"Yeah, I know what I'm doing. I'm a scientist, remember? It's

not brain surgery." He disconnected the camera and the painting was left with an odd little hole where the wire came out.

"Now," Brent said, "I just need to access the cables behind
the monitor. It should be just behind this panel." He lifted a
small door in the wall, just below the monitor, that Jeremiah
had never noticed before.

"Is this going to take long?" Jeremiah asked. "If that monitor is disconnected when the viewing starts, someone's going
to notice."

"We have time. I'll have this hooked up in a few minutes.
Why don't you go make me a smoothie or something?"

"Fuck you."

"Then leave me alone and let me do this." He pulled a thin
cable out from the wall until he had enough slack to work with,
hooked the end of it to something on the back of the camera
and smiled. "There," he said. "Done. Turn it on."

Jeremiah moved in front of Brent, grabbed the remote and
hit the button. With Brent standing directly behind him, aim-
ing the camera at the monitor, what appeared before him was
mesmerizing: an image of the back of his own head, watching
the monitor, which showed an image of his head watching the
monitor, which showed his head again watching the monitor,
and so on, seemingly into infinity. The effect was dizzying, so
much so that he thought he might topple over if he looked at
it too long.

"Well, it works," Brent said.

"Turn it off," Jeremiah told him. "Put it back."

"It's kind of cool, isn't it?" Brent began moving the camera
slowly back and forth, making the image on the wall—and all
of its infinite reflections—waver, until Jeremiah thought he
might actually get sick.

"Knock it off, Brent." Jeremiah hit the button on the remote.
The wall monitor went black and Jeremiah sat down while

Brent put everything back to where it had been. When he was finished, there was no indication anything had been tampered with.

"So, what do we do now?" he asked when Brent sat down on the couch. "Now that we know it's real?"

"Nothing," Brent told him. "Like I said, we just be careful. We be ourselves and we do our jobs. That's all."

"Easy for you to say. But I actually live here."

"Well," Brent said with a smirk, "then I wouldn't dance naked in front of the painting if I were you, difficult as that may be."

A few minutes later, the monitor switched on. As Jeremiah watched the clone stumble through four hours of his workday, he found it unsettling to realize that he was now the watcher and that his double had no idea.

# CHAPTER
# 17

## DAY 94

Jeremiah spent an uncomfortable week in his rooms. He ate his meals standing at the counter in the kitchen, and spent a lot of time in the bedroom, but he couldn't stay out of the living room forever. There wasn't much to do anywhere else. But whenever he was in there, on the computer or the treadmill, or practicing *IF*, he found himself trying not to look in the direction of the painting and hoping it didn't appear obvious. Eventually, he realized he could move one of the chairs out of the camera's view. It was an odd-looking arrangement, one chair pushed up against the wall on its own, but it afforded him a sense of semi-privacy and a place where he could read. Despite everything, Jeremiah was often happy for the long, quiet stretches when he could read. He had devoured half the *New York Times* bestseller list in the space of a few weeks, and had a growing log of books to request, ones he'd never found the time for in his old life. He was absorbed in a true-crime thriller when Charles Scott walked in the front door, unannounced, on a Friday afternoon.

"Mr. Adams," he said, "we need to have a talk."

In his own mind, Jeremiah sneered back at Scott: *You're damn right we need a talk, you spying piece of crap.* In reality, he just looked up at him blankly from the chair.

If Scott had any suspicions about the new furniture arrangement, he didn't mention it.

Jeremiah laid the open book down and walked over to the couch. He sat and put his feet up on the coffee table. "About what?"

"I've just come from a meeting with Natalie Young. She tells me you've been asking a lot of questions about taking Meld."

"I don't like taking it so often."

"She sets the schedule for when you take it, Mr. Adams. That is part of her job."

"How do we know that's safe?" Jeremiah put his feet down and leaned forward slightly. "She keeps saying it's fine. But there isn't enough documented information on that. I would know. I doubt anyone has taken this drug more than I have."

Scott sat down on the couch across from him and looked Jeremiah hard in the eyes with an unreadable expression.

"She is taking it with you, Mr. Adams," he said. "And she has no concerns about the frequency."

"She's not the one being probed. Maybe it's different. She's isn't even taking the same drug I am. I just don't see the point in taking so much of it. I'm not convinced it's safe. In fact, I think it might be taking a toll on me."

"How so?" Scott asked.

"I'm having trouble sleeping, for one thing. Who knows what else it's doing to me."

"We can have Dr. Pike check you out," Scott told him. "I can set that up for tomorrow."

"Pike's already checked me out. He says there's nothing to worry about. He told me it's stress. He prescribed a sedative."

"Then I would advise you to take your sedative and stop worrying. You will take the Meld according to Dr. Young's schedule. It's imperative to the project. We need to know how the cloning is impacting you. I'm afraid that is part of your contract, Mr. Adams."

"Ah, yes," Jeremiah said. "The contract." He would have liked to add that spy cameras weren't part of his contract, but he bit his tongue.

"What is it about the Meld that you don't trust?" Scott asked. "I understand from Mr. Higgins's recent reports that you're also upset about the idea of your mother taking the drug. Meld is a miracle drug. It may actually help her, you know. There's no telling what it will uncover."

"You might feel differently if it were your mother," Jeremiah told him. "Taking Meld isn't all it's cracked up to be, you know. You don't know what it's like."

Scott let a trifling, contemptuous laugh escape his lips. "What makes you so certain?"

"You've taken Meld?" he asked. "Why?"

But Jeremiah knew exactly why Charles Scott would take the drug. With Pike's help, it was a way for him to get a copy of his own mind while it was still relatively sound. He would need that, presumably, to implant into his own, healthy clone when the time came.

Jeremiah leaned forward, elbows on his knees, to assess the man's expression when he lied about his reasons. He was close enough to be certain of it when he saw Scott's head suddenly jerk to one side in an uncontrollable way, his lips tightening and his eyes darting and blinking rapidly for a good second or two. Jeremiah was silent, but the look on his face must have said enough. Scott looked strangely flustered for an instant, and then stood up and turned his back to Jeremiah without explanation.

"Is something wrong, Dr. Scott?" Jeremiah asked. "Are you okay?"

"You will take the Meld as you are instructed, Mr. Adams,"

Scott said firmly, and he strode across the room and out the door without turning around again.

Jeremiah sat, stunned, staring at the door after it closed. There was no mistaking what he'd seen. That was some sort of spasm, a seizure or something. Had Jeremiah been looking the other way, he might have missed it. It was that brief, but it had happened, and it was proof of everything he suspected.

# CHAPTER

# 18

## DAY 100

Early on a Thursday afternoon, Jeremiah and Brent settled in for a viewing he was certain would show the clone alone at his desk. He was surprised, then, when the cameras opened up, not in his ViMed office, but once again in his mother's room at the assisted living home.

"Now what?" he asked cautiously, not really wanting to know the answer. Brent said nothing.

The clone, dressed in his work clothes, was standing just inside the doorway, his back to the camera, and his mother was flitting purposefully around her small room, gathering clothes from the closet and the drawers and stuffing them, unfolded, into a suitcase, which lay open on the bed.

"Mom," the clone said, and Jeremiah was surprised at how much it continued to bother him to hear the word come from his double's mouth. The only person in the world who had a right to call her "Mom" was Jeremiah. "Stop packing. I didn't say you had to leave right this minute."

"Well, if they're throwing me out, then why wait?"

"No one is throwing you out, Mom. Will you just stop for a minute and listen to me?"

"You're working with them," she said, a small, sardonic laugh escaping her lips. "You're not fooling me. You think I don't know. But I see everything."

An exasperated sigh escaped the clone's lips just as Jeremiah sighed in exactly the same manner in the lab. Brent typed something into his laptop.

"I think you're imagining things. No one is working against you, Mom. We're all just trying to help."

"Do you take me for a fool?" she asked. "They've been stealing my things. Putting drugs in my food. And now you tell me I have to leave. I say good riddance! I'll leave right now. The sooner, the better. It's not safe here."

"Just slow down, Mom," the clone said, moving toward her and taking a balled-up blouse from her hands. "No one is trying to hurt you. No one is putting anything in your food. This is foolishness."

The clone led her by the shoulder and eased her to the edge of the bed. She looked away from him and shook her head.

"Foolishness," she said. "That's what you'd like me to believe. But I know what's going on." As if to illustrate that point, she poked a bony finger at her temple and repeated it. "I know what's going on."

"This is what I'm talking about," the clone said carefully, and he sat down beside her on the bed. "You aren't thinking clearly. This is why you have to move. You need to be in a place where they can handle these things. Somewhere they can take care of you."

"I can take care of myself."

"No, Mom," he said. "You can't."

"I need to talk to my son," she said. The clone stopped and stiffened slightly. Jeremiah could see the muscles of his back tense up and the sight mirrored what he felt in his own body. "He'll know what to do about this. Just go and call my son."

"I am your son, Mom," the clone said. "Don't you know who I am? I'm Jeremiah. It's me."

She looked at the clone for a long moment, as though trying to decipher something in the face.

"You can't fool me," she said at last. "You think I'm crazy? You're not my son. I don't know you. I think I'd know my own son." She got up off the bed then and went back to stuffing articles of clothing, one at a time, into the suitcase.

"Mom," the clone said, and left it at that.

In the lab, Jeremiah closed his eyes and said nothing. Brent was typing again.

"What the hell are you writing? Knock it off, Brent."

"Did you hear what she just said?"

"She's got dementia, for Christ's sake! She doesn't mean *that*!"

"I have to put it in there," he said. "It kind of jumps out."

Jeremiah turned back to the screen and watched as his double sat like stone while his mother moved back and forth again between the closet and the bed.

Jeremiah could barely move, either. In all the time since her memory had first begun to falter, there had never been a moment when his mother hadn't known him. It was brutally upsetting. And in that moment, Jeremiah knew his clone was grappling with the same substantial shock. In a strange way, he had never felt more connected to the man on the screen.

"I'll be back, Mom," the clone said. "I need to speak to someone in the office and then we can talk about this more."

A few minutes later, the clone was seated in Dr. Waterson's office, leaning forward, elbows on his knees, holding his chin in his hands.

"I think we'd better go ahead and use the Meld on my mother," he said. "She's getting worse. Do you know, just now, she didn't even recognize me? She had absolutely no idea who I was."

Dr. Waterson blinked and stared at the clone for a brief moment.

"Mr. Adams," he said, "your mother and I already took the Meld. Last night, in fact."

"So, you know that the dementia has progressed," the clone said.

"Actually, Mr. Adams, I'm not certain now that we're dealing with dementia at all."

"What do you mean?" the clone asked.

"What the hell is he talking about?" Jeremiah asked no one in particular.

"No," Waterson said. "There are memory issues, certainly, that much we knew. But they are not consistent with what we typically see in dementia. They aren't impacting the same areas of the brain. In fact, some of those areas actually seem somewhat improved, I think. Her short-term memory, for example, is fine. We may be looking at something altogether different."

"What do you mean? Different, how?"

"You must remember, I am not a psychiatric doctor, Mr. Adams. I am not the right person to diagnose anything, but I have been trained in the use of Meld. I know what to look for. I saw clear evidence of mild depression, some definite paranoia and perhaps even schizophrenic disorder. We'll need a brain scan to be absolutely certain, but the synaptic activity I sensed seemed well above what we'd expect in dementia. I actually feel her memory is fairly sound, under the circumstances."

"How can this be possible?" the clone asked. "You've been talking about the onset of her dementia for a year now."

"This guy is cracked," Jeremiah said. Brent started typing again.

"If I'm not mistaken," Waterson said, "there is a family history of schizophrenia, isn't there?"

"Yes," the clone told him. "My uncle. Her brother. But she's never shown any signs of that."

"It's not completely out of the question, though. These episodes of hers, the things I saw with the Meld, it may point to a latent tendency toward schizophrenia. Earlier signs of the disorder might have been missed for all we know."

"I just never thought it would touch her," the clone said. "I thought that, after all this time, she was fine in that respect."

In the lab, Jeremiah wondered about the implications of that possibility.

"As I said," Waterson told the clone, "I'm not the right person to diagnose this. I'm just relaying my impressions from the Meld experience."

"Does this mean she won't have to be moved, after all?" the clone asked.

"For the moment, I wouldn't be opposed to her staying here with us. Emotionally, it might be best for her to stay. I'd like to bring in a specialist, perhaps even put her under the Meld again. That's quite an exhilarating drug you've got there."

"So I've heard," the clone said.

For the next few hours, Jeremiah paid hardly any attention to the monitor. He had no desire to watch the clone drag through his day at the office after what he'd just seen. Instead, he allowed his mind to wander to thoughts that twisted back in on themselves until he felt dizzy: If his mother could slip so quickly into mental illness, what did that mean for him? Or had the Meld sparked something that had lain dormant in her all this time? What if he'd been wrong all these years about her? What if the things he'd always thought of as eccentric—all her moving around, her restlessness and curiosity—pointed to something more serious than simple quirks? He'd taken the drug more times than she had. Was it having the same impact on his own mind? Could the Meld suicides be related to some dormant insanity?

And far more troubling, if his mother didn't have dementia, why the *hell* did she suddenly not recognize the clone as her son?

Did she know?

# CHAPTER
# 19

## DAY 102

On the night of their wedding anniversary, the ViMed cameras caught the clone and Diana upstairs in the midst of getting ready to go out. Diana was wearing a green top and black satin pants Jeremiah had never seen before. At the moment, she was shoeless, and the hems of the pants were getting caught under her feet as she walked back and forth between the mirror and her jewelry box. He wondered if they were going to the new restaurant in the shipyard that she had wanted to try. That he didn't know these details annoyed him more than he thought it should.

"Did you give Parker money for a pizza?" the clone asked her.

"Yes."

"And you checked the reservation today?"

"Honestly, Jeremiah," she said. "It's a Wednesday night at eight o'clock. I doubt there's going to be any problems. Quit worrying."

"Okay," the clone said, "just checking."

Jeremiah could understand the clone's concern. They hardly went out at all anymore. He was out of practice at the art of securing a table anywhere nicer than a pizza place.

"Your wife is pretty when she wants to be," Brent said.

"Even when she doesn't want to be," Jeremiah told him. She was. That much had never changed.

On the wall, the clone straightened his tie in the mirror and Jeremiah vaguely wondered whether he'd even bothered to comment on how Diana looked. He doubted it. He wouldn't have thought of it himself if Brent hadn't brought it up.

Diana checked her lipstick in the mirror, grabbed her purse and a black sweater and headed out to the hallway.

"I'll meet you downstairs," she said. "I just want to make sure Louie gets out to pee before we go."

Ordinarily, it would have been him taking Louie out before they left. Jeremiah figured nothing had changed with the dog's distrust of the clone, even with the medicine they were giving him.

The clone stopped at Parker's closed door, knocked once and opened it before he went downstairs.

"We're leaving," he said. "We'll be home around ten."

"Yup," Parker said without looking up from his computer monitor. "Have fun."

"Is the homework done?"

"Yup."

"Okay. Don't forget to order that pizza before it gets too late. And keep an eye on Louie."

"Yup, I will."

The clone closed the door and headed downstairs and to the garage, where ViMed cameras followed him seamlessly. Jeremiah wondered for the hundredth time exactly how many cameras Scott had hidden around his house. By his best estimate, there must have been at least a dozen. His double hit the switch on the wall to raise the garage bay door and then the button on his key chain to unlock the car. Diana came into the garage holding Louie by the leash, her arm outstretched to keep him away from her clothes. The dog took a wide arc around the clone as he went to the door to be let back in. The clone glanced down at him with something Jeremiah recognized as unhappy resignation, and for the first time, he understood that Louie's sudden aversion toward him must be hard on the clone. Jeremiah sincerely loved that dog so, presumably, the clone loved him, too. It must be awful. He'd never thought of that before.

When they got into the car, the cameras switched on from somewhere near the rearview mirror. For twenty minutes, Brent and Jeremiah watched as the clone and Diana rode in relative silence to the shipyard.

They parked and got out, and the camera stayed on inside the empty car, the only light coming from the red blinking car alarm signal on the dash. This was their view for the next two and a half hours while the clone and Diana were inside the restaurant. Presumably, Scott hadn't anticipated the need to arm every eatery in town with surveillance equipment. During the lull, Jeremiah and Brent played crazy eights and poker and glanced sidelong at the wall every few minutes for signs of activity.

When the clone and Diana came back out to the parking lot, Jeremiah heard them before he could see them, Diana's voice so belligerent that it startled him. He straightened, paying attention.

"Well, maybe you shouldn't have had that second gin and tonic before dinner," she snapped. "You know you can't drink on an empty stomach. Every time you do, it turns into a scene. Honestly, it's embarrassing. We won't be going back *there* again any time soon."

"Good," the clone said as he unlocked the door with some degree of difficulty. "I mean, come on, Diana. Two hundred and twenty dollars for dinner? For two people? For that price, they should have had someone cutting my steak and putting every bite in my mouth for me!"

"It's our anniversary," Diana said, her voice softening in volume if not in pitch. "Don't you think we can afford to have one nice dinner on our anniversary without you complaining about the cost?"

"It's ridiculous. And that was without a full bottle of wine."

"Jeremiah," she said. "Nice things cost money. That's just the way it is. I hope you gave that poor waiter a decent tip. God knows he earned it."

"I gave him the customary fifteen percent."

"Honestly, Jeremiah. In a place like that, customary is more like twenty percent. You really are uncouth sometimes, aren't you?"

"Am I supposed to answer that?" the clone sneered. "Or was that a rhetorical question? Sometimes I'm too uncouth to know the difference."

"Can we just get home in one piece, please. I have to work early in the morning."

"Of course you do," the clone said, venom slipping into his tone. Jeremiah leaned back, exhaling. He was really walking on thin ice now. He'd do better to just stop talking and drive.

"He is definitely not getting lucky tonight," Brent said.

Jeremiah could have told him that three hours ago, before they'd even left the house.

"Remind me next year," Diana said to the clone, "that we should just stay home and have pizza on our anniversary."

"Will do," the clone said. "Sounds good to me."

The remainder of their ride home was silent, except for intermittent stifled huffs coming from Diana. At first, Jeremiah thought she might be crying, but her indirect glances at the clone held more anger than anything else. She was seriously pissed, Jeremiah thought, and then decided he didn't blame her.

"Happy anniversary," the clone muttered when they pulled into the garage. He stopped the engine, got out of the car and was halfway into the kitchen before Diana had even unbuckled her seat belt.

# CHAPTER

# 20

Charles Scott did not often visit Jeremiah after-hours. When he did, he certainly never bothered to wait at the door until Jeremiah invited him inside. So, when he did just that, after eleven one night, Jeremiah was more than a little surprised. The encounter was made more awkward by the fact that he'd been practicing *IF* in his underwear again and hadn't bothered to fetch his pants before Scott opened the door.

"Forgive me for the late hour, Mr. Adams," he said, a slightly arched eyebrow his only obvious opinion on Jeremiah's attire. "Something has happened, and I wanted to be sure you heard it firsthand before tomorrow's viewing."

Jeremiah stood up, intending to go to the bedroom to retrieve some clothes, but Scott put a hand up to stop him.

"What is it?" Jeremiah asked, suddenly alarmed.

"Perhaps you should sit." Scott motioned toward the couch. Jeremiah stared at him and remained standing. Scott sat down and inhaled deeply.

"What is it?" Jeremiah asked again. "Is it Parker? Diana?"

"Your wife and son are fine, Mr. Adams," Scott said uneasily. "But I'm afraid your mother has passed away. It happened just over an hour ago. The clone hasn't even been notified yet, but I thought you should know as soon as possible. I'm very sorry." He looked at him with an expression that was difficult to read, but leaned more toward curious than sorry, as though he was studying his reaction.

Jeremiah half sat and half wilted onto the couch.

"What happened?"

"They're still looking into it," Scott told him, "but it appears that she may have been given another patient's medication."

"What? I don't understand. How could something like this happen? Why wasn't anyone watching her? How the hell do they mix up her medication in a nursing home?"

"There is also the possibility that it might have been intentional on her part," Scott said.

"No. Impossible. My mother would never do that."

"Correct me if I'm wrong," Scott said, "but didn't the doctor mention he'd seen signs of depression under the Meld?"

The Meld. Suicide. A shiver ran up Jeremiah's spine. Could his own mother be the latest victim of Meld?

Scott stared at him quietly as if waiting for him to speak, but Jeremiah said nothing. He just sat with the knowledge for a moment more, letting it sink in. He was his mother's only surviving family. There would be arrangements to make, he knew, and it would be up to him to see to that. Financially, there was little left to do. He had taken care of all that years ago, but there would be a funeral and other loose ends. He didn't know where to start.

She had often tried to initiate a conversation with him about this very topic, from the time he was in high school, and he had always refused to discuss it. It had seemed morbid to him, and premature. He hadn't wanted to think about it and was always put off by the casual way she'd just start talking about it, as though her own death really wasn't that big of a deal.

"Oh, Jeremiah, everybody dies," she told him. "If we thought we'd be around forever no one would ever *do* anything. Life is short. Knowing that is what keeps you going. But I want to make sure you know what to do with me when the time comes. I don't want to end up somewhere in the middle of nowhere, buried next to people I don't even know."

He had told her to write it all down. She very likely had and, hopefully, it was somewhere in her personal belongings. Someone at the home would know.

"I'll need to speak to the nursing home," Jeremiah told Scott, "as soon as possible."

"I am afraid that will not be permissible, Mr. Adams."

"Excuse me?"

"We cannot allow any contact whatsoever with the outside world," Scott said. "You know the rules. We've been through this."

"But under the circumstances, you have to allow me to leave."

"Leave? I'm afraid we simply cannot permit it. No. We are on a very strict timeline here, as you know."

"A strict timeline? This is my mother, for God's sake!" He was astonished. Anger rose up in his throat and nearly choked him. "I need to be at the funeral! You can't keep me from that!"

"I am sorry," Scott said, rising. "I understand you are upset, Mr. Adams, but the contract clearly states that you are to remain in the lab for the period of one full year. Under no circumstances are you allowed to leave this facility. I'm afraid that includes the death of your mother."

"Dr. Scott, I am her only family. I've got to make the arrangements. I need to be there."

"The clone will take care of everything as well as you would do yourself. I am certain that the whole affair will be handled precisely to your satisfaction." Scott got up and walked to the door, opened it and then turned again, as though a thought had just occurred to him. "This might actually be a unique exercise for the project," he said. "I wonder if you might write down the details of how you would make the arrangements for your mother's funeral. You know, the readings, the music, that sort of thing. Maybe the photo you'd choose for the obituary. It would make an excellent test, to see the comparison. I think it could be quite fascinating. I'm certain our investors would be interested."

With a great deal of difficulty, Jeremiah managed to be silent, but wanted nothing so much at that moment as to punch Charles Scott in the teeth. Once Scott was safely out the door, he settled for punching the living room wall instead. He didn't even make a dent in it, but felt the sting in the knuckles of his hand, which he ignored.

He picked up a lamp and threw it hard against the far wall and watched shards of blue ceramic scatter onto the floor and couch. Seething, he surveyed the room for something else to break, but there was nothing in the immediate vicinity except a computer monitor, which was bolted to the table, so he started on a stack of books, hurling them one by one against the locked door. And then, spent for the moment, he fell back down onto the couch, and put his face in his hands.

No one was supposed to die while he was in here. That wasn't part of the deal. Why had the damned clone agreed to let her take the Meld? If this was suicide, it had to be connected to that, he thought. His mother would never have done it. There was no way. It may have been in her genes, but suicide wasn't in her character. No matter how upset she might have been about the move, her memory, all of it, there was simply no way he could reconcile that she'd killed herself. She'd always been one of the most contented people he'd ever known, almost to a fault. There was no way.

Jeremiah ruminated on the clone's visit with his mother when she hadn't even recognized him. He had no way of knowing for sure whether the clone had seen her again since then, but he found himself hoping their final moments together weren't clouded by her failing mind. The Meld had shown she didn't have dementia, but there was surely something wrong.

What occurred to him next was so shocking it made him bolt upright again. Charles Scott had heard the conversation about what the doctor had seen when she took the Meld. He must have been monitoring these viewings, either in real time or taped playbacks. And so he knew Patricia Adams hadn't recognized the clone. She had looked right at the thing and declared that it wasn't her son. Scott must have seen it. If not, all of it, every word of it, was in Brent's report.

And now she was dead.

If it wasn't suicide—and he couldn't accept that it was—then what was it?

Standing frozen in the middle of the room, still in his underwear, surrounded by the mess he'd made, a kind of dread washed over Jeremiah. He wanted to vomit. He retched and heaved, but it was no use. There was nothing inside him.

Charles Scott was desperate that this experiment continue without interruption. But was he desperate enough to kill? By getting involved with all of this, had Jeremiah sacrificed his own mother?

# CHAPTER
# 21

DAYS 106-109

When he was a child, Jeremiah had loved his mother ferociously. Without a father, she had, by necessity, filled many roles for him—hero, teacher, best friend. She'd done a good job at all of it. They had been close, and she made sure to teach him things a father might have taught a son. Most of which she likely had to learn first for herself. By the time he was fifteen, he could fix a toilet, drive a stick shift and sweet-talk girls, and all with guidance from her. He could talk to her about anything, and she was always honest with him—except for the one thing that came to matter more and more as he grew up.

"It doesn't matter why your father left," she'd told him once. "The only thing that matters is that he isn't here, and that's his loss, not yours."

How she managed to stay so optimistic, so full of life, even with the hand she'd been dealt, Jeremiah would never fully understand. But his mother had a real knack for making even the most commonplace things seem extraordinary and full of possibility.

They used to play a game she called "Imagine," which involved her scavenging the house for three random objects and hiding them in a shoebox. She'd run past him, in and out of rooms, giggling and marveling at the treasures she'd collected, and Jeremiah could hardly contain his excitement. When she was finished, she'd present the box to him with a flourish, and he would close his eyes and take the objects out, one by one, and had to make up a story about whatever he found there. Ordinary things, items they'd looked at and tripped over ten times a day, were suddenly magical and full of mystery. The stories he told began as nonsensical little things: *The pencil and the fish food finally found the car keys and went for a long ride*, and he'd look up at her, disappointed that all the anticipation and excitement— all her treasure hunting—had resulted in something so dull. But she would get excited and spur him on with ridiculous, wonderful questions: *Which one was driving? Where did they go? Did they stop to eat along the way?* It would turn into a long, involved tale, replete with dinosaurs or aerial acrobatics, and he'd add details to it sporadically, right up until bedtime, until he knew he'd never look at a pencil the same way again. It was a wonderful game. He used to try to play it with Parker when he was little, but it never came out the same way, and he'd finally given up. He realized now that he'd never actually told his mother, later in life, how much that game had meant to him. It hadn't even crossed his mind in years. But he remembered it.

Stuck in the lab, he was struck by the notion that his clone might be remembering the exact same thing, and that possibility infuriated him. It felt like a violation. That was his memory. She was *his* mother.

It must have been just before seven in the morning when Brent came into the apartment without a knock. He found Jeremiah still sitting on the couch, still in his underwear, cradling his bruised hand in his lap.

"I'm sorry," Brent told him.

Jeremiah said nothing but looked at Brent with a sort of contempt he hadn't felt toward him before. As far as he was concerned, anyone involved in this experiment, including Brent, was just another of his captors. Just someone else who wouldn't give him the keys. And Brent was certainly complicit with that report he'd written for Scott. *Sorry,* he thought. *Yeah, right.*

"I just wanted to see if you were all right," Brent said. "Besides, we have a morning viewing. Basically, I'm just here early."

Jeremiah turned away from him and stared at the wall.

"Have you eaten? I'll make something, or I could pick something up if you want. I could probably smuggle in some more doughnuts."

"No."

"You want to talk about it?"

"No."

"Look, I want to help."

"You want to help? Then open the fucking door and let me out. Get me to my mother's funeral. That's how you can help."

"You know I can't do that. I wish I could. Believe me."

"Then shut the fuck up and leave me alone. And I am not watching that fucking monitor today, either. I won't do it."

Brent sighed heavily and sat down on the edge of the coffee table, taking in the broken lamp and the books scattered across the floor.

"I know you're upset," he said. "You have every reason to be."

"Fuck you," Jeremiah told him quietly.

"Look, maybe we can arrange for you to at least view the funeral. That would be better than nothing, wouldn't it? Maybe give you some closure."

"I don't want to watch my mother's funeral on TV! I want to be there. It's my mother!"

"I know, I know, but they aren't going to let you go, Jeremiah. If it were up to me, I'd find a way. But at least this way you'd be able to see it." It didn't go unnoticed that Brent had attempted to distance himself from Scott and the rest of them, but Jeremiah wasn't buying it. Not anymore.

"There's so much I wish I'd said to her," he admitted after a moment. He rubbed at his eyes vigorously with his hands. He stood up and walked into the kitchen. Infuriatingly, Brent followed him.

"I think it's important that you watch the funeral," Brent said. "I think you need to."

"How would they do that?" he asked. "I don't even know where it's being held."

"Yeah, but they certainly will. Believe me, Charles Scott keeps very close tabs on that clone. He knows where he is every minute of the day. Nothing escapes him."

"Brent," Jeremiah said, and then paused. He grabbed the blender and a handful of ice cubes and turned it on full blast. He couldn't afford any other ears on what he was about to say. "What exactly did you write in your report to Scott that day we saw my mother with the clone?"

"The usual." Brent's voice rose over the din. "An overview of what we saw, your reactions."

"But you wrote something about my mother not recognizing the clone, right?"

"Well, yeah. I had to."

"And Scott saw that report?" Jeremiah hit the pulse button.

"Yeah. He sees them every day after the viewing, or the next morning."

"And he must see the same things we see, right? I assume these viewings are recorded for him."

"Maybe," Brent said. "Probably. So what?"

"So, presumably, he also saw what that doctor said, that my mother didn't have dementia, after all. The Meld showed no sign of it."

"Yeah, I guess so." Brent looked at him sideways. Jeremiah got more ice for the blender.

"It must have looked to Scott like my mother knew something," he said. "He must have thought she suspected something about the clone. Something that could threaten this whole thing."

Brent stared at him blankly.

Jeremiah said nothing but looked at Brent in a way that he hoped completed his train of thought.

"What? No. Jeremiah, come on! I mean, he loves the experiment and all, but come on. This is science. That's crazy."

"But all of this is so goddamn important to him. I mean, if he thought there was a chance that someone knew, that someone suspected, who's to say how far he'd go to save the thing?" He stopped short of revealing to Brent what he knew about Scott's illness. He couldn't risk that. Not yet. "He needs that funding from those shadowy investors he keeps talking about. If that money dries up, it's finished."

"No way in hell." Brent was adamant. "The people involved in this, those investors, I mean, Jesus, it goes up a pretty big ladder behind the scenes. They'd never stand for it. Scott wouldn't risk it. No way. Put it out of your mind. This is crazy. You're just emotional. You need some rest."

Jeremiah looked Brent hard in the eye for a moment. It was obvious he believed what he was saying. He sighed and turned the blender off. Brent was right about one thing: he was exhausted. His head was pounding. He wanted this whole thing to be over. He wanted to go home. If he were at home right now, he'd have made some excuse to walk with Louie, which he knew would have calmed him down some. A long, quiet walk in the woods with a dog can do more good than most people know. Here, he had no such option. He wondered if that's what the clone was doing at the moment. But no, Louie wouldn't walk with him. Louie was no traitor. While that thought should have made him feel better, it didn't.

"Why don't you just try to get some sleep," Brent said. "I'll get you up in time for the viewing."

Jeremiah nodded. In the bedroom, he fell heavily onto the bed, but thoughts of his mother—the way she'd get excited over seeing a blue jay, the glint in her eye when she smiled at him—kept swimming through his mind, keeping him awake. His growing conviction that Charles Scott was a monster finally drove him out of bed and into the shower. He stood under the water for a full fifteen minutes, hoping it might clear his head, but he emerged as groggy and distressed as before.

When he walked into the living room, Brent was gone. So was the considerable mess from the night before. Jeremiah went to the kitchen, deciding to go with strong coffee if he couldn't get any sleep. Before he'd poured a cup, Dr. Young arrived at the apartment, coming in, as usual, without so much as knocking.

"I'm so sorry for your loss, Jeremiah," she said, motioning him immediately toward the couch. "Let's talk for a while." Her demeanor and tone were such that Jeremiah was instantly skeptical of her sentiments. She was, in typical fashion, all business, and he had the sense that her desire to talk was more for the benefit of the experiment than for him. He didn't trust her. He didn't trust any of them anymore.

Jeremiah didn't feel like talking. There was nothing to say. And if there were, he didn't want to say it to her.

"It might help you to remember that your clone is grieving every bit as much as you are," she said. Jeremiah wanted to swear at her but refrained and was silent.

"Tell me what you're feeling, Jeremiah."

"You know what?" he asked harshly, "Why don't you tell me how I'm feeling. My mother is dead and I can't even bury her. So, how do you *think* I'm feeling? How would you feel, Natalie, if it were your mother? She doesn't have anyone else, you know. I'm the only one."

"I understand you're angry. It may help to talk about it."

"I don't want to talk about it."

"Mr. Higgins came to see me. He seems to feel that you might benefit from viewing the funeral," she said. "I agree. I will suggest to Dr. Scott that he arrange it. And then maybe you can take a day or two off from the viewings after that. But soon, Jeremiah, I'd like to take the Meld with you again. It's almost time for it, anyway, but I think it's even more important now, under the circumstances. I can't have you holding back your feelings from me. This is all part of the experiment, you know. I have a job to do."

He looked away from her and clenched his fists to keep from speaking. He didn't trust the Meld. He didn't trust what would come out of his mind. He couldn't risk her seeing what he knew.

Two days later he watched on the wall monitor in the laboratory apartment as his mother was laid to rest.

He recognized instantly the Church of Saint Paul in the small New Hampshire town he'd lived in for a brief time as a child, the only Catholic church in which he'd ever attended an actual service. He remembered staring up at the stained-glass windows, trying to decipher their images, making up little stories about them in his head while the priest talked in a way he couldn't follow. Neither he nor his mother were members of this church, but she'd taken him here a few times. Although she had been raised a Catholic and had raised him with a quirky sort of spiritual foundation, they were not formal members of any particular church—or of any faith, for that matter. He'd never been baptized. She took him to churches of different denominations sporadically, for what she termed "soul visits." Every now and then they'd just show up at a different church "to hear what they have to say." It had made him uncomfortable as a child. He always felt conspicuous sitting in a place he didn't belong, surrounded by people for whom the service was a sacred weekly ritual. The thought of it now, though, made him smile. She had always felt right at home, no matter where they were, so confident and comfortable. They'd been to Lutheran, Methodist, Unitarian and Latter-Day Saints. She even took him to a synagogue once, but they couldn't understand half of what was said in the orthodox service. Afterward they tried to imitate the words and burst into fits of laughter at how badly they managed. But his mother said the sound was beautiful, even if they didn't know what the words meant.

Her favorite had always been the Baptist churches, because of the music. She loved how the entire congregation would stand and join in the singing, hands clapping, heads swinging and eyes half-closed, as though the music was the main event of the day.

"If God doesn't hear that," she'd say, "then He just doesn't have ears."

Jeremiah never liked these Baptist visits. It seemed too disorderly to him, with everyone in the place erupting in an "Amen" or a "Hallelujah" at totally unpredictable moments. How were you supposed to follow that? How did anyone know what to do? At least in the Catholic church he could fake it, following the lead of the people around him to know when to kneel, when to stand and when to sit down again. He never knew where he should be with the Baptists.

It came as no great surprise that the clone had opted for a Catholic church funeral, but in the lab, in front of the monitor, Jeremiah found himself silently wishing for a full Baptist choir to sing her off, and everybody clapping and letting loose with an "Amen!" She would have liked that, he thought. But he knew the clone wouldn't have entertained the idea for a moment, and neither would he have done at that point. It wouldn't have seemed proper. He would have insisted on a certain decorum. He would have used words like *dignity* and *reverence*. Funny how he could picture himself throwing all that out the window right now. If it had been up to him, right this minute, he wouldn't have cared what anybody thought, and everyone in that place would have been stuck shouting "Hallelujah" at the rafters, right up to God's ears.

Brent, uncharacteristically respectful, sat beside him while he watched, dressed in a suit and tie, his lab coat in the closet and his laptop nowhere to be seen. They were silent as they watched a small procession of people enter the church. The clone, flanked by Diana and Parker, stood at the entrance and endured handshakes and tentative hugs. Both Brent and Jeremiah noted, but didn't mention, the sparse turnout. All but the front few pews in the church were empty. They listened to a priest who had never met his mother talk about what it meant to live life well.

"Life is a gift," he said. "As miraculous as it is brief. And we must use that gift to its fullest advantage, use our flicker of existence to make the world somehow better than it would have been without us. How do we do that? Is it through grandiose gestures of charity and service? Or rather the small acts of kindness we commit when we think no one is watching? Will we be remembered for the pomp and circumstance of our lives, those fleeting moments of greatness? Or rather for all the quiet moments when we are fully and truly present in the world and with those around us? Patricia Adams lived a quiet life. She was a mother, a sister, a friend. She did nothing that the whole world will remember her for. She will never be immortalized in poetry or song; no flags will fall to half-mast for her passing. The annals of history will not devote even a footnote to her life. But to those who knew her, Patricia made the world a better place, and she will be remembered. She will be missed. She lived fully, honestly, with a purpose and with passion. She lived not to impress, but she left an impression. She followed not the rules and obligations of the world, but the rules and obligations of her heart. She lived well."

The words struck Jeremiah in a way he didn't expect. Although the man didn't know her, he spoke about her in words that rang true. Jeremiah's mind went back to all the times his mother had tried to show him the world through her eyes, a world worth exploring, worth knowing, worth figuring out. When, he wondered, had he lost that? How had he come to be so timid and awkward in his life? As he listened to the priest, he began to look for his own quiet impact on the world. It bothered him, more than a little, that he couldn't see it clearly. Where was the impression he'd leave? When the time came, would some priest he didn't know stand in front of a half-empty church and talk about the cloning? The money he left behind? His big house? How he did what was expected of him, met all of his obligations? What if the best thing anyone could say of him, after everything was said and done, was that he toed the line?

The clone didn't get up to speak at all, and Jeremiah knew it was because he just didn't know what to say. But Jeremiah would have said something, given the chance. He would have talked about the things she sacrificed, the things she loved, the way she tried to make him a better person. He would have said he was glad she'd been his mother. He might have even taken a moment to say he was sorry he hadn't been a better son.

For the next two hours, he and Brent watched uncomfortably as the clone attempted small talk with a smattering of distant relations he barely recognized and a few residents of the assisted living home who had come to pay their respects. Nurse Nichelle had come. She shook her head in that way she had and offered the clone a hug and whispered words of comfort that Jeremiah couldn't hear over the monitor. For once, Jeremiah didn't envy his clone. He looked somehow small, deflated—

even on an six-foot wall. He almost wished he could help him. Finally, the clone thanked the priest for his eulogy and, sitting in that laboratory apartment, Jeremiah silently thanked him, as well, and tucked away his words for later.

A few minutes after it was over, Brent retrieved his laptop from the closet and posed to Jeremiah his usual three questions about what he'd just seen. Jeremiah's answers, every one of them, were uttered with robotic precision and a complete detachment: "No."

"No."

"No."

# CHAPTER
## 22

Jeremiah had trouble sleeping again that night. For a couple of hours, he tossed and turned in bed but finally gave in sometime after midnight. He found himself in the kitchen rooting around in the fridge for something to eat. He didn't find a thing that appealed to him. He wasn't even really hungry. He stood in front of the open door letting his mind wander back to what the priest had said about his mother. There was something quietly satisfying about the way he'd described her, the way he focused on the many small ways her life had been important, the way he made it feel as though that had been enough. And it struck him now that, for her, it always had been enough. Growing up, Jeremiah had often felt sorry for her and had pushed away nagging feelings of guilt that she'd had to spend the best years of her life raising him on her own. He used to wonder what she might have done with her life if she'd ever had the chance. It hadn't really occurred to him that she'd been perfectly content, that she'd considered it a valuable, good and worthwhile thing simply to know who she was and to be herself.

He was startled out of his thoughts when Brent came in

through the front door and straight into the kitchen when he noticed the lights on.

"You're still up," he said. "Good." He put a six-pack of craft beer on the counter.

"You're taking an awful lot of chances with my diet," Jeremiah told him, grabbing a beer. "What the hell are you doing here, anyway? We don't even have a viewing tomorrow. Scott, in his magnanimous kindness, has arranged a day off, remember?"

"You had a rough day," Brent said. "Thought you might want some company."

"Brent," Jeremiah began. He was genuinely moved by the sentiment. "You didn't have to do that. You have your own life. You don't have to worry about me."

Brent shrugged and opened a beer. "No one should be alone after his mother's funeral," he said. "Besides, I have a proposition for you."

"Last time someone said those exact words to me I ended up with a clone," he said.

"This is a different kind of proposition."

"I don't know, Brent. I mean, I like you and all—but I'm a married man, and think of Mel."

"Keep dreaming, pal. You're way too old for me."

"Let's hear it, then."

"I've been thinking about what you said," Brent began, "about your mother, about how she died...your suspicions about Scott."

"You said I was crazy, as I recall."

"You probably are," Brent said. "But you shouldn't have to deal with those thoughts. Not after everything that's happened. I think we should go on a little secret mission, see what we can find out. See if we can put your mind at ease."

"Secret mission?"

"There's no viewing tomorrow. That means everyone's got a little time off, right? There's no one here except for one security guard and he's probably asleep by now. And I know that because I split a six-pack with him just before I came here."

"So, this is at least three beers talking, then. What exactly does this secret mission of yours entail?"

"We go into Pike's office," Brent said. "Hack into his computer, see what we can find out. There's bound to be something there that will prove to you that no one is out to get you."

"Sounds pretty risky to me," Jeremiah said. "Not your best idea."

"Come on, where's your sense of adventure? You're the one who thinks there's all kinds of devious plots going on behind the scenes. Why not be a little devious ourselves? Why not just find out?"

"You think you can really hack into Pike's files? With half a six-pack in you?"

Brent snickered. "Really?"

"What if we're caught?" Jeremiah asked. "I don't want to get you in trouble."

"We won't get caught. I know where every security camera is."

"Just like you knew about the one in Mel's painting."

"That's different. No one has any reason to hide them outside your rooms. Believe me, if we stay close to the walls, right up against them, they probably won't even pick us up on camera. But this is our only opportunity, Jeremiah. The place is empty. If you want answers, we need to get them now. Tonight. We're not going to get another chance like this."

Jeremiah nodded. Brent was right about one thing—he did need some answers. He needed to know what happened to his mother. He needed to know if he was going crazy, if the Meld was messing with his mind. And if there was anything in Pike's files about Scott's illness, he thought, Brent might be more inclined to believe this whole thing wasn't what it appeared to be.

"Okay," he said at last. "Do we need to put panty hose over our faces or something? Because I'm afraid I'm fresh out."

Ten minutes later, after having inched their way down the hallway, creeping along against the walls, Jeremiah stood nervously behind Brent in the dim light of Pike's empty office. Brent had been typing feverishly on Pike's keyboard without any apparent success.

"Hurry up," Jeremiah whispered.

"It's going to take a bit of time. Calm down."

"I am calm."

"Then shut up and let me do this."

"What is it you're doing?" Jeremiah asked. "Trying to guess his password? How are you even going to do that?"

Brent turned to him with an expression of slight annoyance. "You've been watching too many bad spy movies," he said. "I worked in the IT department, remember? I never changed my access codes. But I have to cover my tracks here, delete the time stamp on my actions. I can get in no problem if you'll stop breathing on my neck."

Jeremiah stayed where he was but turned his head a little and strained to listen for anyone coming down the hallway.

"Got it," Brent said after another few minutes. "I'm in."

Jeremiah peered over Brent's shoulder and scanned the file names that appeared on the screen. He saw several with his own name attached, probably notes on his physical exams, he figured, and an entire folder devoted to "low-fat food options."

"This one looks promising," Brent said, pointing to a folder on the monitor. "Department of Defense Correspondence: Confidential."

"Department of Defense?" Jeremiah said. "What the hell is Pike's involvement with that?"

"I told you," Brent said, "there are some powerful people involved behind the scenes. He's probably making regular reports to someone. It doesn't surprise me in the least."

"Open it. Let's see what's in there."

Brent clicked on the icon to no avail and looked back at Jeremiah in annoyance. "You just assume something like this wouldn't be protected with a password? For the Department of Defense? Really?"

Jeremiah grunted. "Now what do we do? Do you have that password, too?"

"No," Brent said, "but I bet I can find it."

He rooted around on a shelf just above Pike's monitor until he found a thin red notebook and started riffling through the pages.

"IT got tired of the execs always locking themselves out of their own files," he said. "So we developed this very high-tech system for them. Nice to know they're still using it."

He began systematically trying each password from the note-book and, in under a minute, he had access to the file.

Inside the folder were several dated files. Brent clicked on the most recent one, which was dated just two days before. It was an email exchange between Pike and an army general. They read together in shocked silence.

From: General Matthew McGavin
Re: Project Mirror update
To: Philip Pike

Dr. Pike,
We are pleased with the Meld-induced behavioral aspect of the project and look forward to a successful third test. This is of particular interest to us, as it will demonstrate parameters of control for clones of key personnel in the future. Along with viability, complete control of these clones is obviously para-mount to our needs.

One presumed security risk to project now neutralized.

Keep me advised on any additional security threats. Continued funding of the project depends on no one becoming suspicious of the clone's identity. We can handle any threats as they arise.

Gen. M. McGavin, United States Army

m.mcgavin@usarmy.mil

On Tuesday at 8:32 a.m., p.pike@ViMed.com wrote:

To: General McGavin

Attachment: Monthly report on Project Mirror

Physical viability of clone: Within expected parameters. No organ/muscular degradation.

Meld-implanted memory synapses of clone: Within expected parameters. No noted deviation.

Meld-induced behavioral testing: Two of three Meld-implanted suggestions executed successfully to date with no noted hesitation.

a. On day 21, clone made waffles for breakfast

b. On day 98, clone deviated from normal route to ViMed offices

Final test scheduled for day 239: clone will sing the third verse of "Come Fly with Me" in the hallways of ViMed offices.

Respectfully,

Dr. Philip Pike

Jeremiah read the emails over a second time and felt his stomach fall. His eyes settled on a single, sinister sentence: *One presumed security risk to project now neutralized.*

"A security risk? They're talking about my mother, Brent. It's exactly like I said. They thought she knew something and now she's dead."

Brent said nothing, but Jeremiah could hear him take in a deep, labored breath.

"They killed her," Jeremiah said, his hands raking through his hair. "Neutralized. They murdered my mother. Tell me you see that."

"I'll admit it does look pretty bad," he said. "But jumping right to murder? I don't know."

"I need a copy, Brent. Make a copy."

"That'll show up in the print queue," he said. "I'll take a picture." He took out his phone and snapped two quick photos, adjusting the copy on the screen to make sure he got it all. Jeremiah noticed a slight tremor in his hand as he did so.

"Someone has to pay for this," Jeremiah said. "These people are murderers. She wasn't a threat, Brent. My mother didn't know anything about the clone. It was just her mind. She couldn't remember. That's all. And they fucking killed her for it."

"We don't know anything for sure yet, Jeremiah. We need more. There's not enough here to prove anything. We have to be careful. And we have to keep this to ourselves. Everything. I do agree that this just became dangerous."

"But you believe me now that this whole thing is definitely more than it appears, right? That there's something more to all of this."

Brent nodded and turned off the computer.

"And they're talking about clones of key personnel," he said. "What do you suppose that means? Who are these key personnel?"

"World leaders? Diplomats? Hell, for all we know they want to clone the president."

"And from this, it looks like they can totally control them with the Meld," Brent added.

"These aren't just clones. They're making avatars." Jeremiah was astonished at the realization. "They're making totally controllable fucking avatars."

"But ten times worse," Brent said, "because these will be real. These will be out there in the world and no one will even realize it. This is freaking huge. No wonder they're willing to kill to protect this thing. We don't even know how far up this goes."

"Don't delete these photos, Brent. And back them up somewhere. We may need them. If we're going to stop them, this is useful. But for God's sake, don't let your phone out of your sight."

"Count on that."

"Well, I can tell you another thing you can count on. No one is ever going to see me singing Sinatra in the hallways of ViMed. I am getting the hell out of here long before day 239." He shook his head. "I don't even know the words to that song."

# CHAPTER
# 23

DAYS 113-127

A few days later, Jeremiah and Dr. Young took the Meld again. She was silent as she prepared for it, bringing in the two syringes on a metal tray and making sure to lock the door to the office to guard against someone else coming in and contaminating the connection. But no one had ever come into the office in all the times Jeremiah had been here. He sat sullenly and waited for the needle and hoped he'd be able to hide his secrets. The more he knew, the more he feared the Meld.

There was a momentary jolt immediately following the injection and Jeremiah was hit with a vivid sense of being in water. The impression was so real that it completely threw off his equilibrium, as though he were instantly not on solid ground. He kicked his feet and had to catch himself to keep from falling off the chair. His breath caught in his chest. The sensation was real enough that he could almost taste the salt from the ocean on the tip of his tongue and lifted a hand to shield his eyes from the sun glinting off the waves.

"I'm sorry," he heard Dr. Young say from very far away. "My mind wandered. I'm just thinking about a trip to Jamaica last year. Focus on the light."

An hour or more seemed to pass in a few minutes. Before he knew it, he was fully aware of his surroundings again, the effects of the drug completely gone from his mind. The memory of what he'd seen was hazy, half-remembered and retreating fast.

"Well?" he asked. "What did you see?" He hoped he didn't sound as nervous as he felt.

"I do detect some change in you," she said, and a fleeting look of perplexity crossed her face. "There's something a little bit more, I don't know, settled. You aren't as meticulous with your responses to stimuli. I sense more instinct…something *different*."

"Is that bad?"

"Not necessarily," she told him. "But it is a change, and that could be important to the experiment. I also sense a marked increase in your emotional depth, but I think that's to be expected after the loss of a loved one. A lot of it may be perfectly normal reflection, a period of introspection. That is actually a useful coping mechanism. It means you're working out your grief in a healthy way. I'm glad to see it, but…" She paused in a manner that made Jeremiah suddenly uncomfortable.

"Was there something else?"

"I'm not sure," she said, and leaned in to look him hard in the eyes. "Jeremiah, are you absolutely certain there's no suspicion at home? No one who might be questioning the clone's authenticity?"

*Oh, shit*, he thought. Had he let his mind wander? Had she detected thoughts of his mother? Of the emails he'd read? Of Louie? He'd tried to be so careful, but there was no telling what he'd been thinking about under the Meld. If he'd thought about these things for even a moment…

"No," he said flatly.

"I'm sensing something. It's quite strong, but I can't pin it down. Meld isn't an exact science, mind you, but I have a distinct feeling that someone close to you knows something is wrong.

And it's very possible that I am detecting something that you yourself are not even consciously aware of. But somewhere in your own mind, Jeremiah, I think you have the same suspicions. There's someone who isn't fully convinced. I'm almost positive."

In his head he wanted to tell her yes, he had plenty of suspicions. You bet there was someone who wasn't convinced. But he kept his cool. He had to.

"I don't think so," he tried. "Maybe I'm remembering something about my mother again. Memories, maybe, some jumbled-up thoughts? You remember how upset I was when she didn't recognize me…or the clone, rather. I haven't been myself, you know?"

"Maybe," she said thoughtfully, and leaned back into her chair. "Maybe it is related to that. Let's talk about something else."

He breathed an inaudible sigh of relief, happy she was off the topic for the moment.

"Like what?"

"In Brent's reports, I see the clone and Diana have been at odds lately. Something about an argument on your anniversary?"

Jeremiah steeled himself against the onslaught of prying he knew was coming. But at least this was something he could handle.

"It wasn't anything serious," he told her. "Just one of those things. I think the clone had a little too much to drink, is all."

"Is that typical?" she asked. "Was drinking an issue before?"

"No," he said defensively. "It's not a big deal."

"Is the clone drinking more than you usually did at home? Has that become a problem for him?"

"No, not that I've seen. Look, Natalie, this isn't anything to worry about. I'm sure it's blown over by now. They looked okay at the funeral. They've probably already forgotten about it, with everything that's happened."

"Perhaps," she said, her eyes narrowing. "Still, anything out of the ordinary could be important data. Any atypical behavior by the clone, or anyone close to him, needs to be looked at."

"You're reading too much into it," he told her. "Haven't you ever had a drink on an empty stomach? It happens."

She was quiet for a moment and then shrugged as though agreeing with him. She changed the subject abruptly, as she often did. It always gave Jeremiah the feeling she was connecting dots he couldn't see. It made him nervous. Especially now.

"What do you miss most about your life, Jeremiah? What's the first thing that comes to your mind when you think about that?" she asked expectantly.

"To tell you the truth," he said, "it's mostly little things that I miss. Sitting at the kitchen table on Sunday mornings. Dinnertime. Talking with Parker about school. I even miss bugging him about homework or cleaning his room. I suppose I miss being a father. I miss Parker most of all. That gets worse the longer this goes on."

"Worse, how?"

"You know how it is with kids. Things change so fast. I feel like I'm getting more and more disconnected from him. I don't know what he's thinking about. I don't know what new game he's playing or what music he's listening to. I don't have all those little details anymore. I feel cut off."

For a moment, Natalie's expression looked almost sympathetic. Her eyes lingered on his, and her mouth tightened in a way that suggested she understood. But the expression was fleeting and she got right back down to business.

"I'd like to do another session with the Meld in a week or so, just to keep up with what you're feeling," she said. "But let's call it a day for now. You look like you could use some rest."

Rest was the last thing Jeremiah got over the next several days. Every time he tried to sleep his mind would spin in fifteen different ways. He now knew, without a doubt, exactly how far Charles Scott and the people working with him would go to save this project. And somewhere in the back of his mind he wondered what role Meld had played in all of it. Was it the drug that had made his mother so confused? Was that what made her question the clone? His own role in bringing it to the public, in assuring the world it was perfectly safe, was eating at him. There was blood on his hands, he realized. He was complicit in every single death, including that of his own mother.

Underneath it all, Jeremiah worried about what he might have revealed to Natalie through the Meld. Did she sense his suspicion? His memory of what happened under the drug was, as usual, foggy at best. He couldn't be certain about what she'd seen, about how well he'd managed to control his own thoughts. And the prospect of taking the Meld with her again was looming. He couldn't let her see what he knew about Scott. He had to hide what he knew about the greater scope of the project. He couldn't afford to rouse her suspicion.

And he was still fixated on the notion that he had to keep Louie a secret, too. As he watched the clone every day, infiltrating and taking over every aspect of his life, it was his dog's loyalty that somehow kept him tethered. He needed it more than he thought was logical, but with everything that had happened, it seemed like all he had left.

No matter what that clone did to coax and cajole him, Louie wanted nothing to do with him. There was no aggression anymore—the medicine had seen to that—but there was a stubborn reluctance that could not be broken, and Jeremiah delighted in that. It felt like some sort of small victory. And it gave him some inexplicable gratification to know that Charles Scott's grand experiment wasn't as infallible as he probably thought it was. Every morning the clone would attempt, and every morning he would fail, to lure Louie onto the leash. Finally, he'd just give up and wake Parker to walk him before school, which never went over well.

"You know, it's been scientifically proven that teenagers need more sleep than adults," Parker informed the clone. "What the hell did you do to make this dog hate you, Dad? Kick him or something?"

Keeping that secret—just one small thing that he could be certain belonged, securely, to him—was becoming increasingly important to him. As Jeremiah obsessed on it, that knowledge almost came to signify his last remnant of personal self under this microscope. He wasn't going to give it away.

So, some nights, when he couldn't sleep, he'd find himself at the computer, searching for a way to control his own thoughts, even under the influence of Meld. In the dim glow of the monitor, he'd fuel himself on French roast and study articles on self-hypnosis, meditation and astral projection. He'd sit in the dark and practice sending his consciousness in willful directions until he realized the futility of it. He didn't believe in any of this.

He'd usually end up trying to exhaust himself with an hour on the treadmill, staring blankly at vistas as dull as he could think to program into the monitor—an empty suburban street, a high school parking lot, a construction site left padlocked and vacant overnight. And if all else failed, he'd finally settle on the couch, put on the headset and play *IF*, blowing things up in satisfying blasts of virtual obliteration, not caring who was watching or what they might have thought. In time, all that practice gave Jeremiah enough confidence to challenge Brent outright.

"You really think you can take me?" Brent said after a particularly dull weekday afternoon viewing. "You're on." He opened two beers and took a seat on the couch.

"I've made a few adjustments," Jeremiah told him. He turned on the game and donned his headset, and his avatar appeared on the wall in all his menacing glory. "Meet Clyde," he said.

"Whoa, you have been busy. He looks pretty tough."

"Indeed. He's a mercenary for hire. Kills first, asks questions later. He's a Gulf War vet, watched his CO get blown to bits in front of him and then ate lunch. Came back from combat a little whacked out and his wife left him six months later. Took his baby girl. Ever since, the only thing keeping the demons away is a little more action. He never says no to a job."

"Jesus, Jeremiah," Brent said with a smirk. "Does he have a favorite color, too?"

"What's wrong with a little backstory? Gives him substance, I think. It makes him seem more real."

"Yeah," Brent told him, wide-eyed. "Except he's not real. He's made of pixels and photons. And maybe a little bit of crazy."

Jeremiah just shrugged and started shooting.

"Hey," Brent said after they'd gone a few rounds, "you want to really test Clyde out?"

"Yeah. Start shooting."

"No, not with me, I mean with someone else."

"In case you haven't noticed," Jeremiah said, "you and I are the only ones here. You want me to call Scott? Challenge him to a game? Maybe get a pizza?"

Brent smirked. "I accessed the beta platform. Been playing with this guy who's pretty good. Better than me, honestly. I still can't beat him."

"Do you really think it's a wise move to take a risk like that? So you can play a game?"

"I know what I'm doing," he said. "I'm not a complete idiot. Besides, I think Scott and the rest of them have bigger things to worry about right now than me getting on the beta. Believe me, they're not even looking at this."

"Okay, then," Jeremiah said. "What do we do?"

Brent began a series of fast maneuvers with the handset, typing in lines of code that appeared in rapid succession on the side of the screen. It looked like gibberish to Jeremiah.

"There," Brent said. "We're in. Now I just need to send this guy a request. He's usually around in the afternoons."

He typed a screen name with the handset and Jeremiah's eyes grew wider as each letter appeared on the screen: *L...o...u... D...o...g...1...2...3.*

That was Parker's screen name. Jeremiah was certain of it. It was the same name he used for everything—every password, the combination for his locker at school and every game he played online. Jeremiah had told him more than once that he ought to vary it up a little, but he never did.

"LouDog123?" he asked. "That's who you've been playing?"

Brent looked at him sideways. "Yeah. So what?"

"Brent. That's Parker. You've been playing *Infinite Frontiers* with my son."

"No."

"That's Parker," he said again. "Remember? He asked the clone for the beta? That's him. I'm sure of it."

On the screen, LouDog123 accepted the game request and an avatar somewhat less sinister looking than Clyde appeared blinking on the screen, waiting for battle.

"What do I do?" Jeremiah asked, a sudden wave of worry momentarily paralyzing him.

"I suggest you begin with a grenade," Brent said. "Just play. He won't know it's you."

For the next half hour, Jeremiah engaged in a gleeful, surreal and violent battle with Parker. Despite how much he'd been practicing, he was hard-pressed to even keep up with his son. Parker was good at this, and Jeremiah had to work just to keep the tenuous connection going. One mistake and he feared the game would be over. He resisted the considerable urge to stop firing and just start typing all the things he wished he could tell him. He wanted so desperately to talk to him, to have even a casual conversation—to ask him about school, music, other games he'd been playing—but he knew he couldn't do that. Instead, he let Clyde do the interacting for him. Every grenade he launched, every blast from his gun, every duck and cover, felt like a little step closer into Parker's life.

When it was over—only when Parker's avatar accidentally stepped on a land mine and blew himself to bits—Jeremiah was caught off guard by his own disappointment. He could have stayed there all night.

Good game, Clyde, Parker typed onto the side of the screen. Jeremiah looked at Brent.

"Answer him if you want to," he said. "Go ahead."

Thanks, he typed, his hands shaking visibly. You, too.

The connection severed, Jeremiah slumped back against the couch and took off his headgear. He sighed heavily and didn't even attempt to stop the tears he felt stinging the back of his eyes.

"I don't think I can do that again," he said to Brent. "It's just too hard."

# CHAPTER
# 24

On a Tuesday evening, Jeremiah and Brent sat down to view the clone as he was arriving home from work. Jeremiah leaned back against the couch and opened his third light beer of the evening, hoping it might help him sleep later, and Brent, businesslike and dressed in his lab coat, pretended he hadn't been counting. Jeremiah didn't care one way or the other.

The camera came on and showed an inside view of the front door of Jeremiah's home opening onto the hallway, a patch of evening sunlight illuminating the dust bunnies on the floor. He heard Louie's tags jingle and saw the dog walk sheepishly into the room and yawn when he saw it was the clone and not someone more interesting, like the mailman or a complete stranger.

"Hey there, pal," the clone said uselessly, leaning down to scratch the dog behind the ears. Louie acquiesced, but just barely, and shook his head away after only a second or two. "Where is everyone?"

Tossing his keys on the small table in the hallway, the clone walked into the dining room and through to the kitchen, calling as he went. "Diana? Parker? Anybody home?"

No one answered. He opened the refrigerator and grabbed a

soda from the door. He looked around the room for a note or some hint of dinner in the oven, but the lights weren't even on. It appeared that no one had been home all day. Jeremiah could see the clock on the oven. It was twenty past seven. There should have been someone home by now. Parker should have been pretending to do homework while playing some computer game in his room. The clone called out again as he went upstairs. Louie followed slowly, keeping his distance from the clone, but wondering, certainly, whether anyone was going to even consider letting him outside.

"Dog's probably got to pee," Jeremiah said out loud.

The clone walked through the upstairs hallway and opened the door to Parker's room. The light was off there, too, but Jeremiah could see a swath of typical clutter on Parker's floor—books, laundry, dog toys—and it made him flinch for a moment to remember how much he missed his son. The clone stood there in the doorway, thinking about God knows what, looked down at Louie again and sighed.

"Where is everyone?" he asked again, as though the dog not only had that information but might somehow answer him.

Back in the kitchen the clone made himself a tuna sandwich and filled the dog bowl with food. Jeremiah noted again that Louie likely had to pee and shook his head. No one was taking care of his dog.

The clone took the sandwich into the living room, slumped back in his chair and turned on the news. For about ten minutes Jeremiah and Brent watched as he sat there, unmoving, Louie lying down unheeded by the front door, and they listened, along with the clone, to the headlines and weather report. When the door opened, Louie jumped up with an exuberant welcome for Parker, who bent down to kiss him on the head and then finally let him out into the yard.

"Is Mom with you?" the clone asked.

"No. Why would she be with me?"

"She's just later than usual, is all. Second night this week, isn't it? Where have you been?"

"At a friend's house, working on a science project."

"What friend?"

"You don't know him," Parker told him. "A kid from class."

Jeremiah turned away from the monitor when Brent let out an involuntary chuckle.

"What?" Jeremiah asked.

"That kid has been smoking the ganja," he said. "Look at his eyes. He's totally wasted."

"No," Jeremiah said, and looked closer at the image of his son on the screen. "Parker's not into drugs. He doesn't smoke pot. There's no way he's stoned."

"Sure," Brent said with a grin. "And I don't drink beer. Look at him!"

"He's not!" Jeremiah insisted, noting Parker's glassy gaze with growing concern.

"It's not that big of a deal," Brent said. "Tell me you didn't do the same exact thing at his age."

"He's never been into drugs. Who is this kid he was with?" Jeremiah leaned in closer to the monitor and willed the clone to push for information. He didn't, of course. He wouldn't. Idiot.

"Did you finish the science project?" the clone asked, clueless.

"Yeah. Is there any dinner?"

"There's tuna. Have you talked to your mother today?"

"No." Parker let Louie back in and disappeared into the kitchen. The clone followed, hopefully, Jeremiah thought, to barrage him with questions and accusations, shake him by the shoulders, maybe ground the kid or throw him into a cold shower. Instead, he just stood in the doorway and watched his son make a seriously munchie-size sandwich. Yeah, Jeremiah admitted to himself, he was totally stoned. From the look on the clone's face, he knew it now, too, and the fact that he still said nothing made Jeremiah want to jump through the wall and just take over. What was he waiting for? *Say something! You're supposed to be his father!*

"You've been staying after school a lot lately," he said, a hint of accusation lacing his tone.

"I told you, I was working on a project. You're the one always saying I need to get my grades up."

Parker started to devour his sandwich and slipped Louie a bit of tuna from his finger. The dog wagged his tail delightedly and sat rigidly at Parker's feet, staring up at the food as though he could make it fall to the floor by the power of his own rapt attention.

"Oh, for Christ's sake!" Jeremiah said to the monitor. "He's not going to just let him get away with this, is he? What the hell is wrong with this asshole?"

Brent scribbled something down on his notepad, glancing at Jeremiah from the corner of his eye.

"Oh, knock it off, Brent!"

"What? This is my job, remember?"

"Fuck you," he said, and turned back to the scene in front of him.

Parker made a move for the back staircase, Louie at his heels, and the clone asked where he was going.

"I have more homework."

"Why don't we go get an ice cream first? We haven't done that in a while. What do you say?"

*Good move,* Jeremiah thought, *have a nice talk in a non-confrontational way.* For a moment, he was almost sort of impressed, knowing that, had it been him standing in that kitchen, he might not have played it so cool. He might have started screaming and searching Parker's pockets for a pipe.

"I can't, Dad," Parker said, avoiding the clone's eyes, and went up the stairs, two at a time.

"Follow him!" Jeremiah urged uselessly.

Instead, the clone just started cleaning the mess Parker had left on the counter and, infuriatingly, began humming a mindless tune into the heavy silence of the kitchen. For a moment, Jeremiah entertained the idea of playing another game with his son. Maybe he could tweak Clyde's outfit, swap the Ramones T-shirt for something with a subtle antidrug message: Drugs Are for Absolute Fucking Losers. Do You Want to Destroy Every Brain Cell in Your Head? But he knew he couldn't parent his son through a video game, and he couldn't trust himself to make contact again.

Once the counter was sufficiently cleared, the clone reached up to a high cabinet over the refrigerator, took down a bottle and fixed himself a tall gin and tonic, light on the tonic. Jeremiah winced. A mixed drink on a Tuesday was unheard of. The clone must have been feeling the strain, he thought.

Settling back in front of the TV, the clone rotated through the channels and sipped his drink until the front door opened again sometime around ten o'clock. Diana came in without a word of greeting, dropped her purse on the floor by the hall table and went straight to the kitchen. The clone got up and followed her. Jeremiah could see his face had settled into a hard expression, his brow furrowed and his lips tightened.

"He looks pissed," Brent said.

"Can you blame him?" Jeremiah snapped. "He's probably sick and tired of this by now."

"Working late again?" the clone said. Diana turned and offered him a half smile.

"Yeah," she said. "That same case. Is Parker home?"

"In his room."

"Did you eat?"

"I made sandwiches."

"I had something at the office," Diana said, although the clone hadn't bothered to ask. "I'm exhausted. I think I'll take a shower before bed."

"I bet you're exhausted." There was a hint of accusation in his voice. "All these late nights. Takes a lot out of you."

In the lab, Jeremiah scrutinized the monitor. Was the clone finally going to do what he himself could never do? Was he finally going to confront her?

Diana stared at the clone for a long moment without a word and then shook her head and started toward the stairs.

"Wait," the clone said. Jeremiah held his breath. "Why don't we have a drink? You can tell me all about this case that's been keeping you away every night."

Diana's eyes narrowed. "I'm tired, Jeremiah. I don't want a drink. Besides, it's nothing you'd be interested in."

"Oh? Try me," the clone said. "I think I'd be very interested. Especially if you decided to—oh, I don't know—actually tell me the truth for a change."

Her silence felt like it filled both the kitchen where she stood and the lab beyond. Jeremiah could feel Brent staring at him, but he kept his eyes on the monitor, waiting.

"What are you talking about? Tell you the truth about what?"

"About what it is that's taking you away from your family," the clone said. "What is it that's so much more important to you than your own son? Or should I ask *who*?"

Diana glared at the clone in a way that Jeremiah had never seen before. It was as though he could see something physically shift in her as she held him in her gaze. And that shift smacked of something final. For a minute, he wondered whether she was about to lash out and slap the clone across the face. If she had, it wouldn't have surprised Jeremiah.

Instead, she took one measured step closer to the clone and, when she finally spoke, her voice was low and cool, almost devoid of emotion. "You've changed, Jeremiah," she said. "I don't even know who you are anymore. But you're not the same man I married."

Jeremiah felt a wave of dread rise up inside him. Why, of all the things she might have said, had she decided on those exact words? He understood why she'd said it. She was angry. She'd felt trapped. In any other scenario, it would have meant nothing. But it echoed eerily what his mother had said just before she was murdered. Those were words that could get her killed.

Jeremiah closed his eyes and covered his face with his hands. He could hear Brent typing something rapidly into his laptop. He sat up, startled, and looked at him.

"Brent," he said quietly. "Don't."

"Jeremiah, this has to go into my report. You know that. They're going to see it. If it's not in my report it'll look suspicious."

Jeremiah let his eyes linger for an instant on Mel's painting and then looked again at Brent. "Come in the kitchen for a minute," he said. "I'm going to make a smoothie."

"We're not done with the viewing. There's still twenty minutes left."

"Fuck that," Jeremiah said. "Come in the kitchen."

Over the racket of the ice in the blender, Jeremiah implored Brent to leave Diana's words out of his report.

"Look, Jeremiah, I'm sorry, I really am. But I have to put it in."

"You know what happened with my mother. You know as well as I do what those words will sound like to Scott and his goons. You can't put it in there."

"Look," Brent said, "I know you're upset. I know you're worried about this. But I think they're going to be focused on something else here. They're going to be looking at the fact that the clone thinks she's having an affair. Maybe that's what's really got you all riled up here. That isn't an easy thing to hear."

"No, that's not it," Jeremiah said.

"You know, maybe the clone's got it all wrong. We don't know for sure that she's having an affair."

Jeremiah sighed. "No," he said sarcastically. "Maybe she's joined a knitting circle and she's going to surprise me with a new blanket for my birthday. She *is* having an affair. I already knew about it. I've known about it for a long time, before any of this even started. But that's not what I'm worried about. You know what I'm worried about."

Brent added more ice to the blender and hit the button. "It was just something she said in the heat of an argument, Jeremiah. It isn't that bad. She didn't mean it like that."

"And what my mother said was just because her memory happened to be failing her. It doesn't matter to them. We both saw those emails. They're prepared to neutralize any threats. You know what that means. You saw it. You have to leave her words out of your report."

Brent sighed. "Maybe I can gloss over them and focus on the affair. But they were said, you know. They're going to see the tape of that viewing. They'll see it whether I put it in the report or not. But I don't believe they're going to hurt her because of this. It was just an argument."

Jeremiah added more ice to the blender. "You know, Brent, there are things you don't know about Charles Scott. He's not just in this for the science, to make a better future for mankind. This is personal to him. Believe me. And I don't think he'll stop at anything to see this through. He's got too much to lose. More than you even know."

Brent looked at Jeremiah with an odd mix of confusion and pity and shook his head. "Let's just finish the viewing," he said.

"Then I suggest you take one of Pike's sedatives and go to bed. You've got to relax. You'll drive yourself crazy."

Reluctantly, Jeremiah followed him back to the living room, took his place on the couch and averted his eyes from the screen and from Brent. He had to do something. But without Brent's help, he didn't see what he could do.

He had to find some way to warn Diana, to warn the clone. There had to be a way to stop this.

# CHAPTER
# 25

Two days later, standing in the little galley kitchen in the lab, Jeremiah tried again to convince Brent the whole situation was spinning dangerously out of control, and again, Brent seemed reluctant to see it.

"It's been two days and nothing's happened. Diana is fine. You're just under a lot of stress," he said. "Between your mother, and the affair, it's a lot to handle. Maybe you ought to talk to Natalie about your marriage. That is part of her job, after all. You should take advantage of it."

"My marriage is my business. It doesn't have the slightest impact on the clone or this project or anything else. And I don't care about the affair. It doesn't matter. What I care about is Diana. Why can't you understand that?"

"I do understand," Brent said, annoyance creeping into his tone. "But why can't you understand that we need to be careful with this. We can't afford to do anything that would raise suspicion right now. Let's just play along for now and keep our eyes open."

"Play along? We have to do something, Brent. If Charles Scott has the slightest suspicion that Diana knows something, she's in trouble. Real trouble. You have to help me."

"You keep saying that Scott is behind this," Brent said. "But we don't know that. What we saw implicates the army, the people behind the scenes. Scott is a scientist. He's in this for the science, Jeremiah, and that science is sound."

"You're being played for a fool, Brent. Charles Scott isn't the champion you think he is. He's not in this for the betterment of the species, for the good of mankind. There are things you don't know. You have to help me."

"What do you expect me to do?"

"I don't know. Find her. Just tell her to watch her back. Tell her she has to stay at home. Scott won't try anything with all those cameras around. She's safer in the house. If you could just tell her. Just try."

"I can't do that! I'd lose my job if I so much as glanced at Diana on the street. Are you out of your mind?"

"Your job? That's what you care about? Your job?"

"Well, yes, actually. I do. And so should you. If I'm gone, Jeremiah, you have no one on the inside."

Jeremiah shook his head. "You still believe in this, don't you? Even after what we saw in those files. You still believe in this project? Are you out of your mind?"

"I'm a scientist. There's still some merit in this, some intrinsic value. That's what I believe. Cloning is inevitable. It's the future."

"Even with all of the ethical implications? The laws against it? That doesn't concern you?"

"Well," Brent said, "they make a lot of things illegal that probably don't need to be. I'm not talking about whole clone armies or cloning the pope. There are good uses, too. I think that's worth preserving."

"Like what?"

"I don't know, what if we could clone da Vinci or Albert Einstein or Shakespeare?"

"Yeah, but it wouldn't really be them. Without the Meld they don't actually have minds of their own. How do we know what they'd decide to do? Who's to say a clone would even come close to the genius of the originals? What if a clone Shakespeare started writing zombie fiction? What if Einstein's clone decided he'd rather just be a barber? Besides, you saw the emails. We both know they don't want to clone Shakespeare."

"This technology works," Brent said. "In the hands of the right people it could still do a lot of good. I'm sorry, but I still think that's why Scott is doing this. That's the point of this whole thing."

Jeremiah laughed. "That's not the point. Why is Scott actually doing this? What is he getting out of it? Ask yourself that. What's his end game? Why is this so important to him? It isn't the science. Believe me."

"Fine. If you want to look at it like that. There's money to be made. There are patents and rights. There's power. ViMed is going to get the lion's share of that for the next hundred years or more, and Charles Scott is at the helm. What's so wrong about that? Jesus, they'll probably call the whole procedure the Scott Method or something. That's immortality, Jeremiah."

Jeremiah shook his head and smiled. How could someone manage to be so correct and so off the mark at the same time?

He wasn't going to be able to convince Brent of anything. Not yet. Not in time to help Diana. If he was going to do something, he'd have to find a way to do it on his own.

"Immortality," he said finally. "You're probably right."

They went to the living room, where Brent took his lab coat from the closet, and Jeremiah fell heavily onto the couch and put his feet up on the coffee table, trying to appear more relaxed, even as his mind was racing for a solution.

"Another exciting afternoon watching my very successful double duplicate my every move at the office," he said. "The suspense is killing me. You think he's going to dial the phone with his left hand or his right? Yeah, this science is all so important."

"Quit complaining," Brent said. "If you're that bored, then we'll just play cards while he works." He sat down and began dealing out cards for poker. "Stud High," he said, and threw a beer bottle cap into the pot, in lieu of money, which Jeremiah hadn't seen or needed in several months.

Two rounds in and several bottle caps richer, Jeremiah looked up from a lousy hand when the clone took a phone call that, judging from his expression, was anything but good news. It was a quick and one-sided conversation, but Jeremiah heard enough to grasp that the Meld shit was about to hit the fan again in a big way.

"...and you're certain this was the same doctor who saved that kid in the coma?"

"...and they're sure it was suicide?"

The clone hung up the phone and ran a hand through his hair. The look on his face mirrored Jeremiah's own alarm.

"Holy crap," he said to Brent.

"What's he talking about?"

"Just watch. I have a feeling this won't be pretty."

On the screen, his clone picked up the phone again and dialed.

"We have a problem," he said. Jeremiah could only assume he was speaking to his department director. "That doctor who was singing Meld's praises all over the news, you know the one with the comatose kid? Yeah, well, he killed himself this morning. And he left a note. He mentioned Meld."

For the next two and a half hours, Jeremiah and Brent watched as the clone and everyone in ViMed's Communications department rallied to build a wall against a media onslaught. Judging from the newsfeed in the background, it wasn't helping. The news was reporting that the doctor, after his stint as a medical superstar, had abandoned his hospital post for a private practice focusing entirely on Meld-induced treatment of brain injury. He'd made quite a success of it, but there were indications he might have taken the drug too many times. A talking head read a critical passage from the good doctor's suicide note.

"Meld showed me a monster. How can we look at ourselves through someone else's eyes and not be fundamentally changed? I cannot defend what I've seen. I cannot live with the monster. I cannot escape him. We are not meant to see this. We're not equipped. It isn't right. My only solace is that at least I can take him with me."

The clone had gathered a small group of writers and PR reps in his office. "This is the first suicide in a clinical setting. This is where we need to focus. We need to turn it around. Maybe we can spin the idea that this guy was abusing Meld outside of his practice, using it wrong, maybe even addicted to it. There's got to be someone out there—some disgruntled patient, a jealous rival, a jilted lover—who will talk if we plant that idea in the right ears. You need to find those ears. Now."

Brent whistled through his teeth. "Wow," he said. "Clone's gone all cutthroat. No mercy there."

"Seems a bit aggressive to me," Jeremiah said. "I mean, this doctor has a reputation. A family. He just killed himself, for Christ's sake. I think a little mercy is in order."

More to the point, Jeremiah thought to himself, Meld was still killing people, and the clone was still trying to push it on the public. And, for all anyone knew, that clone was Jeremiah. Those were his own hands bloodied in every one of those deaths.

It had to end. He had to end it. Somehow. But Brent was right about one thing: if anyone realized he was no longer a willing player in all of this, if he showed his hand at all here, he'd be even more stuck than he already was. They'd make sure of that.

He had to play this cool.

Brent typed something into his laptop.

"Come on," Jeremiah said, agitated by the idea that everything he said was being used against him. "Don't you think this is overkill? I mean, you don't need to ruin a man's name to save the company's image."

"That's his job, though," Brent said. "That's your job. Isn't that what you're paid to do?"

"I'm just saying, there's no need to be so cavalier about it after a man has just died."

On the wall, the clone wiped a bead of sweat from his brow and chewed on a pencil as he listened to the writers shoot off a series of ideas that wouldn't work.

"Maybe he just has it in for ViMed," someone said. "Maybe looking for a lawsuit."

"Maybe the suicide note was a fake," someone said. "A forgery."

"What are we supposed to do?" the clone asked. "Prove it was murder? That won't fly. We're not detectives. No, we need to put the focus back on the idea that Meld is safe. That's the key here. We need to keep the focus on safety—drive that point home."

"I doubt the FDA is going to be much help there," another writer said. "I don't think they want to keep talking about how safe Meld is right now. And honestly, I don't think people want to hear it."

"Then we find another way to prove it's safe," the clone said thoughtfully. "Maybe it's time we stop *talking* about it and start *showing* it."

"How are we supposed to do that?" someone asked. "Take it ourselves?"

"Not you," the clone said, looking up at the group with renewed energy. "Me. I can take it. I'll take it on national TV, with a doctor. It'll be all on the up-and-up. Supervised, monitored, everything. And I'll let someone else select the doctor, someone independent. Christ, we'll invite the FDA to oversee it themselves."

"Could work," someone said. "But wouldn't it be better for some bigwig to take it? Someone higher up? Or maybe a scientist?"

"I don't think so," the clone said. "I think it says more if it's just some regular joe who isn't afraid to take the Meld. If I do it, I think it'll go a lot farther to prove there's nothing dangerous about it."

"Is he out of his goddamn mind?" Jeremiah was stunned. After everything, the clone still believed in the Meld, believed the company was in the right. He was still toeing the line.

"I think it sounds like a pretty good stunt." Brent laughed.

"I think it sounds like he's an idiot!" Jeremiah stood up and turned away from the monitor. He paced back and forth in agitation. "After all these suicides and he wants to take the Meld? He's crazy! He has a family to think of. *My* family! What if something goes wrong?"

"Obviously, he doesn't think anything will go wrong, Jeremiah." Brent looked genuinely confused. "Now you don't trust the Meld, either?"

"I think it's a mistake," he said. "It might be good marketing, but this is a bad idea. For the clone."

"Since when are you so concerned about the clone?" Brent asked.

"Think about it, Brent. If something happens to *him*, what happens to *me*? How can I go home again?"

Brent said nothing, but a change of expression showed he understood.

On the monitor, the clone was just hanging up his office phone.

"It's a go," he said to the writers. "We need to set this up as soon as possible. I'll call CNN right away. Someone get on the phone with the FDA and get one of them on board with this. I want this to happen in prime time. Tomorrow. And I want it well advertised. Saturate social media. Call every one of the affiliates."

The group dispersed quickly and the clone, a self-satisfied grin spreading over his face, sat down and picked up the phone. The wall went dark before he finished dialing and, a moment later, Charles Scott entered Jeremiah's living room without knocking.

"It would appear we have a situation," he said. He stood in front of them with an expression that appeared perfectly calm, but Jeremiah could sense a trace of uneasiness in his demeanor.

"Damn right we have a situation," Jeremiah told him. "That clone is making a mistake. He shouldn't be taking the Meld."

"I agree, Mr. Adams," Scott said, moving farther into the room now. He stood in front of a chair without sitting down. Jeremiah shot a quick I-told-you-so glance at Brent. "We have no definitive data on how the drug might affect the clone. This is untested territory. There is a real possibility that, under Meld, your double may become privy to information he must not have. Whoever takes the Meld with him might see something, as well. The risk is simply too high."

"Don't you think," Jeremiah asked, "that maybe it's time you considered taking Meld off the market?"

"That is not an option," Scott said firmly. "Meld and the money it generates are crucial to this project. That must be preserved. At any cost."

It wasn't lost on Jeremiah that Scott had not directly dismissed the implication that Meld was dangerous and had been released too soon.

"So, what do we do about it?" Jeremiah asked. "How do we stop this?"

"We don't," Scott said thoughtfully. "We can't. The wheels are already in motion, I'm afraid. But we can ensure that it won't be the clone who is taking the Meld."

"How's that?" Jeremiah asked.

"You will need a shave and a haircut, Mr. Adams," Scott said with a slight gleam in his eye. "You're taking a trip."

# CHAPTER

# 26

Less than an hour later, Jeremiah found himself sitting on the cold, metal table in Dr. Pike's office, trying to calm his own heartbeat. He couldn't believe his luck. He was getting out, if only temporarily, and that impossible opportunity wasn't lost on him. He had a chance to save Diana. He had a little, slim, tenuous piece of hope. He wasn't going to squander it.

Pike was to perform a full medical examination to ensure that Jeremiah and the clone were as physically indistinguishable as possible when he went to the other side. While he waited, Jeremiah considered his options. They weren't many. He was certain Scott would be with him out there, or watching him, at least. They weren't going to just let him wander. But if he could evade them long enough for a phone call, or if he could somehow slip a message to someone who would relay it to his clone or Diana, he might have a chance. There wouldn't be time enough to plan anything elaborate beforehand, he decided. He'd just have to keep his eyes open and take any opportunity he could find.

Pike entered the room staring at a computer tablet in his

hand. He didn't even look at Jeremiah as he mumbled a distracted greeting.

"I assume you'll want to get me on the scale," Jeremiah said. "I think I've lost enough weight on the Dr. Pike diet."

"Yes, yes," Pike said, looking up at Jeremiah now and assessing him with a quick glance. "The weight. That is an issue. I think we'll be able to hide the discrepancy with your clothing. You won't be there long. We have a more pressing matter right now, I'm afraid."

"What's that?"

"You're going to need a tooth pulled. The clone had a right molar extracted a few weeks ago and we'll need to take the same tooth from you. I was going to wait on this, but circumstances have changed. It needs to be done today. Right away."

"What?" Jeremiah asked. "There's nothing wrong with my teeth!"

"I understand that," Pike told him. "But this is unavoidable."

"If I can hide my weight, I certainly ought to be able to hide a tooth," Jeremiah suggested. "I don't want a tooth pulled. Can't I just keep my mouth closed or something?"

"You're going to be on national TV," Pike said. "All over social media. And you'll be scrutinized. We can't risk it. We can get away with the assumption that the camera adds five pounds. Last I checked, though, it does not add extra teeth."

"Nice to see all the trouble you people can suddenly handle to get me out of here."

"We can't be too careful, Mr. Adams."

"Right, not when it suits your own agenda, I suppose. Different story, isn't it, when I want to get out to bury my mother?" Jeremiah stared hard at Pike, who looked momentarily uncomfortable, averting his eyes and shifting his weight from one foot to another.

"This is different, Mr. Adams," Pike said quietly. "You know that."

"For you, maybe. Not so much for me."

"These decisions aren't up to me," Pike told him. "If you'll hold out your left arm, I need a sample of your blood."

"Sure," Jeremiah said, holding his arm outstretched. "Take my teeth, my blood. Is there anything else? You want a kidney?"

Pike carried out the rest of the examination in silence, checking and rechecking vital signs and scanning for viral infections with a handheld device that Jeremiah surmised worked something like a Geiger counter. When he stepped on the scale, Jeremiah was pleased to see he'd lost a little more than six pounds, which had him still about four pounds heavier than his double, but one step closer to cheese.

Finally, once Pike was satisfied with the readings, he ushered Jeremiah into an adjacent office that had been outfitted as a dental suite. Jeremiah had been here once before for a routine cleaning.

"Please have a seat, Mr. Adams. I will administer a sedative to put you under, if you like."

"No," Jeremiah told him flatly. "Just numb me up. I want to be awake so I can see your face when you yank a perfectly healthy tooth out of my mouth."

Pike sighed. Fifteen minutes later, Jeremiah stood wobbling to his feet, a blood-soaked cotton ball clenched between his gums and one hand cradling his numb jaw.

"Now that that's over with," Pike said, "I believe you've earned those three food choices."

"Sure," Jeremiah mumbled through the cotton. "Now that you've seen to it I won't be able to eat anything for three days. Just get me some decent beer."

When Pike returned Jeremiah to his rooms, he found Charles Scott waiting for him with a dark-haired, impossibly thin woman he'd never seen before. They were standing in the middle of the living room. The woman had an oversize tote bag slung over one bony shoulder and was nearly dwarfed by its girth.

"It's time for your haircut, Mr. Adams," Scott told him. "Miss Phillips here will do the honors." He handed the woman a photograph of the clone. "This is what we're looking for," Scott told her. "He needs to look precisely like this. Make it as exact as possible. No deviation."

"Sure," the woman told him, a substantial Boston accent making the word come out more like "Shoo-wah."

"Can't we do this another time?" Jeremiah mumbled through the soggy cotton in his mouth. "I need to lie down."

"Now, Mr. Adams," Scott said. "You can lie down afterward."

"Pike just pulled a tooth out," he said. "I'm in no mood for a shave."

"Don't worry," the bony woman said. "I'll be very gentle. You just sit yourself down and we'll have you done in no time." She patted the back of one of the kitchen stools, dragged in to serve as a barber chair, and Jeremiah reluctantly sat down.

"Accuracy is more important here than speed," Scott told her, a hint of warning in his tone. "Precision is crucial. He needs to look exactly as he does in the photograph."

She shrugged. "It's a guy's regular and a clean shave," she said. "It's not rocket science." She took a plastic cape out of her tote bag and draped it around Jeremiah's shoulders, fastening it behind his neck.

"Just make sure you're meticulous," Scott said. "That's what you're being paid for." He shot a quick, stern look at Miss Phillips.

When Scott retreated into the kitchen, dialing his phone as he went, Jeremiah toyed with the idea of writing a note for Diana, slipping it to this woman and imploring her to get it into the right hands. But he couldn't risk it. Not with Scott in the next room, and not with someone as chatty as this girl. It would take him too long, he decided, to make her understand.

"Jeepers," she said, rolling her eyes toward the kitchen. "He's a real a worrywart. Good thing he pays so well. I don't usually do house calls, you know, but Dr. Scott there is paying me more for this one haircut than I'd make all day at the salon. And that includes tips! You must be someone pretty important. You famous or something, Mr. Adams?"

"No."

"You live here?"

"For the time being." Every time he spoke, Jeremiah had to suck in on the cotton and swallow a nauseating mix of saliva and blood.

"It's pretty fancy for a basement apartment. Me, though? I couldn't stand living without windows. I like to let the sun in, you know? It's been proven that a lack of sunshine can make you depressed. You ever get depressed here?"

He wanted to tell her yes. Yes, he got depressed all the time. This wasn't a basement apartment. He was a prisoner here. But he said nothing and just shook his head.

He was surprised Scott had let in a total outsider for something as simple as a shave. Everyone else involved in the project so far had been painstakingly vetted and probably made to sign an airtight nondisclosure agreement. But the urgency of the situation likely had left Scott little choice. He had to look completely like his double when he walked into ViMed. Scott needed a pro for this job. There was no way around it. In a way, he thought, it was nice to talk with someone who was unconnected to the whole thing, who didn't know him as the guinea pig. Under different circumstances, he might have even enjoyed it.

She took her supplies out of the tote and laid them meticulously on the coffee table.

"I'm going to warm this up for you in the kitchen," she said, grabbing one of the towels. "We'll start with the shave before that mouth of yours swells up anymore."

The steaming towel felt good on his aching jaw. Miss Phillips stopped talking and set right to work. As promised, she was very careful with the shave, lifting and angling his chin with a gentle touch and paying particular attention to his swollen right side. After a few minutes, Jeremiah began to relax.

She went on to the haircut, starting with wild chopping and then more precise snipping and, finally, tight shaping behind the neck and ears, the last of it with a razor. It was easily the most time he'd spent with a barber in decades. He had almost forgotten how long he'd gone without a haircut. When she was finished, and held a mirror up for his approval, Jeremiah was shocked to see the clone staring back at him. That's what it felt like at first glance—like he was seeing someone else's reflection. He hadn't realized, until that moment, how successful he'd been at distinguishing himself from his double. It had been a conscious decision at the start, to grow a beard, but then it had become as much laziness as anything else. He'd gotten used to the scruff. Here he was now, clean shaven and cropped, and he looked like the man he'd been watching on the wall every day. He turned his face back and forth and quickly decided he didn't like it. He looked older, and much more dignified than he felt he had a right to be.

"What do you think?" Miss Phillips asked with a grin.

"I look like a completely different man," he said.

Jeremiah swallowed three pills to help ease the swelling on his jaw and nodded sullenly as Scott went over his "ground rules" for his brief foray back into his life the next evening. The man seemed genuinely worried.

"You are not to speak to anyone at ViMed at all," Scott repeated for the third time. "Just get in, do your stint with the Meld and get out of the offices as quickly as you can."

"But what if someone talks to me?" Jeremiah asked. "Am I just supposed to pretend I don't hear them or something? Ignore them?"

"Keep it as brief as possible, Mr. Adams. And don't, under any circumstances, say anything that might raise suspicion. Be succinct and then make an excuse to move on. We can't have you starting any conversations that the clone will not remember."

"If I am taking his place for this publicity stunt," Jeremiah said, "it seems to me there will be a lot the clone doesn't remember."

"Leave that to us," Scott said. "We'll use the Meld for that. We'll do a quick download after the broadcast. He will remember everything you do exactly as if he'd done it himself. There will be no discrepancy there. But you need to hold up your own end. You can't do or say anything that might throw him off track. You can't raise suspicions in anyone. Keep everything simple."

"So I'll be taking the Meld twice? In one night?"

"It's necessary."

"I still don't see how you're going to pull this off," Jeremiah said. "How do you propose to make the switch?"

"Those details do not concern you."

"They sort of do. I mean, at least I ought to know where to be, what to do." He was fishing for some indication that he'd have a chance to reach out to Diana.

"Again, Mr. Adams, that doesn't concern you. Leave that to me. You need only to do precisely as I ask of you. Nothing more, nothing less. Follow my direction and this will all go smoothly."

"So you'll be there the whole time? How's that going to work? I mean, as far as he's aware, the clone has never even met you.

And suddenly, you're going to be hanging on him like you're his best friend?"

"I have already arranged to act as ViMed's scientific liaison to this endeavor," Scott said. "I'll be overseeing everything. But there will be several ViMed executives milling around, as well. Almost your entire marketing team. That's unavoidable, I'm afraid. You are not to talk with them any more than necessary. A few of them know all about this project, but the great majority do not."

That surprised Jeremiah. Who else in ViMed, he wondered, was involved in this?

"And I suppose those details don't concern me, either," Jeremiah said.

"They do not." Scott scrutinized Jeremiah for a long moment, as though he were trying to decipher his thoughts. "Remember, Mr. Adams," he said. "Right up until the moment you take the Meld, I will be right beside you. When you take the drug, I will be close by and I'll be watching you."

"But you won't be there for the actual demonstration?"

"No one will be in the room with you when you take the Meld. No one but you and the doctor administering the drug. As usual, anyone else in the room would risk contaminating the connection. Even the film crew will be working remotely for that portion, and I will be watching from a monitor in another location along with the other spectators. You can be assured I will be paying attention."

Jeremiah considered trying to get a message across to the doctor under the Meld. Something silent and telepathic. He'd never been able to exert any control when he took the drug with Natalie, though, so he didn't hold out much hope. Still, he thought, it might be his only chance.

As he spoke, Scott's left hand began to shake, just the slightest tremor that anyone else might have mistaken for simple fidgeting. Jeremiah knew better.

"There's no need to be so nervous," Jeremiah said, allowing his gaze to linger on Scott's hand briefly before meeting his eyes.

Scott immediately tucked both his hands into the pockets of his suit jacket, his arms stiffening perceptibly in an effort to quell the spasm. It was a gesture no one else might have noticed. Jeremiah noticed.

# CHAPTER
# 27

Jeremiah was still half-asleep and dressed in his underwear making coffee the next morning when he was startled by Brent coming through the front door without knocking.

"What the hell, Brent? Why are you here so early?"

"Good morning to you, too," Brent called. He laid his laptop on the couch and came into the kitchen, stopping short as soon as he caught sight of Jeremiah. "Whoa," he said, "you look exactly like him without the beard and the hair. That's amazing."

"Well, not really, Brent. He's my clone, after all."

"How's the tooth?"

"Still gone, thanks." Jeremiah rubbed his jaw. It ached a little, but the swelling seemed to have gone down considerably. "So why are you here at this indecent hour? Did Mel throw you out or something?"

"We're supposed to monitor the clone for the whole day today," Brent told him. "It goes on at nine, which gives us just enough time for breakfast."

"The whole day? What the hell for?"

"Scott wants you to see as much of his day as possible in case there's anything you'll need to know once you take his place tonight. You're to pay meticulous attention—his words, not mine. It's pretty exciting, don't you think?"

"I'm all a-tingle," Jeremiah said.

"I thought you'd be glad to get a chance to go back home for a while."

"I'm not going home, Brent. I'm going to the office. I'm literally going up twelve floors in an elevator. And I've been duly cautioned not to speak to anyone. I don't see why I have to watch him all day. I won't be interacting much."

"I don't know," Brent said. "What if he spills mustard on his tie at lunch or something? You'd have to know that, right?"

"Presumably he'd change his tie before he goes on live TV."

"Exactly. And we'd know which tie to get for you."

"I suppose," Jeremiah said. "Fix yourself some breakfast. I'm still nursing my goddamn mouth."

Brent got eggs from the refrigerator and put bread in the toaster. "Any idea when we can get some bacon around here?"

"I've lost six pounds, I'll have you know. I got the green light to get a few things back on the menu. One of them, at your request, was beer."

"I don't want beer for breakfast."

For several hours, they watched the clone at the ViMed office, and Jeremiah found himself scrutinizing the space more than he did his double, looking for a place to stash a note, if it came down to that. He studied the desk every time the clone was near it, memorizing the exact location of pens and paper, the precise position of the center drawer. If he got the chance to be in that office, to sit at that desk, seconds would count.

As the clone went about his morning, Jeremiah found himself mesmerized by the windows. Even though they only offered a view of a parking lot and the backs of two other buildings in the compound, he fantasized about the chance to stand there for a moment, maybe open it and feel actual fresh air on his face.

He entertained the ridiculous notion of jumping out, risking it all and running back home to protect his wife. But it was a twelve-story drop to the pavement. He wouldn't get very far on two broken legs.

There was more than the usual level of activity in the clone's office all day. The place was on hyperdrive. The entire communications team worked to put the finishing touches on the Meld publicity stunt. The broadcast was scheduled for 7:00 p.m. and would take place in a ViMed conference room, where news crews had been busy for several hours setting up lighting and equipment. Before and after he took the drug, there was to be a panel discussion with officials from both ViMed and the FDA. Charles Scott, obviously, had been "selected" to represent the company. Jeremiah figured the FDA official would be someone handpicked by Scott.

The whole event was one big sham.

ViMed executives were buzzing about it. Big guns—people Jeremiah wouldn't have guessed even knew his name—streamed in and out of the department, offering praise and shaking the clone's hand.

"This is an A-plus idea, Adams," a portly VP with glasses told him. "If this little demonstration doesn't convince people that Meld is safe for the public, I don't know what will."

Jeremiah couldn't stand that the clone looked so smug. *Idiot,* he thought, *you won't even be there.*

Three of the major cable networks had agreed to air the demonstration live, and online streaming sites on both sides of the issue were gearing up for record traffic. Jeremiah understood, with some concern, that much of the hype involved the ghoulish possibility of a live broadcast suicide. He had no doubt that there were people absolutely hoping to see someone freak out and knife himself in front of the cameras as soon as the Meld took effect. They'd be disappointed, though. Because Jeremiah was used to the drug. *Sorry*, he thought, *you sickos will have to get your kicks somewhere else.*

Just after six o'clock, Charles Scott entered the lab carrying a garment bag in one hand.

"It's time to change into your work clothes, Mr. Adams," he said.

They had to walk up a flight of stairs that was hidden behind a locked door before taking a freight elevator to the twelfth floor of the building. Jeremiah was nervous. As the car made its way up, he could feel his stomach fall. Charles Scott and Dr. Pike stood by without a word. Pike held a syringe securely in his right hand. Scott stared at his shoes. When the car stopped and the doors opened, Scott went out first, holding Jeremiah back with an outstretched arm, and surveyed the back hallway in both directions. Satisfied that there was no one in sight, he motioned for Pike and Jeremiah to follow him out. Some two hundred feet to the right was a door that Jeremiah recognized as a supply room. He'd been there only once or twice in over ten years. Typically, it was Brenda's domain. Scott opened the door and ushered Jeremiah inside.

"Lock the door," Scott told him. "Dr. Pike and I will head off the clone and, once we have him secured, I will come back here and make the switch. Do not open this door unless you hear my voice. And be quiet. This should only take a minute or two."

A minute or two might be all the time he'd need, he thought.

When they left, Jeremiah quickly locked the door and looked around. The room was narrow and stifling, without windows. A long table took up much of the floor space, and the walls were lined with shelves containing reams of printer paper, water jugs and a host of things Jeremiah had always taken for granted. Cardboard boxes were stacked up in one corner of the room. He tore at one and found only old printers and a mountain of ink

cartridges. Finally, on a high shelf, he saw what he was looking for—spare telephones. He had to climb to reach one and
winced when it fell to the floor in a clattering riot. Scrambling
back down he picked the thing up and scanned the room for
a phone jack so he could plug it in. He saw none. Damn technology, he thought. Much of what the office used now was
wireless. He began pulling boxes away from the walls but still
couldn't find a jack.

He heard footsteps in the hallway, coming to a stop just outside the door. He watched the doorknob wriggle and held his
breath. It couldn't be Pike and Scott, he thought. They wouldn't
have tried the door. And there was no way they could have ac-
complished their task so quickly.

"Now, how did this door get locked?"

*Brenda.* A fine time for her to fetch a box of pens, he thought.
His first instinct was to find a place to hide, but the only obvious
place was under the table where he'd be in full view as soon as
she walked in. It would have looked absurd if she'd found him
there. He took a step backward and braced himself, frantically
trying to come up with some reasonable explanation as to why
he would have locked himself in the supply room.

She turned the knob a few more times and then he heard her
footsteps retreat at a quick pace back down the hall. She'd gone
to her desk for her keys, he figured, which would mean she'd
likely be inside the supply room in about forty-five seconds. It
wasn't even enough time for him to slip out and hide somewhere
else. He'd just have to let her come in and find him, he thought,
and hope she hadn't just walked by his clone out in the hallway.
He tightened his lips and decided his best option was to simply
pretend he was looking for something. The sound of her heels
coming back toward the door made his heart jump. He ditched
the phone he was still holding, turned his back to the door and
started shifting boxes around on the shelves.

"Excuse me, ma'am." It was Charles Scott's voice, just on the other side of the door. "I'm looking for Jeremiah Adams. I'm Charles Scott from Engineering. I'm supposed to be involved in the broadcast tonight, but I'm afraid I've become quite turned around. Am I on the right floor?"

"Oh, my, we all know who you are, Dr. Scott. You want the eighth floor," Brenda told him. "Mr. Adams left just a few minutes ago. They needed him for a sound check or something. But you'd better hurry."

"I'm somewhat hopeless navigating this building," Scott said. "Perhaps you could escort me?"

"Sure," she said, and Jeremiah could almost hear the smile in her voice. No doubt she was happy to suddenly find herself playing a crucial role in the whole production. "You just follow me. I'll get you there in a jiffy."

Jeremiah started breathing again when he heard them leave. An instant later, Pike was at the door, knocking and calling out in a hushed but urgent tone.

"Mr. Adams, open the door. We have to hurry."

Jeremiah opened it, and Pike nearly pounced on him in his effort to get him out of the room.

"That was a little too close for comfort," Jeremiah told him.

"Yes, and if we don't get you downstairs we're going to have another close call." Pike had him by the arm as he hurried down the hallway, back toward the freight elevator. The doctor leaned on the button. "We've got to get down there before they send out a search party."

"Where's the clone?" Jeremiah asked.

"Unconscious in a janitor's closet where I left him," Pike said.

"A janitor's closet? What if someone finds him? I thought you were supposed to take him downstairs to the lab."

"Yes, well, there was a glitch, as you know. Dr. Scott had to come and save you from being found out."

"Don't act like this is my fault," Jeremiah told him testily. "None of this was my idea."

The elevator door opened, and Pike pushed Jeremiah inside and started hitting the buttons on the panel. When it landed on the eighth floor, Charles Scott reached into the elevator and grabbed Jeremiah by the arm before the doors had even fully opened. He pulled him out into the empty back hallway. Pike stayed behind, presumably to retrieve the clone from the closet and hold up his end of the plan.

"They've been waiting for you, Mr. Adams," Scott whispered as he ushered Jeremiah through a doorway and into the main corridor. "Follow my lead and there won't be any questions."

As soon as they walked through the door, Scott with a hand lightly on Jeremiah's elbow, there was a rush of activity. Jeremiah thought it looked like a movie set. It was surreal to see ViMed's hallways so chaotic. Camera and sound technicians were taping wires down along the walls, several people rushed back and forth hurrying papers and cell phones from one person to another, and a skinny blonde woman, whom Jeremiah instantly recognized as a prime-time news anchor for CNN, was noisily testing her microphone in a corner. She looked much smaller in real life than she did on TV. A lunchroom had been transformed into a makeup area and, as they passed the doorway, Jeremiah caught a glimpse of a long-limbed young man in a bright blue smock bent over someone, applying powder with an artist's brush.

"I've found him," Scott announced loudly to no one in particular. "He was hiding out in the back hallway. I think he has a case of the jitters."

"Get him in here!" The lanky makeup artist was patting an empty seat with one hand and waving to Scott with the other.

Jeremiah went in and took a seat next to Natalie Young, who looked at him demurely and held out her hand.

"I'm Dr. Natalie Young," she said. "I'll be taking the Meld with you tonight. It's nice to meet you, Mr. Adams."

Jeremiah shook her hand and said nothing. So much for telepathic messaging, he thought. But of more immediate concern to him was the question of what she would detect under the Meld. She was almost certain to discover his suspicions and his plan to warn Diana. He had to nip that in the bud.

Leaning in close to her, speaking just above a whisper, he told her bluntly about his wife's affair.

"I know," she told him. "I read the report. We'll discuss it later."

"I just thought you should know before the Meld," he said. "You know, in case you pick up on anything strange. I thought you should understand I'm sort of upset about everything. There's bound to be something."

She nodded. "Noted," she said. "I'll look past it."

Jeremiah leaned back in his chair and tried to clear his mind of anything incriminating, focusing instead on the fact that someone was applying color to his cheeks.

# CHAPTER
# 28

The eighth-floor conference room had been emptied of its furnishings, except for several chairs, which were arranged in a semicircle. Facing those were of a bank of cameras and bright lights mounted on metal stands. Jeremiah took his place in the center chair. Dr. Young took the seat on his left, Charles Scott, to his right and an FDA agent who introduced himself as Nathan Christopher sat next to Scott. Jeremiah didn't recognize him, but that, he knew, meant nothing. For all he knew, the man might have been privy to the entire experiment. Three network news anchors sat on the other side of Dr. Young. There was no audience to witness the event, but a small number of ViMed executives and scientists stood in a quiet huddle in a far corner of the room, out of the camera shot. To his dismay, Jeremiah also saw two older men standing off to the other side of the room, both in what appeared to be full-dress army regalia. From the number of medals on them, they looked to be fairly high-ranking. He swallowed hard. They weren't here to provide security, he knew. They were here to make sure no threats would need neutralizing.

A balding producer who smelled heavily of cough syrup fastened a microphone to Jeremiah's lapel and talked to him in clipped, hurried sentences.

"Let the anchors set it up. They know what to do. When you speak, look at them and not at the camera. Be yourself. You'll do fine." He stood up and moved quickly out of the frame. "In three. Two. One," he said.

Charles Scott shot a severe glance at Jeremiah. There was no mistaking what he meant.

The lead anchor, an impeccably dressed and angular man, began by introducing the participants, ending with a direct question to Jeremiah.

"Are you nervous about taking the Meld today?"

Jeremiah stammered for a moment. "N-no, not really," he said. He was momentarily distracted by the producer rolling his hand in the air in front of him, as though to encourage him to elaborate. "Meld is perfectly safe when used in a clinical setting. I'm sure I'm in very good hands with Dr. Young."

"And even with all these suicides connected to the drug, that doesn't worry you?" the anchor pushed.

"Well, as ViMed has always maintained, those deaths occurred while taking Meld in an unsafe manner, without medical supervision. And we also suspect the drug was adulterated once it hit the streets. I am not worried."

"Why are you doing this, Mr. Adams?" the anchor asked. "Why you? Why now?"

He wanted to say he had absolutely no idea, that he'd been asking himself the same questions and couldn't find an answer. To any of it. But he felt Scott's eyes boring into him, so he said what he was supposed to say.

"I want to demonstrate that Meld is not only safe, but to remind people that this is a drug that saves lives," he said. "Meld has already had tremendous impact on treating mental illness, Alzheimer's disease and reaching the conscious minds of comatose patients. There is reason to believe that this drug might have other benefits we aren't even aware of yet. Imagine the implications for people suffering from ALS—people who become trapped, essentially, in their own failing bodies, who've lost the ability to speak. Meld could help them, too."

The last bit was entirely ad-lib and meant for Scott's ears. But if Charles Scott was worried about it, he didn't let on. Still, Jeremiah was pleased with himself that he'd found the nerve to throw it in.

At this point, the news anchors, spectators, film crew and producers began to file out of the room, along with Charles Scott and the man from the FDA. All of them would watch the actual Meld demonstration from the safety of a remote location to guard against any of their thoughts being accidentally picked up. While Jeremiah was relieved he wouldn't have to risk getting an intimate view into the mind of Charles Scott, he couldn't help wondering if it might have answered some questions and confirmed his suspicions.

There was absolute silence when Natalie Young finally injected both Jeremiah and herself with the two different compounds of Meld and then moved her chair to face him head-on. Jeremiah closed his eyes and waited for the initial barrage of images he knew would come—snippets from her internal dialogue, odd bits of conversation with people he didn't know, random yearnings and shadows of things she'd rather hide. But the first, fleeting image he saw from Natalie's mind was something unexpected—a vague sense of shock. There was distinct hesitation from her. Almost the instant it appeared, she retrieved it and pulled it back. He didn't understand what it was, what it meant, but Jeremiah was certain she'd been genuinely surprised by something she'd seen in his mind. Had she picked up so quickly on his suspicions about Scott? His desperation to warn Diana? Had those thoughts been that close to the surface? He fought to empty his mind, to think of something else, but before he could do it, she had already switched gears. She reined in her own emotions, and her mind began to bore into his as it usually did when they took the drug. He was helpless to do anything but give in to it. She was adept at this. The next thing he knew, he was cognizant, alone in his mind and free from the Meld's hold. The panel filed back into the room and allowed him a few minutes to compose himself before rifling him with questions.

"How do you feel, Mr. Adams?"

"What do you remember?"

"Can you describe the experience for the viewers at home?"

"Do you feel any sudden depression?"

Jeremiah answered warily, saying all the things he was supposed to say, hitting all the buzzwords and, generally, behaving exactly as he was expected to. He tried to steal a glance at Natalie, to see if he could determine what she'd seen in him, but she took pains, it seemed, not to catch his eye. She answered every question directly to the interviewer.

"What I saw in Mr. Adams was a levelheaded, rational man," she said. "Nothing out of the ordinary. Nothing unexpected. I was able to probe his thought patterns, his self-perception, and see a bit of how he views the world. To me, he seems content. He is a perfectly normal man."

Whatever she saw when she looked at his mind through the Meld, Jeremiah thought, it wasn't that.

Once the cameras were off and the producers began guessing at the viewership, Jeremiah found himself in the middle of a group of ViMed executives. Charles Scott was at his elbow.

"Great job," someone said to him. "I think this is going to work."

"Let's hope so," a nervous older woman said. "We've got too much riding on this."

Jeremiah nodded and shook hands with several people without saying much.

"Come, Mr. Adams," Charles Scott said. "I'll walk with you to your car."

He was likely in a hurry, Jeremiah thought, to get back and hook him up to the clone. Jeremiah's stomach turned at the realization he'd have to undergo the Meld twice in a single hour, and this time with his double. He didn't even want to imagine what that would be like, seeing what was basically his own mind reflected back at him under the drug. He turned on his heels, said his goodbyes and followed Scott out of the room and into the hallway.

They almost ran headlong into Brenda.

"Oh, Mr. Adams," she said, "I'm glad I caught you before you left."

Jeremiah said nothing but looked to Scott for some sort of cue. Scott looked ruffled for a moment and then quickly regained his composure.

"Ah, it is my heroine," he said with a smile. "Do you know, Mr. Adams, I might have missed the entire event tonight if not for this charming lady. She was kind enough to come to my aid when I was hopelessly lost."

"Brenda's good at that sort of thing," Jeremiah said, and then turned to her, hoping he sounded less anxious than he was. "You're here late. I thought you'd be gone by now."

"Well, the phones were ringing off the hook as soon as the broadcast finished," she told him. "I just stayed to field the calls. Everyone wants a quote or an interview."

"I'll get to them in the morning, Brenda," Jeremiah said. "Let the broadcast speak for itself for now."

"That's what I told them," she said. "But I thought I'd bring you the messages, in case you want to contact anyone tonight. Your friend from the *Times*, Walt Thompson, called twice."

She handed Jeremiah a sizable stack of notes.

"Thank you," he said. "I don't know how I'd ever get anything done without you, Brenda. I have a lot to thank you for."

The look of slight surprise on Brenda's face made him instantly aware that what he'd said was completely out of character for him. But he'd felt compelled to say something nice to her for once. Thankfully, though, the surprise left her face and she just smiled and shook her head.

"Just doing my job, Mr. Adams. I'll see you in the morning."

As soon as she was out of earshot, Scott leaned into him with a stern warning.

"Be careful, Mr. Adams," he said. "That could have gone very badly. Let's get back to your office before we run into anyone else."

"Why don't you tell me first, Dr. Scott," he said, sensing his momentary upper hand, "what the hell the army was doing here?"

"Certain military people have an interest in all of this. Beyond that, it's none of your concern."

While Scott led him roughly by the elbow toward the elevator, Jeremiah took a certain delight in his own brashness. It felt good just to see Scott squirm.

Pike was pacing back and forth in front of the doors as soon as the elevator opened on the twelfth floor.

"Come, Mr. Adams," he said tensely. "We need to get your memories into the clone as quickly as possible. The sedative won't last much longer. We'll do this in your office. It will make more sense if the clone regains consciousness there."

The entire floor was empty at this time of night, and the silence made Jeremiah uncomfortable. The hum of the water cooler and printers reverberated through the deserted hallways.

"We had a brief encounter with the administrative assistant just now," Scott told Pike. "That will need to be implanted." He turned to Jeremiah. "Wait in your office, Mr. Adams. And put those messages where he'll see them."

He'd almost given up on another chance. But they were leaving him alone in here. It wasn't over.

When the door closed and he was alone in his office for the first time in several months, Jeremiah felt so strange that he hesitated and wasted precious seconds just taking it in. He turned to look out his office window, but by now it was so dark outside that all he saw was his own reflection, looking disoriented and quite out of place here. He snapped back into clarity and grabbed for the phone, dialing his home number with barely a glance at the keypad. He cupped his hand over the mouthpiece and listened anxiously as it rang three times, never taking his eyes off the office door.

Parker picked up.

Jeremiah froze for an instant at hearing his son's voice on the phone. A wave of regret washed over him as he thought of all the things he wanted to say to his son. There wasn't time.

"Parker, get your mother to the phone."

"She's not home, Dad. Hey, I watched you on TV. I can't believe you took that stuff."

"Where's your mother?"

"Working, I guess."

Jeremiah hung up the phone without even saying goodbye to his son and tried to remember Diana's cell phone number. He'd only ever dialed it by pressing one button on his own cell. He had no idea what it was.

When he heard Scott and Pike in the hallway, progressing slowly with the dead weight of the unconscious clone, Jeremiah grabbed a pen. He had seconds to consider what he would write. He flipped to an empty page in the middle of a yellow legal pad on the desk and scrawled a message for his double: *Diana is in danger. There are NO ACCIDENTS! Keep her home!*

He righted the pad, quickly pocketed the pen and nearly toppled over at the sight of the two men dragging the drugged clone into the office. It would have been an unnerving thing to see even if he hadn't been frantic. He tried to steady his breathing while they settled his double at his desk.

The downloading of the evening's memories from his mind to his clone took all of fifteen minutes. Pike affixed several wires connecting Jeremiah's head to that of his double, and then attached an additional connection to himself. He hastily explained that, this time, the Meld would feel different.

"This is a one-way transfer," he said. "But you may sense something from the clone. Anything you pick up should be minimal. To be honest, I'm not entirely certain what you'll experience. We never prepared for this."

"What do I need to do?"

"Nothing," Pike said. "The hard connection will allow me to control the download. I'll be able to filter everything. I can implant only what we need. Try to relax."

During the transfer, Jeremiah was hardly aware of anything except a vague sense of false confidence from his double. The sensation was hazy, hovering just in the background. But what he could sense from the clone's mind was eerily familiar, as though his own random thoughts were flitting through his head. Afterward, he was shuffled out of the room by Scott and into the freight elevator, on his way back to the lab before the clone was even fully awake. Jeremiah wondered vaguely what they'd implanted in his mind to reconcile that he was about to wake up at his desk.

# CHAPTER
# 29

Jeremiah had told Brent about the note he'd slipped to the clone. During the viewings over the next several days, both of them watched the clone with renewed interest and scrutiny to see if it had worked.

"You've got some balls on you," Brent said. "I'll give you that." He'd seemed impressed and worried at the same time, but they weren't able to talk about it out loud in front of Mel's painting and the camera. They had to be careful.

Jeremiah was desperate to know if his risk had made a difference, whether he'd managed to get a warning to Diana. He held his breath for any glimpse of her during the viewings, any mention of her name or her whereabouts if she wasn't present. It infuriated him that none of the viewings were at home while she was there.

Much of what they saw took place in the clone's office where he continued to be lauded for his brilliant public relations ploy. It had evidently been a resounding success. The doctor who'd killed himself was being referred to as little more than a Meld-crazed addict on most of the mainstream news outlets. Hold-outs from the web and fringe press, though, were still skeptical and continued questioning the drug's safety. Jeremiah silently applauded them, something he'd never have believed he'd ever do. But he made a point to keep all thoughts to himself during every viewing, unwilling to give Brent any additional fodder for his report. He was more immediately concerned with Diana.

If he could have just seen her, he would have been able to relax a little. She was safe so far, he had gleaned that much, but that could have just been chance. He found himself peering into the eyes of his clone, trying to find some small measure of change in him. Every faraway glance, every hesitation when he spoke, suddenly took on new importance to Jeremiah. Had he found the note? Was he trying to work out the impossible discovery of such an ominous warning in his own handwriting? Was he aware of anything?

For his part, the brief foray back into his own life had had a profound impact on Jeremiah. He could still hear the echo of Parker's voice on the phone. It pulled at him. And he remembered the look on Brenda's face when he'd thought to say a single kind thing to her. Most of all, he remembered the fleeting things he'd been able to see of his clone's mind during those few minutes when they'd been connected under the Meld. His double seemed to hold himself in high regard, to be so confident in his position with ViMed, his place in the world. But what was troubling was what he'd seen just underneath that: the clone seemed to understand that he was lying to himself, that none of that confidence was actually true. There was a real sense of doubt there, and although it had only been the briefest of flickers, Jeremiah had instantly recognized that doubt as his own. It had always been there, just under the surface, pushed away and rejected. It was a difficult thing to have seen, and he kept those thoughts to himself, too.

Instead, as each four-hour segment passed with every indication that Diana was safe, Jeremiah clung to the profound satisfaction that his note had worked. He'd taken a risk and had made a difference. He might have foiled Scott's plans for his wife. He might have actually done something. He savored that victory alone.

At the end of another viewing watching the clone still basking in the glory of his publicity stunt, Brent traded his lab coat for a beer and seemed ready to settle in for the evening.

"I'm tired, Brent," Jeremiah said instead of engaging in the casual conversation. "Finish your beer and go home to Mel. I'm going to bed early."

Thirty minutes after Brent left the lab, Jeremiah all but collapsed onto his bed and fell into the first sound sleep he'd had in days. Sheer exhaustion finally won out over his own fretting.

When he awoke in the darkened room, it took him a full minute to comprehend that someone was knocking impatiently at his front door in the next room. From the sound of it, they'd been trying to get his attention for a while. No one ever knocked like that on his door, he realized through a fog. Once his eyes adjusted, he saw by the clock on his bedside table that it was 2:28 in the morning.

"What the hell," he mumbled, and threw off the covers. "Yeah, just a minute!" he called.

As he approached, pulling tight the belt on his bathrobe, he heard the familiar buzz and click of the electronic lock and the door eased open. Charles Scott stood in front of him, dressed uncharacteristically in a white T-shirt and khaki pants, as though he, too, had been roused from his sleep. His hair and demeanor, however, were in their usual state of perfection.

"I'm sorry to wake you, Mr. Adams." Scott stepped inside and the door closed slowly behind him. "I'm afraid something has happened."

Jeremiah rubbed at his eyes and yawned.

Scott put two fingers to Jeremiah's elbow and decisively led him to the couch. Jeremiah sat down and tried to shake the sleep from his head.

Scott scrutinized him with narrowed eyes and inhaled deeply through his nose before speaking. "I have terrible news," he said. "Your wife, Diana, was in a car crash about an hour ago. I'm afraid she didn't survive."

Jeremiah stared up at Scott blankly and tried to determine whether he was actually fully awake. He couldn't comprehend the words. They made no sense to him. He couldn't connect them with any kind of truth. He had written the note. He had warned his clone. He had saved her. He had made a difference.

Diana.

"Did you hear what I said, Mr. Adams? Your wife was killed in a car accident tonight."

"Parker..." Jeremiah started to rise up from the couch before falling back down again.

"She was driving alone. Your son is safe at home with the clone."

Jeremiah shuddered at those words. There was no such thing as safe anymore.

"An hour ago? In the middle of the night? Where was she going in the middle of the night? What happened?"

"The accident occurred just a few blocks from your home," Scott told him. "We don't know whether she was coming home or going away. There were no other cars involved. Apparently, she lost control and went off an embankment. She was pronounced dead at the scene. We're still trying to piece together the information. You know about as much as I do at this point, I'm afraid."

Jeremiah fell silent again as the news took shape in his mind. There should have been rage. He should have lunged toward Charles Scott and strangled him where he stood. But all he could feel in that moment was a horrifying sensation of falling, of being engulfed. Hot tears began to sting the back of his eyelids. He didn't know how to react to this. He buried his face in his hands and pushed hard against his forehead and temples to keep from crying outright. None of this made any sense.

"I'm so sorry, Mr. Adams. If I could have foreseen all this tragedy happening in your life in these few months… Well…we never know what the Fates have in store for us, do we?"

Jeremiah almost welcomed the anger those words began to coax from him. Fate? This was murder! But his shock and a sudden shred of senseless hope pushed it down again.

"Are you sure about this?" he asked. "I mean, are they sure it was her? Maybe it was some sort of mistake. How do you even know? I mean, unless you were watching her, how do you know?"

"We're sure," Scott said, his voice uncharacteristically quiet. "We have safeguards in place so that we are warned about things such as this. I'm sorry."

"She was only forty-six, for Christ's sake. She can't be dead."

"I know. It's a terrible loss. Terrible."

"You're planning to let me out now, right?" Jeremiah looked the older man hard in the eyes. "I mean…this experiment is over. It's done now."

"Right now, Mr. Adams, I would like to turn on the viewer. The police should be arriving at your home to inform the clone. Dr. Young thinks it's important that you experience this in real time. I want to make certain that happens."

Jeremiah looked up at the wall without words as an image appeared of his double switching on the hallway light and opening the front door. He was dressed, like Jeremiah, in a bathrobe, his hair messy and his face tired. Two uniformed police officers, one male, one female, stood on the front steps, hats in their hands in front of them.

"Jeremiah Adams?" the woman asked, turning the volume down on a radio hooked to her belt.

"Yes."

"Is your wife Diana Adams?"

"Yes."

"Sir, I am Officer Mahoney, this is Officer Towle. May we come in?"

The clone opened the door wider and stepped aside to give them entry. Jeremiah noted the clone's eyes darting nervously back and forth, from one officer to the other, and his face grew markedly paler. Police holding hats in the middle of the night will do that to a man, he thought, even to a copy of a man.

"Sir, we regret to inform you that your wife was killed in a car crash tonight on Route 18, about an hour ago."

On hearing the words, the clone instantly wobbled, as though his knees had given out, and the male officer caught him by the arm and gently led him to a nearby chair. Jeremiah felt hot waves of renewed pain sweep over him, as though hearing it from the police somehow made it more real. As a man, he and his double hung their heads and lifted identical hands to their eyes. Scott, quite out of character, tentatively touched Jeremiah's shoulder. He shrugged violently to be rid of that treacherous hand.

"What happened?" the clone asked weakly. "What do you mean a car crash? Where?"

"Just down the street, sir," the male officer told him. "It looks like the car lost control, went off an embankment and hit a tree."

On the screen, the female officer handed the clone a card. "I'm afraid you'll need to identify the body at this address," she said. "We could take you now, or you could go in the morning if you prefer. There's no rush, sir."

"N-no, no," the clone stammered. "My son is asleep upstairs. I'll go in the morning."

"I'm very sorry for your loss," she said, and her sincerity

showed in her face. "You can reach me or Officer Towle at the station if there's anything you need. If you have any questions. Anything at all."

"Yes, of course. Yes. Thank you."

They let themselves out the front door, closing it softly behind them, and left the clone sitting, half-slumped, in shocked disbelief.

"Turn it off," Jeremiah said.

"Are you sure, Mr. Adams? The clone may be about to speak to your son. You'd want to see that, I think."

"No. I don't want to see it. What I want is to be there with my son. Turn it off. Just turn it off."

He did, and without another word, Charles Scott left the apartment. The door closed slowly but absolutely behind him. Jeremiah didn't even look up.

# CHAPTER
# 30

He remained on the couch, unmoving, wondering how it could have happened. Not just Diana, but everything. How could his life have come so undone in such a short span of time? How could he have let that happen? For forty-seven years, it seemed, his world had moved steadily, mostly in a predictable straight line, everything happening pretty much as expected. There were hurdles and hiccups, but nothing he couldn't see beyond, nothing without an answer. What was it about him, he wondered now, that had so easily swayed him to leave? What kind of weakness was that? What kind of selfishness? How could he pick up the pieces now? How was he supposed to walk back in? What was he supposed to do?

In a way, since this whole thing began, right up to this moment, he'd been able to pretend all of it was happening to someone else. He could look up at that screen and almost convince himself the clone was a different, separate person. But not now. Now he felt buried under all of it. The weight of his own ruined life was crushing. His own blame in that was overwhelming. So, he sat there, unable to move, and wondering why he wasn't sobbing.

Sometime around 6:00 a.m. Natalie Young knocked once and then came in through the door in his living room. She was dressed in a neat red dress with matching heels, her white lab coat unbuttoned over this, and her hair pulled back in its usual tight knot. She looked every bit as though the world was still exactly as it ought to be. She took a seat across from him, pulling up the chair and sitting on its edge, so that her knees were almost touching his. She waited a few minutes in silence, looking at him with pursed lips and a cool, somewhat studious expression.

"Oh, Jeremiah," she said at last, and left it at that.

"I don't want to talk right now."

"I think we need to."

"I don't want to talk."

He stood up then, tightened the belt around his bathrobe again and walked into the kitchen without looking at her. He switched on the light and busied himself with the coffeemaker, measuring French roast with slow, purposeful movements, and filling the carafe with water from the refrigerator dispenser. He laid the preparations on the counter, and closed his eyes, breathing deeply, putting his hands before him to steady himself. After a moment, she followed him, and stared at his back until he finally turned around.

"Talk to me, Jeremiah. Tell me what you're thinking."

He was silent. She didn't want to know what he was thinking.

"I need to make sure you're coping with all of this. I need to make sure you're all right."

"No."

"We could take the Meld. I can see it that way, if that would be easier for you than talking right now."

"I'm not taking the Meld. I've taken too much of that stuff already. And the last time it was twice in one day. I don't like letting you peer into me like that." He hesitated just a moment and looked her hard in the eye. "I don't think you understand what you're seeing," he told her. "I think you made mistakes."

"What do you mean?" she asked. Jeremiah thought he detected a hint of apprehension in her voice.

"I think you should go, Natalie," he said, turning back to his coffee. "Please. Just go."

"Mr. Higgins will be here soon," she told him. "Talk to him. I'll see you tomorrow, Jeremiah, for our scheduled session. Please try to get some rest today. If you need me, let me know."

He said nothing and watched her walk out the door. Without conscious thought, in sure, robotic motion, he got himself showered and dressed. When he came back out to the living room, Brent handed him coffee and motioned him to the couch without a word.

"I told you. I tried to tell you," Jeremiah said.

"I know."

"You didn't listen."

"I know."

"She was my wife. What am I supposed to do now? This isn't even my own life I'll be going back to anymore. Everything's just so fucked up now."

"I know."

"And Parker. Jesus. What happens to Parker?" Jeremiah could hardly get the words out. He didn't even try to hide the tears on his cheeks. He just let himself cry. Brent put a hand firmly on his shoulder and said nothing. After a moment, Jeremiah wiped his eyes roughly and pulled himself together enough to speak again. "Parker is alone with that clone now. He needs his father. He needs his *real* father."

"I get that," Brent said. "But they're not going to let you go."

"They have to. This is finished. I am not leaving my son alone with that thing."

"He's not alone. For all Parker knows he's with his father.

He's going through this with you. I mean, Parker doesn't know the difference. He's okay for now."

"What do you mean?" Jeremiah stared at Brent. "He's not okay. Nothing is okay. Don't you get that by now, Brent? Don't you understand? I have to do something."

"Let's play a game of *IF*," Brent said, out of left field.

"What? I don't want to play the fucking game, Brent. Just go, will you? I want to be alone."

"I think it will help," he persisted, and proceeded to turn on the controllers and the headsets.

"How the hell is that going to help? You're crazy!"

"It'll be a diversion. Come on. Just one quick game. Please? Humor me." Brent's eyes were fixed on Jeremiah, his mouth tensed in a straight line across his face, urging him to accept. "Please." Something in his eyes was deadly serious. "I want to help you."

Reluctantly, Jeremiah took the headset and put it on. The wall in front of them morphed into an image of the virtual battlefield, fixed at the precise point they'd left it several days before. Brent didn't touch the avatar but began typing a message with his controller. Jeremiah watched as words appeared on the sidebar.

Type. Don't talk. Natalie told me she saw something under the Meld. She saw that someone out there knew.

Knew what?

That it wasn't you.

Diana didn't know.

Are we sure? Maybe she did know. Maybe what she said was true.

Diana didn't know. It wasn't her.

Who, then?

Doesn't matter.

Who?

Louie.

Dog?

Yes. He knows. He knew from the first day.

She must have seen that. She must have thought it was Diana. Then they saw the tape, heard what she said. I should have listened to you. I should have helped you. I'm sorry.

Jeremiah didn't type a reply. A dread washed over him as Brent's words sunk in. He read them over again, then took his headgear off and laid it gently on the table in front of him. He walked out, through the bedroom and into the bathroom, where he thought he might vomit. He was shaking, and his reflection in the mirror was ashy. He steadied himself against the sink and breathed in and out slowly, trying to settle his churning stomach.

All of this was his own fault. He'd been so smug, so self-righteous, trying to keep secrets from them. It was impossible to keep a secret under the Meld. From his suspicions about Charles Scott—his illness, the fact that he'd released Meld to fund his personal clone—to the emails he'd read about the army's involvement, it was all there in his head. The Meld just distorted all of that, mixed it up and spit it back to her as vague red flags.

And Louie, he thought. Why had he held on to that so hard?

Like it was some twisted trophy, as though it were the last remaining vestige of his own identity. He'd been a fool to think it mattered, arrogant to think he could keep it hidden. It wasn't the clone who'd destroyed his life. It wasn't Charles Scott, even. He'd done it himself.

And Parker was out there. Under their scrutiny. Unprotected. Alone.

Brent began knocking at the bathroom door. "Are you all right?"

Jeremiah turned on the shower full blast, hoping that would get rid of him, and said nothing. Brent eventually stopped knocking.

The mirror began to fog over, and Jeremiah wiped at it with the sleeve of his shirt and studied his own face in the swath he cleared. He looked old. He looked tired. He looked different than he had when this whole thing had started several months before, and not just physically. He wasn't the same man he saw on that monitor every day. He was separate. He was different. He was changed. And something in him welcomed it, accepted it, for better or worse.

For a few startling minutes Jeremiah seriously considered the idea of killing Charles Scott.

Never in his life had he been prone to violent thoughts, but they came easily to him in that moment. He imagined strangling the man with his bare hands, delighting in the agonized contortions of his face as he gasped for air and realized he was dying. The man was evil. He deserved it. And part of Jeremiah longed for that revenge, so much so, that his hands balled into tight fists as he considered it. But another part of him, a surprisingly logical part, understood that this wasn't the answer. He stared into his own eyes and, with considerable effort, reined in his anger. If he killed Scott, he went to jail. Or worse. And that would leave Parker alone with that clone, helpless under the scrutiny of these people. Jeremiah couldn't allow that, no matter how much he wanted Scott dead. This wasn't about what he wanted. This was about Parker. This was all about Parker.

He was going to get out of here. He was going to get to his son. And if they wouldn't let him out, he'd find a way to break out. If they wouldn't let him *trade* places with the clone, he would have to *take* the clone's place. He knew that. Looking at his reflection, he realized he would have to do something drastic. For once in his goddamn, miserable excuse of a life, he would have to take action. No more halfhearted attempts. He would make his own decisions, take control and create his own ending.

Jeremiah was going to kill his clone.

Somehow.

He lived quietly with that knowledge for several hours, growing into it, getting comfortable. He rolled the words over on his tongue, becoming familiar with their shape: *Kill. Murder. Dead.* He allowed himself ample opportunity to back out, to change his mind, but even when he looked for a reason not to do it, he couldn't find one. This was the only way. As the idea took root in him, it became more focused and seemed to give him purpose. He saw it like a shield, solid protection against anything else this experiment could throw at him.

They had largely left him alone after the news about Diana. Apparently, the abbreviated viewing with Charles Scott would count as the full four hours for the day. Even Brent had disappeared by the time Jeremiah had finally come out of the bathroom, and he used the solitude to formulate a plan. He wanted to research all the various ways a person could be murdered, to find the cleanest, most reliable method. But he knew they'd certainly be monitoring his internet use. Googling *murder* probably wasn't the best idea. Instead, he played *IF* on his own, morphing into his avatar, steeling himself for the task taking shape in his mind. He tried to think like Clyde, to push away every trace of sympathetic thought. Clyde wouldn't think twice about killing that clone. He probably would have done it a long time ago. Brent had left a final message on the sidebar of his screen: I'll be there tomorrow. Keep quiet. Stay calm. I'm going to help you.

Eventually, he realized, he'd have to tell Brent what he was planning to do. The only conceivable way out of here would be with his help. And Brent knew the truth. He could be convinced. Maybe.

It would prove difficult, he knew, to hide his state of mind from Natalie Young. But he had the motivation he needed to do it. He'd have to concentrate, lock his intentions away in some dark corner of his mind and just fake his way through their conversations.

While he waited to be escorted to her office for their scheduled session the next morning, he took a few deep breaths and practiced a calm, unreadable expression.

"I know you're hurting," Dr. Young said before he'd even settled onto the couch. "You've had some time alone with it now. How are you coping, Jeremiah?"

"Fine," he said. "I'll be all right. I'm more concerned about Parker right now."

"And you didn't want to watch when the clone broke the news."

"I didn't think I could stand it," he told her. "I didn't want to see."

"Why?"

"Because I wouldn't have been able to say anything. I should be the one to tell him his mother died. I don't want to listen to someone else do it. Don't you see that, Natalie? I'm his father. It's my job. They took that away from me."

"Okay," she said thoughtfully. "I suppose I can understand

that. Have you thought about how you would have handled that conversation? What you would say to Parker if you were there?"

"Why should I?" he asked, his voice rising slightly. "What good would it do? I'm not there and, evidently, no one is going to let me out."

"We can't let you out. You know that."

"That's funny." He smirked. "They didn't have a problem letting me out when it suited their own interests."

"That was different, Jeremiah. But you signed an agreement, remember."

"Yeah, I signed a fucking contract. I know. The almighty contract."

"You're halfway through this, Jeremiah. You need to see it out to the end. I know it isn't easy for you, with what's happened, but quitting now isn't going to change any of it. And these next months can give you some time. Some perspective."

"I don't need perspective," he said. "I need to go home and be with my son."

"These next six months here might be useful to you," she said. "It may help to prepare you for the life you'll be going back to. Things will be different now. You'll be raising your son on your own. You might take some cues from the clone. Watching how he handles things might make it easier for you."

"How he handles things? Really? You think that's what I'm worried about? I know how to handle things. I want to get out of here and handle them. I want to get back to my son. He needs me. He needs his father."

"This project needs you. There are billions of dollars in government funding at stake here, Jeremiah. Surely you can understand that this is worth a few more months of your time. It is worth finishing. And I'm here to help you. And you have Brent, too. You're not alone, you know."

Jeremiah cringed and balled his fists on his lap.

"You think I care about this experiment? I don't give a fuck about the money or the science." He stopped himself before he gave anything away out of anger. He took a deep breath and looked at the wall.

"Jeremiah," she said after a moment, "I think you and I should take the Meld again. I need a closer look."

He tried to conceal his alarm. Meld was the last thing he wanted right now. He couldn't hide anything from her under the Meld.

"I don't know," he tried, "I don't like that idea. I don't think I want to go through that right now. Besides, we just took it." He looked her square in the eyes. "Surely you can see that it's dangerous, Natalie."

She said nothing at first. But she didn't deny it. She couldn't.

"I know it can be frightening to face your own feelings," she said finally, "but it's important. I need a comparative baseline here. I think it's warranted, under the circumstances. You've been through a lot. We need to really see how you're doing, Jeremiah. This is all part of the program, and I believe it will help."

"Well, when would we take it exactly?" he floundered.

"Now."

He scrambled for a way out of it. There was absolutely no way he was taking that drug now. He couldn't risk her catching a glimpse of what he knew, of what he was planning.

"If it's all the same to you," he said in as calm a tone as he could muster, "I'd rather hold off on it for a while. I want to think about things privately for a few days, maybe a week. I need a chance to think about what's going on in my life, sort my thoughts out in my own head before I have to share them."

She was silent, but his request didn't seem to set off any noticeable alarms in her.

"No," she said at last. "We need to do this now. Let me just go and get the injections. I'll be right back."

She left him alone in her office. He knew from experience that it would take her only a few minutes to return with the necessary supplies. Before panic could fully set in and paralyze him, Jeremiah did something he'd never done in his life. He stuck a finger in his throat, as far back as he could manage, until his eyes watered and he gagged and he finally vomited all over the carpet, narrowly missing his own feet.

"Oh, my God," she muttered when she returned. She stopped in midstep and stared down at the mess on the floor, syringes in hand and a look of confusion and mild disgust in her eyes. "Are you ill, Jeremiah?"

"Maybe. With everything that's happened, I think it might just be nerves," he said. "God, I hope I don't have something contagious."

She looked at him coldly for a moment and then pursed her lips and shook her head.

"Perhaps it might be best if we waited, then. We'll do this at our next session in a few days. Maybe you should go lie down while I find someone who can clean up this mess."

He mopped at the sweat on his face and tried not to look as though he'd just dodged a bullet.

"Yeah, I think I will," he said.

# CHAPTER
# 32

Back in the apartment, Jeremiah paced the floors. He'd bought himself a few days, maybe, but he no longer had the luxury of meticulous plotting. He had to settle on a plan and make a move. It was time to act.

He'd pretty much decided on stabbing. It was quick, quiet and completely controllable. He'd seriously considered poisoning at first. A lot of murder mysteries he'd read used this as the least traceable method of killing someone, but he didn't need to worry about that. If he did it right, there wouldn't be any indication of a murder at all and there wouldn't be anything to trace. The clone would be gone, and he would take its place. Besides, poison was too unpredictable, and it might take too long. The idea of shooting the clone appealed to him on some level, too. It was violent, explosive, and the idea of blowing the thing away like that gave him a surge of satisfaction. He liked to imagine Charles Scott's reaction to that kind of violence against his creation. But gunshots would attract too much attention on his suburban street. Besides, Jeremiah had never used a gun in his life, never even held a gun, and how would he even get his hands on one? Stabbing was the way to go, he decided. A knife was a simple, instinctual weapon, and something about the proximity involved in stabbing was enticing to him. He liked the idea of using his own hands to do this. It seemed poetically appropriate.

His kitchen was equipped with all manner of knives to choose from. Evidently, he mused, no one had ever considered the possibility that the lab rat might think to arm himself. All he needed was a sure way out of here.

Brent was due for a viewing early that evening. Jeremiah was dreading what they'd have to watch. His heart sank at the thought of seeing Parker's face, of watching the clone fumble to comfort him. He wasn't sure he could have done a better job, but he wished more than anything else that he could have the chance to try. Parker certainly knew about his mother's death by now. The news had been broken to him and the first sting of shock subsided enough for it to feel real to him. Jeremiah imagined he was out of school for a few days while arrangements for the funeral were being made and details were taken care of. His double would be busy with that. He'd have that needed distraction. But Parker would have nothing but long stretches of time to wallow and grapple with the untamed emotions of an adolescent boy. The idea of it broke his heart.

When Brent walked in before 5:00 p.m. he carried two white-handled shopping bags that he placed on the counter in the kitchen.

"Dinner," he told Jeremiah. "I figured you haven't been eating. I smuggled in Chinese, and plenty of it. Screw the goddamn diet."

He emptied one bag of several steaming cartons, which, Jeremiah admitted, smelled good. He hadn't realized how hungry he was. From the other bag, Brent took a good-size bottle of whiskey.

"And dessert," he said.

"I'll have dessert first, in that case."

Brent nodded and got two small glasses from a cupboard, filled them each halfway and handed one to Jeremiah, who downed it and held his glass out for a refill.

They ate in relative silence in the living room, in front of the empty viewing wall. Soon enough it switched on automatically, and Jeremiah saw an image of his own kitchen table where, ironically, his clone and his son were eating directly from white Chinese food cartons. For a while, there was no discussion between them, either.

"When do I go back to school?" Parker asked at last.

The clone looked up from his food in surprise. "The wake is Friday, day after tomorrow," he said. "And then the funeral is Saturday. Maybe Monday if you want. You can take a few more days, though. I've spoken to the school. It won't be a problem."

Jeremiah winced. He understood at once his son's desire to get back to a routine, to trick the mind into thinking everything was normal again. Parker didn't understand that it wouldn't work that way. How could he?

"No. I'd rather go back," Parker told the clone. "And you didn't need to call the school. I'm not in kindergarten, you know."

"I thought it might help if you didn't have to worry about that," the clone said. "And besides, I didn't call the school. They called me. Someone there must have heard about the accident. It's been on the news."

"Who called from the school?"

"Your counselor. He seems to think you might need some help dealing with all of this. With your mother, I mean."

Parker stared at the clone without expression. Jeremiah couldn't tell if he was about to hit him or start crying.

"I don't need any help," he said finally. "Especially not from that idiot counselor. He's always on my back about my 'emotional landscape.' Every time someone gets a paper cut, he thinks it's a 'plea for help.' I'm not talking to that whack head about Mom. I hate him."

"Actually," the clone said, "he thinks it might be a good idea for you to see someone outside of school. You know Meld, right? That's the medicine my company makes. He thinks it could help for you to take that with a doctor, just to make sure you're handling everything. I think it might be a good idea. I told him I'd talk to you about it."

"What?" Jeremiah jumped up from his seat.

"Oh, yeah, that's a great idea," Parker said sarcastically. "That's the stuff everybody takes and then kills themselves. I don't think so. You might have fooled everyone else about that stuff when you took it on TV, but I don't want anyone giving it to me."

Jeremiah could have jumped through the wall and high-fived Parker. At least someone was thinking clearly. The clone didn't see it in exactly the same way.

"Well, those people weren't using it properly," he said. "It's perfectly safe when you take it with a doctor. And it really can help. Let's see how you feel in a few days. You have your suit all set for the wake?"

"You already asked me that. I already told you, I do."

"And your shoes? What shape are they in?"

"It's not a problem, Dad. My shoes are fine."

"We don't want any last-minute surprises. We've got to be on time, and we've got to look good."

"I don't see why it matters what I'm wearing."

"It's out of respect, Parker. It's customary. Wouldn't you want to make your mother proud?"

"It's not like she's going to care. She's dead. Remember?"

"Parker…" The clone looked at the boy with a mix of pity and shock. "Don't talk like that."

"Well, she is dead, Dad. She's gone. She's not going to give a single fuck what I'm wearing. She's not going to be proud of me. Ever again."

Jeremiah cringed and looked away from the screen. The kid was reaching out for some sort of comfort in the only way he knew how. If his clone saw that, too, he didn't act on it.

"Parker, watch your mouth," he said angrily. "There's no reason for that. How do you think your mother would react to that kind of language? Pull yourself together."

Parker pushed his food away and got up from his seat noisily.

"I'm gonna take Louie for his walk," he said. "Someone around here needs to keep things going."

The clone said nothing. Jeremiah wanted to reach right into the wall and pull Parker out of there, give him a hug, swear right along with him, tell him he understood exactly what he was feeling. Let him know it was okay to be angry, and it wouldn't always hurt like this.

Instead, he could only watch helplessly as his son leashed the dog and stormed out into the evening alone. His double sat motionless for a few minutes at the table and finally got up, leaving the cartons where they were, and poured himself a hefty measure of Jeremiah's good bourbon. He sat down, turned on the TV and stared into thin air until Parker came back an hour later. He stood and started to say something, but Parker didn't even stop to look at him. He just went upstairs and both Jeremiah and his clone heard his bedroom door slam closed. Soon afterward, the clone went upstairs himself. He hesitated outside Parker's door for a moment, and then went to his own bed, where Brent and Jeremiah watched him toss until the wall monitor switched off two hours later.

"There is no way my son is taking Meld," Jeremiah said when the wall went blank. "Absolutely no way in hell. I can't believe the clone is even thinking about it! He's not giving it to Parker."

"He probably doesn't know what else to do, Jeremiah. I mean, what would you have done?"

"Not that!" he said. "Maybe he could, oh, I don't know, actually *talk* to him or something? And you can put that down in your goddamn notes for tonight. I would absolutely not have acted the same way as that moron of a clone just did. I actually have a brain in my head."

Brent looked at Jeremiah with a warning in his eyes. Jeremiah didn't care. But what he had to say next, what he finally had to tell Brent, couldn't be said out loud. "Let's play the game, Brent," he said. "I feel like blowing shit up."

As soon as the battlefield flickered into view, Jeremiah began typing in the in-game chat.

I need to get out. I need to get to Parker.

How? You can't go back. There can't be two of you.

There won't be.

??

I'm going to take his place.

What?

I'm going to kill him. I will take his place.

!!

No other option. I have to get out.

How?

You can help.

Too risky.

You just get me out. I'll do the rest myself.

No.

You said you would help me. Parker is alone!

This is murder.

Diana was murdered. My mother. This is something else.

I can't help.

Why?

The project is still important.

The project is a lie.

??

You've been lied to. All of you.

??

Charles Scott is sick. He wants to clone himself. This? Practice run. I'm a guinea pig.

Sick?

ALS. Something. He's dying.

Brent took his headgear off and turned to look at Jeremiah with an expression of utter confusion.

"How do you know?" he asked aloud. "Are you sure about that?"

"I'm sure, Brent. The signs are subtle, but they are there." He nodded at Brent to put his headgear back on and then resumed their conversation in the game.

Pike is giving him stem cells. You know what that means.

The coffee cup, Brent typed, looking at Jeremiah with widened eyes.

You understand?

Brent paused for a long moment before typing his reply, as though the realization of it all needed time to sink in.

He's desperate.

So am I. I have to get out of here. You have to help me. I have to get out. Help me.

They'll kill me. They'll kill Mel. I can't help.

They won't know.

??

We fight. You let me win. I get out. No blame.

They'll know. No.

I'll knock you out. Steal your key card.

Won't work. You'd have to kill me.

Okay…?

Really?

No. Help me. How can we do it?

Or almost kill me. Stab me.

??

Not fatally. Enough to get me taken out of here.

I can't!

Only way it will work. I know how to make it safe but look real. You stab me. Steal my key card and, in the confusion, you'll have time.

No.

Trust me.

I can't. No!

You want out? You will. Trust me!

Okay.

Okay. How will you kill clone?

Stab him, too.

Too much blood?

MY blood. No one will question.

The body?

I bury it. Need it for insurance against Scott.

??

If they try anything I go public. They go to jail. Insurance.

When?

Has to be soon. Dr. Y wants to do Meld.

How soon?

A few days. We need a plan. Need to get to my house. How?

I'll get you there.

You can't. You'll be stabbed, remember?

Mel, then. I'll get it done.

No. Too risky. Don't involve her.

Only option. She won't know more than she has to. Trust me!

I do.

Start shooting. Game too calm. Looks bad. Talk tomorrow. I will have more.

For the next hour, they finished the bottle and battled. Jeremiah lost miserably, misfiring and screwing up his aim at every shot. He didn't have it in him to shoot his friend at the moment—even in a virtual way.

# CHAPTER
# 33

DAYS 164-165

Two days later, at eleven in the morning, Brent and Jeremiah sat solemnly on the couch together and watched as the clone shook hands and awkwardly embraced a steady line of mourners at Diana's wake. Jeremiah only caught a few brief glimpses of his son the whole day. Each time, Parker sat sullen and sunken in his dark gray suit and scuffed black shoes. He hardly looked at anyone and only spoke when absolutely necessary. Even then, he said as few words as possible. As far as Jeremiah could tell, Parker didn't shed a single tear. It was hard to watch. He found himself wondering whether Parker had even spoken to the clone since the last time they'd watched them. Despite how it made him feel, he hoped he had. A kid shouldn't have to go through this alone. No one should.

The day after that, they viewed her funeral and Jeremiah wept openly in front of Brent. His sobs, though, were punctuated with the sting of determined anger, as he steeled himself for what he was about to do. It wasn't going to end this way, he told himself. The anger was the only thing that kept him in one piece.

In the kitchen afterward, Brent took two beers from the

fridge and looked at Jeremiah with an unreadable expression on his face. Jeremiah thought he'd rattled him with the crying.

"I'm fine, Brent. Don't worry."

"It's not that."

"What, then?"

"I wish I'd listened to you sooner. About all of this, I mean."

Jeremiah got a few handfuls of ice from the freezer. He wanted to alleviate some of Brent's guilt, but he had to do it under the din of the blender. This wasn't for anyone else to hear.

"I don't know that it would have done any good. I got the note to the clone. It didn't help. It's not your fault, Brent."

"It's not your fault, either," he said. "You know that, right?"

Jeremiah didn't answer.

"There was nothing you could have done," Brent told him. "You couldn't control what you were thinking under the Meld."

"I shouldn't have been thinking about the dog," he said. "I shouldn't have tried to keep that a secret. It was pride, some ridiculous sense of power. It was stupid of me. And Diana paid the price for that. This is on me. This is all on me."

"You didn't know," he said. "There was no way you could have known."

"I did try." Jeremiah was fighting back more tears. "I tried to warn her, I tried to tell the clone to protect her."

"I know you did."

"I wanted to save her. I thought I could. I thought I could do something."

"You're doing something now," Brent said. "Just get through this and it will be over. I'm going to help you. You're not in this alone anymore."

# CHAPTER
# 34

DAY 166

They were scheduled to watch the clone at home on Sunday afternoon. Jeremiah didn't want to see it. A day after he'd buried Diana, after all the planning and details and gatherings were behind him, the clone would be forced, finally, to deal with the reality he was left with. Jeremiah didn't want to witness that.

There is so much ritual involved after a death, he thought. People come together for the wake, stiff handshakes and teary hugs giving way, after a while, to more boisterous reminiscing and a few stifled bouts of uncomfortable laughter right in front of the casket. Then the funeral, all solemn, righteous and wooden, filled with quiet, pious reflection, until everyone goes off to have a few drinks afterward. All of it, of course, as a means to some sort of closure.

But there's never any closure. Not really. All the ritual is nothing more than a way to stave off the inevitable finality of the long goodbye. It's easy to stand for hours at a wake, surrounded by people who've come to help ease the burden. You feel sheltered. Getting out of bed on the morning of a funeral isn't hard, precisely because it's necessary. What's hard, Jeremiah understood, is the day after. And the next day, and the next, when there doesn't seem to be any reason to get out of bed at all, and there isn't anyone around anymore to tell you they're "terribly sorry for your loss."

He didn't want to have to watch and be made to feel all of that along with his double, along with his son. He didn't want to get swallowed up in that kind of sorrow. He couldn't risk losing the jagged edge of his anger if he wanted to carry out his plan. He had to stay angry. He had to stay sharp.

So, when Brent arrived about an hour before they were set to watch, he told him to call Charles Scott and ask for a reprieve.

"Tell him I need a few days," he said. "Tell him whatever you want, but I don't want to see it. It's going to turn me all around. I can't."

"I don't know, Jeremiah. I doubt he'd go for it."

"He must have seen your report from yesterday, right? You must have put down that I cried. Just tell him you think it'll do me some good. Tell him I just need some time. He's got to understand that, doesn't he? Just call him. This is important, Brent. I need to stay focused. Watching this isn't going to help."

Brent shook his head and took out his cell phone. "I'll try," he said.

Fifteen minutes later, Scott walked into the living room, a look of feigned concern on his face.

"Mr. Adams," he said, and he nodded his greeting to Brent. "Mr. Higgins tells me you don't want to watch your scheduled viewing today. This is rather unorthodox."

Jeremiah tried to swallow his anger before he spoke.

"Look, Dr. Scott, I just need a little time, a few days without watching. After yesterday, it's just hard, is all. You gave me a day after my mother died. This is the same thing. I just need a little time."

Scott tightened his lips into a failed attempt at a smile and sat down on the edge of a chair across from Jeremiah.

"The viewings of the wake and the funeral were not monitored," he said. "That can be considered your time off in this case. You are required to watch for four hours every day, Mr. Adams. The continuity is crucial to this experiment. I can understand that you're in mourning, and I'm sorry for that, but we can't just take more time off because you don't feel up to it. I've allowed you too much already with the shortened viewing we saw together the other day. I've made that concession. Now it's time we get back to work."

Inwardly, Jeremiah was reveling in a fantasy that ended with Charles Scott in a bloody heap on the floor. It almost made him smile.

"With all due respect, Dr. Scott, everyone is entitled to bereavement time. Isn't that a law or something? ViMed is giving the clone time off, aren't they? You don't see him being called into the office. I'm only asking for the same thing. I mean, come on, he's just going to be sitting around moping at home. I don't see how my watching that will be of any benefit to the project. What difference does it make? I already know what he's going to do. I can tell you right now that I would do exactly the same thing."

"Dr. Young feels the continuity is important for your own well-being," he said.

Jeremiah wanted to spit. No one other than Brent gave two shits about his well-being.

"I think I know something about that, too," he told Scott, masking the venom in his tone, "and I'm telling you it'll do me good to take some time for myself. Just a couple of days."

Scott pursed his lips and looked at Brent, who just shrugged his shoulders. "Maybe he's right," he said. "You read my report. It could help."

Scott said nothing and, in that moment, with Brent looking directly at him, Scott's eyes became momentarily unfocused. For an instant his whole face looked unnatural, went slack in a way, as though he'd completely lost control of it. Jeremiah looked at Brent and saw a stunned surprise in his eyes. He'd seen it, too.

Scott smoothed his hair in a useless effort to hide what had happened. He hesitated and then looked back to Jeremiah with mild exasperation in his eyes.

"All right, Mr. Adams. A few days. That's all. And I will have to insist that Mr. Higgins remain here during that time."

"I don't need a babysitter," Jeremiah said for good measure. Inwardly he saw the benefit of Brent having to stay.

"You need to be monitored. I'm afraid that point is not open to debate." He turned back to Brent. "Mr. Higgins, you will clear your schedule."

"Of course. I'll just go home to pick up a few things and be back within the hour."

"One hour," Scott told him. "No more." He stood to leave and Jeremiah stood up, as well.

"Thank you, Dr. Scott," he said, the words almost sticking in his throat, and with considerable effort he put out his hand to the murderous worm of a man. "I appreciate this."

Scott shook his hand and took his leave without another word. Brent exhaled deeply and stared at Jeremiah.

"He is sick," he said.

"I told you."

"And you are good," Brent added. "You just got two days off and all the time we need to see this through."

# CHAPTER
# 35

In less than an hour, Brent returned with a suitcase, a bag of burgers and two more bottles of whiskey. Jeremiah tore at the food, realizing as soon as he smelled it that he was ravenous again, despite everything. He'd been pacing the apartment since Brent had gone, a nervous ball of energy. He'd logged more time on that treadmill in the past forty-eight hours than he'd typically done in a week. Something in his stomach, he thought, might help him calm down.

"I don't know about the whiskey," he said. "We need our wits about us."

"I have a distinct feeling I am going to need it before this night is over. In case you've forgotten."

"Oh, yeah. Right."

"Besides," Brent said, "we have ample time now. Might as well have one good bender while we can."

"I drink like a fish now, thanks to you."

"You're welcome."

"You're a terrible influence on me. I'm too old for this."

"At least you're not a stiff old asshole anymore, like your clone.

I think I've been a very good influence on you. I've turned you into someone who's actually cool."

"Just like *My Fair Lady*. In reverse."

"Well, my name *is* Higgins, after all."

"So it is." Jeremiah smiled. "What do we do now, Mr. Higgins?"

For the next few hours, they played *IF* at full volume on the wall monitor and got slowly but sufficiently sauced, going through an entire bottle in record time. Jeremiah hadn't drunk like this since his college days and he began to regret doing it on top of the three greasy burgers he'd wolfed down earlier. It wasn't long before he was leaning back on the couch alternating between a beer and bottled water, ruing the headache he was certain to have in the morning. He took off his headset and put down his controller, letting Brent tackle the battlefield on his own for a while. The game had started to make his head spin. He closed his eyes and listened to the muffled explosions coming from Brent's headset. As usual, it was on too loud.

He had to admit, though, it felt good to let loose. They hadn't typed a single word in the in-game chat and had not—even for a minute—discussed the actual issue at hand. It was an understood, shared decision to avoid it entirely. Jeremiah welcomed the distraction, and, for his part, Brent obviously realized just how much a distraction was needed. He was a good friend, Jeremiah thought, and the irony of that gnawed at him. He hadn't had a real friend in a long time. He hadn't made the effort. But Brent had stepped up to help him when he should have refused and run away. Jeremiah wouldn't have blamed him. He was a kid. He had a lot to lose if something went wrong. He had everything to lose. And there was plenty that could go wrong. It was a big risk. And in return? Jeremiah would be *literally* stabbing him in the back. In twenty-four hours, he'd have to take a knife to the man and very likely never see him again.

"You know, Brent," he said, loud enough to cut through the din of the game, "I have a lot to thank you for."

"Yeah. I am pretty amazing."

"I mean it. Most people wouldn't do something like this."

"Most people don't find themselves in this kind of situation. Special circumstances."

"You still think I'm doing the right thing?"

Brent took his headset off and turned off the controller in his hand. The sudden silence in the room was almost startling. "Do we need to make another smoothie for this conversation?" he asked.

"No," Jeremiah said. "I just want to make sure I said thank you."

"Don't worry about me. Don't go all sappy on me."

"I'm not. I won't."

"Everything's going to work out, Jeremiah. Don't worry. And now that we know the truth, I don't see that we have much choice."

Jeremiah nodded. Brent was right. But as the moment got closer, and with the alcohol clouding his mind, he found his thoughts drifting in unexpected directions.

"Do you think the clone has a soul?" he asked after a moment.

"A soul? I think you're asking the wrong guy. I don't buy in to any of that stuff. But I guess *he* thinks he has a soul."

"Is that enough, do you suppose? Just to *think* you have a soul?"

"I think it has to be enough," Brent said. "For most people that's all you get."

"But does that make us human?"

"Maybe it does," Brent said.

"I don't know," Jeremiah said, leaning back and closing his eyes. "It can't be that simple. That clone's not actually human. Just thinking he is doesn't make it true. He's just a copy."

"Yes," Brent said, "but he doesn't know that. He thinks he's you. So, whatever you feel, that's what he feels, too. And all I'm saying is that, when you come right down to it, it's the same thing. If he thinks he's human, maybe he is."

"Well," Jeremiah said after some reflection, "he can believe anything he likes. Doesn't make it true."

"So," Brent asked after a moment, "are you asking because you're worried about your *own* immortal soul?"

Jeremiah pondered this for a moment. He remembered a time when he was very young, six or seven at most, and his mother found him in the backyard running hose water into an anthill and laughing as he did it. He'd felt a certain giddiness in watching that hole flood and all the ants come scurrying out, most of them only to drown where they stood. His mother had never liked the ants in the yard, so, at first, he couldn't understand why she'd been so angry with him. But she turned the water off, yanked him by the arm and dragged him back into the house. He remembered she'd had real tears in her eyes while she scolded him harshly for what he had done, spouting off about how those ants were only going about the business of being ants and didn't deserve such cruel treatment.

"You're a *good* boy, Jeremiah," she'd told him. It felt more like a plea than a character assessment. "You're a *good* boy."

He wondered now what kind of a mark it would leave on his soul once he killed the clone. What, exactly, was it he'd be killing? After all, he considered, wasn't this thing just going about his business of being Jeremiah? He didn't know he was a clone. It wasn't his fault. In fact, he thought, the clone might be the only one completely blameless in all of this. He tried to push those ideas out of his mind. He couldn't afford to get stuck. He had to stay focused.

"No," he said finally, but without conviction. "I have no concerns about my own immortal soul."

"Let's drink to that," Brent said.

"I'm done. I'd like to be able to see straight. You drink like this out there?"

"Nah, Mel's not really much of a partyer. If I want a bender, I go out with the boys. You know how it is."

"No. I don't know. I don't have anything remotely resembling 'the boys' at home."

"No?"

"Not for a long time, anyway. You ever see my clone going out with any boys after work?"

"Well, you're keeping up with me just fine, for an old fart."

"Yeah, well, I wasn't always this way, you know. I logged some epic nights, back in the day."

He recounted for Brent a story from the summer he'd graduated high school.

"A group of us had depleted our beers but we weren't ready to call it a night," he said. "We were all pretty obviously underage but there was one guy who sometimes had some luck with a fake ID. Unfortunately, he was, at the moment, completely passed out on the couch. Absolutely comatose."

"What'd you do?"

"Well, the first thing we did was grab a green magic marker and we drew a handlebar mustache on his face," Jeremiah said. "Then we woke him up and sent him to the package store to buy a six-pack."

Brent laughed so hard he nearly fell off the couch.

"We watched the whole thing through the window," Jeremiah said, laughing so hard at the memory he could barely get the words out. "And when he came out, he couldn't understand why the clerk was so quick to tell him to fuck off. It was hilarious!"

"And you never see those guys anymore?" Brent asked.

"Not in years. We didn't keep in touch. I haven't even thought about them, to tell you the truth. That's pathetic, isn't it?"

"It kind of is."

"I don't think I have one single friend," Jeremiah said after a moment. "Not one actual fucking real friend."

"That's really pathetic," Brent told him.

"Well, maybe I do have one friend."

"If you say it's me," Brent said, "I think I might cry or something."

"No, not you. Louie. That dog is my best friend."

Brent laughed. "I hate to break it to you, pal, but that dog hates you."

"No," Jeremiah told him. "That dog loves me." He wanted to reiterate that it was the clone Louie hated, not him. But somehow he had the wits, even in his drunken head, to stop talking about it in front of the camera.

"You know, Jeremiah," Brent said finally, "I *am* your friend."

Jeremiah opened his eyes to gauge Brent's expression, but he was still leaning back with his eyes closed, so he couldn't tell if Brent was being serious.

"Yeah, well, I was kind of forced on you. You didn't have much choice in the matter. If you met me before, I *would* have been that uptight asshole we watch on the monitor every day. I would have been the clone. You'd have hated me. God, he makes *me* hate me."

"You're probably right," Brent said. "Sometimes I almost forget you're the same person. What the hell happened to make you like that?"

"I don't know," Jeremiah said. "Maybe I take after my father."

"Was he an uptight asshole, too?"

"Beats me," Jeremiah told him. "He took off when I was a kid. Up and left. Walked out on us and never came back. He was probably an asshole, though. He was probably king of the assholes."

"That's harsh," Brent said, his voice laced with a barely concealed yawn.

"Damn right it's harsh. I mean, what kind of father does that?"

"Maybe he had his reasons," Brent said. "I mean, who knows, maybe your mother was cheating on him."

"Fuck you."

"Sorry. That came out wrong. I just mean, well, with Diana and all. When you found out she was cheating on you, did it make you want to leave?"

"I thought about it, sure, but I'd never actually do it."

"If you think about it, you did actually do it. You never talked to her about it. You never faced it. You left. You walked out. It just took you a little longer. And you did it in a way that would leave you blameless."

The truth in the words stung.

Jeremiah got himself up off the couch to pee. He continued the discussion, turning his head and bellowing out the open bathroom door.

"I don't know what happened to me. When did I become such a wimp? I wasn't always like this, you know. Things are going to change. You hear me?" He waited, but Brent said nothing.

"No wonder I didn't have any friends," he said as he stumbled back into the room. "Don't ever let yourself get weak, Brent. Don't ever forget that you have to face things like a man. Stand up and just face it. Problems don't just go away on their own. You have to do something."

He was slightly annoyed to see Brent was completely passed out on the couch and had missed out on all of his sage advice. He considered for one minute trying to locate a green magic marker. Instead, he just went into the bedroom and slept, fully clothed, but soundly, for the first time in what felt like months.

# CHAPTER

# 36

### DAYS 167-168

The next morning, while Brent still snored on the living room couch, Jeremiah went into the bathroom and made a ritual of shaving off the scruff of the beard he'd been working on again, first carefully trimming and then pulling the razor over it twice. He wanted to look as much his clone's double as possible when he finally confronted him. It would add a certain drama to the moment, he thought, and he'd certainly earned a dramatic moment.

Once they were both moving, fed and sufficiently caffeinated, he and Brent spent the whole of Monday afternoon and much of the evening in careful, deliberate preparation for the task ahead. Over breakfast, with the otherwise empty blender pulverizing the rest of the ice from the freezer, Brent asked Jeremiah to repeat the cell phone number he was to call when the deed had been done. Jeremiah told him it would have been far easier to just program the number into the burner phone he'd secured for him.

"It's too risky. If anyone finds a cell with my number in it, what's that going to look like?"

He went over and over the maze-like path from the apartment to the exit doors.

"Right down the hallway, out one set of double doors and into the parking lot," Jeremiah said. "I know."

"Two sets of doors, Jeremiah. The second set of doors gets you outside."

After lunch, Brent paced the floors of the apartment, his brow knitted in worried concentration, and muttered to himself under his breath. It was a far cry from the carefree, whiskey-fueled confidence of the night before.

"If this is going to work," he told Jeremiah. "It has to be exact, down to detail. Nothing gets left to chance. We need to go over it again. What time do we start arguing?"

"At two-thirty in the goddamn morning. And I'm going to need some sleep before that. Or a few pots of coffee."

"And where do you aim the knife?"

"Right shoulder. Away from the neck."

"Jesus, Jeremiah! *Left* shoulder! I'm right-handed!"

"Right," Jeremiah said. "I mean, correct. Your left shoulder. Got it."

"Let's play *IF.*"

Jeremiah sighed and looked at the ceiling. "Can't we just keep the blender going?"

"I'd rather play the game," he insisted, and had his headset on before Jeremiah even sat down on the couch.

"This is ridiculous," Jeremiah told him.

"We can practice our moves," Brent insisted, handing over a headset and glaring at him.

Jeremiah sat down on the couch and put his gear on. "Fine," he acquiesced. "We'll practice."

If Scott *were* watching, he'd see only two men nursing massive hangovers and playing an inexplicably long video game. They were meticulous about keeping their eyes to the screen so as not to give anything away with their faces.

You know what to do when Mel takes you to your house? Brent typed.

I wait in bushes until clone opens garage door in the morning. About 7 when door opens, I go in. Hit kill switch to bring door down. Kill clone. Call you.

Camera!

Sorry. Hit camera above my right shoulder. Then door. Got it.

That's important!

I know!

Hit ViMed camera!

I know! Okay! Shut up already!

Okay. You ready for it?

Sort of...except stabbing you. That's tough.

Don't worry. That's why we're in here. Let's practice.

Fucking stupid, Jeremiah typed. It wasn't the practicing he was worried about.

Humor me. Let's go.

For an hour or more, their avatars battled in hand-to-hand combat amid the scream of AI grenades and mortar blasts. Jeremiah was expert, by now, at manipulating Clyde's movements

and deftly had him overpowering Brent's man with high ka-
rate kicks and undercut punches that nearly knocked his head
off. He couldn't, of course, add any such ninja-style flourishes
in real life, but it felt cathartic to do it in-game. He could wield
the virtual knife pretty well, too, after a while, unsheathing it
from a halter at his side and twirling it, baton-style, in one fluid
move. But the first few times he stabbed it, he killed Brent's avatar, once actually severing the entire arm, and the simulation
would pause and start all over again.

Oops, he typed. Sorry!

Another time, Brent's guy kicked Clyde's feet out from under
him and ended up with the knife at Clyde's throat.

Stop that, Jeremiah typed. That won't happen.

I'm going to fight back.

Eventually, he figured out that he needed to overpower
Brent's avatar first with a few well-placed punches, get him
to the ground, pin him there and go for one quick jab in the
shoulder. No fancy moves, just a series of careful actions. They
practiced it over and over until Brent seemed satisfied and finally took off his headset.

"There!" Jeremiah said triumphantly, adrenaline still pumping. "Satisfied? Had enough yet? I can beat you every time."

"You say that like it's going to be easy or something," Brent
said. "Don't get cocky about this, Jeremiah. Remember, you're
not Clyde. You are a middle-aged marketing manager from Mas-
sachusetts. You're not a warrior. It won't be that easy."

By early evening, Jeremiah found himself lying on the bed,
unable to sleep. His mind was racing, Brent's pacing in the
kitchen sounded like line-dancing, and he was seriously doubt-
ing whether he'd be able to take a knife to his only friend once
the time came. Stabbing him a hundred times over in virtual

reality was one thing. In the real world, there was blood and guilt. Brent had reassured him that he'd "take care of it." Jeremiah had no idea what that meant.

He closed his eyes and tried to clear his mind. He practiced the breathing exercises that he'd used so long ago, when he was first connected to the clone through the Meld. It had helped him then to stave off the terror of being sucked into the dark emptiness of his double's blank mind. It didn't work for him now. The moment he began to relax, new questions cropped up to trouble him: Where would he bury the body of the clone? What if the clone screamed and a neighbor came over at the wrong moment? What would happen once he took over his life again? How was he supposed to just seamlessly ease back into a life he hadn't actually been living for six months? And how was he going to handle Parker? What if *Parker* noticed something was different?

After a few futile hours, Jeremiah got out of bed and went into the kitchen to find Brent putting two low-fat frozen dinners in the oven. His attempt to get a beer from the fridge was met with quick disapproval.

"Don't start drinking now, Jeremiah. We still have a few hours to go. You need your wits."

"Look who's suddenly found his inner teetotaler? You're right, though," he said, and took a bottled water instead.

They ate in relative silence. There was little left to say. The only thing they had to do was wait.

Sometime after 1:00 a.m. they each took a single shot of whiskey and sat down on the couch, waiting for it to take effect. They had to force an argument, and if it was going to be enough for Jeremiah to take a knife to Brent, it had to be real.

"So," Jeremiah began tentatively. "*You're* an asshole."

Brent rolled his eyes. "Sticks and stones," he said, and leaned back on the couch. "You'll have to do better than that."

"Too much pressure," Jeremiah told him. "I can't argue on command."

"Let's just talk, then. You know, you never really told me how you got involved in any of this. What made you agree to have yourself cloned?"

"I don't know," Jeremiah said thoughtfully. "A lot of things, I guess. I needed a change. Something different. I think I was stuck, you know? Nothing was exciting to me anymore. I wasn't going anywhere. Too many problems. Too many headaches. Then there was the $10 million, of course. That didn't hurt."

"So, they bought you right out of your life?"

"Yeah. For $10 million, they did."

"And look where it's got you," Brent said with a smile that looked more like a sneer. "Your job is on the line, your kid is a punk and your wife is gone. Your life is in ruins. You're worse off now than you ever were. And now, after all this, now you won't even get the money. Kind of sucks, doesn't it? Everything was for nothing."

"None of that was my fault," he said, real defensiveness creeping into his voice. "I didn't do any of that. It just happened."

"It just happened? That's a lame excuse. Of course it's your fault. You're the one who walked out on your life, left it in the hands of some copy, a facsimile. This is all on you." Brent reached for the bottle, poured himself another shot and threw it back.

"That's not fair. The other day you were all, *It's not your fault.* Besides, what happened to changing the future, all your spouting off about bettering mankind, saving the world? What happened to the power of your precious science? That's why you signed on, isn't it? Isn't that what you're doing here?"

"Yeah, well, I didn't walk out on my life and my family. Nobody bought me. And I actually *am* a scientist, remember? This is actually my job."

"Fuck you, Brent."

"You ever wonder why they picked you for this?" he asked, unrelenting. Jeremiah felt the back of his neck grow hot. "You ever ask yourself that?"

"Because they knew I could handle myself, I suppose. Because I'm levelheaded. Careful. Probably not a concept you would understand."

"Because you're easy," Brent said, moving forward on the couch to make his point. "Because you're a pushover and you let the whole world just walk all over you. Because you don't have a backbone. You have no balls. You're a wimp."

Jeremiah stood up and glared down at him.

"Look at yourself!" Brent said, not threatened in the slightest bit. "Look at your life. I've seen it. I've watched that clone day in and day out for six months. And that's you up there. You know that, right? You just do what you're told, what's expected. You just go along with it. The people you work with don't give a crap about you. Your son basically ignores you. Your wife could barely look you in the eyes. And you just pretend it's all hunky-dory. You're weak. You're hollow."

"Shut the fuck up! You don't know me. You don't know me at all!"

"I guess that's what comes of having no father," Brent pressed on, not missing a beat. "Then again, that's probably why he left in the first place. Maybe he saw the same thing in you all those years ago. Maybe that's what drove him away. He figured it was hopeless and just took off."

Jeremiah's whole body clenched, and he grabbed Brent by the shirt collar and pulled him off the couch to his feet. Brent laughed. From this distance, Jeremiah could see his eyes were glassy and smelled the whiskey on his breath.

"And then you did the same exact thing," Brent pushed. "You just took off. Walked out on your family the first chance you got. Don't you see that? Don't you get it? You can't escape your own destiny. You were doomed from the start to repeat the same mistakes of your father. It's a never-ending cycle and you can't stop it. Your son will end up the same way: Weak. Pathetic. Hollow."

Jeremiah couldn't contain himself another minute. Before he even had time to think about his own actions, he pulled back his right arm, holding Brent's shirt with his left, and punched him hard and square in the face. Brent's head reeled to the left and he fell backward, hitting the back of his head on the arm of the couch, blood already coming out his nose, his mouth. And before he could get his balance back, Jeremiah hit him again, pulled him forward away from the couch and then pushed him back hard. He fell on the floor.

Brent shook his head and slowly got on his feet. He took two or three unsteady steps toward Jeremiah, looked him right in the eye, almost nose to nose with him now, and showed blood-stained teeth behind a deliberate, joyless smile.

"Diana probably crashed her car on purpose," he snarled. "Just to be rid of you."

Jeremiah stood still for another instant, his breath coming out in slow, shallow spurts. He pushed Brent back hard against the wall and burst past him into the kitchen. He grabbed a knife from the counter—only half recollecting in that moment that this had all been carefully planned—and then he went back and jabbed the thing three inches in and out of Brent's left shoulder. Somewhere in the back of his mind he wondered how he'd remembered to put the knife into Brent in exactly the way they had rehearsed. Brent went silent. His face went slack and his eyes went wide and finally closed. Something in his expression seemed to relax and he fell slightly forward, right onto Jeremiah, and uttered a single word into his ear before falling limply to the floor.

"Sorry."

It was enough to snap Jeremiah back into his senses. He looked down in dismay at his friend, who was slumped now at his feet, but still awake and perceptibly smiling, despite his injury.

Jeremiah bent down to fish Brent's key card out of his pocket, taking time to let his hand linger on Brent's shoulder for just an instant. Then he slipped the bloody knife into his sock, opened the door and ran. Without thinking, he somehow made it down the hallway, out the doors, through the dark woods and into the next empty parking lot. He was standing under a broken streetlight just as a young woman pulled up in a silver Volkswagen Beetle.

# CHAPTER
# 37

DAY 168

Jeremiah was crouched behind the tangle of an overgrown rho-
dodendron bush at the side of his house, the knees of his pants
already soaked through from the damp ground. A chill in the
air kept him from sweating, but the tension in his muscles and
his frantic heartbeat were harder to control. He fingered the
smoothness of the knife handle between his thumb and fingers
and tried to slow his shallow breathing with a sort of meditation. After all the trouble to get himself here, all the sleepless
nights he'd spent imagining this very moment, all he wanted
now was to have it over with. The sun had been up for more
than an hour, but it offered little warmth. He'd been hiding
here since 5:00 a.m. and his body shook with the simple desire
to stand up and stretch. He shifted his weight from one knee to
the other and rolled his shoulders and neck to get a little relief.
The last thing he wanted was to cramp up at the crucial moment. He'd only have seconds to get himself under that garage
door if he wanted to do this right. He needed to take the clone
by surprise. The shock factor was crucial. He figured he probably could have stood up for a second or two—after all, any of

his neighbors would only see Jeremiah in his own side yard—but he didn't risk it.

From this angle, he had a clear view of his bedroom window. He'd seen the light come on some twenty minutes ago. Once it went off again, he'd know the clone was on his way down to the kitchen, and then out to his car in the garage. At least that used to be the routine. It couldn't have changed much. He'd only been thankful he hadn't seen the car parked in the driveway, where Diana used to park. That would have changed everything.

A minute later he heard the once-familiar squeak of the kitchen door opening and, before he could prepare himself for it, he saw Parker barrel down the steps to make the school bus. He hadn't even considered that he might catch a glimpse of his son. He'd seen Parker on the monitor fifty times or more, but this was different. This was harder. He was right there, almost close enough to touch. As he passed the bush, Jeremiah held his breath and resisted the urge to jump up and call out to him, to grab him by the arm and hold him there. He noticed, with some aspect of resentment, that Parker had grown a couple inches taller since he'd been gone, and there was a certain breadth to his shoulders that hadn't been there before. He swallowed the wave of regret that rose up in his throat and watched his son turn the corner and disappear from view. Then he breathed again. He'd see Parker soon enough, he thought, if everything went right. He turned his attention back to the matter at hand, just in time to see the light go out in the bedroom window. He swallowed hard and tightened his grip on the knife.

Minutes passed as he waited for the first whirring of the garage door opener, his signal to spring. Every muscle in his body tensed, and he worried that his own heartbeat might be enough to obscure the tiny sound he was straining to hear. *This is almost over,* he told himself. *You can do this.*

He hadn't anticipated the sudden fear he felt in his gut. Every time he'd thought about this moment, calculating the plan down to the last second, imagining his every action, it had been fueled by anger and a fierce sense of righteousness. It had also, he admitted, been tempered by the likelihood of absolute impossibility. Somewhere inside him, even as he had clung to the idea of killing his clone, he never fully believed he'd actually get here. And here he was. He closed his eyes and tried to push his anger back to the surface, hoping it would be enough to crush the tiny web of doubt that inched out in all directions now and threatened his resolve. *You can do this*, he told himself again. *You have to do this.*

The instant Jeremiah heard the small mechanical sound he'd been waiting for, it was as though a switch had been pulled in his brain. His movements were quick and unhindered by thought. He darted out from behind the bush, dropped and rolled the few feet over the driveway and across the threshold of the garage. While the door was still in its upward motion, he sprang to his feet and hit the kill switch hard with his fist, the overhead light glinting off the six-inch blade in his hand. As the door came down behind him, he saw the clone jump and turn toward him in alarm, recognition not yet registering on his face. To his right, above his shoulder, Jeremiah found the small, innocuous gleam of the camera lens embedded in the concrete wall, exactly where Brent told him it would be. He took the blunt end of the knife handle and smashed it in with one quick jab. No one was watching now.

Jeremiah said nothing, but inched forward a little. After months of watching the clone across the impossible distance of the cameras, they were now separated by the length of a single car. The figure before him was no longer that towering image projected across an entire living room wall. He was exactly, down to the last molecule, evenly matched with Jeremiah. Looking at him now, though, he seemed even smaller. Jeremiah stared into familiar eyes and the rage he felt beginning to boil back up in him made him feel almost giddy.

The clone backed up against the door that led to the kitchen, his hand grappling behind his back for the knob. Jeremiah saw the clone's eyes widen in a mix of terror and desperate confusion as the shock of recognition settled there. He blinked hard and his mouth began to move as if to ask a question, make a plea, but no sound came out. He pressed his back hard against the door, fumbling, unable to turn away, until his knees gave out and he began to crumple to the ground.

Jeremiah moved slowly toward him, blade first, and stared him down, unblinking. A slow smile spread across his face when he saw the fear tighten its grip over the clone, pinning him to the floor. That fear seemed to feed something in Jeremiah. The more the clone cowered, the more intense Jeremiah's own fury burned.

"Who are you?" the clone whimpered. "What do you want?"

Jeremiah stopped a mere two feet from him and almost laughed.

"Who am I? Don't you know?" He took a heady delight in taunting him. "Here, take a closer look."

He spanned the space between them in a few steps and knelt down at eye level, the knife so close to the clone's face the steel began to fog with his breath.

"Now do I look familiar?" Jeremiah sneered. "Recognize me?"

"How can…" The clone arched his back and craned his neck away from the blade, his eyes wild with confusion. "Please," he moaned, "please, I have a son!"

The words hit Jeremiah like a slap in the face. He pushed the flat of the knife under the clone's chin, so tight against his neck that he could feel the pulsing of his veins right through the handle, as though the weapon had become some sort of conduit connecting them.

"No!" Jeremiah spat the word out like venom. "No, *I* have a son! *You* have nothing!"

He watched in fascination as the clone's face twisted in terror, the blood visibly draining from his cheeks, the eyes darting frantically, looking for escape.

"Please," the clone barely managed, "please."

It would have been so easy to kill him then. It should have been so easy. One little push into that pulsing vein on the neck. One little slice.

But the sight of that face and the terrified eyes rattled Jeremiah, just for an instant. Just long enough to make him hesitate. Long enough to register the sudden, startling sensation of looking into a mirror. Jeremiah pulled the blade just slightly away from the clone's neck as the realization spilled over him like defeat. He couldn't do it. He wouldn't kill this thing. His hand began to tremble, his breath heavy and hard in the clone's sniveling face. He hated him. He wanted to do it. He wanted him gone. But something in him held back. This must be, he thought, what people go through in the seconds leading up to suicide. He'd always considered it a cowardly act. In that instant, though, he understood the steely resolve it must take.

Just a few months ago, he thought, this might have been him. This *was* him. This cowering, frightened mess of a man was *him*. And Jeremiah knew that. A few months ago, he would have reacted in exactly the same way, pleading for the sake of Parker, terrified at the thought of leaving him—everything relating to the fate of his son. And it was this, Jeremiah supposed, that finally snapped his will. Simple recognition. That, and empathy. A thing he never figured on, but there it was. He had been willing to kill to get Parker back. The clone was begging to stay with him. For all his faults and weakness, for all his mistakes, this clone loved the boy every bit as fiercely as Jeremiah did. It connected them, he thought; like it or not, more than any other of a million similarities, this was what made them the same.

But even as his murderous intent ebbed away, the anger and loathing still gripped his gut. Except that, for the first time, it felt more like what it actually was—*self*-loathing. It was something sharp, focused inward. It felt like regret. It was a hatred for every time he had ever ignored his own best interest, for every time he'd allowed himself to be swayed off course by propriety and appearance and someone else's ideas. He was disgusted by what he saw in front of him. And Brent's words came flooding back to him in that moment, words that had been uttered in a forced performance, but now rang achingly true in his ears. For the first time, perhaps, with his eyes wide open, he accepted this as himself. Standing there now, he had the sensation of choking on every single desire he'd ever forced himself to swallow. Everything he'd wasted was stuck in the back of his throat. Jeremiah suddenly found himself wanting not to *kill* the clone, but to *change* him. He wanted to warn him.

He grabbed his double by the necktie and pushed his head back down into the unforgiving cement floor with a thud. The clone let out a grunt at the impact and closed his eyes in agony.

Jeremiah got to his feet, stood over him, fuming.

"Stand up!" he shouted, and punctuated the command with his boot in the clone's shoulder. "Stand up and fight! You used to fight! What the hell happened to you?"

He kicked him again and then a third time until the clone struggled to get his hands underneath him and push himself up to a sitting position. He sat there for a moment, dazed, and then began to scoot away backward. Jeremiah kicked him again in the side and the clone grunted and fell back down in a heap, his face buried in his arms.

"Stop sniveling!" Jeremiah shouted. "Do something! Why the

hell do you just lie there and take it? You let the whole goddamn world trample on you—kick the shit out of you—until there's nothing left! Look at me! Hit me! Fight back!"

The clone kept his face buried and Jeremiah heard muffled sounds as though he were actually sobbing on the floor in front of him.

"Look at me!" Jeremiah commanded again. The clone turned his head slowly and looked up at him, red-faced and wheezing, trying wordlessly to beg for his life, attempting to make sense of what he was seeing. But there was no making sense of this.

"I don't know who you are," the clone moaned. "I don't know who you are."

Jeremiah knelt down on one knee, the knife now at his side, and looked him hard in the eye.

"You know," he told him. "You know exactly who I am. You just won't see it. You'll never see it because you're too afraid to really look at anything. You're too weak. Or maybe you're just crazy. Am I really here, Jeremiah? Or have you completely lost your mind? Maybe they'll put you away, just like Uncle Charlie!"

The clone paused and Jeremiah knew he'd struck a chord. Just like him, his double must have been plagued by the constant, menacing threat of some hereditary lunacy.

"Who *are* you?" the clone asked again, more frantic now, almost defiant. Hearing it satisfied something deep inside Jeremiah.

"That's the question that will haunt you for the rest of your life," he said. "That's what you'll ask yourself over and over again, every night as you lie there in the dark and try to wrap your feeble little mind around this moment. This moment! Right here! This is the moment that will define you—take over the rest of your life. Is this real? Did it really happen? Until all that's left is that question!"

The clone just looked up at him, his expression completely blank and vacant, which only served to push Jeremiah on.

"But this isn't the question that matters. This is meaningless. This is nothing! You need to pay attention to the right things— the questions that actually mean something. Did you read my note?" Jeremiah barked. "About Diana? Did you do what I said? Did you try to protect her? She's dead because you didn't pay attention! She's dead because you're too arrogant to believe anything that doesn't fit in your stupid little box of a mind. That actually fucking *means something*!"

The clone just stared up at him stupefied, his expression tortured. Something in his face made Jeremiah certain he had read the note. Jeremiah snickered and shifted as if to leave, convinced he wouldn't get through to him, couldn't make him understand. How could he see if he wouldn't open his eyes? But before he even stood up, something made him stop. He needed to do something, he decided, leave him with something to think about, something real and unforgettable to make him understand. He needed something to make him believe. Jeremiah shifted his weight again and brought one knee hard down onto the clone's wrist, pinning his left hand flat against the garage floor. Without pausing, without a flicker of consideration, he raised the knife high above his head, machete-like, and brought the full force of it down onto the clone's index finger—cutting through skin and flesh and halfway into the bone. The scream was high-pitched and prolonged and the clone's whole body writhed and then buckled as the color drained from his face. From somewhere inside, Jeremiah could hear Louie barking frantically, scratching at the door. Jeremiah had to hack three more times, using the blade as an ax, before the finger was fully off the hand. Then he picked it up and put the warm, slippery thing into his pocket.

He stood up, breathing heavily after the exertion, and watched the blood pool onto the floor and pick up little swirls of incandescent dust. The clone pulled his mangled hand in tight to his body, curled up and rocked back and forth in a fetal position. Jeremiah could tell, more from his motion than from any sound he emitted, that he was sobbing. He patted his pocket and felt the warmth of the clone's blood on his own hand.

"I want you to remember," he said flatly. His voice sounded quiet and cold, terrible, even to his own ears. He repeated the words, softer this time, almost pleading. "I want you to remember."

He dropped the bloody knife and left it where it fell, right beside the clone. *Have fun explaining that*, he thought, knowing any fingerprints or DNA would point irrefutably to self-mutilation. He knew the clone wouldn't report anything to the authorities. What would he say when they asked for a description of the assailant?

He turned around, almost calmly, and walked through the side door of the garage, up the length of the brick walk and around to the back of the house. He kept walking until he reached the woods and found the familiar path that he had walked so many times with Louie. Once he was deep enough in the trees, he took the cell phone from his back pocket and, with shaky hands, dialed the number Brent had made him memorize.

"Change of plans," he said when Brent answered on the first ring. "Meet me in the woods behind my street. Park at the top, go in behind the first house and just keep walking. Stick to the path. I'll find you."

# CHAPTER
# 38

Jeremiah leaned hard against an oak tree and slid down to a sitting position. The morning air was still cold, but he didn't feel it. What had he done? How had he managed to blow his one chance? And, more importantly, what was he going to do now? It was almost eight o'clock. By now Scott and the others knew he was missing. Certainly, they were already searching for him, and were likely starting to suspect Brent, too. And the clone was still alive.

He looked around him. There was little chance anyone would find him here. He could count on one hand the number of times he'd ever run into another person in these woods. But he couldn't calm his nerves. If anyone—one of his neighbors— should happen to come by, it would be a problem. He couldn't afford to be seen. He needed to wait for Brent and come up with another plan. But he didn't have another plan. He hadn't thought he'd need one.

He sat still for a few minutes, trying to focus on the sounds around him. It was silent except for a slight breeze rustling the leaves and the sporadic trill of chickadees in the trees. After a few minutes, he stood up and began walking along the path toward the top of the hill, looking for Brent.

He heard him before he caught sight of him, stumbling through the undergrowth and fallen leaves, obviously out of his element. His left shoulder was hanging limply in a sling and he held his arm gingerly against his chest as he tramped up the path.

"What the hell happened? What do you mean there was a change of plans?" Brent called breathlessly as he approached. "Is he dead?"

"No."

"Fuck. What?"

"I couldn't do it," Jeremiah admitted.

"And what are we supposed to do now?" Brent was frantic, gripping the top of his head with his good hand, turning circles as though the trees themselves might offer some solution. "Scott has called me four times since they discharged me from the hospital! He keeps asking me to walk him through that fight again."

"Does he know?"

"No, I don't think so. But it won't take him long to figure it out once he realizes I'm not at home convalescing like I'm supposed to be. Jesus! They're probably at my house as we speak!"

"Is Mel there?"

"No, thank God. She's already at work, none the wiser. She doesn't even know about this yet." He looked down at his own injured arm. "Jeremiah, we are royally screwed. We need to get you back to the lab and just take our chances. Maybe they'll go easy on us if we just get back there. There's nothing else we can do. The clone isn't dead. Maybe they'll just look at this as a drunken rampage or something."

"I can't, Brent. I can't do that. Look, I didn't kill him, but I do have this." He took the bloody finger from his pocket, cold now, and stiffened into a slight curl, so that any way he held it, it looked like it was pointing at Jeremiah. Brent turned his head violently at the sight of it and then turned back to Jeremiah with a shocked expression.

"What the hell? You cut off his finger? His fucking finger? What the hell?"

"I don't know, I wasn't thinking. I just did it."

"Put it away. Jesus!"

Jeremiah slipped the thing back into his pocket and ran a hand through his hair, thinking.

"Maybe we can use it," he said. "Maybe, between this and those emails, maybe it will be enough."

"Use it how? What are you going to do with a finger? Wave it around? What good is it? You were supposed to have a body! You were supposed to kill the clone, Jeremiah! A finger isn't going to do us any good. It isn't enough to prove anything!"

"It might be," he said. "We need to think. It might be enough. I mean, I have a finger in my pocket with my *own* DNA and ten more of them on my own hands. We can use this. We can. We just have to figure out how."

"You go back to them with that and they're just going to lock you up and take the finger. And that's if you're lucky. It isn't going to work," Brent said.

"I can bring it to someone," Jeremiah said. "I can use it to show someone what they've done. We can prove it with this. I think this can work. At least it's something."

Brent's phone rang, the sound startling them both more than it should have. Brent looked at the number.

"Scott again," he said. "We've got to do something fast, Jeremiah. We can't stay in the woods forever."

"I know a guy on the *New York Times*," he said. "Walt Thompson—a science editor. I know this guy—he'll go public with it. He is convinced that corporate America is to blame for everything from global warming to peanut allergies. Believe me, he'll jump at the chance. He fucking hates Meld."

"Yeah, and how do you propose we get to this science editor of yours?" Brent asked as his phone rang yet again. "They're looking for us. We can't risk it. They have too much at stake here. Who knows how far they'll go to bring you back."

"We'll mail it to him, then. Pack it up on ice, with a note explaining the whole thing. He'll know what to do."

"Yeah, he'll know exactly what to do when some lunatic conspiracy nut cuts off his own finger and sends it to him in the goddamn US mail—because that's what it's going to look like, you know. He's going to think it's *your* finger. He's going to think you're crazy and that you're stalking him. Then he'll have you arrested. It won't work."

"Wait a minute," Jeremiah said with a sinking feeling in his gut. "That's it, Brent—that's exactly what we have to do."

"What?"

"I have to send him my own finger. We have to have both of them. Mine *and* the clone's. Same finger from the same hand. We put them together, that'll prove it. That's what we need."

"Are you insane? You're not going to cut off your own finger! Besides, your friend won't have any reason to think you didn't just cut off a finger from each hand."

"No, this will work," Jeremiah told him. "If we cut off the same finger—he ought to be able to tell. The fingerprints will match up. As far as I know, the prints are the same for me and the clone. It will be two of the *same* finger. Last time I checked, it's not very common for someone to have *two* left index fingers! This will work. It's our best chance."

"You're crazy. I'm not going to sit here and watch you cut off your finger."

"You're not going to watch—you're going to have to do it."

"Absolutely not," Brent said. "No fucking way I'm doing that!"

"Brent, I can't do it myself. I won't be able to do it. I know my limits."

Brent's phone rang again. "I have to take this," he said. "It's Mel."

Jeremiah listened as Brent's voice quickly became agitated. "What do you mean Charles Scott is coming to see you? At work? He's coming to the museum?"

Jeremiah gestured for him to put the call on speaker.

"No, to my studio," she said.

"Mel, where are you? Are you there now?"

"Yeah. Like I told you, I've been here all night, since I dropped that weird old guy off like you asked me to. And where the hell are you?" she asked. "Your boss, Dr. Scott, was asking all kinds of questions."

"What questions? What did you tell him?"

"Like when I saw you last, whether you'd left town. You told me you were working through the next two days. Why wouldn't your boss know that? What's going on, Brent? Where have you been for the past two days?"

"Mel, what did you say to him?"

"Nothing! I told him I haven't talked to you since Sunday. That the last time I saw you was when you asked me to help out with that friend of yours. And he was asking all about that, too. What's going on, Brent? But he made it sound like there was some kind of problem or something. He made it sound like he thought you were at home. Where the hell are you?"

"I can't tell you, Mel. Everything's fine, but I can't tell you."

"Are you in some kind of trouble?"

"No, nothing like that, there's no trouble," he said. "But, Mel, you have to listen to me. You have to listen carefully. Get out of your studio. Right now. Don't meet with Charles Scott. You can't meet with him. Just trust me on this. Don't go anywhere near him."

"What do you mean? What's going on?"

"Mel," Brent pleaded, "just listen to me. Get out of there. And don't go back to the museum. Don't go home, either! Look, just go somewhere else, go to the mall or something. Take a drive somewhere. Go to your sister's in Rhode Island. Just don't let him find you."

"What the hell is going on? What are you talking about? I have to go back to work. I can't just take off. You need to tell me what this is about. You're scaring me, Brent."

"There's nothing to worry about, Mel. I just need you to do this, okay? I need you to stay away from Charles Scott. I'll explain it all, but not now."

"Brent..."

"And turn your phone off, Mel. Turn it off and keep it off, you hear me?"

"What if you need to reach me?"

"Call me tomorrow," he said. "By tomorrow this will all be over. One way or another."

Brent hung up on her before she could say anything else and looked at Jeremiah with real desperation in his eyes.

"There's no other way, Brent," Jeremiah told him. "We have to do this. We have to do this now."

"I can't cut off your finger!"

"I didn't think I could stab you in the shoulder, either, but I did it. You have to."

"This is going to hurt a hell of a lot more than that did."

A little more than an hour later, they were in Brent's car, parked in the service area behind a strip mall, hidden between two trailer trucks. Brent had gone to three different stores to buy several packages of dry ice pellets, two large bath towels, four nips of vodka, an insulated lunch box, a large assortment of bandages, gauze and first aid supplies and a small ax.

Fifteen minutes after that, Jeremiah had fainted outright in the front seat and Brent was vomiting behind one of the trucks.

# CHAPTER
## 39

By the time Jeremiah came to, Brent, his face a ghastly, grayish white, was visibly shaking as he attempted to bandage Jeremiah's hand.

"Jesus, there's a lot of blood," he said, tearing at a strip of gauze with his teeth. "We need to get you to a hospital. This was a stupid idea."

There was a blood-soaked towel in Jeremiah's lap and another on the floor by his feet. He didn't even remember seeing the blood. He figured he must have blacked out the instant the ax went down. His only recollection was of a sudden white-hot pain that seemed to engulf his entire body all at once.

"No, it's fine," Jeremiah managed, his head spinning. "Just use more of the gauze. Get it good and tight. It'll be fine. God, Brent, you look worse than I do."

"Yeah, well, I've never cut off someone's finger before. And you should look in a mirror. You're not exactly going to win any beauty contests, either."

Jeremiah had downed two of the vodka nips before the amputation and opened a third one now with his teeth, hoping it would help to dull the fiery pain in his hand. He gave the last bottle to Brent, who drank it down without hesitation.

"Where is it?" he asked. "What did you do with my finger?"

"It's in the lunch box with the dry ice."

Jeremiah took the clone's finger out of his pocket and handed it to Brent, who, at the sight of it, instantly looked like he was going to get sick again. He took it gingerly and turned his head away as he slipped it quickly into the lunch box with its twin. Jeremiah closed his eyes and put his head against the cool of the window.

"I need to get back to ViMed," he said. "I need to talk to Scott."

"You need to rest," Brent told him. "I think you can afford to take a few minutes."

"You'll need to package that lunch box, address it. Have it ready to go. Once I'm in there, give it one hour. If you don't hear from me by then, you mail the package, get Mel and get out of town. Understand?"

"Yeah, I understand. But let's try to avoid that, okay? I have enough explaining to do already without telling Mel we have to leave town and go into hiding."

An hour later Brent pulled the car over as close to the ViMed lab as he dared and turned off the engine. He didn't want to risk being spotted by the security cameras, so Jeremiah would walk the last quarter mile or so.

"You ready for this?" Brent asked. "Are you okay?"

"I'm as okay as I'm going to be," he said, looking down at his bandaged hand. Brent had wrapped it in so much gauze it looked like he was wearing a boxing glove, which felt appropriate for what he was about to do. Even then, blood was just beginning to seep through on one side. It hurt like hell, but at least it was a dull ache now and had stopped throbbing.

He got out of the car and looked at the building he'd been

trapped in for so long. He was struck by the strangeness of looking at it from the outside. He'd been so focused on escaping the place, and here he was about to walk right back in.

He patted his pocket and felt for the phone, which contained photographic evidence of the package that was now in Brent's care. It had to be enough, he thought. This had to work. If it didn't, he didn't know what would happen. Would they simply put him back in the lab and carry on with the experiment? Doubtful. Once they realized he couldn't be trusted, they'd likely do a lot worse than that, he thought. He turned back to Brent, who had started the car but hadn't pulled away yet.

"Don't go too far," he called. "Wait for my call."

"One hour."

Jeremiah took a few uneasy steps in the direction of the lab, his head spinning from blood loss, adrenaline or both, and readied himself for what he had to do. If this was going to work, he knew he had to go in strong. He could show no doubt, no hesitation. He needed to face Charles Scott with confidence and in full control.

About twenty paces before he reached the building, Charles Scott came striding swiftly out the front door, flanked by two serious-looking armed security guards. Scott said nothing as the guards took Jeremiah, one by each arm, and hurried him through the entrance, down the hallway, through the two locked security doors Jeremiah had come through the previous night, past three uninterested secretaries and directly into Scott's office. When Scott nodded at the guards, they let him go with a shove and swiftly left the room, shutting the door behind them. Scott stood silently, taking Jeremiah in with a venomous glare.

"Mr. Adams," he said finally, "do you have any idea the resources we've wasted trying to locate you?"

"Do you have any idea," Jeremiah asked, "how much I do not care?"

"What happened to your hand?" Scott said, glancing at the bandage. Jeremiah said nothing, but smiled slightly. "Sit down, Mr. Adams."

Jeremiah knew he should have remained standing, asserting his confidence, but he was still light-headed. Better to sit than to faint, he decided, and took a seat in front of Scott's desk. Scott remained standing.

"Would you care to tell me where you've been for the past several hours?"

"I have a distinct feeling you already know the answer to that," Jeremiah said.

"I am assuming you went home. Did he see you?"

Jeremiah just smiled again, enjoying the anxious look creeping over Scott's face. He'd play this out for a while, he decided, make him squirm for a few minutes.

"Mr. Adams," Scott said, leaning into Jeremiah's face. "I need you to tell me, did the clone see you?"

"He certainly did. Saw me. Talked to me. Fell in a heap at my feet. I don't think he'll soon forget it. I don't think he likes me."

"What did you do?" Scott asked harshly. "What did you tell him?"

Jeremiah went quiet again and Scott straightened up and walked slowly around the desk, stopping and leaning down into Jeremiah with a steady glare.

"All right, Mr. Adams," he hissed, straining to keep the rising anger out of his voice. "Let me tell you what *we* know. We know that Brent Higgins is responsible for your escape last night. There is no way you could have managed it without help, and he was the only person there. And rest assured, when we find him, he will answer for it. Dearly. We know you were at your house this morning at 7:43. We know that because that is the precise moment our camera in the garage suddenly went dark. We also know that the clone did not report to his office at ViMed this morning. And *that* is because he drove himself to the hospital with a serious injury to his left hand. We saw that from our camera in his car. Can you illuminate how the clone came to be so gravely injured? And why you seem to have similarly injured the *same* hand?"

Jeremiah glanced down at his own bandaged hand with a smirk. "Coincidence?" he said.

"I will ask you again, Mr. Adams," Scott said, "what did you do?"

"I did nothing to the clone that I wouldn't have done to myself, I assure you."

"This is not a game," Scott said. "I don't know what you think you're doing, Mr. Adams, but let me make this perfectly clear. Whatever this is, you will not get away with it. Whatever little game you think you're playing, it won't work. We have far too much at stake here to allow you to get in our way."

"Oh, I am quite aware of what's at stake for you, Dr. Scott." Jeremiah waited a moment before elaborating. He wanted to savor this. "You're not feeling too well, are you? What did the doctors tell you—ALS, is it? That's my guess."

"What are you talking about?"

"That's a nasty disease," Jeremiah said. "Slow, but thorough. What did they give you? A year? Maybe two? How long before you can't speak anymore? Or breathe on your own? How long before it starts to eat away at your precious mind?"

Some of the color drained out of Scott's face, which was answer enough for Jeremiah that all of his suspicions had been correct.

"But it doesn't really matter, does it? I mean, presumably, you've got a clean medical scan and a Meld implant of your mind. Everything nice and tidy to put into a clone of your own."

Scott remained silent, but Jeremiah could see his face tense up.

"And the Meld," Jeremiah added. "I know a few people who

would be very interested to learn why it was rushed onto the market, where all the profit was funneled. Now *that* would make a hell of a headline, don't you think?"

"You can't prove any of it," Scott said defiantly. "No one would believe you. It's your word against the corporation's."

"Oh, I don't know about that. You think I'm stupid enough to come here without proof?"

"You've got no proof," Scott said, concern now creeping into his features. "There is no proof."

"Why don't I just show you," Jeremiah said. He took the phone out of his pocket, opened up the photos of the package and its contents and handed it over. Scott took it and sat down again behind his desk.

"What is this?" he asked. "You severed the clone's fingers?"

"Oh, just one of his fingers. The other one is mine." Jeremiah watched as Scott, looking back at the image on the phone, began to comprehend exactly what he was looking at. His eyes went wide and he pursed his lips. He looked back up at Jeremiah with something approaching apprehension.

"And what, pray tell, are you planning to do with these grisly items, Mr. Adams?"

"Look at the next photo," he said, "and you'll see where I plan to send them. And I think Walt Thompson will be very interested in the implications. Have you read his stuff, Dr. Scott? He's not exactly a champion of big business. And he really has it in for Meld and ViMed."

"This won't prove a thing," Scott said. "It's just two fingers in a box. It's nothing but the ravings of a madman."

"Yes, it is just two fingers in a box. Two left index fingers with the same prints and identical DNA. I think all the information is there. I almost didn't see the need to include a note. Those fingers, excuse the pun, will point him in the right direction. He's smart. It won't take him long to figure it out."

Scott stood up and came around the desk again, red-faced and serious. He grabbed Jeremiah by the wrist and began to pull at the bandage on his hand. Jeremiah pulled away and carefully unraveled the bandage himself, displaying his mangled hand, and watched as realization came over Scott's face. As he wrapped his hand back up, wincing with the pain, Scott glared at him and fell silent. He waited for Jeremiah to finish with his hand.

"Have you sent the package?" he asked.

"No. But it will be sent on my behalf in about forty minutes unless I make a phone call to stop it. It's your choice."

"You are stepping on some pretty powerful toes here," he said. "I'm not sure you understand the magnitude of this project— who is involved in this."

"Oh, I understand more than you think I do," Jeremiah said. "I'm well aware of the military involvement. What was his name? General McGavin, right? Waffles, Dr. Scott?"

Scott's face settled into an intense grimace.

"Be careful, Mr. Adams," he said. "You don't know what you're getting into."

"Well, why don't you tell me," Jeremiah said. "Go ahead. We've got time. What do they want from all of this? What sort of plans do they have for human clones?"

"I don't know what their plans are," Scott said. "And I don't care. They put up the money for this, for all of it. I'm not being paid to ask questions."

"Well, then, Dr. Scott. You are a pathetic, selfish bastard, aren't you? It ought to bother you. You ought to be asking questions. Do you think anyone is interested in saving the world with this technology?"

"What is it that you want?"

"I want my life back," he said. "What's left of it. I want my son. And I want your word that Brent Higgins will not be harmed in any way. He walks. Oh, and while you're at it, I'll take my money, too—the whole ten million."

"Your money? You've broken the contract, Mr. Adams. We don't owe you anything."

"Yeah? Take me to court."

Scott sat down again in his leather chair and drummed his fingers on the desk as though waiting for something.

"So, you expect to just walk back into your life? And what would you have us do with your clone, Mr. Adams?" he asked. "Do you expect that we'll simply destroy it?"

"That isn't my problem," he said coolly. "Do whatever it was you planned to do with him before. I'm just pushing up your deadline. And speaking of deadlines, tick-tock, Dr. Scott."

"I need to make some phone calls," he said. "Wait here."

Scott opened a hardly visible paneled door in the wall behind his desk and walked into an ancillary room, closing it firmly behind him. He was gone nearly ten minutes, during which Jeremiah checked his watch at about ten-second intervals. He could hear nothing behind the wall, and by the time Scott came back out there was less than fifteen minutes left before Brent would mail the package to the *New York Times*.

"Well, Dr. Scott?" he asked. "What's it going to be? Do I make that phone call or do you start packing for federal prison?"

"My partners have suggested a compromise."

"No compromise," he said firmly. "I want all of my demands met. I want my son. You have just over ten minutes."

"You'll have your son—and your money, Mr. Adams. But we would like the opportunity to salvage at least part of this experiment. Surely you can appreciate that. There is too much at stake. We need to continue it in some capacity."

"You mean *you* need to continue it. What's your idea?"

"You can have your son. We'll get him out for you. But we'd like the chance to clone your son and place that clone with your

own. That way we would at least be able to continue our monitoring, and perhaps even gain additional insight. Keep the funding coming in. Everybody wins."

"There is no fucking way you are cloning my son! Are you
out of your mind? No."

"Hear me out," Scott said quickly, "just hear me out." There
was a distinct hint of desperation in his voice. "We would get
your son and establish new identities for both of you. There are
high-level officials from the CIA and FBI who have a stake in
this, Mr. Adams. It could be easily arranged. Totally fresh start—
anywhere you wanted—with enough money to do whatever you
like for the rest of your life. All we ask in return is the chance
to see this thing through to some conclusion. And Higgins—
he'll walk away with a $1 million bonus in hand. You have my
word on that."

Jeremiah glanced at his watch. He had about seven minutes
left to make the decision or the package would be sent and everything would be decided for him. If he did nothing, the truth
would come out and Scott and the rest of them would certainly
go to prison. On some level, he thought, that would be satisfying. It's what they deserved. But he'd be implicated, too, for his
role in the thing. He'd likely get off on some sort of whistle-
blower protection, maybe even vindicated as a hero, but that's
not what he wanted. And for once in his life he was going to get
what he wanted. He wasn't going to let anyone decide for him.
And he wanted the money. Without that, the last six months—
everything he'd been through—would have been essentially
for nothing. He felt like he'd more than earned the money. He
deserved at least that much. More importantly, though, and the
thing that tugged at him now more than anything else, was
Brent. If that package was sent, they both knew Brent would
be implicated right along with everyone else. He'd go to prison,
too. Jeremiah wanted to avoid that. In his mind, Brent was in-

nocent, lured into this thing by a guileless belief in the power of good science, and he had been willing to risk everything to help a friend. He couldn't let Brent go down with the rest of them. He wouldn't be responsible for that.

"How would this work exactly?"

"We have people in place that could gather the necessary DNA from your son as quickly as this afternoon. We could expedite the cloning process and then make the switch. You'd have your son back within seventy-two hours."

"I don't want him harmed. I don't want him snatched out of his bed in the middle of the night by some thug on your payroll."

"Nothing of the sort, Mr. Adams, I assure you. We could arrange it so you could simply collect him from his school tomorrow morning. You would bring him back here yourself, where he'll undergo the Meld with his clone. We'll fit you both with new identities. He would need to be told something, Mr. Adams, but we can leave that up to you."

"And his clone?"

"We would simply return his clone back to the school a few hours later, in time to go home that same afternoon and be none the wiser. We can arrange everything, just as we did with your clone. The transition would be seamless. And you and your son would then be free to go."

Jeremiah considered the idea for another moment. He would have liked more time to think it through, understand the finer points and implications, but he realized he didn't have that luxury. The clock was ticking.

"Make the call, Mr. Adams." Scott was holding out the cell phone Jeremiah had given to him. He took it and dialed Brent's number.

Brent picked up on the first ring.

"Hold off," Jeremiah said. "We're all set."

# CHAPTER
# 40

DAYS 171-172

The locking mechanism on Jeremiah's door had been taken offline. The door stood partially open now, out to the empty hallway. He could come and go as he pleased, but there was nowhere he wanted to go. For several hours, he had been getting the apartment ready for Parker's arrival. He'd had the kitchen stocked with frozen pizzas, chips and soda, and had someone procure a new gaming console that was supposed to be impossible to get at the moment. He also made a point of ripping the camera out of Mel's painting on the wall, smirking directly into it as he did. No one was going to be watching him anymore, he thought, and they certainly weren't going to be watching Parker. He didn't know why he was making all these preparations. Parker would only be here for one night. But keeping busy took his mind off the problem of what the hell he was going to tell him.

Brent was grinning ear to ear when he stuck his head around the door late that afternoon.

"I didn't expect to see you back here so soon," Jeremiah said.

"I wanted to collect my paycheck in person," he said. "I wanted to feel it in my hands. I'm a goddamn millionaire! Besides, I have the package here. I wanted to put it in your hands. I'm glad to get rid of it, tell you the truth. It gives me the creeps."

Jeremiah took the lunch box from Brent and looked around the apartment for a place to stash it. He supposed he ought to hide it somewhere, just in case Scott had any last-minute ideas to double-cross him. Finally, he settled on the freezer, scooping a gallon of Rocky Road into the sink and stuffing the whole thing inside the sticky container. He shoved it into the back, behind three pizzas and a frozen lasagna, and closed the door.

"You're not worried they'll find it in there?" Brent asked. "It's kind of a lame hiding place for something like this."

"Scott's convinced I stashed it somewhere else. I showed him a photo of a storage place. He doesn't need to know I got that photo off the web."

"Smooth, Jeremiah."

"Brent," he said, "I'm going to need your phone. I need that evidence if we're going to stop them."

Brent hesitated for a moment and then handed it over. "Why can't I just forward the photo to your phone?"

"Scott took my phone as collateral already."

"I can save it to the cloud."

"No," Jeremiah told him. "I want control of this. I don't want it out there. It's risky."

"Fine," Brent said. "I'm glad to be rid of that, too. I've been sleeping with it under my pillow. What are you going to do with it?"

"I'll get it to Walt Thompson. He'll know what it means. He'll figure it out."

"A lot of people are going to burn for this."

"Which is why you need to leave, Brent. You and Mel need to get away. I'll do what I can to make sure you're protected, but once this hits the fan, it'll be out of my hands."

"I'm getting away. Believe me."

"What are you going to do with the money?"

"I'll tell you one thing—Mel and I are going to have one hell of a honeymoon!"

"Good," Jeremiah said, "that's a good idea."

"So, I suppose this is goodbye."

"I suppose it is," Jeremiah said. "And, as I understand it, I won't be able to contact you again. They're setting us up with entirely new lives, new names, everything. Very cloak and dagger."

"What are you going to do?"

"I have no idea. Write, maybe, or travel. After I take care of the evidence, I just want to go somewhere with Parker and be a dad. That's all I really care about right now. That's all I want to do."

"I won't even know your name," Brent said. "I wouldn't be able to find you if I tried."

"Maybe I can get word to you somehow. Maybe, if they ever finally release the update of that damn game, you can look for Clyde."

"Clyde is a badass. So are you. How's the hand, by the way?"

Jeremiah shrugged casually and looked at his bandage. Dr. Pike had seen to the wound—made a cleaner cut, this time under heavy anesthesia, sutured it and put him on powerful antibiotics to guard against infection. Brent's boxing glove bandage had been replaced with something slightly more manageable.

"Sit down, Brent. Let's have a drink—one for the road." He got two beers from the fridge and they sat down in the kitchen. "I don't know how to say thank you," he said.

"You don't have to."

"If it weren't for you, I'd be stuck here another six months. God knows what would have happened to Parker, the way things were going. I might have gone back to nothing. You gave me a second chance. And you risked everything to do it."

"You gave yourself a second chance," he said. "I just opened the door for you."

"Look, Brent, I don't mean to go all fatherly on you or anything, but can I offer you some advice before I leave?"

"Sure, Pops."

"I'm serious. This is important. You've got to learn something from all of this."

"I have," Brent said. "If you think you might have to cut off someone's finger, don't eat a breakfast burrito in the morning."

"As useful as that may be, I hope you learned something from my mistakes. I hope you realize that it doesn't have to be that way for you. Don't ever become the kind of asshole I was."

"C'mon, Jeremiah," he started.

"I mean it. All of that stuff you said when we were arguing. That's all true. I know that. And somewhere, you do, too. Or else you wouldn't have been able to come up with it so quickly. You're not that good of an actor, pal." Jeremiah took a breath. "If you ever start to doubt yourself, promise me you'll take a good hard look at your life and turn it around before it's too late. You get to decide who you are and who you're going to be. Don't let anyone else decide for you."

Brent raised his beer bottle to Jeremiah's and smiled.

"Parker's a lucky kid," he said.

"Maybe. But I've got a lot to make up for. That starts today."

Natalie Young knocked on the frame of the open door a half hour later and came into Jeremiah's rooms without an invitation.

"I wanted to see how you're coping," she said. "Make sure you're okay with all of this, you know, before you leave."

Jeremiah snickered and shook his head. "How thoughtful of you," he said.

She came farther into the room and took a seat on the edge

of the couch, an unspoken bidding for him to join her, which he ignored.

She sighed heavily and looked at his face for a long moment before she spoke.

"Jeremiah. I thought you and I should have some closure. I thought I might be able to help you prepare for what comes next."

He almost laughed.

"What comes next? Really, Natalie? What comes next is none of your damn business. I don't need any help from you. You've done quite enough already, I'd say."

She pursed her lips and said nothing.

"You know what, though?" He moved closer to her but remained standing, enjoying the feeling of looking down on her. "I'm glad you're here. I think maybe we *could* use some closure. But not the kind you're thinking of. There are things you need to hear."

"Go ahead," she said. "I'm listening."

"Do you even realize there's blood on your hands?"

"Jeremiah…"

"My mother? My wife? Their deaths are on you, Natalie! You, and that godforsaken Meld."

He saw her swallow hard and avert her gaze for a moment, but he moved himself back into her line of vision and continued. She would face this.

"The things you thought you saw when we took that drug, that wasn't the truth, was it? They never knew anything. They never knew."

"I know that now," she said. "Meld isn't perfect. Perceptions can be imprecise. But I had to report what I thought I saw. Even unfocused, vague implications had to be reported." She looked at him with a pleading expression that sat uncomfortably on her face. "You have to believe me, Jeremiah. I had no idea they would… I didn't know what they'd do."

He was quiet for a moment and turned away from her. "Meld should be banned," he said, and then turned back to her to get his next point across. "That drug is dangerous. Maybe people were never meant to peer into each other's minds and make assumptions. Maybe we were never meant to see into our *own* minds that way, to see that kind of ugliness. Meld crosses a line we should never have crossed. It's dangerous, Natalie. You need to know that."

"I know I saw something," she said, flustered. "I'm sure I saw something when we took the drug. Someone knew something. I'm certain of it."

"Maybe you did," he said. "But it wasn't them. They were innocent."

The tears that wet her cheeks surprised him for a moment but didn't soften him.

"If I could take it back," she said, "I would. I wish I could make it right somehow. All I can do is tell you I'm sorry. I know that's not enough."

"No," he told her. "It's not."

He left her there and went into the kitchen without another word. A minute later he heard her get up and walk out the door.

Charles Scott came in before nine the next morning, exactly on schedule, with a suit and tie on a hanger. "I thought it best," he said, "if your son sees you dressed for work as he would expect. Best not to make this any more confusing for him than it already is."

Jeremiah had hardly slept the night before and had already been up for hours. He had no idea what he was going to say to Parker once he saw him. How could he explain this? How would he make Parker believe any of it? Jeremiah went to change and shave in the bathroom. Scott paced nervously back and forth, grappling, Jeremiah assumed, with his own issues of making this work.

Jeremiah scanned his reflection in the bathroom mirror. He looked more or less exactly as he had six months before, exactly as his clone looked when he'd left for work that morning, down to the same bandaged left hand. It felt odd to look so much like his old self and feel like someone completely different. He never could have imagined, when all of this began, that so much could change in a matter of months. He took a deep breath and tried to calm himself. Breaking out of the lab, confronting the clone, cutting off his finger—all of it felt easy compared to the prospect of facing his own son.

Scott knocked on the bathroom door. "Let's go," he said. "The car is waiting."

They had secured an exact replica of Jeremiah's car, right down to the coffee stains on the front carpet and the dent on the bumper. He'd be picking Parker up in that. Scott would follow close behind. "Just to be safe," Scott said, which Jeremiah understood to be a precaution against any sudden decision he might make to flee. He had no such plans, though. They were holding his money, just as he was holding on to the package. They'd agreed to make the swap at the last possible moment. "Just to be safe," Jeremiah had said.

Since he'd last been to Parker's high school, a locked-door policy had been implemented. Jeremiah had to press an intercom button and tell a receptionist his business there before the door would be unlocked.

"Jeremiah Adams," he said into the speaker. "I'm here to pick up my son. He has a doctor's appointment." The door buzzed open and he went inside and through to the front office.

Waiting by the front desk, Jeremiah was preoccupied with trying to act normal. He didn't know why. He'd never seen this

receptionist before. She didn't know who he was. But he couldn't
shake the feeling that he'd somehow give something away, ruin
everything in the final moment. He stood there imagining an
intricate scenario that involved her pressing some secret button
under her desk and alerting the police that there was an imposter posing as a parent.

When Parker walked into the office, Jeremiah almost didn't
recognize him. The height he'd noticed the day before was more
jarring up close. Parker was nearly as tall as he was now. He
was dressed in torn jeans, a flannel shirt open over a light blue
T-shirt and the ever-present earbuds around his neck. His red-
dish hair had grown shaggy, and Jeremiah noticed, maybe for
the first time, that it was the exact same shade as Diana's hair
had been. To his dismay, there was the first hint of a mustache
over Parker's lip. He tried not to stare, but it wasn't easy. Parker
shrugged his shoulders and looked at Jeremiah with some agitation.

"What's going on?" he asked sullenly. "I don't have a doctor's appointment today."

"Yeah, it's just your physical. They called right after you left.
Must have been something Mom scheduled and didn't tell me
about." Parker cast his eyes down slightly at the mention of his
mother, and Jeremiah cringed. "She probably meant to tell me,"
he said, his voice catching in his throat.

It had been so long since he'd spoken a single word to his
son. He found it disgusting that the first thing he said to him
was an outright lie.

"You know, Parker," he said after a moment, "I know you
miss your mother. I miss her, too. But I'm here for you. If you
ever want to talk. You don't have to go through this alone."

"Whatever," Parker said, and turned to leave. Jeremiah looked
at the receptionist, who smiled and waved at him. It seemed
she'd decided against pushing her secret button.

In the car, Parker slumped into the front seat, tossed his backpack into the back and grunted.

"You're the one who needs the doctor's appointment," he said. "I didn't cut off my own finger with a chain saw." Jeremiah had wondered what story the clone would concoct. It sounded fishy and desperate to him. What would he possibly have needed a chain saw for first thing in the morning as he was leaving for work?

Halfway back to ViMed, Parker informed him this wasn't the way to his doctor's office.

"It's a different doctor," Jeremiah said. "A new guy."

When they pulled into the complex, Parker was thoroughly confused.

"Isn't this your office, Dad? What the hell?"

"Some new thing with the health insurance," he told him. "Routine exams can be done right here at ViMed now for everyone in the family. It's the best health care money can buy. A new perk—very high tech. Wait and see. It's cool—like one of your video games."

Parker shrugged. "Whatever," he said. "How long is this going to take?"

"Not too long," Jeremiah told him.

They walked through the front entrance, followed at a discreet distance by Scott and a lone security guard, and were met in the hallway by Dr. Pike.

"Good morning, Mr. Adams," Pike said with a bit too much enthusiasm. "This must be Parker. Nice to meet you, young man. If you'll both follow me."

Parker looked at Jeremiah with a puzzled look. "That's kind of weird," he said. "We don't even have to check in or anything? No waiting room?"

"Like I said, this is only for employees and families," Jeremiah told him. "They aren't exactly overbooked around here."

He followed Dr. Pike and Parker into a small examination room and Parker climbed up on the table and stared at his father.

"You don't have to stay, Dad," he said. "I can take it from here. I'm not five, you know."

"No, I'd rather stay," he said. "In case the doctor here has any questions. Isn't that right, Dr. Pike?" He wasn't about to leave Parker alone with anyone.

"It's customary for a parent to remain in the room during this part of the exam," Pike said. "Nothing to worry about, young man. I assure you, this part is all routine. No embarrassing questions. I'll save all of those for when your father is out of earshot."

Parker stripped from the waist up and Pike began a typical check of his vitals.

"Am I going to need any shots?" Parker asked.

"I doubt it," Pike said, and directed Parker to take a deep breath. "If you're not up to date the scan will detect it."

"What scan?"

Pike removed the stethoscope from his ears and opened the side door that led into the scanning room Jeremiah had entered so many months before. He directed the boy to take a seat in the hydraulic chair and Parker looked at him quizzically.

"What's all this?" he asked. "This doesn't very seem routine to me."

"It is a high-velocity bio-scanner," Pike explained. "ViMed created it. It is the only one like it in the world. In fact, you're one of only a few people to ever use it. This machine can detect all manner of illness and disease right down to the cellular level. It even gives a full medical history. It can do the work of ten doctors in a fraction of the time. It's quite safe. Nothing to worry about. Take a seat."

He handed Parker a pair of dark glasses to guard against the lasers and told him to buckle up. Jeremiah tried to act unconcerned as Pike closed Parker in the room and he followed the

doctor to a complicated panel of controls in an adjoining hallway. There were no windows between Parker and the control
panel. He couldn't see his son, but he could hear him clearly
through a speaker system connecting the rooms.

"There will be a series of bright lights, Parker, and a lot of
movement as the machine begins to scan your body. Remain
still and don't be alarmed."

"Dad?"

"I'm here, Parker," he said. "I can hear you. You okay in
there?"

"What the hell is this thing? What's this for? Do I have cancer or something?" The tinge of real fear in his son's voice was
alarming, and Jeremiah swallowed hard before answering.

"Oh, my God—no, Parker, you don't have cancer! You're
fine. Everything's fine. This is all just routine. I'm telling you,
it's nothing to be worried about. I've done this myself. It doesn't
hurt."

About an hour later, Jeremiah steadied his son with a hand
on his shoulder and they walked back into the adjoining examination room.

"Pretty cool, huh?" Jeremiah said, trying to sound as casual
as he could.

"Not really," Parker told him. He looked a bit pale. "Can we
leave now? Can you just take me back to school?"

Jeremiah looked at Pike, who nodded quickly toward the
door as he began looking through the test results.

"Yeah, we can go, Parker. But there's only a few hours left of
school. Why don't you just take the day off? We can grab some
lunch and you can spend a few hours with me at the office. I'll
show you around. It's pretty cool." He still had no clear idea of
how he was going to explain all of this, how he was going to
tell Parker he would never be going back to his school again.
That he would never be going back to the life he knew again.

Back in the apartment, Parker looked around excitedly, taking in the sleek design of the place.

"Whoa," he said. "This is where you work? Is this your office?"

"Check it out, take a look around."

"This is awesome," Parker said as he went into the kitchen and opened the fridge. Rooting through the freezer, he immediately went for the ice cream and Jeremiah almost tripped in his rush to physically push the boy away and close the door.

"That's for later," he said with a bit more force than he liked. "Go ahead and take a soda, though. Make yourself at home."

Parker took his bottle into the living room and stopped short when he saw the video game console, which Jeremiah had placed conspicuously on a table.

"That's a Sparx Four," he said, stunned. "That isn't even supposed to be released for, like, another six months. No one has that yet. How did you get one of those?"

"Parker," Jeremiah said. "Sit down for a minute. I need to talk to you. You can check that out later."

But Parker had gone over to the console and picked up the headset. "This is amazing," he said. "Are there any games?"

"Yeah, later, though. I need to talk to you. Put that away for a minute and come and sit down."

# CHAPTER
# 41

## DAY 172

"I think you must have lost your mind along with that finger, Dad. Clones? Really?"

Jeremiah had just spit the whole thing out without taking a breath, and Parker had listened with a blank expression and then burst out laughing.

"Parker," he said, "I'm serious. I know how it sounds, but this isn't a joke. I haven't been home in six months. I've been here. I've been watching. I saw the whole thing with your mother. I saw everything, right there on that TV set on the wall. But I'm back now."

"Yeah, whatever, Dad, very funny," he said. "Can I just play a game on this thing now?"

"Think about it," Jeremiah said. "Louie knew it. Remember how he just suddenly turned on me? Started growling at me for no reason? He knew that wasn't me! When have you ever known that dog to treat me like that? Remember how you thought that was so weird? You asked me if I kicked him or something."

Parker said nothing, just picked up the headset again and tried it on for size.

"Look, I can prove it to you, Parker. I can show you that

everything I've told you is the absolute truth. But you need to be prepared. You need to understand. I don't want you to freak out on me."

"I don't think I'm the one freaking out, Dad." He twirled a finger at his temple.

Jeremiah touched a button on a remote control Scott had supplied him with, and the entire wall in front of them flickered on like a television, resolving into a clear image of the clone sitting in his ViMed office, twelve floors above them.

"That's him," Jeremiah said as Parker stared at the wall and then back at his father. "That's him, right this minute. He's at work. He's up on the twelfth floor, and I'm sitting here with you."

Parker said nothing, but a slow smile crept over his face. "What is this?" he asked. "Are we on one of those TV shows on the Science Channel or something? Okay, you can come out now Mr. Announcer Dude—I don't believe you! You failed!"

"Parker." Jeremiah took him by the shoulders and looked him directly in the eye. "Look at my face. This isn't a trick. It isn't a joke. There's no TV show, no secret announcer dude. This is the truth. You've been living with my clone all this time. The whole thing was a ViMed experiment, something for work I agreed to take part in. But it's over now. And you and I need to leave. We have to get away from here. Everything's been taken care of. We're going to start over. Have a new life, just the two of us. Everything's going to be different now. Everything's going to be better."

As he spoke, he watched several expressions come and go over his son's face: disbelief, confusion, shock, something approaching acceptance and then finally full disbelief again. He looked at the scene playing out on the wall and then back at his father several times and shook his head. Jeremiah never let go of his shoulders.

"That's just a video or something," he said. "You set this whole thing up."

"Look at the clock on the wall behind him," Jeremiah pointed. "It's the same exact time, down to the minute. It's true, Parker."

"Dad," he said, and didn't finish the thought.

"Do you have your phone on you?"

"Yeah, of course I do."

"Call me."

"What?" Parker looked even more confused.

"Call me at my office right now."

Parker slowly took his cell phone from his front pocket, pushed a few buttons and held it to his ear, staring at Jeremiah the whole time.

"Um, hi," Parker said into the phone. "Can I speak to Mr. Adams? This is his son, Parker."

On the wall, they both watched as the intercom sounded at the clone's desk and he picked up the receiver.

"Thanks, Brenda," he said. "Put him right through."

Parker looked again at Jeremiah and then back at the wall.

"Hey, Parker," the clone said. "What's up? You okay?"

Jeremiah watched as shock crept over his son's face. It was obvious that he heard the same words uttered in his ear exactly as they heard them from the monitor. The boy was absolutely silent as the impossibility of it set in.

"Parker?" the clone said, a look of slight concern on his face. "You there? Everything okay?"

"Y-yeah," Parker stammered into the phone, eyes fixed now on the clone's face. "I, um, I just wanted to let you know I'm staying after school today."

"Oh, well, that's fine," the clone said. "Thanks, I guess. I'll be home at the usual time. You sure you're all right? You need to talk or anything? I have time."

"Yeah, no, I'm all right," Parker said, looking at Jeremiah

again with an expression that entirely contradicted the remark. "I gotta go, though. I'll see you tonight."

"See you tonight." The clone hung up the phone with a shrug. Parker let his own phone fall from his fingers and remained absolutely still.

"This is incredible," he said. "I can't believe it."

"I know," Jeremiah told him. "I know it is. You all right?"

"Yeah, I think so." Parker looked at him with a thousand questions in his eyes. "Dad," he finally said, his voice unusually hushed. "Dad, was Mom a clone, too? Was that a fake Mom in that car? Is Mom here somewhere?"

Jeremiah's heart sank.

"No," he told his son as gently as he could. "No, Parker. That was really Mom. I'm sorry."

"How could you do something like this, Dad?" he asked after a moment. "Why did you do it?"

"I don't know, Parker. I'm still trying to figure that one out. But in a strange way, despite all of it, part of me is glad I did. Because now things will be better. I missed the hell out of you, though. I can tell you that." He put an arm around his son and gave him a quick kiss on top of his head and Parker didn't even flinch.

"Better, how?" There was a hint of anger in Parker's voice. Jeremiah could see he felt betrayed. He didn't blame him.

"Not better," Jeremiah said. "Different, maybe. Watching that clone, I got to see where I went wrong. I've made mistakes, Parker. A lot of mistakes. I wasn't the best father to you, and that was wrong. I should have done better. I should have been more involved, paid more attention. Now, I will. I only wish I could do the same with your mother."

Parker let his head fall.

"I know you're angry, Parker," Jeremiah said. "I know all of this is confusing and a lot to take in after what you've just been through. I'm angry, too. I wish your mother was still here. I wish a lot of things. But that's why this whole thing has to end. Now. I couldn't have you alone with the clone, after your mother and all. It had to end. We need each other."

"So, now what?" Parker asked. "What did you say about starting a new life? About getting away from here?"

"Just me and you. We're going to start fresh. Just the two of us."

For a long minute, Parker said nothing, and he looked as if he were fighting off tears.

"Hey," Jeremiah said, "I know you like this game *Infinite Frontiers*. I've been playing it a bit myself, you know. It's pretty cool. I want you to see my guy. He's totally badass."

With the remote, Jeremiah switched from the clone monitor to the new gaming console and the scene on the wall filled with the image of a simulated battlefield. As soon as Clyde materialized on the screen, larger than life, Jeremiah looked at his son, who was staring at the avatar with a look of complete bewilderment.

*"You're Clyde?"* he asked. "That was *you*?"

Jeremiah nodded.

"I kept looking for you. You were never online again."

"It was just that one time. It was sort of a fluke," he said. "But yeah, that was me."

"And you beat me," Parker said. Some of the anger seemed to fade from the boy's eyes.

"Only when you tripped over that land mine. I'm not anywhere near your level. Not yet, anyway."

"Yeah," he said. "Stupid move."

Jeremiah smiled and bumped Parker's shoulder with his own. "I'd have nailed you, anyway," he said. "You want a rematch?"

Each of them put on their headgear and took a controller. Parker glanced at his father with some wariness and then back at the wall. For the next forty minutes the room vibrated with simulated bomb blasts and laser fire and it was only then, immersed in his own element, that Parker finally began to relax. More than anything Jeremiah had shown him or said, it seemed like it was playing the game that finally convinced him of the impossible. Jeremiah decided to let him win. As Parker wiped out Jeremiah's last stronghold with a bright blue blast of plasma fire, Parker turned to his father and looked at him with an expression Jeremiah couldn't read. But there was an element of trust in there, and something bordering on respect.

"This is insane," Parker said finally. "I can't believe you play *Infinite Frontiers*. And you're good at it. You sure *you're* not the clone?"

Charles Scott came into the room just as they turned off the game. He nodded to Jeremiah and held out a hand to Parker.

"I've heard a lot about you, young man. It's nice to finally meet you." Parker shook his hand with some uncertainty and then looked back at Jeremiah.

"It's time for the Meld," Scott said, and Parker flashed a look of shocked concern at both men.

"It's fine," Jeremiah told him, and then turned to Scott. "I haven't told him about this part yet. You came in before I had a chance."

"Nothing to worry about, son," Scott said. "Meld isn't illegal when it's used under clinical circumstances. It's medicine, and I'm afraid it is necessary."

"Necessary for what?" the boy asked, agitation in his voice.

"Parker," Jeremiah began, "there's something else I haven't told you. These men have agreed to help us make a new start. They're giving us plenty of money, brand-new identities, just like one of those witness protection programs you see in the movies. But before they can do that, I've agreed to let them make a clone of you. Your clone will be going back home, staying with my clone. To them, it will seem like nothing's changed at all. I should have told you sooner. I'm sorry. But this was the only way I could make this work. The only way I could get back to you."

Parker stared at Jeremiah for a long moment.

"They're going to make a clone of me?" he asked, a conflicted smile spreading across his face. "An actual clone?"

"Yeah," Jeremiah told him, still unsure of how his son was taking the revelation. "That's all this world needs, right? Two Parkers."

"And he takes my place, like at school and everything?"

"That's right," Jeremiah said.

"Why can't the clones leave? I mean, I don't know if I want to leave school and all my friends. I don't want to leave everything. Maybe we could stay and send them somewhere else."

"I know it's hard, Parker," Jeremiah told him. "I know. But it's the only way this can work."

"But that's where Mom was, Dad. It's our house. We can't just leave." Parker looked again as though he were trying not to cry. Jeremiah felt instantly guilty for not considering that aspect. He'd been trying to treat it like an adventure, like a game. It wasn't a game to Parker. Jeremiah was asking him to leave the last place he'd had his mother. It was a heartless thing to do.

"I'll have someone go to the house for a few things," he told his son. "Some photographs, maybe a few personal things for you to hold on to. Any ideas?"

Parker shrugged and considered it. "Her hairbrush, maybe? Or one of those bracelets she liked?"

"We'll get both," Jeremiah said, looking to Scott for some assurance. Scott nodded, a look of slight irritation flashing over his face.

"Okay," Parker said reluctantly. "I guess so."

"It'll be okay, Parker," Jeremiah told him. "You'll see."

"Well, at least there's one good thing," Parker said.

"What's that?"

"At least the clone will have to take my French midterm."

Jeremiah smiled. "I suppose he will," he said, and he stood up to walk with his son to Pike's lab. He was eager to get a look at his son's clone, which had been in incubation for forty-eight hours, grown from a few cells from Parker's cheek at school as part of a bogus health screening.

Scott stared at him. "You can't be present for the Meld, Mr. Adams. You know that."

"I don't need to be in the same room," Jeremiah said, "but I want to go with him."

"Even your proximity could threaten the purity of the download," Scott told him. "We need to be precise about this. It's the final step."

"I don't feel right about this."

"This is the way it must be done," Scott said. "Besides, you're needed here. You are to meet with our agent in charge of your new identities. There are matters you need to discuss before the proper documentation can be fabricated. Once that has been completed, you and your son will be free to go directly after the Meld process. We are seeing to the final details as we speak."

"That can wait."

"No, it cannot wait," Scott said firmly. "We've gone to great lengths to procure this agent from the FBI. He's taking a considerable risk even being here. Time is of the essence, you understand. You have my word, Mr. Adams. I will return your son to you safely. It shouldn't take more than an hour. Two at most."

A thin, serious-looking man, dressed in a dark-colored suit, entered the room behind Scott. Jeremiah would have pegged him for a federal agent a mile away. He might as well have been holding a sign that read Secret Agent.

"Is there a problem?" the man said, casting a dire glance at Charles Scott.

"Not at all," Scott assured him.

"Look," the agent said, this time to Jeremiah, "we do this now or we don't do it at all. It's your choice."

"I'll be fine, Dad," Parker said. "I'm not afraid. And to tell you the truth, I sort of want to get out of here as soon as we can. This whole thing is sort of freaking me out. You take care of that agent dude. I'll go and do this."

Reluctantly, Jeremiah allowed Parker to go with Charles Scott. As he headed out the door, though, Parker stopped suddenly and turned back to Jeremiah.

"Dad," he said. "Are we going to get Louie? We can't just leave him there. We have to take him with us."

Jeremiah turned the question back to Charles Scott with an urging glance.

"Your dog? I don't think that would be a problem," Scott said. "I'll dispatch someone to your home to collect him and the mementos from the boy's mother. The dog will be waiting for you after the Meld."

"I'm Agent Glen Jasper," the agent said once Scott and Parker had left. "We have a lot to do and not much time to get it done."

"Jeremiah Adams," he said, shaking the man's hand.

"Not for long you're not, sir. I'm here to change that."

Jeremiah hadn't even begun to consider new names. With everything else he'd had to contend with, the thought hadn't even crossed his mind. But the enormity of the decision suddenly weighed on him. This was important. Whatever names he chose now would be with them for the rest of their lives, might influence, in a way, everything that came after. Jeremiah sat down slowly and started to think. He wished he'd thought to discuss this with Parker. It would have been nice to ask for his input on something so fundamental as his name. But now there wasn't time. He had named his son once, he decided, he'd just have to be trusted to do it again.

"Some people find it helpful," the agent offered, "to retain something from their original name in the new one. Samuel Johnson, for instance, might become John Samuelson. In my experience, it makes the transition a little easier."

Something in that logic appealed to him, and Jeremiah mumbled out loud as he worked out variations in his mind.

"Adam Jeremiah… Jeremy Adamson… Jeremiah Parker… How about Adam Parker for my son?"

"Adam Parker," the agent said, spelling it out as he typed it into a laptop. "And a middle name?"

Jeremiah hardly had to think before he said it.

"Brent."

"Adam Brent Parker," the agent repeated as he typed. "And you? What is your first name, Mr. Parker?"

"Jeremy, I think," he said. "Yes, I like that. My name is Jeremy Adam Parker."

For the next hour, Jeremiah answered an endless procession of questions, which touched on everything from what he had studied in school to whether he'd ever had measles, while the agent took fastidious notes on every answer and barely looked up from his laptop.

"Now we'll cross-reference this with your existing records," the agent said, still typing at lightning speed, "and input photos here, and here." He handed Jeremiah the laptop and a stylus. "And if you could sign here and again over here," he said, "with your new name, of course."

Jeremiah had to stop and think before signing his name. After the agent had him sign no fewer than twenty-six more times, however, it almost became easy and the scrawl took on the characteristics of an actual signature.

"Very good, Mr. Parker," he said as he stood to leave. "All of your documents will be waiting in your vehicle for you within the hour—one packet for you, another for your son."

"What documentation will be included exactly?"

"Birth certificates, social security cards, passports, a driver's license for you, school transcripts, the title to your vehicle, immunization records, medical and dental histories, eight years of tax returns, bank account verification and two library cards, one of them expired. We'll even have a few old utility bills thrown in for good measure. You will also receive two cell phones, complete with a two-year carrier contract under your new name, as well as a detailed biographical history. You will need to read that and become familiar with it. It's everything you'll need."

"I'd say so." Jeremiah whistled. "You're certainly thorough. Don't we need to change our appearance—dye our hair or something?"

The agent came very close to smiling.

"Don't believe everything you see in the movies, Mr. Parker," he said. "That is very rarely necessary. You must remember, however, that neither you, nor your son, will be allowed to come within a one-hundred-mile radius of Boston again—ever. One of the documents you've just signed agreed to that. I'll get a full copy into your folder. And the federal government now has an excessive amount of information on you." He glanced pointedly to the laptop in his hand. "If you try to come back here, we will find you. Aside from that one restriction, you are free to go where you will. Do what you want. But stay out of trouble. And stay under the radar. Don't get famous or anything."

"I understand," Jeremiah told him, and he shook his hand.

"It was very nice to meet you, Mr. Parker."

# CHAPTER

# 42

Parker and Charles Scott were back in the apartment soon after the agent left.

"You okay?" he asked his son. "How was it?"

"It was weird," he said. "Really weird. Dad, you wouldn't believe it—the thing looks just like me. I mean *exact*! Like looking in a mirror. Man, I wish I could be there when he shows up for school! He is gonna fool everyone!"

"Believe me, I know how you feel. And the Meld? How did that go?"

"I guess it went fine," Parker said. "I didn't really feel anything. It was sort of like being hypnotized or something, I guess. I don't feel any different. I don't really remember it. I guess it isn't as bad as everybody keeps saying."

"The jury is still out on that," he said.

Jeremiah asked Charles Scott if he should start packing and realized only then that he had neglected to take any of Parker's clothes with him.

"It isn't necessary, Mr. Adams…or Mr. Parker, is it now?" Scott told him. "You'll find everything you need is already in your car—enough clothes to get you started, some cash, all the basics. You can get anything else on the road. We took the liberty of securing a Mercedes for you. Well-equipped, top of the line. I drive one myself. I'm sure it will be to your liking. If you'll just follow me. We can take care of our final transaction outside."

"One second." Jeremiah darted into the kitchen and grabbed the package from the back of the freezer and took it out of the ice cream container. He put a hand on Parker's shoulder and ushered him out behind Charles Scott.

"And Louie?" he asked. "Did you get the dog?"

"The dog is waiting for you."

Almost the instant they were out the front door, before they were even halfway across the circular drive where the chocolate-brown Mercedes was waiting, Louie had bolted away from the man who held his leash and nearly knocked Jeremiah over with a wild greeting. With two paws up on his chest, he whined and whimpered as though he were literally trying to speak. Jeremiah laughed and tried to turn his face away from the dog's exuberant kisses and attempted to calm him down. Louie was literally shaking with joy at the sight of him. Jeremiah felt almost as happy. He'd almost forgotten how much he'd missed this dog. He was glad Louie was coming with them. He knelt down and allowed himself to be kissed, and talked in soft, low tones until the dog stopped whining.

"It's okay, boy," he said. "I know. I know. I missed you, too. It's okay."

Parker got into the front seat of the car and Louie stayed at Jeremiah's side as he looked to Charles Scott for what he sincerely hoped would be the last time. Scott was staring down at the dog with some confusion.

"It would appear that someone has forgotten to give that dog its medication. He seems overly exuberant considering, in his mind, he saw you leave for work just a few hours ago."

Jeremiah smiled slowly. Part of him wanted to tell Scott that Louie had known all along, that the clone hadn't fooled him for one minute. He wanted to see Scott's face when he realized that maybe his precious experiment wasn't airtight, after all, that there were some things even science couldn't account for. It would have felt like one final triumph—a twist of the knife before he left. But he resisted the urge. It wasn't worth the risk. He'd have to be satisfied, he decided, with the victory he'd already won.

"I don't know," he told Scott, "after your people took him out of the house, he's probably just happy to see us again. Poor thing is just confused."

Scott pursed his lips and scrutinized the animal for a long moment. "A loyal companion," he said at last.

"You have no idea." Jeremiah absently tightened his grip on Louie's collar. "So how do we do this?"

Scott took a phone from his pocket and tapped a quick series of buttons.

"You'll notice an icon for a bank account on the home screen of this phone, Mr. Adams." Jeremiah took the cell phone from him as he continued. "The initial password has been set as '*replica 321.*' You will see the transaction has already been made to the account in the amount agreed upon. Once you're satisfied, you can change the password and relinquish the package."

Jeremiah opened the file and nodded when he saw the account balance was just slightly in excess of $10 million.

He handed over the package. Louie leaned in hard against his knee as Jeremiah changed his bank password to Brent's cell number.

Scott tore the paper away from the package, letting the wrapping fall at his feet, and unzipped the top of the lunch box to view the contents. He looked away with a sickened but satisfied expression and nodded once. He then extended a hand to Jeremiah.

"I must say, Mr. Adams," he said. "You surprise me. I never would have thought you capable of this sort of willful deceit when we first met. If I had, I think I might have selected another test subject."

"Yeah, well, I guess you never really know a person as well as you think, do you?"

"I have a feeling you may be right about that, Mr. Adams. You may be right."

Jeremiah opened the back door of the car and Louie jumped in and settled himself down on the leather seat, still panting with excitement. Jeremiah took his place behind the wheel, looked once at Parker and drove away from the ViMed lab for the last time.

He had no real idea where they were headed. But it didn't matter. He'd just keep driving until they decided to stop somewhere. As he turned onto the expressway, heading away from the city, away from everything, he felt an intense excitement rise up in him—a feeling he'd almost forgotten he was capable of. Everything ahead of him seemed so full of potential, vivid with possibility. The fact that it was unknown, untested, only made it that much sweeter. He had Parker. He had a second chance. A single finger seemed suddenly a small price to pay. No matter which direction they chose to go, a new beginning would be waiting like a blank page ready to be filled, and Jeremiah was holding the pen. It was exhilarating, so much so that he actually laughed out loud.

"I've always wanted to see the Grand Canyon," he said to his son. "Maybe we should head west."

"Sounds awesome," Parker said, "and maybe rafting on the Colorado River."

"Why not? This is going to be a good life. We're going to do it right. I promise. But you do realize, I hope, that once we get settled somewhere, you're going to have to go back to school, right? You're going to have to graduate."

Parker didn't answer him. His head was turned toward the back seat of the car.

"What the hell is up with Louie?" he asked.

Jeremiah looked up in the rearview mirror. What he saw made his heart stop. The dog was baring his teeth, growling almost inaudibly, his ears pulled slightly back against his head.

The dog was looking directly at Parker.

# CHAPTER
## 43

He'd told Parker they needed to stop at home to pick up Louie's things. That the people from ViMed hadn't known what to get.

"His bed, an extra leash. It'll only take a few minutes," he said, "and then we'll hit the road." He had to work to keep the tremor from his voice.

Why the hell had he let Parker go off alone with Scott for that cloning? What the hell had they done with his son?

His mind raced as he tried to get hold of the situation. They'd switched them and left him with Parker's clone. And they'd used the Meld to pump every single memory—everything Jeremiah and Parker had been through over the last several hours, the cloning, the conversation about Diana, and all of it—into the mind of this thing.

"I thought we weren't supposed to go back here. I mean, what if your clone is there? Or mine? That'll be a bit awkward."

"I think we'll be okay," Jeremiah said. "But just in case, I'll park down the street a bit and you stay in the car. Head down." He tried to smile. "Sort of like spy stuff."

Parker's clone shrugged.

Natalie should have been here by now, but he didn't see her

car anywhere. When he'd pulled off the road and thought for a few frantic minutes about who to call for help, he'd quickly realized that she was the only one he could trust now, the only one who could possibly put this right. And she owed him. He wasn't leaving without his son.

"Meet me at my house in a half hour," he'd told her. "Bring Meld and whatever else you need to put back all of those memories into my son. I want him back the way I left him. Intact."

Jeremiah peered into the garage door window of the house. There was no car inside. He glanced at his watch. The clone would be at work for at least another hour. Parker, no doubt, was in his bedroom playing video games. He tried the kitchen door. It was locked. Looking around in as casual a manner as he could manage, he saw no neighbors on the street. There was no one to see what he was doing. He balled his good hand up inside the sleeve of his suit jacket and easily shattered the bottom pane of glass, knocking away the remaining shards so he could reach in and turn the doorknob. Once he was inside, he stood stone still, hardly daring to breathe, and listened for any sign that Parker had heard something. After a moment, he let out his breath and eased the door closed behind him as quietly as he could. Thank God for those expensive headphones, he thought.

He remembered the cameras. ViMed had eyes all over the house. If anyone were monitoring, they were probably looking right at him. And, he considered, they'd have no reason to believe they weren't seeing his clone. If he played this cool, if he could just get his wits together and act casual, as though he were in his own house doing nothing suspicious, he could probably fool them for long enough. Unless, he thought, they were monitoring the clone at the office at the same time. That would certainly rouse someone's suspicions. His only option was to destroy the cameras. Or at least turn them off.

He crossed the room quickly, opened the door to the base-

ment and went to the breaker box. Standing there in the sudden pitch-blackness, he hoped Parker was on his laptop and still
engrossed in his game. With a little luck, he probably wouldn't
even notice that the lights were out in the middle of the afternoon. But he worried about some sort of alarms going off at
ViMed. He had no idea whether he'd done the right thing. But
at least he could be sure no one would see him make the switch.

Back in the kitchen, he stood for a nervous few minutes until
he saw Natalie approach the door, looking over her shoulders
in a ludicrously conspicuous way. He let her in quickly and put
a finger to his lips.

"Where's Parker?" she asked in a whisper.

"Upstairs, on his computer," he said.

"And his clone?" she asked.

"In the car, down the street."

"And you're sure about this? You're absolutely certain you
have the wrong one?"

"That kid in the car believes he is Parker," he told her. "He's
not. You think I wouldn't know?"

"All right," she said, "I believe you."

"How are we going to do this?"

Her eyes widened. "I thought you had a plan!"

"I didn't exactly have all day to think of every single detail,"
he said. "Did you bring everything you need?"

She nodded toward the leather bag slung over her shoulder.

"This is extremely precise work," she told him. "Implant-
ing memories with Meld is Pike's job. I'm not even sure I can
do this."

"Well," he said, "you'd better figure it out. This is my only
chance. You said you wanted to help me. I need your help now."

She inhaled deeply, a kind of resolve coming over her face.

"We're going to have to bring them together for this transfer,"
she said. "It will be easiest if the real Parker is under sedation

to receive the memory implant. Luckily for you, I thought of that." She took a syringe out of her bag. "The clone will need to be conscious during the procedure and then sedated just before the end, so he doesn't remember seeing his own double."

"I'll get the clone," Jeremiah said. "What do I tell him?"

"I don't know. That's up to you, Jeremiah. Let's take care of the real one first. Then at least we can stop whispering."

Taking the stairs as carefully as he could, avoiding the few spots where he knew they would squeak, Jeremiah led her to the second floor and down the hallway to where Parker's bedroom door stood slightly ajar. Parker was inside, his back to them, obliterating video enemy forces with severe concentration, entirely oblivious to the fact that his own father was standing there about to subject him to Meld and essentially kidnap him.

Natalie wasted no time, but inhaled deeply, readied the syringe and walked up behind him with long, determined strides. She jabbed the needle into Parker's right shoulder. He jumped violently and turned with a terrified expression, but slumped over onto his desk before he could utter a single word. Natalie settled the boy's head into a more comfortable position and Jeremiah let out the breath he hadn't been aware he was holding in.

"I'll go get the clone," he said. "Wait here."

Halfway down the stairs he ran headlong into his own clone coming up.

# CHAPTER
# 44

For a moment they stood there, facing each other without a word, neither of them fully comprehending what they were seeing. For his part, Jeremiah was simply surprised to see the clone home so quickly. He hadn't considered this contingency at all and the shock of it stopped him in midstep. He imagined his clone's concern was a little more urgent, as he'd literally walked in on a home invasion. He was probably also wondering whether he'd lose another body part.

It was the clone who spoke first.

"You!" He stared at Jeremiah while his face raced through a series of expressions from fear to confusion to rage and back again. "Parker?" he called over Jeremiah's shoulder. "I swear to God if you've hurt him… Parker!"

He pushed past Jeremiah with a sudden show of strength and took the remaining stairs two at a time, almost tripping in the process, and burst into Parker's bedroom to find Natalie Young standing over the boy. Jeremiah came in at his heels. Natalie looked from one identical face to the other and then settled on Jeremiah.

"Jesus!" she said. "This is all we need. You didn't think to lock the door?"

"He has a key, remember?"

"What the hell is going on here! What have you done to him? Parker!" The clone rushed past Natalie and grasped the boy by the shoulders, a look of absolute terror creeping over his face when he saw Parker's head fall awkwardly to one side.

"Oh, my God! No. No. What have you done?" He began slapping the boy's cheeks in an attempt to rouse him.

Jeremiah rushed up next to his double and tried to pry Parker from his grip.

"He's okay. He's just sleeping," he said. "He's fine."

"We haven't hurt him," Natalie said, holding her hands out in defense. "It's just a mild sedative. That's all."

"Who the hell are you people?" Although he addressed both of them, the clone's eyes were fixed on Jeremiah's face. "I'm calling the police."

"You won't do that," Jeremiah said. "If you didn't do it before, when I had a knife to your throat, I don't think you'll do it now. Think about this. What are you going to tell them when they ask for a description? We're not here to hurt anyone. Parker's not in any danger. But you and I need to talk. It's time I filled you in on everything that's going on. It's time you knew the truth."

Natalie shot a warning look at Jeremiah, which angered him.

"What else are we supposed to do, Natalie?" he asked. "We're sort of backed in a corner here and time is running out. The project doesn't matter anymore. Fuck that. Besides, he has a right to know."

"A right to know what?" the clone asked, looking from one of them to the other. His hands still gripped Parker's shoulders. He let go, turned to Jeremiah and lowered his voice. "Who the hell *are* you?"

"That," Jeremiah said, "should be as plain as the nose on our identical face. Come with me."

Five minutes later, back in the hallway, Jeremiah's clone was shaking his head.

"You're insane," he said. "Human cloning?"

"Yeah, yeah, I know. Illegal, immoral, all of that. But scientifically possible, and that's what this is. Look at me! Look at my face. What do *you* think this is? What else can this possibly be?"

Jeremiah locked eyes with his double and watched as some sort of understanding eventually fell over its face. The clone's eyes began to twitch, and he pulled at the hair on the top of his head, in exactly the same way that Jeremiah had always reacted to bad news.

"You know it's the truth," Jeremiah pushed. "You've known it since the minute you saw me. Now you just need to admit it. And time is running out. I'm afraid we can't have your existential crisis right now."

"You expect me to believe this?" the clone said. "How do I know that *you're* not the clone? Maybe you're the clone and you're trying to steal my life, my son!"

"I'm not stealing anything. I'm trying to take back my own son, my real son. And believe me, I don't want your life. You can keep that."

"But Parker is *my* son," the clone said. "I remember the day he was born. I remember every first day of school, every argument, every time he ever cried. I remember everything. He's my son."

"And Parker's clone will remember all of it, too. Those memories won't go away. You lose nothing. In some weird way, that clone is your real son," Jeremiah said. "I just want to make this right again. For both of us. For *all* of us. We don't have time to debate this. We have to do it now."

Natalie's voice pierced the silence between the men.

"We need to hurry this up, Jeremiah. We need the other clone."

"Get him. He's in my car, down the street." He tossed her his keys as she brushed past them and started down the stairs. "Be careful," he added. "Don't give him any information. Just bring him in."

He turned back to his clone, who was leaning heavily now against the wall and still shaking his head.

"My entire life? Everything I remember? My childhood? My marriage? You want me to believe it's all been a lie? That I'm not the man I've always thought I was?"

"If there's one thing I've learned from all of this," Jeremiah said, "it's that no one, none of us, is ever really who we think we are. We tell ourselves lies to feel better, but they're just lies. The truth is a lot harder to look at. But the trick is, you can't let it crush you. You either accept who you are, or you change it. In your case, you just have to accept it. And you have to do that now."

"Just accept all of this and hand over my son?"

"You don't have a choice," Jeremiah snapped. "Right this minute there are people on their way here who'd kill all of us in a heartbeat to keep this thing quiet. Including your son. And mine."

The clone said nothing.

"You're his father," Jeremiah said. "Every bit as much as I am. Act like it! We've got to do this."

The anguish still there on his face, the clone closed his eyes and offered a feeble nod of his head in reluctant acceptance.

Relief washed over Jeremiah just as Natalie started back up the stairs. Parker's clone came up cautiously behind her and stopped as soon as he saw the scene in the hallway.

"Dad...? What?"

"Parker," he said. "We need to do one more thing. You need

to go with Dr. Young. Do exactly as she tells you. You can trust her."

The boy looked at him in utter confusion, eyes widening in alarm, and Jeremiah laid a reassuring hand on his shoulder. "We need to do this, Parker. No one's going to hurt you. We just need to fix this one thing."

"And then we can go?"

"Then we can go," he said. "Anywhere we want."

Jeremiah felt a lump in his throat as he watched the boy follow Natalie into the bedroom as though he were walking toward a firing squad. His own clone made a move to follow, but Jeremiah stopped him with a hand to his shoulder. Natalie closed the door behind them.

"That's your son," he said. "He's every bit as real as you are."

"And he won't remember anything about this?" the clone asked. "Nothing about the experiment, about seeing two of us? About seeing his own clone in there?"

"If everything goes right, the only thing he'll remember is that he came home from school, fell asleep and you woke him up in time for dinner."

They listened in silence to a few muffled sounds coming from the bedroom, none of them as worrisome as they thought they ought to be. They exchanged anxious glances, but everything that needed saying between them had already been said.

It was only a few minutes before Natalie emerged from the room, struggling with the slumping body of Parker against her shoulder. He looked awake, but zombie-like, and was able to walk uneasily under her guidance. She nodded back toward the room.

"You take care of him," she said. "I'll get this one in the car and then I'm leaving."

"Did it work?" Jeremiah asked. "Is it all done?"

She shook her head slightly. "I hope so. I did my best. But

you should both be prepared for some overlap in memory. Some gaps. You'll just have to work with it."

She started slowly down the stairs with her burden and turned when Jeremiah spoke again.

"Natalie. You should know that I have evidence about all of this. I plan to turn it in. If I were you, I'd get far away before this all comes out. You may still have a chance."

She nodded.

"Good luck, Jeremiah," she said. "Both of you."

Jeremiah and his clone went into the bedroom where they found Parker's clone limp in a chair, his head lolling uncomfortably to one side. Together, they lifted him up and laid him carefully onto the bed, each of them pulling off one shoe and positioning a leg.

They stood there, sharing a long, silent exchange, and Jeremiah held out his hand to his double. It felt strange to shake his hand, but appropriate somehow.

"I don't know if I can leave you out of this when the truth comes out," he said. "I can try, but you need to be prepared for it. People may come looking for you."

"If everything you've told me is true, then they'll have no reason to believe I'm not who I say I am. And you won't be here to dispute it. Where will you go now?"

"I don't know. A fresh start. Somewhere new."

Jeremiah started out of the room, leaving his clone to pick up the pieces of the shattered life he was walking away from. He turned back then, a final question occurring to him.

"Will you ever tell him?" He nodded toward Parker's clone on the bed.

The clone hesitated for a moment and then looked back at the boy with a thoughtful expression.

"No," he said finally. "I don't think I will. I really don't see the point."

★ ★ ★

At the car, Parker was in the back seat now, looking slightly dazed. His head leaned heavily against the window and Louie's head lay contentedly in the boy's lap. Jeremiah breathed a sigh of real relief at the sight.

"You all right?" he asked.

"Let's just go, Dad. I'm okay."

Jeremiah nodded, turned the key and adjusted the rearview mirror. Before he drove away toward a future that held as much hope now as it did uncertainty, he took a moment to peer into his own eyes. It seemed to him that it was the first time he ever really understood what he was looking at; all at once, he saw the man he'd been, the man he had become and, more importantly, the man he was going to be. He actually smiled.

"Okay," he said. "Let's go."

★ ★ ★ ★ ★

# ACKNOWLEDGMENTS

Writing a novel is a task done mainly all alone. Bringing it from a wisp of an idea to a solid thing you can hold in your hand, however, takes a small army. There are many I have to thank:

My agent at The Gernert Company, Will Roberts, for his meticulous eye, sustained encouragement and enthusiasm, and the ability to gently keep me on the right track. Margot Mallinson, my editor at Mira, for her belief in this story, in me as an author, and her amazing capacity to make a book shine. Libby McGuire, whose expertise I was so fortunate to enjoy during her time as an agent. Michelle Meade, who helped to polish my story in ways that truly mattered. Thomas Hess, Leanna Hamill and Jennifer Harris, collectively known as The N.I.P.s—the best and most demanding writing group ever—and good friends, to boot. Stacie Julian and Linda MacKinnon—you know what you did, and I thank you from the bottom of my heart. My incredible group of girlfriends for all the laughs, good times, and so much encouragement. To my father, Charles Arena, and my whole gigantic family, but especially to Isabelle, Julian and Greg, who supported me, cheered me on, and probably heard 27 different iterations of this book. They never once said "no" when I asked if I could read them just one more scene—even though I'm sure they really wanted to. You should know it made a difference. And thanks, finally, to Louie, who made sure I was never *really* working all alone. I miss you more than words can say, buddy, so I'll just leave it at *Woof!*

My apologies to anyone I may have omitted. It's never intentional.